D0232986

WINDSHIFT

First published in the United States of America in 2006 by
Rizzoli International Publications, Inc.
300 Park Avenue South
New York, NY 10010
WWW.RIZZOLIUSA.COM

© 2006 Andrea De Carlo
© RCS Libri S.p.A., 2004 Bompiani

All rights reserved. No part of this book may be reproduced,
stored in a retrieval system, or transmitted in any form, or by
any means, electronic, mechanical, photocopying, recording,
or otherwise, without prior consent of the publishers.

2006 2007 2008 2009 / 10 9 8 7 6 5 4 3 2 1

ISBN-13: 978-0-8478-2881-4
ISBN-10: 0-8478-2881-6

Library of Congress Control Number: 2006927070

Printed and bound in the United States

Andrea De Carlo participates in the campaign
"European Writers Against Forest Destruction" launched by Greenpeace.
This book will be printed on forest-friendly paper (recycled using
post-consumer waste) for which no tree will be destroyed.
WWW.ANDREADECARLO.COM

WINDSHIFT

Four friends. A weekend in Umbria.
An adventure that is going to change their lives.

A Novel

ANDREA DE CARLO

RIZZOLI
NEW YORK

Alessio Cingaro is sitting in his bathroom, on a little arm-chair with an ultra-low backrest that he bought on a whim in a trendy furniture shop, not so much because he needed it but because its nonfunctional look, that of real, pure luxury, attracted him. It's perfect to sit on, his back upright, his face thirty centimeters from the radiating lamp of a next-generation home tanning set, whose safety and effectiveness is guaranteed by a series of acronyms referring to the most recent European regulations. His eyes are covered by a pair of yellow plastic goggles, the kind they put on chickens, to protect his eyesight without leaving big telltale white patches. As an additional benefit, they make him feel he's under the sun on a tropical beach with his eyes closed. Within reach of his right hand is a vaporizer filled with demineralized water, which he gropes for every few minutes to hydrate his face and neck. The terminals of an electronic stimulator are making his abdominal muscles contract, with a rather pleasant, regular rhythm. It's a little early to tell whether it really works, as he purchased the thing over the phone only a week ago, after having seen it in countless TV ads, applied to the bellies of bodybuilders on steroids and to the bottoms of girls apparently unaware of the erotic effect of their buttocks vibrating in on-screen close-ups. The two preamplified loudspeakers on a nearby shelf blast out music he downloaded last night from the Net, although he would be hard-pressed to say who plays it; he usually clicks the mouse too quickly to fully register the names of the musicians. It's like the ongoing beat of life, it makes him nod his head and shake his knees and tap his hands at the base of his neck, where he places them so they will match the color of his face; it helps him from getting too relaxed or too tense. He once read that a Greek billionaire famous for his heavy eyeglass frames claimed that the secret of his success came down to just two points: getting up at six every morning and always being tanned. Alessio found this a precious tip, because it was so easy to apply to real life, and until now it has worked for him. The important thing is to not be deceived by the fan blowing in his face and to stick to the prescribed times of exposure, thus avoiding any permanent skin damage and the loss of credibility that would come with it.

The timer alarm rings, the ultraviolet lamp and the fan simultaneously go off; Alessio detaches the terminals of the electro-stimulator, dries his face and torso with a soft towel. Dabbing, not rubbing. He doesn't have time for a second shower after the one he took when he woke up, but he carefully applies a French skin cream containing Siberian ginseng and hyaluronic acid. Then he sprays deodorant under his armpits, and perfume on his neck and wrists. All these products belong to the same brand, which simplifies things and gives him an idea of thoroughness as he looks at the row of tubes and small bottles on the shelf under the mirror. As for his chest, he waxed it a couple of days ago so it's still as smooth as those of the male models who smile at themselves on the covers of the lifestyle magazines he buys every now and then, and there's no trace of southern Mediterranean monkey-man hairiness. He rubs his hair with anti-hair-loss lotion and combs it so that it sticks up a little higher on his head. This, together with the longish sideburns, also helps to make his face look more oval, minimizing the rather childish look he still tends to have at thirty-two. Finally, he looks at himself one last time in the mirror: full face, both profiles. He arches his eyebrows, tries out two or three of his standard smiles: they work.

He walks into the adjacent bedroom, where a forty-two-inch wall-mounted plasma screen is showing a morning talk show, in which a few second-rate guests respond to the questions of a second-rate host who's mostly concerned with the nods and gestures of his offscreen assistants. The studio audience is a drab mixture of housewives and retired or chronically jobless people, the type who tend to doze off as soon as they are off camera, only to wake up with a jerk when the APPLAUSE sign goes on. The female assistant has an embarrassed mommy's-girl face which contrasts with the red-and-black, South American brothel-style, wasp-waisted corset she's wearing. It takes her a huge effort to respond to the few words directed to her every once in a while, as she's never really sure which camera to face. Her movements are wooden and she has the eyes of a mouse; it's no surprise that her sexy calendar didn't do as well as those of her colleagues.

In the meantime, on Alessio's computer monitor, a high-pitched, tire-screeching, gun-blasting movie flashes from a pay-per-view channel which Alessio can watch for free thanks to some simple software he downloaded from the Net. The sounds of the two TV programs mix in a curious way with the music coming from the bathroom, but Alessio isn't at all bothered or confused by this: he's used to skipping between concurrent bits of information, registering only those which for some reason or another catch his attention. And this is nothing compared to the evenings, when the TV sets in the kitchen and in the living room also are turned on and he has to answer all the e-mails and the sms and the calls on his cell phone and the landline, often in less than an hour before going out to a restaurant or the movies. The fact that his attention span is getting shorter year by year, if not month by month, doesn't worry him in the least. He sees it simply as an additional spur to make the best use of his time, leaving no blank spaces that could be filled by boredom and all kinds of depressing thoughts.

Alessio opens his walk-in wardrobe, running his hand over a series of suits arranged in a subtle graduation of shades from gray to blue. The one he picks out could easily do in situations either formal or trendy, and then he selects a shirt and necktie to go along with it. His jackets are mostly double-breasted, for the same reason that the prime minister favors them: they give him a sense of protection that no single-breasted jacket could ever provide, confirming his status twice over. His suitcase has been ready by the door since early morning; it doesn't look bad either, with its porous pigskin and the brass corners that shine as if they were gold. Alessio fiddles with the computer as he dresses, reducing the size of the movie window to open up new ones that display the weather forecast for central Italy (changeable), the New York stock exchange (not too bad) and the Milan exchange (negative, but it did well yesterday), and he starts to download eight movies of which four are not yet released in the cinemas, and, while he's at it, a batch of twenty-or-so songs. It's gratifying to think that the computer will be doing this work by itself while he is on his trip, all at high speed and for the low, fixed cost of an ultra-wideband connection.

When he's about to knot his tie, the door opens and his mother appears, wearing an imploring expression on her face. "Alessio," she says, "will you eat a little spaghetti before leaving? Just basil and tomato, light and simple?"

"Mamma, I told you I don't have time!" says Alessio, in a rather hard tone. It's too bad, but this is the only tone that she's going to understand. It's noon, and this must be the third time she has pestered him about eating.

But his mother doesn't give up so easily. "You can't leave on an empty stomach, Alessio! At least let me make you some veal and a little salad!"

"Mamma, stop it!" he shouts, and it seems to him that nobody could blame him now for raising his voice. "I'll eat something on the highway, in some roadside restaurant!"

"They only feed you rubbish in those places!" says his mother. "It's junk food!"

"Let me get dressed, I'll be late for my clients," says Alessio, his tone of voice lower but with even more firmness. He pushes her out of the room.

Then, while putting on his shoes, he feels sorry for the disappointment he read in her eyes as he closed the door in her face. But it's just one thought among many. He presses the remote control to turn up the volume of the TV, where some girls clad in sequined bikinis are moving to a childish dance, choreographed to make the best use of the cramped space of the studio as well as to showcase their bodily curves. Alessio puts on his jacket and buttons it up, then does a few steps as if he were dancing with them—waving his arms, humming along to the playback song left over from last summer.

The architect Enrico Guardi is standing on the sidewalk in the city center, observing Milan as it pursues its many interconnected activities in the Friday noise and traffic. His wife, Luisa, is lost in thought, with her thin tortoiseshell glasses and her light brown hair drawn back in an elegant little bun, her charcoal-gray coat over her smoky-colored pantsuit. He asks her, "So? When are they coming?"

"I have no idea," she says, in the tone of someone who doesn't want to be held responsible for the organization, nor for the other participants' possible shortcomings.

"We could have gone tomorrow, instead of today," says Enrico, looking at his World War Two-style submarine commander's watch.

"Oh, stop it," snaps Luisa. "You're not the only one around here who works."

Enrico gestures to the street, he says, "Why don't you give Margherita a call? You know there's no limit to how late she can be."

Luisa puffs out her cheeks, and punches in the number on her cell phone with nervous fingers.

Enrico thinks of the prominence that the most minute details can acquire in a long-term relationship, of how reassuring or irritating a single gesture or facial expression can become when you are able to accurately anticipate it.

In the meantime, a cab pulls up; Arturo Vannucci gets out of it, with one of his red-and-blue striped sailing bags. Of the three of them he's the only one who's dressed appropriately for the occasion: an Irish tweed coat over a gray-brown turtleneck sweater and rust-brown moleskin pants, and yellowish heavy-duty boots. Holding Luisa and Enrico in his usual super-energetic bear hug, he says, "So! How is it going?"

"Fine," says Enrico, responding with just a little less strength.

Arturo makes a questioning gesture. "What about Margherita?"

"Apparently she's on her way," says Enrico, thinking of how reassuringly and irritatingly familiar are his thickset person, his practical attitudes, his basic balance, his constantly optimistic disposition.

Luisa says, "She's sorry for being late."

"As if we weren't used to that," says Arturo. There's no trace of impatience in his tone, just a mixture of worldliness and good character, clarity of thought, and the self-assurance that comes from an unshakable economic background.

Enrico thinks of all the business trips they've made together—of the basic division of roles they established from the very first one and then perfected over the years.

A large silver minivan pulls up, indicator lights flashing. Alessio Cingaro jumps out, in a royal-blue coat, his face tanned as if he were just back from a two-week holiday in Barbados. He walks up to them with his right hand outstretched.

"Good morning, Mrs. Guardi! How are you, Mr. Vannucci? Mr. Guardi, you're looking great!"

"Thanks," says Enrico, his eyes going past him to catch Arturo's ironic glance.

Alessio turns around and asks, "What about Miss Novelli?"

"On her way," says Luisa. She's tense, vibrant, elegant, exposed, attentive—as always.

Enrico is about to make some scathing remark about Margherita and her always being late, but the cell phone in his jacket starts to ring. He takes it out and presses it against his ear, moving a few steps away from the others. He ends the conversation as soon as he can, the moment that a cab pulls up at the curb.

Margherita emerges from it in a rather elaborate way: giant insect-like wrap-around sunglasses, pink lamb's wool cap over bleached hair, white lambskin coat, stonewashed, sequined jeans cut very low on her hips, cruelly pointy boots. She takes her lilac fiberglass trolley-suitcase from the driver, goes through her pockets looking for money but can't find any; she turns to Arturo for help, smiling half gratefully and half absentmindedly as he dashes forward, wallet in hand.

Enrico taps his fingers on his wristwatch with a reproachful expression. "We've been waiting here for half an hour."

Margherita pulls up her sunglasses, makes a face and gestures like an affection-starved child. "The traffic was terrible," she says.

"Oh, really? That's *so* unusual," says Arturo, in a mocking tone.

"Give me a break, you guys," says Margherita. She embraces the three of them, then spins around a few times, clapping her hands excitedly. "Isn't this *amazing*? The whole gang, back together again! I can't believe we're finally doing it!"

Enrico, as the only child of two very boring parents, has always dreamed of having a small group of friends; he thinks that for this he should be grateful, instead of feeling bored and annoyed.

"Good morning, Miss Novelli!" says Alessio, smiling like a salesman. "I saw you on the program, the other evening!"

"Ah," says Margherita, suddenly back in the world of grownups.

"Congratulations, eh? You were awesome, as always," says Alessio, his adulatory tone so exaggerated he sounds almost mocking.

Margherita doesn't seem to notice, or perhaps she's simply not interested. "Well, they drove me crazy with those phone calls from home. I couldn't hear a damn thing, I kept being cut off. It made me want to sue the producers—*and* the phone company." She looks at her friends, not expecting any comments on this subject: she knows only too well they're not part of her audience, they would never admit to having seen her program if not by mere chance.

Enrico says, "What say we get started?" He just wants to speed things up, be done at least with the preliminaries.

"Mr. Guardi is right," Alessio points out. "That way we'll arrive in the area in good time, have a nice dinner and a good night's sleep, and be all refreshed tomorrow morning, when we'll go to see your houses."

"Can we all fit in there?" asks Luisa, pointing at the silver mini-van as if her question implied more extensive doubts.

"Of course, Mrs. Guardi!" says Alessio. "There are seven super-comfortable seats. Airplane-style, really. I had the agency reserve it just for this trip." He goes to open the back door, grabs the nearest suitcase, helps the others put theirs in. Then he opens the sliding door at the side, and makes a ceremonious gesture of invitation.

Everybody gets in, Enrico last—with a long, nostalgic look at the frantic movements of the cars and the people in the street.

Luisa observes the merciless squalor of the Milanese out-skirts: the sidewalks and buildings indicative of public indif-ference and private resignation to the point that she can't help feeling its contagion. It's what Enrico calls her "self-injuring sensi-tiveness"; she merely needs to glance along the gray facades to imagine the sounds and smells at the other side of the windows, the weak light and the suspended dust filtering each color into greenish and yellowish and reddish shades of cloths and couches and bedspreads and people's faces. She can picture them waking up amid the ugly furniture, the bitter espresso cups sipped while sitting at sad kitchen tables, the descents in elevators permeated with bad smells and cheap perfumes, the maneuvers in smog-encrusted cars, the waits for crowded buses, the extenuating home-to-office journeys, the detestable hierarchic relationships, the gossips and pressures and disloyalties among colleagues, the lunches gulped down while standing, the interminable rides home in the half-paralyzed traffic, the sick expressions seen through opaque car windows, the neurotic gestures, the nose-pickings, the swearwords, the fake thin-lipped smiles, the frantic rushing to shops on the verge of closing time, the carbon monoxide and pol-lution-imbued clothes, the TV sets tuned on to virtual parlors hosted by circus owners and brothel madams with their courts of clowns and prostitutes, the desolate dinners made up of

microwaved deep-frozen food and third-hand opinions and fragments of sentences and elbows on the table and fixed stares at the
TV, with its representations of allegedly more alluring lives, the
oxygen-deprived nights perturbed by the squeaking of springs and
the roaring of engines, the feet-dragging Sunday strolls on sidewalks littered with spit and dog shit, the circular thoughts aimed
at soccer matches or disappointing sexual activities inspired by
porn videos or by columns in magazines, the cultural misunder-
standings and the pitiless pressures of the open market. There's
nothing she can do about it. She's always had this excessive vulnerability to a sense of desolation, and the place she grew up in
certainly did nothing to relieve it. Sometimes, when she was a
child, her father would take her through particularly bleak parts
of the bleak city, telling her, "Now don't you start registering too
many details," his preemptive aggressiveness aimed at protecting
her. She asks herself whether it was the same attitude that attracted
her to Enrico when she first met him; are the choices someone
makes in life really free, or are they determined by chains of inter-
locked reasons?

Alessio turns on the radio, a silly tune pervades the minivan.
Margherita gives him an intolerant look; Alessio immediately
turns the volume down.

"Even better, turn it off," suggests Enrico, in the unfaltering
tone Luisa finds alternately reassuring or embarrassing, depend-
ing on the circumstances.

"Of course, Mr. Guardi," says Alessio, turning the radio off.

Luisa thinks that she would never bring herself to make such a
peremptory request. She would be restrained by her decency, her
tact, her formal courtesy, her considerations about the other's
point of view. She thinks that ever since she was a child she had
the tendency to tone down her reactions, even when they stemmed

from very definite impulses. Always seeking a kind of moral balance, she would, for example, sympathize with the point of view of the driver in a car crash who rear-ended her. She asks herself, is this due to her being a woman, or to her specific temperament, her education, her parents' characters? She also asks herself whether she's learned to live with it or is increasingly more exasperated by it—if she can tolerate her own contradictions thanks to Enrico's attitude.

Alessio takes a green folder from the glove compartment and hands it to Enrico. "Mr. Guardi, the drawings you asked me for." His cologne is even more overpowering than Margherita's perfume, and with every movement he makes, a kind of scented halo surrounds him.

Enrico takes the folder, and says, "Ah, at long last."

"They faxed them to me only this morning, Mr. Guardi," says Alessio. "I just had the time to print them. They're pretty slow, out there at the Turigi agency. The provinces, you know?"

"Is it them who'll be taking us to see the houses, tomorrow?" says Enrico, pulling the printouts out of the folder.

"No, no," says Alessio. "*I'll* be taking you, Mr. Guardi. Alone."

"So you won't have to share your commission with them, eh?" says Margherita, in the winking, artificially intimate way she's developed as a TV reality-show host.

"Not at all, Miss Novelli," says Alessio. "I just don't want anybody bothering you. Those guys at the Turigi are like cavemen. You know the pushy, nosy type of real-estate agent?"

"I sure do," says Margherita, casting a malicious glance at Luisa.

Luisa thinks that Alessio could very well be a politician for the new generation, with his limited but effective knowledge of marketing and communication techniques, his determination to pursue a few very well-defined personal goals rather than chasing some vague, vast vision. It doesn't take a lot of imagination to picture him talking about international relationships or agricultural politics or information assets, with his double-breasted suit and his automatic smile and his slightly obtuse but perfectly functional way of looking you in the eyes.

Alessio says, "Mr. Guardi, if you don't fall in love when you see it, it means I don't know my job. I'd bet anything on it."

"Anything?" says Margherita.

"Really, Miss Novelli," says Alessio. "It's such a totally perfect piece of property."

Enrico studies the drawings with a mixture of skepticism and technical attention. "They're not very easy to read, these drawings. What does it say here, is it twenty-five or twenty-six?"

At that moment, a jaunty little tune goes off, but it's not from the car stereo, it's Alessio's cell phone. He says, "Excuse me, Mr. Guardi," quickly puts an earpiece into his right ear, and murmurs, "Debby. No, with the customers. Yeah, sure, in the car. I don't know. Buy the white ones. Buy them *both*, then. Do what you want, honey. I told you, Debby, I can't talk right now. Okay. Big kiss."

Margherita turns her head, an ironic look in her eyes; Arturo in the back is smiling. Luisa recalls that even at her publishing house she's constantly receiving e-mails that end with "a hug" or "a big hug" or "a kiss" or even "a big kiss" from authors and collaborators with whom she has such a low level of intimacy that in any face-to-face conversation they would find it awkward to be on a first-name basis. She wonders whether such affectations are only a transitory social tic, or whether they could be an unconscious compensation for the steady impoverishment of everybody's day-to-day life. Such expressions are part of phone conversations, too—a proliferation of empty signs of affection that run through the telephone lines every minute, evoking for brief moments corporeal pressures and temperatures and textures and breathings to millions of increasingly lonely, self-centered people.

She turns to look at Enrico, absorbed as he is in the technical drawings in his hands. He seems competent, serious, unfathomable.

Arturo looks at the that landscape insignificantly slipping away at both sides of the truck-infested highway. The Pianura Padana, Italy's vastest, most affluent flatland: densely populated, given over with equal, dull fervor to industry and agriculture. The minivan's airplane-type seats are comfortable and isolating, there's no contact whatsoever with anybody else's shoulders or knees. This physical separation has the effect of accentuating the mental distances between them, or so it seems to him; conversation is fragmentary, contstantly interrupted by cell-phone calls. Arturo thinks of other, infinitely more uncomfortable and promiscuous trips they have made together in the past: the nonstop tensions of looks and words and gestures, the continuous lateral adjustments in the progression toward the horizon; the laughs, the communal breathing. Now, if he were to peer into the car from the outside, they would probably look to him like the result of an incomplete metamorphosis, which made them different from what they were but not entirely, still holding on in a desperate and futile way to what has kept them together for so long.

Luisa says, "Is the main building really habitable as it is?"

"Mrs. Guardi, you could go live there tomorrow, if you wanted to," Alessio assures her.

"Mmmh, I doubt it very much," says Enrico. His cell phone rings; he fishes it out of his jacket and leans slightly forward to answer. "Yes? Hello? *Hello?*" He looks at the display, shakes his head, puts the phone back into his pocket.

Luisa gives him a quick glance: there's just the slightest attrition when their eyes meet.

"The basic structure is as solid as a rock," continues Alessio. "It's been standing there for centuries. The monks were living there in the year 1200. The walls are a meter and a half thick. To keep you cool in summer and warm in winter, better than air-conditioning."

Arturo is about to say something, but now his cell phone starts ringing. Just reading the name on the display causes him a stabbing pain in his liver. The voice at the other end is charged with claims and intentions of vindication—it penetrates his right ear in a sharp crackling that fills him first with dismay and then with anger. He thinks of cutting off the communication, but then is swept away by his feelings. "Giulia, this is *your* weekend! If you don't tell me anything until the very last moment, I take it for granted that the children are staying with you!"

The others pretend not to hear, they go on talking or looking out of the car windows. But they've all known Giulia for ages, ever since Arturo courted her and invited her out for dinner and kissed her and danced with her and set up two houses with her and had two children with her and discussed and disagreed and fought with her with increasing frequency and intensity: they have every reason to be participant spectators.

Arturo raises his voice again, not something that he does very often. "No, I can't! I'm not even in Milan any more! You should have told me earlier, Giulia! I had the children last weekend, when it was my turn!"

The others are now visibly embarrassed, try as they may not to show it. Luisa forces herself to ask other questions about the houses; Alessio gives a few of his reassuring, professional answers.

But Arturo is brought to complete exasperation by his ex-wife's arguing. "You must stop blackmailing me, Giulia! You only do it to ruin my life and keep me constantly on tenterhooks! I've had enough of this game! I've already talked to your lawyer, last month! I did everything you wanted me to and more, you know it perfectly well! You've won on all fronts, now leave me alone! Leave me alone! *Leave me alone*!!!" He presses a button on his cell phone to cut off communication, then he turns it off. He looks around, his vocal cords aching, his heart full of poison. "Sorry, guys," he says.

How he'd love the others to burst out into a collective laugh, or even make ironic comments and provocative observations, or tease him with affectionate nastiness. Instead, there's a shuffling about and looking away, pretending not to have heard anything or at least having no opinions about it. The fact is that for years they've considered Arturo and Giulia a single entity: a person with two names and two faces and two sexes and two roles but the same life and the same aims in life, the same social facade. He's aware of the strain they have to endure to rearrange their mental land-scapes; he feels guilty and embarrassed about it.

Luisa's cell phone emits an old-fashioned ring-tone; she rummages through her bag, finally fishes it out, and says "Hi. Yes. No. I think it's just a shrewd, self-congulating little soufflé of a book."

Arturo glances at Margherita, who, in an exercise of non-intrusion, turns toward Enrico and asks, "Do you really think there's enough space? So we'll be able to be close to each other without being *on top* of each other?"

"Well, at least on paper, we should," says Enrico.

"Not just on *paper*, Mr. Guardi" says Alessio. "Miss Novelli, you'll get four fully independent units of about two hundred and fifty square meters each, just as you wanted, and one is more beautiful than the other. You'll be fighting over who is getting what, you'll see."

"I'm sorry, but that's what I *think*," says Luisa into her phone. "There's nothing I can do about it. I just find it empty, presumptuous, and terribly irritating."

"I want the tower, I said it first!" says Margherita, in the voice of a spoiled child she's always had but which recently took on a more exasperating nuance.

"No, *I* want the tower," says Arturo, mostly to tease her.

"Wait till you've seen it," says Enrico. "It's the most problematic space in the whole arrangement. We'll get a room per floor out of it, at the most. It'll be all stairs."

"Not all stairs, Mr. Guardi," says Alessio. He seems about to launch himself into some technical disquisition about what can be termed problematic in real estate, but instead he points out the satellite navigator's screen to Margherita. "Have you seen this, Miss Novelli? It's the new 3-D version."

"It looks like a videogame," says Margherita without really paying much attention, one ear listening to Luisa who keeps talking to her editorial director about a book she doesn't like but will have to publish anyway.

"I know perfectly well," says Luisa. "But it can't be the only standard, the market."

"Is the area really beautiful?" asks Arturo. "I've been to Umbria several times, but never around Turigi. I know Perugia pretty well, and Orvieto and Gubbio and Assisi, though. I was happy enough with my house near Greve in Chianti, but my dear ex-wife is keeping it." He thinks of the years he spent improving the rather cold renovation his parents had made to the old Tuscan farmhouse, the painstaking search for the right materials, the long conversations with the local artisans, the many attempts to find the right solutions. Having lost the house also means never seeing again the big straw baskets under the patio or the ancient barrels in the cellar, the light stone slabs he had personally laid down one by one along the path in the garden. Giulia will probably end up giving it all a tacky glazing or she'll bring it to ruin, or maybe she'll sell it to some idiot who'll never know the amount of care and attention he devoted to it, when he was still deeply hypnotized by his misunderstanding of family life.

"Beautiful?" says Alessio. "Mr. Vannucci, it's one the most enchanting areas in Italy. You can't find such pristine landscapes, unless you're prepared to go among the wolves, in the mountains of Abruzzo."

"What's exactly your definition of 'pristine'?" says Margherita, a suspicious look on her face. "You don't mean too rustic, I hope?"

"Not at all, Miss Novelli!" says Alessio. "Not at all! I mean natural, unspoiled, just what you've been looking for. You've seen the pictures, haven't you?"

"Yeah, well, pictures are one thing, reality is another," says Margherita.

"And you should know," says Arturo.

"What?" says Margherita.

"Just kidding, come on," says Arturo. "In any case, the landscape over there is wilder than in Tuscany, that's for sure. Not as cultivated, or populated. More woods, less vineyards. I would say that Umbria is medieval, compared to Tuscany being Renaissance."

"And the prices are less than half those of Tuscany, Mister Vannucci," says Alessio. "At least for the time being. But just wait until the Germans and the Japanese realize it; the prices will go sky-high in a matter of months. As things stand today, this is the best investment in real estate you could make."

"It's not to make an investment that we want those houses,"

says Margherita. "It's to *use* them. Spend time in them, relax and enjoy ourselves in them."

"Yeah," says Arturo. "Still, we wouldn't be terribly disappointed if it turned out we hadn't thrown our money away." This is the role the others have given him since the beginning of their friendship, and he's held on to it through the years without wavering, even when the others were bored or not paying attention or maybe wanted him to be different, because he knew how important it was. He's always felt like the group's drummer, never aspiring to the charisma of the guitar player, nor to that of the lead singer. It's enough for him to know that without his steady, grounded beat the band would soon lose cohesion and fall apart.

Margherita, in the meantime has withdrawn from the conversation. She's pressing her cell phone to her ear, saying, "I don't care if you're sorry! It's me looking like a poor deaf who can't even get the callers' names right!"

Arturo would like to comment on her tone, but he doesn't know to whom, because Enrico is still looking absentmindedly out of the window and Luisa is still carrying on to her editor: "A publisher has the duty of making choices, every now and then! Otherwise we should just stick to the trashy instant books by the TV comedians!"

"Exactly, Mr. Vannucci," says Alessio, unperturbed. "I'm pretty sure you won't be sorry if in a couple of years your property is worth three times what you're paying now."

"Three times, huh?" says Arturo.

"Mr. Vannucci, let's write down today's date, okay?" says Alessio. "Then in a couple of years you'll give me a call. You'll buy me a coffee, okay?"

Enrico emerges from his thoughts and says, "First let's see what the costs of the renovation will be. It's going to be a rather serious endeavor, you know."

"It's going to be smooth and easy, Mr. Guardi," says Alessio. "Everything's there already, as gorgeous as the sun. Trust me. Wait until you've seen it for yourselves."

Enrico smiles skeptically; then his cell phone rings. He looks at the display with a wary attitude, puts it to his ear, then says, "Of course the passageway is ochre. I don't care, it's the builders' problem, not mine! You talk to them, I don't even want to hear about it. Tell them you haven't found me, tell them I'm on a plane."

"Of course it's my personal opinion!" says Luisa into her phone. "And as long as I'm directing this series, perhaps my personal opinion is of some interest?"

"Discuss it with Di Sorio, then!" shouts Margherita into her phone. "Discuss it with Telecom, discuss it with Cuccioni, discuss it with whomever you like! If you don't have the problem fixed by Wednesday evening, I'm not going on the air!"

The three of them end their conversations almost simultaneously. They sit still and expressionless as the reverberation of their voices dies off in the muffled rumble of the van's engine.

Arturo leans forward with a slanted smile, he says to Enrico, "You know the expression 'traveling light'?"

Enrico turns to look at him, and although he's irritated and thinking of something else, he bursts into laughter. Luisa and Margherita laugh, too. So does Alessio, probably not to be cut off from the general mood.

Arturo thinks that perhaps after all it is possible to keep a friendship alive forever, as long as you don't let it be eroded by time. He laughs louder than the others, his heart warmed by the feeling of sharing.

Margherita thinks that she should have asked the others to postpone this trip, to stay in town until the matter of the phone connections and the more serious situation of sponsors were solved. She knows from experience how worthless are proclamations and vows of friendship and displays of self-confidence among the television people. Countless times she has witnessed their changes of mind at the very last moment due to unavoidable phone calls, their sudden lapses of memory, their fake smiles and pats on the shoulders, their dinner invitations that hover halfway between sexual harassment and offers of compensation, their waving of the company's flag to cover the meanest of private interests. A few of her personal proverbs occur to her, such as "Success has many fathers, but failure is an orphan," or "The good watchdog always anticipates its master's intentions," or "Put your hands forward, so you won't hurt yourself if you fall facedown." But right now one of her aunt's favorite sayings comes to mind: "He who wants shall go, he who doesn't shall send." The trust she has in her agent keeps diminishing as the distance that separates her from him grows; she knows only too well how necessary it is to keep him on a short leash, if she wants to avoid any ugly surprises. She checks the charge status of her cell phone, and anticipates how her right ear will be burning after all the calls she'll have to make in order to reach a satisfactory solution.

Another source of deep distress comes from the disgraceful job her hairdresser did the day before yesterday, when she asked him to lightly trim her hair and refresh the highlights. She knows she should have kept an eye on him, but she was so preoccupied that she had lowered her guard and skimmed through a couple of gossip magazines. The result was finding herself with a yellowish-white head of hair that made her cry out in anger in front of the mirror, to the amusement of the salon's other customers. Even worse was having to go on the air in front of millions of people acting all sprightly, as if it had been her idea to morph into a semi-albino. She pulls her woolen cap down over her forehead; she can't wait to be restored to a plausible shade of blond, first thing Monday morning.

It also has to be said that the others certainly aren't any welcome distraction: the minivan is a hotbed of half gestures and half looks, unsaid words, cell phones continually ringing like electric shocks. She thinks that perhaps at this stage in their lives they are all a little too wrapped up in themselves to make this kind of trip together, the overlapping of their individual anxieties making it impossible to communicate in the simple and funny way they had years ago. She would like to smoke a cigarette, but she knows how the others would instantly turn on her if she did. She's hungry and her head is aching; if they don't let her at least drink a cup of coffee she risks having a fit of nerves.

Arturo is saying, "What I'm really looking for is a new place to go with my children. Ever since Giulia and I split up I've been spending whole days before every holiday studying guides and maps, phoning travel agencies to organize increasingly longer trips, and they always turn out to be a disappointment."

"I can assure you it's like that even if you don't have children," says Margherita, in a useless effort to push away the thoughts that are tormenting her into the background. "You can travel as far as you like, you'll find the same things everywhere."

"Not exactly the same, come on," says Luisa, characteristically seeking a balance between the subjective and the objective—a typical Libra.

"*Exactly* the same," says Margherita. One of the things that working in television has taught her is how pointless it is to try to express your thoughts in nuances. What counts is to put forward one sharp opinion—right or wrong, it doesn't matter—and to do it with great determination. This way you can stir up some controversy, see if others are with you or against you without getting bogged down in a million subtle, ineffective shades of meanings. She goes on to say, "Same hotel rooms, same CNN and MTV, same soft drinks, same junk food, same commercials, same music, same tanning lotions. The only things that change are the landscape and the humidity, which you have to pay for with a dozen hours on a plane and a sick stomach."

Arturo laughs. "My God, what a picture."

Margherita can't really see it as funny. She has all too vivid a memory of her last exotic holiday, in a resort on what is supposed to be the last exclusive island off the coast of Thailand. She had dreamed about it for months, only to see it destroyed in a matter of hours by gastrointestinal problems. It all comes back to her, now: the blinding sun through the windows, the giant spiders on the walls, the sweat-soaked sheets, the boxes of medicines, the brochures and sunglasses and electronic gadgets and useless swimming suits scattered around the bungalow. In a bitter tone, she remarks, "At this point in my life, traveling far is a totally idiotic thing to do."

"I couldn't disagree more," says Arturo. "To me it's idiotic *not* to travel."

"In our case we're talking of a mere three and a half hours," says Alessio, quick to stem any negative considerations before they can taint the notion of buying a small hamlet in the country-side. "These days it can't even be called a trip anymore."

"What would you call it, then?" says Arturo.

"A getaway," says Alessio. "A simple getaway. You know it better than me, Mr. Vannucci."

Luisa looks dreamily out of the car window, and comments, "I could even move there permanently. To live there. If I decided to quit the publishing house, for instance."

"Why on earth would you do that?" says Enrico, alarmed.

"Because at some point one gets fed up with things," says Luisa, giving him a hard look.

"Don't start being moody, now," says Enrico, "just because of that Castruccetto book you don't like."

"It's not just the Castruccetto book," says Luisa. "And I'm not being moody." She turns toward the window again, offering an obstinate profile.

Margherita thinks of some words to lead the conversation back to the subject of the day. It's a kind of acquired instinct, a respon-sibility she takes home from work. But her cell phone goes off with its frantic little march; she fishes it out of her bag, and says with a sigh, "I told you not to call me anymore."

There's an ironic glimmer in Arturo's eyes, as he turns toward Enrico in one of those exchanges he probably feels compelled to have by the rules of their friendship. But Enrico is so wrapped up in his own thoughts, he doesn't even notice.

Margherita hastens to cut the conversation off, "It's none of your business, Ugo. Ugo, *please*. Thanks, I have things to do now. Bye, bye. Bye now!" She presses the OFF button of her cell phone, and scans the others' faces, without detecting any reactions. Still, she knows that almost certainly they're calling up their mental images of Ugo at her birthday party, six months ago: the artificial tan and the extra-wide wing-collared white shirt open to his chest, his jerky little bursts of laughter to fill the voids in the conversation. To be honest, he isn't totally devoid of qualities as a man, in the areas of sex and money, for instance, or in his rather desperate desire for cultural improvement. But no qualities can compensate the atrocious feeling of public humiliation Margherita experienced when she saw his pictures in a magazine, rubbing himself on top of a third-class TV starlet on the deck of his motorboat, off the coast of Capri. She knows that the others must have seen those pictures or at least heard about them, but they are too snobbish to ever admit it.

There goes her cell phone's little march again; she lets it play on for a while, then looks at the display and sees it's not a second attempt by Ugo. She hastens to answer, listens to the agitated voice of her agent piling words upon words in self-justification. Almost immediately she runs out of patience and cuts him off, saying, "And who else was there, besides Menguzzi and Tornante? But wasn't Politanò on our side, until this morning?"

Meanwhile, Alessio continues his telemarketer-type chatter. "Whatever you're going to do with it, it's the quietest holiday place you could ever find in Italy. And should you decide to move there, you can do a lot of things in the country better than in town thanks to cell phones, the Internet, wideband satellite connections. You can even set up a videoconference—it's a thousand times easier and cheaper than flying to New York to meet a client."

"Well, I'm not so sure about that," says Enrico, coldly. Then he, too, answers his cell phone: "No, Akiro. Two forty-five on the whole floor, of course. Of course the corridors are included!"

Margherita can't help listening in, as much as she tries to

concentrate on her own conversation. She raises her voice: "And who's giving us any guarantee on this? I'll believe it when I see it on paper, otherwise it's just empty talk! I know what Tornante's word is worth! I saw him last year, the big fat mozzarella puppet!"

"You may have twelve-centimeter steps in Japan, but it has to be *twenty* here!" says Enrico, as if in a yelling contest. "Yes, Akiro, twenty *centimeters*. What does the handrail have to do with it? The children will raise their little legs up a little, it will only do them good!"

Luisa points outside—the signs tell her that a highway station is some fifteen hundred meters away and quickly approaching. She asks, "Could we stop for a sandwich, maybe?"

"Of course, Mrs. Guardi," says Alessio, with a glance at the others to see if they agree.

Arturo nods his head; Margherita too makes an approving gesture, without interrupting her conversation.

Alessio switches the indicator on and turns into the right lane, slowing down.

Margherita thinks again what a really bad idea it was to leave today, with so many crucial matters still unsolved, as the minivan pulls into the parking lot with its cargo of overlapping anxieties.

Alessio eats a "Riviera" sandwich that drips mayonnaise, leaning with his back against the side of the minivan, cell phone pressed to his right ear. Normally he's rather careful to balance proteins, fats, and carbohydrates in his diet, but these highway restaurants tend to trigger a kind of indiscriminate voracity in him, perhaps because they seem a little like space stations, outside of the everyday earthly precedents. So, even though the cooked ham is way too pale and the cheese is of terrible quality and the lettuce is thin and damp, he actually enjoys it. He leans forward at every bite so as not to smudge his coat, but a few yellowish drops end up falling on loafers anyway. Meanwhile, on the phone, he lets his client do the talking, saying "aha" every now and then with a full mouth, just to let her know he's still there. She's not the kind of client he likes to deal with, with her exaggerated expectations and lack of flexibility and constant attempts to reduce his agent's fee. When he finally manages to end the conversation he mutters, "You ugly face-lifted bitch," bending down to wipe the mayonnaise off his shoes with a paper towel.

Some fifty meters away, he sees Mrs. Guardi and Miss Novelli coming out of the diner's glass doors and down the steps, Mrs. Guardi in front, a small bottle of mineral water in one hand and her cell phone in the other, eyes downcast. She's not bad looking, but she's one of those high-strung, neurotic women that almost scare Alessio, like an English teacher he had in accounting school.

As a client she's pretty worrisome, too, because of the way she oscillates between a rather naïve enthusiasm and sudden bouts of depression which are difficult to predict or control. It's obvious that from an emotional point of view she has a lot invested in this country villa idea, but it's also clear that for him the risky part is now, when it comes to turning ideas into facts.

Miss Novelli follows her, phone pressed tight to her ear, gesturing nervously. Rather attractive, even though of course less so than on TV. In real life she's shorter and with smaller tits and bags under her eyes, and her hair over-bleached. Alessio pegged her type from the first time she came to the agency with the others: the kind of woman who changes her mind ten times a day and thinks that everybody should go along with her because she's a TV star, alternately behaving in a bossy or fragile or seductive manner. But provided he keeps his nerves, she's the kind of client who could pay off, because of the way she tends to act on impulse. It's all a matter of letting her give in to the right impulse at the right moment, allowing her to think that all the choices are hers.

Now she ends her phone call and lights up a cigarette, inhaling eagerly. She says something to Mrs. Guardi, who shakes her head. Most likely it's about work or personal stuff, but then again it might be something else. Alessio watches them from a distance for another couple of minutes, then he walks toward them. It's never a good idea to leave clients alone for too long, right before a purchase. He knows all too well that when a client is about to leave the safety of the "still-thinking-about-it" zone to make the leap and finally sign a contract, the slightest doubt can work its way through the most apparently solid conviction like a worm through wood. He's learned this at his own expense: the closer you are to the final agreement, the more a client has to be pursued and motivated and reassured step by step. As in any other gambling game, no real estate sale is won or lost until the very last move.

Alessio approaches the two women with a casual air, glancing at a black Mercedes SL he's always liked a lot, although this latest model may have lost something in the tail, or then again it may not. Miss Novelli is now acting out with Mrs. Guardi the wise and nice confidante's role she plays in her shows when she's not too busy ripping someone to shreds. "Of course I know," she says, all her facial muscles tensed to show concern. Sure, it's difficult to take at face value her gestures and expressions, when you've seen her a thousand times using them as part of her repertoire in a reality show. Come to think of it, Alessio's job and Novelli's have a lot in common: both risk inspiring mistrust in their efforts to show attention and care.

Mrs. Guardi seems too upset to listen anyway, behind her elegantly understated clothes and intellectual-looking tortoiseshell glasses. She turns toward the diner, to see her husband and Vannucci exiting through the glass doors. The architect has his cell phone in his hand but almost immediately he puts it back into his jacket, smiling at his wife as he walks toward her.

In the meantime a guy with a shaved head and a carefully sculpted goatee has approached Novelli, projecting an admiring or possibly provoking attitude. "Excuse me," he says, "are you Margherita *Novelli*?"

"Yes," says Novelli, on the defensive. She drops her half-smoked cigarette, stubs it out with the sharp point of her right boot.

Alessio gets between them, bodyguard style, a hard expression on his face: gestures like these help you gain a client's confidence.

The guy with the shaved head doesn't even notice him, he's too focused on Novelli. He says, "I would have said so. Congratulations for the show, eh?"

"Thanks," says Novelli, stiffening as if expecting a volley of insults or even kicks from one moment to another.

Alessio asks himself what he should do in case she is attacked.

Would it be enough to stand there as a physical barrier, or would he have to produce some martial-arts motions? He's not very well trained at such things, apart from a couple of karate lessons he took years ago, because they were offered for free by his gym.

The bald guy says, "I barely recognized you, in person. You look taller on TV."

"I know," Novelli says. She turns toward Mrs. Guardi, but she's too lost in her own problems to offer any support.

"Really, congratulations," says the guy. "Would you sign an autograph for my wife? Her name is Fiorella."

Novelli says, "Of course, of course." She's relieved, almost grateful, smiling more than she should. She writes longer than necessary on the brochure the guy is handing her, then shakes his hand, smiling nervously again; as soon as he's gone she lights up another cigarette.

Mr. Guardi and Mr. Vannucci walk up behind her, with teasing expressions she certainly doesn't find amusing. With a laugh Vannucci says, "Can I have an autograph too, for my wife?"

In Alessio's opinion, he's the best client in the whole group: positive, motivated, stable, practical. The architect, on the other hand, is probably the worst, as reluctant and technically competent as he is. Barring any false steps or sudden catastrophes, Alessio should be able to make him sign the contract.

"You bastard," says Novelli to Vannucci. She laughs, too, but it's very clear that this continuous poking fun at her by her friends disturbs her more than she's ready to admit.

Alessio wipes the last traces of mayonnaise from the corners of his mouth and dusts the crumbs off his coat. "Ladies and gentlemen, shall we get on our way?" He holds the minivan's keys up high, like a Japanese tour guide. Nobody laughs or seems particularly amused, but they all follow him.

Luisa is absorbed in the loping curves of the road, after the tension of the highway infested with ferocious trucks roaring like prehistoric animals and shark-faced cars zigzagging between lanes at crazy speeds and the continuous calls on their cell phones, voices and reasons competing for attention all the time. Now the others are silent, too, looking without much interest out of the minivan windows at the cultivated hills and the thickets and the new developments and the old stone houses and the brutally pruned plane-trees, the disproportionately boxy factories and supermarkets, the concrete boulders, the turnpikes apparently going nowhere.

She tries hard to focus on the nice aspects of the landscape, but it's not easy, because there are so many ugly buildings springing up among the cornfields, huge power lines towering over the vineyards. All kinds of human activities seem to have inflicted wounds on the countryside, turning it into a kind of no-man's-land that is neither country nor suburb nor industrial zone. This is what she tries to point out to the foreign authors and publishers she sometimes escorts around Italy: the peculiar discontinuity between a glorious past and a dismal present. It's not that she has an aversion to everything that is contemporary; what hurts her each time is the brutal, totally insensitive lack of grace and intelligence in the choice of materials and shapes and in the placement of the new constructions. It's as if at some point in history the almost instinctive, harmonious care with which Italian buildings and towns had been made for centuries had vanished, gave way to the most stupid and aggressive bad taste, unrestrained by any regulations or even by simple common sense. It's this utterly thoughtless disregard for all matters of style and beauty that makes her cringe now as she looks out of the minivan window. She thinks that the "beautiful Italy" of yore probably survives only in art books and upmarket real estate magazines, where all the interfering ugliness has been carefully blotted out of the picture. Most likely, she thinks she's the only one among her friends to be pained by this, and the thought makes her feel utterly lonely.

Alessio is not talking, as he is concentrating on comparing the real road in front of them to the virtual road on the screen of his navigator. Suddenly he makes a triumphant gesture, saying, "Ladies and gentlemen, we're in Turigi."

Luisa can't help staring at what looks like a shopping mall's building yard: huge supporting posts, iron rods, concrete mixers, cranes.

"How long have we been on the road?" says Margherita. "I don't know about you guys, but my ass is sore and my legs feel like pins and needles!"

"It's only been three hours and forty-five minutes, Miss Novelli," says Alessio; acutely aware of the difference that a quarter of an hour can make in a decision to buy.

"It feels like a whole *lifetime*," says Margherita. "And you haven't even let me smoke a cigarette, you fucking healthnuts."

"That's all we needed, your cigarettes," says Enrico, without taking his eyes off his cell phone as he taps in an sms.

"Excuse me, ladies and gentlemen," says Alessio. "Let's keep in mind that we stopped for at least twenty minutes at the service station. Otherwise, we could have easily made it in three and a half hours."

"Yeah, driving at two hundred kilometers per hour," says Arturo.

Luisa says, "I expected it to be more beautiful here." She has no intention of playing hard to please, but it certainly takes a lot of blotting out to isolate the few nice buildings from the ugly ones scattered all around.

"This is *Italy*, Luisa," says Enrico, sending off his sms. "It shouldn't be such shocking news to you."

"Well, I hoped it was different, at least over here," says Luisa, offended by his patronizing tone.

Enrico says, "All you have to do is put together a largely submerged economy, an overabundance of laws, a general disregard of rules, a widespread corruption of local administrations, then add the horrible taste of the engineers and builders and the dreadful taste of the purchasers, and what you get is this."

"It's also such a long and narrow country," says Arturo. "And it has the highest ratio of cars per inhabitant in Europe."

"And cell phones," says Enrico.

"And TV sets, thank God," says Margherita.

"But ladies and gentlemen, this is the *new* part of town!" says Alessio, alarmed. "You still have to see the old center. All stones and bricks, really ancient and beautiful. Just like your houses. You'll have to see the porticoes, the Zamparini palace, the communal tower with its wonderful antique clock. The square is a veritable jewel, and there's a museum of pottery that'll make your heads turn. We have all of Sunday morning to visit, I can guarantee that you'll be enchanted!"

Margherita yawns and stretches; she says, "How far is the farmhouse B and B from here?"

Alessio glances at the navigator screen, then says, "Eight kilometers, more or less. As soon as we're out of Turigi we have to head southwest, and we'll be there in a matter of minutes."

"And you're sure it's an acceptable place?" says Margherita; she yawns again.

"Acceptable, Miss Novelli?" says Alessio, in feigned shock. "It's the only place in the area that gets three little trees in the guide, eh? Comfortable, quiet, offering typical, fabulous homemade food. When I talked to the hostess, she said she would warm up all the rooms."

"Why, were they freezing cold?" says Margherita. She puts her boots on the dashboard, spread-legged, scratching the tip of her nose.

"Of course not, Miss Novelli," says Alessio, in a professionally patient tone. "She just wanted everything ideally set up. We unpack our suitcases and relax for a couple of hours, make a few phone calls or whatever, then we'll have a nice dinner, with all the good local food and the healthy, organic vegetables you ladies love so much."

"Yeah," says Arturo. "They do have a very tasty cuisine here in Umbria."

"A bit coarse, though," says Enrico.

"Not necessarily," says Arturo. "Perhaps more basic then others, but not coarse, when it's well prepared."

"Still, it's not famous for being subtle," says Enrico. He's never been very interested in food, and it's obvious to Luisa that he's saying this just to distance himself from the whole idea of buying the houses.

"Okay, maybe not *subtle*," says Arturo, "but tasty. It has to do with the environment, as always. This is not Chianti, it's a much rougher territory."

"I wouldn't call it rough, Mr. Vannucci," says Alessio.

"Don't worry, I don't mind rough," says Arturo. "As long as it tastes like the wild boar they cook around here."

"The pastas are exceptional, too," says Alessio.

"That's true," says Arturo. "A few years ago, I had some really wonderful *strangozzi* pasta with trout and black truffles near Perugia," says Arturo. "Most delicious."

"Is somebody hungry, or what?" says Alessio, teasingly.

"Well, that awful sandwich on the highway tasted like plastic," says Arturo. "And you were all in such a hurry to get back into the car again."

"It's been long enough as it is," says Enrico.

"It hasn't been that long, Mr. Guardi" says Alessio.

"Says the salesman," says Margherita.

Alessio tries to bring the conversation back to a more appealing topic: He says, "Wait till you've tasted the Turigi red wine, Mr. Vannucci. Then you'll really fall in love with this place."

"Yeah, they've made great progress with the wines here, too," says Arturo. "Besides the noble Montepulciano, which has long been up there among the best, of course. I drank some outstanding Polego lately, for instance. A truly interesting, fruity, herby taste. It goes well with the local lamb in black-truffle sauce. Or with a nice hare *alla norcina*. That is, cooked with lard, rosemary, juniper, and a couple of freshly picked laurel leaves."

"Exactly," says Alessio. "This is a gourmet's paradise, Mr. Vannucci." He puts all his resources into play to contrast the general feeling of tiredness: smiling, gesticulating, fiddling with the automatic air conditioner to cool off the overheated minivan. Luisa tries not to notice a gas station at the center of an expanse of asphalt large enough for at least twenty articulated trucks. She asks herself whether she should develop a protective screen against such esthetic squalor, or whether it's too late to do so. She says, "And how long does it take to get to our houses, from here?"

"Ah, about twenty minutes, Mrs. Guardi," says Alessio. "Maybe even less."

They're already past the small town now, past the *carabinieri* station, past the last semidetached houses. There are still a couple of ugly modern villas with vulgar fences all around them, and then the countryside finally opens up. Luisa looks at a wonderful old stone-and-brick farmhouse set among the fields extending on both sides of the road toward the hills. Pulling down her window, soaking up the growing harmony of forms and colors she feels an intense kind of relief. This is what she has been waiting for all along: the greens and yellows and browns, the undisturbed hills sweeping up in perfect rolling waves, woods alternating with patches of cultivated land. The balance, the quietness, the timeless care. This is the antidote to the frantic dreariness of the city, to the aggressively sharp-lined and colorless, man-made landscapes. For the first time, after three and a half hours and hundreds of kilometers, she can breath in deeply.

Enrico says, "Do you mind pulling up that window? The air's damned cold."

She pulls up the window, then leans with her forehead against the glass, looking out as far as she can see.

Margherita has one of her sudden bouts of childish enthusiasm. "Listen, why don't we go see our houses before going to the farmhouse B and B?"

"You mean now, Miss Novelli?" says Alessio.

"Yes!" says Margherita. "So we don't have to wait until tomorrow morning!"

"Well, technically we could," says Alessio, unconvinced. "But aren't you all a little bit too tired?"

"I'm not!" says Margherita. "Are you guys too tired?" She turns to look at them, but her cell phone emits a "message received" signal, and she frantically rummages through her bag to read it at once.

Arturo says, "If it's really only about twenty minutes away, I'm in."

"Me too," says Luisa, certain that Enrico would prefer to go right away to the farmhouse B&B.

Unexpectedly, Enrico says, "Yeah, okay. So we can go back to Milan tomorrow, instead of waiting until Sunday. What are we going to do here for two full days, anyway?"

"Mr. Guardi, there's quite a *lot* to do, as you well know," says Alessio. "Inspecting the estate, making measurements, taking notes for the renovation. . . ."

"Is it really such an unbearably long time to you, two whole days?" asks Arturo. "To get a good idea of the houses and of the area around them? And maybe, just maybe, be with your friends for a while? When was the last time we were able to do this, Enrico? And it's not even two whole days, anyway. We only have the whole of tomorrow, and half of the day after."

Enrico says, "You're right. Sure." He nods, raising his hands in mock surrender.

Luisa says, "So, are we going to see the houses right away?"

"Yeah, let's go have a look," says Arturo.

Alessio says, "You're sure you wouldn't rather go to the farmhouse to take a nice shower and relax a little before dinner? Those houses are not going to run away, eh? They'll still be there tomorrow morning." It's obvious he doesn't like the idea of going now, but he doesn't want to contradict his clients either, so all he can do is hope they'll change their minds.

"We can relax later," says Luisa.

"Yeah," says Arturo. "We have plenty of time."

Margherita is still fiddling with her cell phone to answer the sms she's received; as soon as she's done she instantly reverts to the childishly enthusiastic attitude of a few minutes earlier, saying, "So come on! Take us there right away, Alessio!"

"Okay, if you all agree," says Alessio, with a strained smile to mask his aversion. He taps on the navigator's buttons as if he was afraid to ruin it, setting the new coordinates.

"Hurrah!" screams Margherita. "I can't wait to be there! We'll see our very own private hamlet! In the sunset, it'll be so perfect!"

"I don't know about the sunset, Miss Novelli," says Alessio. "The sky is pretty cloudy right now."

"Who cares about the sky!" says Margherita. "I just can't wait!"

"Awright!" screams Arturo, who never backs off when it comes to being one of the boys.

"It's so exciting!" says Luisa, in an outburst of spontaneity that makes her feel a little awkward. "We've been talking about this for about ten years at least, haven't we?" She reaches out for Enrico's hand, squeezing it.

He squeezes hers back, and says, "Yes."

Alessio drives carefully up the dirt road that climbs through the hills. The cultivated fields are well behind them now; woods now cover the undulating landscape almost entirely. Novelli at his right keeps showing her excitement: pointing out at every bend, saying, "Look! Isn't it awesome?" even when there isn't much to see except tree trunks and branches and leaves. Vannucci seems just as thrilled, talking about *boletus edulis* mushrooms in saffron sauce and homemade lasagna *al pesto* and rabbit cacciatore with black olives and cherry tomatoes. Mrs. Guardi leans with her head against the window glass, enchanted by the colors of the vegetation as if they were a balm for her soul. Her husband, the architect, on the other hand seems to be less and less at ease as they venture further into the woods: he doesn't talk, looks at his watch every few minutes.

Overall, Alessio is quite pleased with their reactions. Call it a dream, call it a fantasy, call it what you like, this is what he is going to sell them, and the majority of them seem to like it. The road is narrow and twisty, but at least there aren't any mudslides or serious potholes; the navigator indicates the route clearly enough; the big fuel-injected turbo-diesel engine seems to be turning well. Alessio feels like a ship captain in an ocean of hills: in control of his vessel, half worried, half pleased at the thought of being responsible for the valuable, delicate cargo he's carrying.

At one point there's a fork in the road, which he can identify with some difficulty on the screen. He slows down, cautiously follows the navigator's directions. This electronic assistance is not enough to entirely reassure him, now that for a good fifteen or maybe twenty minutes he hasn't seen a house or a steel pylon or a road sign or any other sign of civilized life.

Then the red arrow on the screen points to a left turn in the virtual road, but the real road takes a slow bend to the right, along a compact front of trees. Alessio stops.

Mr. Guardi immediately leans forward, saying, "Is everything okay? Are we still on the right road?"

"Uh, we should be, Mr. Guardi," says Alessio. He looks at the navigator's screen, then at the woods.

"What do you mean, we should be?" asks Mr. Guardi. "It's either the right one or it isn't."

Novelli taps one of her mother-of-pearl varnished nails on the screen, and asks, "Doesn't it show there?"

"It does, Miss Novelli," says Alessio. "It does."

"So? What's the problem?"

"There's no problem," replies Alessio. He knows perfectly well that if there is an aspect of his job where he can't afford to show any uncertainty, it's this. He shifts the automatic gear-change lever into DRIVE; he makes the tires rasp on the compacted ground.

Behind him, Mr. Guardi says, "It'll be getting dark soon."

Vannucci, from the last row of seats, says, "I'm afraid we can forget about the sunset over our houses. It's really cloudy, too."

"Don't worry, ladies and gentlemen," says Alessio in a reassuring tone taken from his repertoire, forcing himself not to look at the sky. "We'll be there at the right time. With the magical postcard light, really."

"Bah," says Mr. Guardi. "I doubt it very much."

Alessio thinks that perhaps not even a satellite navigator like this one can be one hundred percent accurate when it comes to such a minor little dirt road, so far from the inhabited world. He thinks that perhaps it was a mistake not to bring a couple of paper maps as well. He tries to think of an acceptable way to save face and go back and postpone everything to tomorrow morning, after having gathered some detailed instructions at the farmhouse B&B.

From what he can see between the clouds and the trees, there's little doubt now about daylight fading. The satellite navigator keeps beep-beeping for a turn that simply isn't there, the road keeps climbing through the woods like it could go on forever. Alessio hits the brakes again, and looks out of the side window, drumming his hands on the steering wheel.

Beside and behind him now there's a variety of puffs and coughs, whispers and looks and gestures; he feels a growing pressure on his back and temples.

"Listen, if you got lost you might as well tell us," says Mr. Guardi.

"At this point, I'm afraid, we can be pretty sure of it," says Vannucci from the back.

Alessio points to the navigator's screen, trying to decide to what extent he can place the blame on it. He says, "This thing keeps indicating a left turn, but there's nothing on the left, as you all can see."

"Don't you have a regular, ordinary map?" asks Mrs. Guardi.

"An ordinary one, no" says Alessio. "But we have the virtual maps of all of Europe on the GPU, Mrs. Guardi."

"Forget about that toy," says her husband. "Can't you remember the way by yourself?"

"How did you get there the last time?" says Vannucci. "Try to remember."

"It's not a matter of remembering," says Alessio, in the evasive way to which he resorts on the rare occasions when he can't give an effective answer.

"Well, make an effort!" says Miss Novelli, with the sudden aggressiveness she tends to display when she abruptly stops smiling to attack one of her unsuspecting victims.

"Right now, I wouldn't know," says Alessio. The navigator's unexpected failure has the effect of making him feel strangely tired, slowing down his reactions.

Mr. Guardi says, "Why did you take us out here, if you didn't remember the way?"

"Mr. Guardi, I didn't want to take you here right away," says Alessio, making an intense effort not to fall into a spiral of self-justification. "It was Miss Novelli who insisted. I had planned to take you here tomorrow morning."

"Do you mean it's my fault, now?" says Novelli, in the even harsher register she uses when she's really bent on tearing someone to pieces in front of a few million people. "You're the real-estate agent, here! It's your job to find the way!"

"It certainly is, Miss Novelli," says Alessio. Appeasing, submissive, mild smile, lowered eyes: it's his only possible tactic in a situation like this.

But Novelli isn't appeased at all. She turns to the others and says, "I only suggested that we come. He said there was no problem! You've all witnessed it!"

The architect says, "Yes, well, you could have spared us the suggestion."

"Anyway, we're here now," says Vannucci.

"That's right," says Mrs. Guardi. "Let's just try to find the way."

"At this point it's perfectly pointless," says Mr. Guardi. "It's getting so dark, we wouldn't be able to see anything anyway."

Alessio grabs the opportunity. "Mr. Guardi is right. We go to the farmhouse B and B and come back here tomorrow morning, all rested and refreshed."

"Sure, all rested and refreshed," repeats Novelli, like a pit bull that doesn't want to let go now that it can smell the blood. "Then you'll have to explain how the hell you made it to those houses the other times."

Alessio could easily think of more than one reply to her question, but the intimidating TV technique she's using is making it really difficult for him, demolishing his professional defenses in the most astonishing way. He blurts out, "Well, I haven't actually *gone* there."

"What, what?" says Novelli.

"You never saw the houses you want to sell to us?" says Vannucci, with a simpler, more basic kind of surprise, which has an even more devastating effect.

"Of course I saw them, Mr. Vannucci," says Alessio.

"How did you see them, if you've never been there?" asks the architect.

Alessio tries to revert to the agent-client relationship they had only a quarter of an hour before. "Exactly like you did, Mr. Guardi. I saw the drawings, the photographs, the maps."

"Ah, perfect," says Mr. Guardi, as he looks at the others.

"I don't *believe* it!" says Novelli. She has a coarse voice, the child-actress/smoker/reality-show hostess getting all excited at the thought of publicly massacring somebody.

Alessio says, "Yes, but the people from the Turigi agency have been there," trying to backpedal as fast as he can from the details of his dangerous faux pas.

"But you wanted to keep them out of this," says Novelli. "So you wouldn't have to share your commission with them." At this point she doesn't even have to raise her voice anymore, she's so sure of the public's thumbs-down verdict.

"Please, Miss Novelli," says Alessio. He tries to smile again, but he realizes that his voice is taking on the awful sub-Alpine inflection he thought he had rid himself of when he was eighteen, together with the accounting studies and the narrow-shouldered jackets and the rubber-soled shoes and the hairstyle that still embarrasses him whenever his mother takes out one of his old photographs.

"There's no slinking away, darling," says Novelli. "It's as clear as day what the reason was."

"It wasn't for that reason," says Alessio, his accent going to hell even faster as a result of this "darling" used as a disemboweling weapon.

Mrs. Guardi says, "Come on, Margherita. Let's just go to the farmhouse B and B and come back here tomorrow morning, with all the right directions."

Alessio looks at her gratefully. "Right, Mrs. Guardi. If you just give me a minute to make a U-turn, in a few minutes we'll be back on the main road."

"Just make it quick," snaps Novelli, sitting up straight in her little bitch-queen pose.

"Yes," says Mr. Guardi. "I'd rather not spend the night here."

"No problem," says Alessio. "It's all under control, ladies and gentlemen." He turns the headlights on and shifts into gear, and speeds up along the dirt road among the trees.

Suddenly there's a terrible crash: the minivan comes to an abrupt stop and tilts forward, everybody goes flying from their seats. It's such a violent and unexpected event, it's over before Margherita even realizes she's in the middle of it. Then she moves very slowly in the reverberation of the mechanical noise: she touches different parts of her body to make sure she doesn't have any major damages, and looks at the others doing the same.

"What a *blow*," says Arturo, with a hand on his forehead; when he lowers it there's a red patch under the broken skin.

"Oh my God, you're bleeding," says Luisa.

"It's nothing," says Arturo. True to his sportsman's spirit, he doesn't even look at the palm of his hand.

"I hit my shoulder," says Enrico, perhaps not to be outdone. "What the hell happened?"

"I've no idea, Mr. Guardi," says Alessio, ashen pale, still clinging to the steering wheel. "Must have been a pothole."

Luisa tries to pick up her glasses from the mat where they have fallen, but her fingers are shaking from the shock, she can't get hold of them right away.

Margherita feels her anger surging, now that she realizes what could have happened. "He speeds up at two hundred kilometers per hour on a road like this one and doesn't even see the potholes! If it wasn't for the seatbelt I would have smashed my face on the windscreen!"

"I wasn't speeding," says Alessio. "I was doing thirty, at most."

But Margherita's retrospective scare keeps turning into rage. She says, "You were going too fast anyway! There's no doubt about that!"

Alessio takes his hands off the steering wheel, puts them on his head, paying attention not to ruffle his hair, and moves his lips without answering.

But his unwarlike attitude has the effect of redoubling Margherita's fierceness. "First he loses his way, then it turns out he's never been to the houses he's trying to sell us, then he almost kills us!"

"Margherita, please," says Luisa; putting her glasses back on.

"Yeah, making a scene won't help now," says Arturo.

Alessio tries to use this support to make a last-ditch comeback. He says, "What matters is that nothing serious has happened. We're all still in one piece."

"Not thanks to you, that's for sure!" says Margherita.

"*Margherita*," says Luisa again, in her exasperating, perfectly balanced woman's role, always trying to smooth down any disharmonies she might see.

"I'm sorry if you got scared, Miss Novelli," says Alessio. "I realize how awful it must have been."

"Thank you very much indeed!" says Margherita. "I could be ruined for life, now! I could be totally disfigured! My face could be a bloody pulp! I could be facing months of reconstructive surgery!"

"Please, Miss Novelli," says Alessio.

"Can we get out of this pothole?" says Enrico, rolling down a window to take a look.

"Absolutely, Mr. Guardi," says Alessio. "We've got a one hundred sixty-horsepower engine and a frightful torque to boot." He turns the ignition key. The engine starts, but as soon as he shifts into DRIVE, it dies off again.

"This is useless," says Arturo.

"Let's take a proper look, instead of making blind attempts," says Enrico.

"*Absolutely*," says Margherita, imitating Alessio. "*I realize how awful it must have been*." The more she looks back on the sequence of events, the angrier she gets.

They all get out of the minivan. There are only trees all around them; the sky is dark, with big, lead-colored clouds moved by a cold wind. Enrico and Arturo and Alessio lean down and squat to look at the front wheels: they are sunk into a ditch that runs right across the road, half a meter deep.

Arturo says, "This is no pot-hole, it's a veritable *trench*."

"It can't be," mumbles Alessio, shaking his head.

Enrico says, "How could you not see it, a ditch like this one?"

"It wasn't there, Mr. Guardi," says Alessio, his accent seemingly deteriorated beyond repair.

"Of course, it must have sprung up suddenly," says Enrico. "By some kind of magic."

"Mr. Guardi, I swear it!" says Alessio, like a first-grade student surrounded by older, nastier, richer kids in the schoolyard during midmorning recess.

"You were driving too fast, that's why you didn't see it!" says Margherita. She lights a cigarette, puffs out the smoke, turns in several directions.

"Miss Novelli, I had my eyes glued to the road!" says Alessio, all his professional attitudes gone to hell with his accent.

"Admit you're wrong, you moron!" says Margherita. "It's the least you can do, damn it!" She turns to the others to stress the fact that she's representing their feelings as well as hers, being the only one among them who's not held back by form.

"I'm not wrong," says Alessio, in a low voice. He seems enthralled by the ditch that swallowed the minivan's front axle.

Luisa says, "Is it serious?"

"What do you think, Luisa?" says Enrico, sharply. "Does it look serious enough to you?"

"Can't we push it?" asks Luisa.

"We can try," says Arturo.

Enrico says, "It's rather heavy, this beast."

"Let's try it," says Arturo. "Alessio, you turn the engine on. Keep it in neutral until I tell you."

Alessio goes to sit at the wheel again; he turns on the engine and lowers the window, looking out apprehensively.

"In reverse, eh?" says Arturo.

"Of course, Mr. Vannucci," says Alessio, as if he hadn't tried to go forward just a few minutes ago.

"Do you know how to shift into reverse?" says Margherita, with a renewal of anger that makes her want to dive through the open window and cover his head and shoulders with blows.

"Of course I do," says Alessio, livid.

Arturo instructs the others as to where and how to push, like a skipper organizing his crew for a regatta. "All together now, okay?" he says, then he gestures to Alessio to shift into reverse.

Out of pure male competitiveness, Enrico starts pushing before the others. "Come on!" he shouts.

Alessio revs up the engine. The front wheels spin in the ditch, spraying earth and stones everywhere. They all push in their assigned spots, like healthy and financially secure urbanites who know how to react with energy and even a dose of humor to a catastrophe, provided it's a minor and transitory one. Arturo puts every bit of the strength of his arms and legs into play, shouting, "Step on that pedal, Alessio! More gas!" Enrico shouts, "Come on!" again, but it doesn't take much to see that his push is a lot less effective. Luisa applies her energies with well-directed care, but without saying a word. Margherita pushes with the tips of her fingers, for fear of ruining her fingernails or getting her clothes dirty. She shouts, "Put your damned hoof down on that pedal, you ass!"

But the wheels have no grip and the minivan is too heavy and the ditch is too deep. All their combined efforts produce only noise and oscillations, stones and earth flying in all directions, white smoke and a smell of burnt rubber coming out of the hood.

Arturo stops pushing, he gestures the others to do the same, he shouts to Alessio, "Stop! *Stop*! We'll just end up burning the engine!"

Alessio turns the engine off and gets out of the minivan, and looks at the front axle which seems to have sunk deeper into the ditch.

Margherita says, "How on earth could you not see it, I wonder? How?"

"It wasn't there, Novelli, I told you!" shouts Alessio, with the desperate aggressiveness of a cornered man.

"How dare you talk to me like that?" says Margherita. "Are you totally out of your mind?"

Enrico intervenes with a sharp gesture. "We'll talk about it later, okay? Let's first call someone to get us out of here."

"Yes," says Arturo, touching his bloodied forehead. "Does anybody know the road assistance number?"

"I've got it, Mr. Vannucci," says Alessio, in a futile attempt to recover at least a tiny part of his role. "We're covered 24/7, throughout Europe."

"It's enough if we're covered in Umbria," says Enrico.

Luisa takes her coat from the minivan and puts it on, holding it closed with both hands against the stiff wind. Margherita picks up her lambskin coat, even though she's still burning inside from anger and retrospective fear.

Alessio gets back into the minivan, takes the road assistance booklet out of the glove compartment, and leafs through it. He finds the number, taps it into his cell phone, then moves his right arm in several directions. He gets out of the minivan, crosses the road, spins around, walks on tiptoes, goes toward the woods, comes back. He looks at the others with a blank expression and says, "There's no signal. Zero."

The others stare at him in disbelief, then each of them takes out their cell phone and goes through the same motions, as if in some surrealistic ballet.

"Nothing," says Enrico.

"Not even one dot," says Arturo.

"Zero," says Luisa.

"Tell me it's not true!" says Margherita, as a series of awful mental images race through her brain. "Tell me it's all a joke! There's a candid camera hidden somewhere among those trees, right?"

"We must have landed in a dead spot," says Alessio, still stretching his arm around.

"A dead spot!" says Margherita. "You know where you can stick it?"

"*Margherita*," says Luisa.

"Margherita, what?" says Margherita. "I have some absolutely vital calls to make, in an hour at the most! It's a matter of life and death, fuck! I just can't afford to be stuck in some damned dead spot!" Again she moves her cell phone in several directions, walks up and down; the feeling of entrapment shortening her breath, making her pulse pound at the base of her neck. Her head is full of intolerable distances getting longer by the minute: roads and highways stretching like rubber bands, phone calls going unanswered, hands twitching on increasingly faraway desks, sheets of paper moved out of view, indecipherable handwriting, watch hands turning faster and faster.

Enrico bites his lips and says, "I have some very important calls to make, too."

"Me, too," says Luisa.

"All because of this good-for-nothing swindler!" screams Margherita, looking at Alessio. "Now you'll get us out of this fucking situation at once! You understand? *Now!*"

But instead of throwing himself at her feet and asking for forgiveness, Alessio has a kind of thin, vile smirk on his lips. He says, "Who was the one saying 'Just make it quick,' 'Just make it quick'?"

"If you dare put the blame on me again, I'll *sue* you!" screams Margherita. "I'll have you kicked out of the real-estate agents' association for good! I'll expose you live in front of millions of people!"

Luisa takes her by the arm. "Please calm down, now."

"I'm not calming down!" screams Margherita, even louder. "Do you realize the crazy situation we're in? Do you realize? You probably don't realize!"

"I understand," says Luisa. "But bickering isn't going to help us."

"That's true," says Arturo. "It's not going to get us out of here, that's for sure."

Enrico, who keeps futilely punching the number into his cell phone, says, "Let's try to come to some decision."

Margherita looks at the trees that are becoming a dark mass around the thin strip of the dirt road that seems to get thinner by the minute. "What kind of decision?"

"Like getting a move on," says Arturo. "Before it's totally dark."

"And how do we get a move on?" says Margherita, in a cracked tone. She'd much rather be among her collaborators and technicians now, than among these old friends—demanding immediate answers, threatening recourse to superior authorities to overcome obstacles, meeting reassuring looks rather than these uncertain ones.

"On foot," says Luisa.

"But how far can we get on foot, Mrs. Guardi?" says Alessio. "It took us more than half an hour to come here by car. And it's dark, too."

Enrico says sharply, "Do you have any alternatives to suggest, Alessio?"

"I don't know, Mr. Guardi," says Alessio. "Maybe someone will come through here, sooner or later."

"No one is going to come through here!" says Enrico. "Don't you see where we are?"

"I don't believe it," says Margherita. "I don't *believe* it." She stares at her cell phone, finding it unconceivable that it's no longer inhabited by the sounds and names and voices that have been flowing out of it during the whole trip like indisputable signs of life.

Arturo says, "The worst thing we can do now is just stand here and talk."

"But I can't leave the vehicle here in the middle of the road," says Alessio.

Enrico says, "If you prefer to sit in it until tomorrow, suit yourself."

"Mr. Guardi, please try and understand," says Alessio.

Enrico doesn't even listen to him. "Come on, let's go."

"There must be some houses near here," says Luisa, sounding more worried than she would like to show.

"Of course," says Arturo. "We'll make a telephone call from the first house we find, have a tow truck come and pick us up."

Luisa points to Margherita's boots. "You'd better put something else on, you can't walk in those."

"I *can* walk," says Margherita, with the feeling that a strenuous defense of her boots can protect her in some way from the images of void and distance and exposure to the elements that keep invading her. It's cold, the wind whistles in her ears, and tears get in her eyes.

Luisa shakes her head. Enrico and Arturo retrieve their coats from the minivan and put them on. Alessio takes his blue coat, too, reluctantly.

Margherita says, "What about the suitcases?"

"We leave them here," says Arturo. "There's nobody here to steal them."

"I'm not leaving mine," says Margherita, for the same reason she doesn't want to change her boots. "I've got a lot of valuable stuff in there."

"Are you kidding?" says Luisa. "You can't drag it along on this road!"

But to Margherita this has become a matter of principle: she stands in front of the minivan in the attitude of someone who's not going to give up at any cost. "I'm not leaving it," she says.

"But you're going to carry it yourself, eh?" says Enrico.

"Don't worry," says Margherita. "I'm not expecting any wonderful gestures from anybody."

Alessio opens the trunk, takes out her lilac fiberglass suitcase, and hands it to her with a nasty look, which makes her want to shout a few more insults at him and maybe even give him a kick, putting her pointy boots to good use.

Enrico says, "Are we going?" He follows Arturo, who is already on his way, back to where they've come from.

Luisa waits for Margherita to move, then walks at her side, looking disapprovingly at her boots and suitcase.

Alessio lingers as if he didn't want to detach himself from the minivan, then takes his pigskin suitcase, locks the car, and hurries after the group.

Margherita limps on her high heels, in her mixture of anger and fear and feeling a lack of control. The wind blows harder, the light is vanishing fast; the little wheels of her suitcase scratch the earth and keep wrapping up dead leaves.

The wind moves the black clouds and whistles through the trees, shaking branches and leaves in the growing darkness. Enrico walks behind Arturo and in front of the others, checking his cell phone at intervals: the words *no network* are always on the display. He's never liked walking, ever since as a child his parents would drag him on endless excursions along Alpine paths, his father with binoculars hanging from his neck, his mother with a thermos of sugary tea strapped across her shoulder. To him, walks have always seemed a stupid and pointless thing to do, no esthetic or intellectual compensation for the brutish effort required to drag your own body forward, step after step. The walks that Luisa insists on taking with him almost every weekend make him feel like a hamster spinning in a wheel; the only exertions on foot that make any sense to him being through circumscribed portions of the city or around significant buildings, always with a well-defined goal in mind, and accessible means of transportation at hand.

In any case, right now Luisa doesn't seem too enthusiastic either, as she tensely walks behind him in the dusk, her hands in her coat pockets. Margherita and Alessio, further behind, look like a couple of affluent refugees, slowed down by their trolley suitcases and by their occasional stops to check their cell phones, exchanging a hateful look every now and then. Limping in her cruelly pointed boots, Margherita says in a shrill tone, "Could you perhaps slow down to a more reasonable pace?"

Without even turning, Arturo says, "We told you to leave that suitcase in the car."

"Don't you worry about my suitcase!" says Margherita. "I only asked you humbly not to run!"

Arturo says, "We must cover as much ground as we can before it's totally dark."

Margherita mumbles something, her voice carried away by a gust of wind. She stops, shakes her suitcase which has its wheels stuck and screams, "Fucking leaves!"

Arturo turns, and with an exasperated expression, says, "I'll carry it, as long as you don't stop!"

But Enrico anticipates him: he walks back furiously and grabs Margherita's suitcase by the expandable handle. "Leave it to me, damn it!"

Margherita holds on to it, saying, "I'm carrying it!" However, she almost immediately lets go.

Enrico drags the suitcase behind him with its blocked wheels, surprised at how heavy and unbalanced it is. "Where the hell did you find this?" he says. He kicks at the wheels to free them from the leaves.

"Careful!" says Margherita. "It's a gift from Adriano Remuzzi."

"Oh my God, the fashion designer?" says Enrico, already full of regret for having taken it. "The wheeler-dealer financed by the Mafia to launder dirty money?"

"You don't even know him!" says Margherita. "He's a wonderful person! Hold it straight, you're going to ruin it!"

"There's no way to hold it straight, it's a faulty design!" says Enrico, dragging the suitcase even more angrily. "If you don't like the way I carry it, I'll throw it into a ditch!"

"Give it back to me!" shrieks Margherita, hobbling behind him without getting any closer.

"She's got all her nice little clothes in it," says Alessio.

"What is he saying?" screams Margherita. "Speak louder, you asshole!"

"Don't start again, you two!" says Luisa.

"Yes, save your breath for walking!" shouts Arturo at the head of the group.

They all walk in silence for a while, but the more they walk, the less they are able to discern anything in the mingling darkness of sky and vegetation. The road becomes almost invisible, distances seem to vanish as night falls rapidly over the woods. At one point the piercing cry of some wild animal cuts through the obstinate whistling of the wind.

Margherita says, "What was it?"

"Maybe an eagle owl," says Luisa.

"Or a barn owl!" says Arturo.

"It sounded more like a ground animal," says Enrico, at least partly to make Margherita pay for the unbearable effort it's taking him to drag her suitcase.

"It must have been a giant weasel!" says Alessio. "They jump out of the bushes and grab you at the neck and suck out all your blood before you even realize what's going on!"

"Someone make this shithead shut up!" screams Margherita, desperately trying to get closer to the others. "I'm going to ruin you, just wait till we're back in Milan!"

"Stop it, the pair of you!" says Luisa. "Don't you think this situation is difficult enough without your constant bickering?"

Arturo says, "Very shortly we won't be able to see anything at all." He quickens his pace even more.

Enrico makes it a point of honor to stick close to him, but with the dead weight of the suitcase he's dragging it isn't easy at all. This causes a resentment in him that extends from Margherita to the whole group, to the idea of having been dragged away from a very interesting day to end up in this absurd little tragedy made up of isolation and darkness and fatigue and sweat and cold and total uncertainty.

Luisa says, "I just felt a drop! It's raining!"

"Oh, come on," says Enrico, even though another drop has just hit his forehead.

"What?" screams Margherita's voice, somewhere behind them.

Alessio's voice says, "Mrs. Guardi is right, it's raining!"

"It's raining all right!" says Arturo's voice.

Soon afterward nobody can doubt it anymore, as a heavy rain pours down on them, hard and cold on their faces and on the trees all around, its rustle mixing with the howl of the wind.

Margherita screams, "How much fucking bad luck can concentrate in just one shitty situation?"

"There's no limit!" says Arturo.

"What are we going to do now?" says Luisa in a worried voice, although she tries to keep it under control.

"Keep walking!" says Arturo. "Enrico, are you okay with that suitcase?"

"Yes, yes," says Enrico. With anybody else he would readily admit that his right arm was hurting as if it were being torn off, but with Arturo he just can't; there's always too much antagonistic teasing going on between them. He gives the suitcase a wild jerk and drags it sideways, hoping it might hit some stone and open up, scattering all its contents in the mud.

The rain and the wind keep getting worse, the elements caught in some kind of detestable match. The little group closes ranks in the ever-thickening darkness. They walk blindly, their feet made heavy by the rain that fills their shoes and soaks their clothes and strikes their foreheads and eyelids and gets into their mouths and noses. There's the flickering of the display of a cell phone, the sound of Alessio breathlessly trying to catch up with the others.

"I can't feel my feet anymore!" says Margherita.

"Don't say I didn't tell you!" says Luisa.

"You always know everything!" says Margherita. "You're such a lucky woman!"

"Stop wasting your breath!" shouts Arturo.

Enrico says, "How can it be there's not one single inhabited house in a radius of kilometers?"

Luisa says, "Do you have any idea, Alessio? Did the guys at the Turigi agency tell you anything about it?"

"I wouldn't know, Mrs. Guardi," says Alessio.

"What do you expect that fuckhead to know?" says Margherita.

"While Novelli of course knows everything!" says Alessio.

"You idiot!" screams Margherita. "You moron! You absolute imbecile! And don't you ever dare call me Novelli again!"

"Stop it, both of you!" shouts Arturo.

Luisa shouts, "Let's hope we're on the right road, too!"

"What do you mean, Luisa?" barks Enrico. "Of course we're on the right road, since there's only one!"

"Don't talk to me in that tone!" says Margherita. "We might be going in circles, for all we know!"

They're all shouting now, to make themselves heard above the noise of the rain and the wind, and everything they say turns into an argument.

With an intense effort, Margherita approaches the head of the group and shouts, "I read that some people can walk in circles for dozens of miles without realizing it!"

"Except we don't happen to be in a desert!" shouts Enrico.

"On the contrary, we're in the most densely populated country in Europe!"

"It doesn't seem so densely populated here!" shouts Luisa.

"I'd say zero inhabitants per square kilometer!" shouts Arturo.

Margherita shouts, "I can't take it any more! I'm tired! I'm scared!"

"Come on, Margherita!" shouts Luisa, in a quavering voice. "What are you scared of?"

"Everything!" screams Margherita. "Today's horoscope said there's an ugly transit of Pluto in Aries!"

Enrico has the irresistible impulse to throw the doggedly resisting Remuzzi suitcase among the trees; he shouts, "Great, all we were missing at this point was some idiotic, childish talk of astrology!"

"Who's the childish idiot, Enrico?" shrieks Margherita.

Arturo stops suddenly, as Enrico bumps into him. He shouts, "A light!"

"Where?" say all the others at the same moment, groping around in the dark like exhausted survivors of a shipwreck.

"Over there!" shouts Arturo. "It's a window! It's a house!"

After a few seconds Enrico sees it, too—a little square of light, flickering maybe two or three hundred meters away across the cold, wet darkness whipped by the rain and the wind. He shouts like the others, with an enthusiasm that only an hour ago he would have considered embarrassing. His feet are already slipping on an irregular incline, in a frantic attempt to shorten the distance.

It's not just a house but a group of houses, even though Arturo can only make out the stones of some walls in the dim light that filters through the cracks of a front door. The others all crowd behind him, soaking wet and panting, desperately looking for shelter. A huge black dog comes out of the darkness, barking in a deep voice: all you can see is a deeper shadow and the flash of his white fangs.

Margherita screams, "Help me!" and presses herself against Arturo.

"Calm down!" shouts Arturo.

"This thing's going to tear us to pieces!" screams Alessio, though it's not clear whether out of real fear or to further terrify Margherita. In fact he seems mostly worried about his pigskin suitcase as he tries to shelter it underneath the overhang of the roof, even though it's completely soaked and this must be breaking his heart.

"He's not going to tear anybody to pieces!" shouts Arturo.

"How do you know?" screams Margherita.

Arturo shouts, "I've been around dogs all my life! Just don't make any sudden gestures, that's all!" The wind moves the rain in gusts, making the little group press even more against the door.

"Ring the bell!" shouts Margherita. "Have somebody open this door, quick!"

They're all getting even wetter than they were out in the open. A veritable waterfall is pelting down from the roof, rebounding on the flat stones, forming a torrent along the wall.

Arturo squeezes his eyes to distinguish something around the door; he shouts, "I can't see any doorbell!"

Enrico shoves him aside and shouts, "Let me knock!" He slams his open right hand on the wood, causing the big black dog to bark even louder.

Arturo comes forward again and bangs his fist with all his strength on the old door, again in some kind of competition with Enrico. Despite this double hammering it seems that nobody inside hears anything; then the door half opens, and a dark face appears in the vertical band of light. It takes Arturo two or three seconds to realize it's an Indian, dressed with a coarse, loose jacket and a pair of equally coarse trousers.

Enrico draws back; Margherita says, "Oh my God"; Alessio says, "Where does this come from?"; Luisa remains silent.

Arturo says, "Good evening." He makes a little bow with clasped hands, like he learned to do during a trek in the mountains of Nepal, when he used to ask the locals for lodging.

The Indian is evidently not impressed: he doesn't bow back, nor does he answer with gestures or words. The big black dog continues barking.

Arturo feels suspended between the rain and wind and cold at his back and the light and warmth in front of him; he says, "Sorry for disturbing."

"Our car ended up in a ditch!" shouts Enrico, his voice partly covered by the noise of the wind and of the pouring water.

"Could you perhaps let us in, please?" says Luisa: her well-educated accent barely audible in the noise.

"So we can call for a tow truck?" says Arturo.

Still, the Indian does not answer; he nods to the big black dog, which slips inside. Behind him appears a child of maybe five, not Indian but with similar hair and clothes; he, too, seemingly belonging to another time or place.

Margherita says to the others, "Let me try," and steps forward. Out of sheer desperation she musters one of her television smiles and even the appearance of an exuberant tone. "Hi! I'm Margherita Novelli! *Crazy Stuff*, Rai One Television?"

Arturo watches her with a mixture of embarrassment and hope. He's witnessed more than once the power of her popularity—the sudden manifestations of kindness and collaborative spirit in people that only a second earlier had seemed totally hostile or indifferent.

But in this case there's no miraculous transformation. The Indian sticks to his remote expression, the child behind him doesn't seem impressed either. Margherita turns toward the others; her smile already melted into a tragic fold, under the continuous shower that washes the last traces of mascara down her cheeks.

Alessio leans toward the Indian, perhaps in an attempt at a surprise redemption in front of the others. He gestures as if addressing a comic-book savage and shouts, "We give you five euros for *Drriin . . . Hello?* Eh? You get my drift?"

The Indian turns to push the child inside, then he slams the door shut.

The dark and the cold and the rain and the wind suddenly seem even worse than a few minutes before; the small group draws closer, everybody looking at Alessio with extremely hostile expressions. Margherita screams, "He was about to let us in, if it wasn't for your fucking idiocy!"

Enrico shouts, "It's really hard to behave more stupidly than that!"

"Or insultingly!" screams Luisa.

Alessio shouts back, "Excuse me, ladies and gentlemen, did you see that guy's face? The way he was looking at us? And his clothes? Did you see when Novelli talked to him? He was about to ask for her autograph, really!"

"You should only shut up, you worm!" cries Margherita, trying to give him a kick. "You maggot, you chickenshit!"

"Calm down!" shouts Arturo, extending his right arm to create a barrier. The closest situation that comes to his mind right now is a shipwreck off the coast of Brittany, in which the skipper had drowned while attempting to save a seventeen-year-old boy while the sailboat sank and Arturo and the rest of the crew miraculously made it into the inflatable raft. He realizes how absurd it is to compare the two events, but the feeling of wreckage is so close, he shudders at the thought.

Margherita screams, "I can't stand this any more! I'm cold, I'm wet, my feet hurt, I want a *hotel room*!"

Luisa starts banging on the door, crying out, "Please open up! You can't leave us out here!"

The door seems destined to remain shut, leaving them out in the wind and rain, but surprisingly, after a few seconds, it half opens again. This time it isn't the Indian: it's a curly-haired girl, with a similarly wild appearance and the same kind of clothes.

In a shattered voice Luisa says, "Listen, our car broke down, we got lost, we don't know where to go. Please let us in."

The curly-haired girl hesitates for an instant, looking at Luisa and at the other shipwrecks clustered around her; then she opens the door wide, motioning them to come inside.

They walk into the warm and dry house as if into a strangely real mirage. It's a large room that's a kitchen and a dining room and perhaps other things, too. Sitting around a long table made of rough wood are the Indian, the child, a woman who could be the child's mother, and a girl of perhaps sixteen who looks even wilder than the others. In front of them are bowls and spoons, vegetables, cheese, a loaf of homemade bread half wrapped in a cloth. The light comes from some oil lamps and candles and a big fireplace. There's a smell which Luisa thinks she knows, even though she can't remember from where: wood smoke and peasant's soup and beeswax and sweat. It accentuates the familiarity and the strangeness of the scene. The chairs and the shelves and the cupboards look as organic as the food and the earthenware on the table: irregularly shaped wood, put together in a primitive but functional way. The big black dog that was barking outside now comes to sniff the small group as they walk across the room dripping rainwater. He rubs himself against Enrico, who cautiously tries to kick him away.

Alessio checks his cell phone yet another time but shakes his head. Arturo looks at the furniture and seems fascinated by it. Luisa's glasses are fogged; she takes them off, tries to dry them with a tip of her wet sweater. Margherita says, "Please excuse us, but the thing is . . ." Her voice breaks down, she can't go on.

Enrico addresses the people sitting at the table in a tone of voice that, surprisingly, survived intact through the storm: "If it's not too much of an inconvenience, we need to make a phone call for a tow truck or a taxi to come here from Turigi."

The persons around the table stare at him without answering, their attention stemming from surprise or suspicion or pure linguistic incomprehension; it's not clear.

Alessio whispers to the others, "Does anyone speak Swahili, by any chance?"

Luisa kicks him in the shin, not as hard as she would have liked to.

The Indian finally moves his lips: "We don't have a telephone."

"You don't?" says Enrico, struck by the sound of his voice as much as by the absurdity of his statement.

Margherita stutters, "What do you mean, you don't have a telephone?" She's pale, her makeup washed away, her woolen cap and lambskin coat soaked; Luisa thinks that not even her most loyal TV fans would be likely to recognize her in this state.

"We don't have one," says the Indian. The others around the table keep staring, their wild eyes shining in the light of the lamps.

"No telephone," says Arturo; he runs the back of his hand under his nose to stop it from dripping.

Enrico says, "Perhaps then you can give us a ride to town? Of course we'll pay for the gasoline, and for your time."

"When you've finished eating, of course," says Arturo.

The Indian barely moves his head; he says, "We don't have cars."

Enrico suddenly seems a lot less self-assured: He looks around with a lost air and stares at the muddy puddle at his feet.

In a harsh, raspy voice, Margherita says, "How do you guys manage? How do you go to town?"

"We don't," says the woman who must be the child's mother.

"Never?" says Enrico.

"Never," says the woman.

"What about a tractor?" says Arturo, an optimistic glimmer in his eyes. "Do you have a tractor to pull our car out of the ditch?"

The Indian shakes his head; the curly-haired girl says, "We don't have any kind of engine."

"We're *against* engines," says the woman with the child.

"Ah, I see," says Arturo.

Alessio mumbles to nobody special, "We've ended up in the Middle Ages, we have."

"You shut up," says Luisa, tempted to give him another kick. "Don't make things worse."

"Worse than this, Mrs. Guardi?" says Alessio.

"He's got a point, there," says Enrico, trying to dry his forehead with the soaked sleeve of his coat.

Margherita collapses on a stool; eyes closed, arms crossed upon her breast, she rocks back and forth.

Luisa says, "Come on, Margherita," but she doesn't know how to console her. Her movements are limited by the cold in her bones and by her drenched clothes, the slippery weight of her shoes, the strangely familiar smell in the air.

The curly-haired girl walks up to Margherita and takes off her woolen cap, revealing the wet, bleached hair sticking to her head. She pulls the soaked lambskin jacket from one sleeve, tries to take it off too. Margherita appears to put up some resistance, then she unbuttons it, lets the girl slip it off her.

The child's mother nods to the others and says, "You, too, take your coats off. And your shoes." It's not clear whether she speaks out of kindness or because puddles are widening at their feet on the ancient terracotta-tiled floor, cracked and polished from use.

Luisa, Arturo, Alessio, and Enrico awkwardly take off their coats and shoes, then look around without knowing where to put them.

The child's mother drags a bench in front of the fireplace and says, "Put them here, so they'll dry a little bit." She puts some more wood in the fire, rekindles the flame.

Luisa and the others place everything down on the bench, even though the coats are so drenched that they should probably be wrung out. Luisa is almost relieved by the bad condition their clothes are in; she thinks that otherwise the contrast with the clothes of their hosts would be unbearable.

Margherita lets the curly-haired girl assist her with her boots, muttering "thank you" in the voice of a seriously ill person. It isn't easy at all: the curly-haired girl pulls with two hands, straining. When she finally succeeds there's the noise of a fish jumping in a lake, a stream of water gushes out onto the floor. The second boot requires even more effort; Margherita touches her feet through the socks with an extremely pained expression. She puts her things down on the bench and limps to the fireplace, where she stands warming herself with her back to the fire, a few centimeters shorter than usual; Luisa realizes that it's been years since she's seen her without high heels on.

Arturo takes his socks off, hangs them on the mantelpiece. Barefoot, he flashes one of his globetrotter's smiles; he says, "My name's Arturo."

The people sitting around the table stare at him in silence; then the curly-haired girl says, "Mirta."

"Gaia," says the mother of the child, a moment later. She points to the child, "Icaro."

"Luisa," says Luisa, clearly articulating each syllable, as she tends to do when she finds herself in an awkward social context.

"Arup," says the Indian.

"Aria," says the young girl.

"Enrico," says Enrico, as if he was making a slightly embarrassing concession.

"Alessio Cingaro," says Alessio, as if it was extorted from him.

Luisa points to Enrico's socks and says, "Aren't you taking them off?"

"No," says Enrico stiffly.

"But they're all soaked," says Luisa.

"I'm perfectly fine, thank you," he says.

Margherita, with the expression of a poor beggar girl, says, "Do you think we could have a bite of something?"

Luisa looks at her in a scolding way.

"Sorry, but I'm *dying* of hunger," says Margherita, the sheer need in her voice erasing any other consideration.

The woman whose name is Gaia goes to fetch a pot hanging by the fire, brings it to the table, and then ladles thick soup into some clay bowls. The curly-haired girl whose name is Mirta cuts a few slices from the bread loaf half wrapped in cloth. The Indian whose name is Arup and the child whose name is Icaro and the young girl whose name is Aria just sit and stare.

Margherita sits down at the table and immediately starts gulping down the soup. The others stand and watch her from some distance, their aloofness diminishing by the second. Arturo sits down and takes a spoonful of soup, keeps it in his mouth to savor it, then swallows it and smiles, his entire body expressing physical appreciation. Luisa dips her spoon into her bowl in the most balanced way she can manage, but still too quickly. She burns her lips and palate with the first spoonful, then lets the feeling of well-being fill her with the taste and the warmth. All her senses are now engaged by the act of eating, her mind filled with a deep, ancient form of gratefulness.

Enrico tries to maintain his imperturbability, but he can't; he sits down with the others, eats with much more eagerness than he would like to. Only Alessio is fidgeting with his spoon, as if he was afraid of being poisoned. Luisa imagines him to be the type of Italian who packs spaghetti and coffee in his suitcase when traveling abroad, with the constant dread of having to experience any cuisine that's different from his mother's.

"This is exceptional!" says Arturo. "The authentic *acquacotta*! There's no way to find it in any restaurant anymore. Onions, tomatoes, toasted homemade bread, extra-virgin olive oil, mint leaves, salt. So simple, and yet so perfect. Unchanged for *centuries*."

Arup the Indian stares at him perplexedly, then goes to fill a jug from a little barrel, pours wine into some clay cups, and hands them around.

Arturo takes a long sip. "*Good*. Do you make this?"

"Yes," says Arup.

"Sangiovese grapes, right?" says Arturo. "And Montepulciano. And . . . there's this wonderful, slightly tannic aftertaste . . . what is it?" Smiling, gesticulating, trying to get the communication across.

"Tintoriello," says the Indian.

"Aha," says Arturo. "A little-known local variety, eh? I bet that's what gives it this deep ruby color, too?"

The Indian nods his head, still with a rather suspicious expression.

"I like it," says Arturo. "I like it. And you age it in oak barrels like that one?"

"We don't age it," says the Indian.

"Of course," says Arturo. "What's the point, anyway? This is a wine to drink daily. Aging would only dull its lovely bouquet."

"Cut it out," mumbles Enrico. "We're not at a wine tasting, in case you haven't noticed."

"It's excellent, really," says Luisa, to cover her husband's voice. "You can taste the grapes, really."

"You can taste the *vinegar*," mutters Alessio.

Luisa gives him a sharp look. She says, "Please stop it."

Margherita has already emptied her bowl of soup and her cup of wine without saying a single word; when she raises her head some color has come back to her, mixing with the last traces of her runny mascara.

Arturo eyes the cheese and the vegetables on the table, but doesn't dare to ask if he can have some. Instead he points to the table and chairs and he says to Arup, "You made those yourselves too, right?"

"Yes," says Arup.

"Nice," says Arturo. "All groove-and-tongue joints, eh? No glue or screws."

"Yes," says Arup.

Luisa handles a piece of whole wheat bread, with a care that's meant to show respect and admiration for the culture that produced it. "How long have you been living here?" she asks.

"Nine years," says Arup.

"Ten," says Gaia.

"Congratulations," says Luisa. "It's a really beautiful place."

"Always with no electricity, and no telephone?" says Enrico, to bring everything into perspective again.

"Yes," says Arup.

"And no engines," says Arturo.

"Yes," says Arup.

Margherita says "Excuse me, where's the bathroom?"

Luisa again feels a pang of discomfort at the idea that there's no limit to her friend's requests. She'd like to tell Margherita to go outside, to pee in the rain.

Mirta says, "It's out there," with a vague gesture.

"Out where?" stammers Margherita, alarmed.

"Come with me," says Mirta. She gets up, and takes an oil lamp from the table.

Margherita tries to put her soaked boots back on, but it's impossible. She gives up almost immediately.

Mirta takes a pair of wooden clogs by the door and hands them to her, then makes her way toward the other end of the big room.

Margherita looks around as if seeking some kind of reassurance or encouragement from the others, but she meets Alessio's eyes and sees only a sadistic glimmer in them, so she slips on the clogs without a word, and follows Mirta.

Luisa thinks that she, too, will eventually need to go to the bathroom but that she can wait, even though it's hard to tell for how long, given the surreal nature of the situation.

M irta takes an umbrella from the wall, and goes to unlatch a door that gives into a paved backyard where streams of rainwater are flowing.

"Where?" says Margherita, in a voice so unstable and frightened, it fills her with anger.

Mirta opens the umbrella, and it's a big, red one; she escorts her under the pelting rain to the door of a small stone building. She hands Margherita the oil lamp and says, "I'll wait for you out here."

"In the dark?" says Margherita.

Mirta doesn't answer, she walks back toward the wall with her big red umbrella, its color fading as it retreats from the halo of the lamp.

Margherita walks into the little stone building and latches the door, terrified at the thought that the oil lamp might blow out at any moment. It's rather clean inside, but the only facilities are a hole in the stone floor and a low basin without a tap, a vase with some branches of satinpod, a bucket, a jar, some colored cloths nailed to the walls, and two towels hanging from wooden rings. The rain drums on the roof and rattles on the small window, leaking through in rivulets at a corner; the wind howls and whistles like a dangerous wild animal.

Margherita puts down the oil lamp with extreme caution, pulls down her wet, sticky pants, and squats above the hole in the floor. She still can't believe the change from the comfort of her TV studio to this slum of medieval discomfort. The contrast sends a shiver through her bones and makes her tremble uncontrollably.

Alessio double-checks his quad-band, photo- and video-equipped cell phone; he puts it on the table, again shaking his head in disbelief. He hands his clay cup to the woman named Gaia and says, "Could I have a glass of mineral water, no gas?"

The woman named Gaia looks at him with a baffled expression, then fills his cup with water from a jug.

Alessio drinks cautiously, but with the corner of his eyes he sees the child Icaro picking up his cell phone. He shouts, "Let go of it!"

The childs eyes widen and he drops the cell phone to the floor.

Alessio screams, "Noooo!" and jumps desperately toward the excruciating noise of his technological jewel shattering on the hard floor. He picks up the pieces, but he can't even bring himself to look at them.

"You shouldn't have left it there," says Mr. Guardi in his cold, upper-class Milanese accent, apparently embarrassed by this inelegant scene.

Alessio says, "Mr. Guardi, *they* should have kept an eye on that monkey!" He gradually examines the disassembled parts of his cell phone, assessing the damage by degrees.

"Will you stop using that language," says Mrs. Guardi, stiffly.

"You're the monkey, anyway!" says Gaia, the child's mother, herself like a big, offended primate.

Bitterly, Alessio replaces the phone's SIM card and battery with meticulous care and clicks the rear cover into place. He presses the "on" button, and holds his breath. To his huge relief the little start-up tune sounds and the display lights up, revealing the Van Gogh sunflowers screen saver that Deborah chose for him. Alessio breathes again, then looks up to see his clients and the wild country people all staring at him as if he was some kind of monster.

"Excuse me, but this is a tool of the trade, for me," says Alessio. "You can't even find it, in Italy. A cousin of mine bought it for me in Singapore. Six hundred dollars, it cost, even though there are practically no taxes over there."

He's about to go into the technical features of the phone, but the front door opens: a bearded, long-haired guy with the same kind of coarse clothes as the others walks in, all drenched from the rain. He has a bow in his hand, a quiver full of arrows across his shoulder; he stops as soon as he sees the group of city folks sitting around the table.

Mr. Guardi says, "Evening," but with far less self-assurance than a moment earlier.

Alessio turns toward Vannucci at his right, muttering, "Who's this, now? Robin Hood?"

Vannucci elbows him sharply, as if they weren't all in the same boat.

The woman whose name is Gaia says, "Lauro." Judging by the way she looks at him he must be the gang leader, or something of the kind.

He stares at her, bow in hand, as if waiting for explanations.

"They got lost," says Gaia. "They were desperate."

"Their car ended up in a ditch," says the Indian.

The Robin Hood type whose name is Lauro puts down the bow and quiver and takes off his wet, loose jacket, grabs a cloth from the wall, and rubs his hair. He looks even wilder than the others, with an added dose of potential danger in his eyes and in the way he moves.

Mr. Guardi sits up in his chair, trying to muster all the dignity he can as a wet, shoeless man sitting in front of a begged-for dish. He says, "We were hoping to call a tow truck, but your friends explained to us that you don't have telephones or cars here."

"That's right," says Lauro. He takes a knife out of a sheath that hangs from his belt and cuts a slice of bread and one of cheese, puts some lettuce on top of it, and gives it a ferocious bite, still looking at the city dwellers.

The girl named Mirta reenters the room, Novelli in tow. Without any high heels or makeup, her wet bleached hair glued to her head, she looks pitiful, to say the least. When she sees Lauro she stops in her tracks and says "hello" in a tone of voice that only this morning would have amused Alessio to no end, but now gives him only the most transitory, bitter satisfaction.

Lauro doesn't answer; he says, "Why did you come around here? What were you looking for?"

"We wanted to see some houses that are for sale," says Mr. Guardi. It's obvious that he would prefer to stand up and be more or less on equal footing with Lauro; but as he must be aware that without his shoes and with his trousers all wet he would cut an utterly miserable figure, all he does is lean back in his chair as nonchalantly as he can.

"A small village we'd like to buy and renovate," says Vannucci, his smile too open for this kind of confrontation.

Novelli has an unexpected resurgence of resentment. She says, "But our great real-estate agent there didn't know the way, and then he managed to drive us right into a ditch and very nearly kill us all. Maybe they don't even exist, the houses he wanted to sell us."

Alessio feels he's being humiliated in front of too many witnesses. "Novelli, joking is fine, but enough is enough! We're not all hosting fake reality shows here, are we?"

Novelli is taken aback by the vigor of his reaction. "How *dare* you?" she says turning around to check the audience's prevailing mood.

Alessio storms off to fetch his suitcase; he opens it and grabs the wet green folder, barely registering the pitiful condition of his clothes. He takes out the drawings and plans of the houses, soft and heavy with moisture but still perfectly readable; he says, "Here: cadastral map, cadastral notes, abstract of land title, certificates of ownership. Here: 'Rustic buildings located at Windshift. . .'"

Lauro walks up to him and grabs the sheets out of his hands. "Let me see." He goes to look at them near an oil lamp; he laughs.

Alessio says, "Would you mind telling me what's so funny? So we can all laugh?"

The guy says, "*These* are the houses you wanted to sell them."

"What?" says Alessio, not understanding whether this is a joke or a provocation or what.

"You mean, *this* is Windshift?" says Vannucci, but he's almost voiceless, he's so surprised.

The guy called Lauro nods, in a half-swaggering, half-sad attitude, like a character out of some pirate movie.

"Of course," says Mr. Guardi. "I thought I recognized the shape of this. . . ." He runs his eyes along the walls of the big room and across the ceiling, up to the ancient oak roof beam.

His wife and Vannucci and Novelli look at each other as if they had just discovered themselves guilty of some capital crime; the wild country-dwellers seem rather disconcerted, too. For a while there's only the noise of the rain pelting on the roof tiles and on the window panes, of the wind whistling and howling inside the chimney.

Alessio thinks that, yes, there are no limits to how much bad luck you can suffer in just one shitty day; his arms fall to his sides. For a moment he'd like to forget about the whole thing, just tend to his ruined suitcase and to his ruined clothes inside it. Then he recovers, with a quiver that surprises even him, and says, "I knew that the satellite navigator couldn't be wrong!"

"Too bad these houses are not for sale," says Lauro. No longer laughing, his expression is purely hostile, menacing.

"What do you mean, too bad?" says Alessio, squinting his eyes, tipping his head.

The guy says, "I mean that as you can see we're living in them, and we have no intention of moving out."

Alessio is a little scared of him, but experience has taught him that the qualities of a really good real-estate agent reveal themselves in the most difficult situations. He says "It's Lauro, right?"

"Yeah," says Lauro, defiantly.

"Now, listen to me, Lauro," says Alessio. "You know better than me that you've been unlawfully occupying this property."

Lauro scowls and turns toward his friends, to show he has no intention of answering him.

The woman called Gaia says, "These houses had been abandoned for years when we arrived here. They were about to collapse, all the windows were gone, the roofs caved in."

"We had to hunt for roof tiles for years," says Mirta. "And we fixed the floors, fixed all the holes in the walls."

Alessio says, "Excuse me, but if somebody finds an abandoned house, he can't appropriate it, just like that! Otherwise what would happen to private property? You've been unlawfully occupying this place; there's a standing order of eviction, signed by a lower-court judge!"

"D'you want to know what we did with the order of eviction?"

says Lauro. "Look." He walks to the fireplace and throws all the drawings into the flames: wet as they are, they take only a couple of seconds to flare up.

Alessio yells, "Hey! Those are official legal papers!" He dashes toward the fireplace but stops a couple of meters short. He doesn't feel up to a physical fight with such potentially dangerous people, and besides, he knows other, more sophisticated techniques of persuasion.

Lauro stares at him in an attitude of stubborn, territorial defense and childish defiance of the laws of the state: it's like an admission of weakness, even though he doesn't realize it.

Alessio changes his tack entirely, with the same careless ease with which he could change his shirt in the morning. "Listen," he says, "nobody here is going to gain anything from a confrontation. Even though you are absolutely not entitled to it, we're willing to pay you a bonus to get out of here. But you must prove to us that you're ready to reason, instead of throwing important documents into fires. I'm here as a mediator, that's my job."

Lauro says in a threatening tone, "Perhaps you don't get it, mediator."

"No, look, *you* don't get it," says Alessio, switching to a more arrogant tone.

"Why don't you shut up, Alessio!" says Mr. Guardi, as if embarrassed by a dumb, overzealous servant. "We have no intention of evicting anyone."

"We didn't have the slightest idea you were living here," says his wife, in an aggrieved, socially conscious tone.

Vannucci says, "For all we knew, these houses were vacant."

"But they *are* vacant, Mr. Vannucci!" says Alessio, shocked by the unbelievable way they're withdrawing support from him just when he needs it most.

"All of you—get out of here at once!" says Lauro. He points to the door, his hand trembling with barely restrained anger.

"What do you mean, out?" says Novelli, sounding like an orphan. "Right now? In the middle of the night? You can't be serious!"

"Try to be reasonable," says Vannucci. "We don't even have a flashlight, we don't know the way, there's terrible weather."

"It's dark outside!" says Novelli. "It's cold! It's raining! It's full of wild animals! My feet are killing me! You can't send us out to die like dogs!"

Mr. Guardi looks toward the door, as if he'd rather tramp through the rain than take part in such a pitiful scene.

The girl named Mirta nervously twists a lock of her hair around a finger, and says, "It's true, Lauro. Where can they go at this time of night?"

"It's none of our business," says Lauro. "We certainly didn't invite them here."

"Yes, but we can't throw them out like this," says Gaia. "What do you think, Arup?"

Arup says, "It's true that it's dark, it's raining, it's a long way to Turigi. . . ."

Mrs. Guardi seems moved by this display of humanity by people who would have every reason to hate her. "If you let us sleep here," she says, "tomorrow morning we'll be gone at first light. We promise."

Lauro stares at her, then turns to his friends. "Who's for letting them sleep here?"

His ragged friends raise their hands one after the other, like they were performing some kind of long-established ritual; even the girl Aria and the child Icaro do so.

Lauro says, "And where are we going to put them?"

"In the last room upstairs," says Gaia. "There are mattresses and blankets there."

Lauro nods, looking far from happy but apparently resigned to having to put up with the majority rule. He tells the city dwellers, "Tomorrow at first light, you get out of here."

"You can count on it," says Vannucci, with one of his broad, international traveler's smiles.

"Of course, of course. Thank you so much," says Mrs. Guardi in a grateful tone, almost with tears in her eyes.

Her husband, the architect, doesn't say anything; he at least maintains a dignified expression.

"Thanks," says Novelli, in a quivering voice.

Alessio says "Excuse me, ladies and gentlemen, I was talking business to these people."

"I don't think it's the right time or place," says Mr. Guardi, without even looking at him.

"Please, just shut up," says his wife.

"We can do without your business talk, right now," says Vannucci.

"You imbecile!" says Novelli. "You've already fucked up enough for today!"

Alessio would like to tell her what he thinks of her, but right now they're clearly all against him, so he just bows his head, contenting himself with mumbling something incomprehensible.

The blankets and pillows have a musty smell; some of the latter are overstuffed, others are flabby and almost empty. Margherita rummages through her suitcase, but it's too cold and she hates to change in front of others. She ends up keeping her wet stuff on, just adding two sweaters layered one on top of the other. She tries to pick the mattress that's least dirty, but it's not easy to choose in the trembling halo of the lamp. She finally makes up her mind and sits on one, then lays down. It's an unacceptably hard and prickly straw mattress that feels like it was taken from some folk museum. She's horrified at the thought of who might have slept on it or had sex on it or given birth or maybe even died on it. She wonders whether parasites might still be lurking under its faded, spotted light blue stripes. Are her clothes thick enough to protect her from fleas or ticks or bacteria or viruses? She gets up and takes a second pair of socks from her suitcase, slips them on top of the others. Her feet hurt as if they had been squeezed under a press; she pulls down a double sock to take a look, but as soon as she sees the reddish skin of her heel she pulls it up again, not even wanting to imagine what the rest might be like.

Arturo looks at her with a slightly ironic expression, as he takes off his trousers and briskly rolls them up, he could almost be in some mountain refuge after a day of vigorous trekking.

Margherita says, "What the fuck are you sneering at?" He just shrugs his shoulders.

The others are fumbling with their blankets and pillows on their straw mattresses, passing each other the oil lamp that Mirta gave them, as if it was a treasure to guard with the utmost care. From his drenched pigskin suitcase Alessio takes out a pair of pajamas so wet they look like a dead cat, he puts them back with a disheartened expression. Margherita feels a little quiver of revenge, but it's not remotely enough to quench the resentment she feels toward him. Luisa shakes her blanket, as if she could put everything back in order with her goodwill alone. Margherita knows that she must be as uncomfortable and disgusted as she is, but that she would never admit to it for fear of being seen as politically incorrect. Her constant efforts at irreproachable conduct irritate Margherita enormously now, as does Luisa's never-ending quest for balance in personal relationships. Still, this is precisely why she's always needed Luisa to counterbalance her all-too-frequent ups and downs. Through these many years they must have had a deep, serious conversation for every crisis she's had, and each time she's come out of it feeling reassured. That's what friends are for, she thinks, even though at times they can be so unbearably hard to put up with.

Arturo does some knee bends on his strong legs, extending his arms straight in front of him, breathing out in an energetic way every time he bends down, without realizing how ridiculous he looks in these circumstances. But they're all ridiculous in their own way, as they try to adapt to the idea of having to spend a terribly uncomfortable night amid the debris of their shattered dream of a place in the country where they might reinvigorate their friendships and their best aspirations. Margherita thinks that only a few years ago this would have been a fantastic opportunity to fling ironic, caustic jokes and observations at each other, laughing like crazy until dawn. Now they are four successful professionals, shocked by a temporary loss of control, and all they can do is put up with a rotten situation and make it through till tomorrow, when in one way or another they'll find a way to get out of here.

Enrico smoothens the folds of his straw mattress, and lays on one side like a disciplined soldier, pulling the brownish blanket over his ears. Luisa lies on the mattress next to his, her head straight on the musty pillow, trying like Margherita to minimize the contact with the damp, rough cloth, stiff on her back. Alessio sits on the mattress they left for him near the door, looking at his shadow on the wall as if he was in some third-world prison cell. Most likely he feels like a martyr for the great cause of real estate; Margherita would like to hit him with a stick just to confirm the idea.

Arturo takes the oil lamp. "Is it okay if I put it off?" he asks. The others answer with barely articulated sounds, as if words were unnecessary. After a brief flickering, the light goes out. Darkness fills the room like India ink, down to its tiniest corners.

Margherita desperately tries to fall asleep, but she's too tired and shaken and worried. She also needs to pee again, but she can't even imagine getting up in the dark room and lighting the oil lamp by herself and walking in her socks down the stairs and through the corridor and out the back door into the storm-tossed back-yard. The smell of her blanket and pillow haunt her with a cease-less evocation of intimate and disgusting aspects of unknown lives, while a frantically updated inventory of the tiny critters that are probably teeming in the straw runs through her mind. She wishes she had at least changed her panties and bra, and put on a fourth sweater, protected her head with her spare woolen cap or with the foulard she had packed just before leaving. She tries to shift her concerns onto some other level, but instantly she's filled with anguish at the thought that most likely her agent is still des-perately trying to call her this very moment. She's almost certain that without her direct instructions things must have degenerated on that front, too, with catastrophic consequences. She can visualize, in every detail, the many faux pas he must have already made: accepting caption clauses without discussion, leaving essential points undefined, overlooking vital details in an exchange of fake smiles and pats on the shoulder. She asks herself whether tomorrow there will still be time to put things back together again and when exactly she'll be able to use her cell phone again. She feels so angry and powerless, she could scream; she kicks under the blanket, the tip of her right foot sending a stab of pain through her entire body, her eyes filling with tears.

The others can't sleep either, judging from the rustling and tossing and turning and grunting that goes on in the pitch dark, mixing with the pelting of the rain and the whistling of the wind through the cracked and disjointed window frames. Margherita breathes slowly, trying to distinguish possible signals of danger among all these noises, her heart beating faster every time a louder creak or squeak penetrates the room with a gust of cold air.

Light filters in through the many cracks in the window shades, forming a reticule over the confusion of bodies and blankets. Luisa gets up, puts on her glasses and trousers and her still-wet shoes, then goes to open the window. A pale sun lights up the clearing where a few stone and brick buildings and a small tower stand. There are puddles from last night's rain, a haze filtering the colors of the landscape, making the tree-covered hills around the house look more distant than they are. Some horses are grazing in a paddock some fifty meters away, next to a vegetable garden, an orchard, some beehives. The girl Mirta is pushing a little herd of goats along with a stick; farther away Arup the Indian is hollowing out a tree trunk with a chisel, the impact of his mallet resonating in the still air. The big black dog is chasing a cat that runs into a group of chickens and ducks and geese voraciously fighting over some grain. Luisa wets her right forefinger and thumb with saliva and cleans the corners of her eyes; she inhales the cold, bracing air down to the bottom of her lungs as she takes in the timeless scene in front of her.

When she turns to look at the others, Enrico, Arturo, and Alessio are all sitting up on their straw mattresses, stretching and yawning. Alessio rummages in his jacket pockets and fishes out his cell phone, looking at the display with totally unfounded expectations, then shakes his head. Only Margherita remains sleeping, wrapped up in her old blanket like a mummy.

Enrico says, "What a dreadful night."

"Hey, this is the country life!" says Arturo, cheerfully.

Alessio says, "My goodness, we're like Kosovo refugees, really."

Luisa turns to look out of the window again, the voices behind her sounding like a radio interference.

Enrico says, "I've been on the alert the whole time. I expected to find myself with a knife pointed at my throat."

"Oh, come on, Enrico," says Arturo.

"Did you hear the mice?" says Alessio.

"No," says Arturo with a yawn.

"There were so many damned noises," says Enrico.

"As big as cats," says Alessio. "Anyway, it just takes a proper de-ratting to get rid of the problem, eh?" He's got back most of his real-estate agent's attitudes, accent included, as if yesterday's debacle had dissolved with the night like a bad dream.

Luisa says, "It's beautiful here." She expects the others to come look out of the window, too, but only Arturo does. He grunts approvingly, taking in the view.

"It sure is, Luisa," says Enrico, "but the sooner we're out of here, the better."

"Mr. Guardi, I intend to have a very frank talk with them," says Alessio.

"With whom?" says Enrico, as he struggles to put on his English shoes, deformed as they are by the rain.

"The wood elves," says Alessio. "The Robin Hood gang. I want to tell them that last night we were too tired to discuss the matter, but that they should be careful not to push their luck too far, because our patience is limited."

"What's the point?" says Enrico, angrily trying to force his heel down into his left shoe. "Did you have the impression they were so eager to listen?"

"They were even too kind with us," says Luisa, "given the circumstances. Imagine offering shelter to some total strangers, feeding them and everything, only to discover that they came to kick you out of where you live."

Alessio gestures with his palms up, saying, "But Mrs. Guardi, it's not *us* kicking them out, it's the *law*. They've been illegally occupying this property for *ten years*."

Luisa says, "You heard them, these houses were abandoned when they arrived here."

"Mrs. Guardi," says Alessio, "if it was enough to sneak into an empty building to have some right to it, it would be the end of everything."

More and more, Luisa feels she's in the wrong company. "Why didn't you tell us that there were people living here?" she says.

"What do you mean, Mrs. Guardi?" says Alessio. "I explained the situation to Mr. Guardi."

"You explained it very badly," says Enrico, a little too quickly. "According to you there were a few poor peasants with a standing eviction order, not a community of fanatics totally determined to stay."

"This doesn't change a thing, Mr. Guardi" says Alessio. "No matter who they are or what they say, they still stand to be evicted."

Luisa says to Enrico, "You mean, you knew that we would be kicking somebody out in order to get these houses?"

"Honey," says Enrico, finally forcing his foot into his right shoe, "all I knew was that the houses were legally available, and that the asking price was reasonable."

"They *are* legally available, Mr. Guardi," says Alessio. "And you're not going to find a price like this one anywhere else, you know it full well."

"I don't care about the price!" says Luisa. "I'm not kicking anybody out of where they live!"

"Not so loud, they are going to hear us," says Arturo. He has no trouble getting into his heavy-duty boots, as they're made for the rain and the mud.

"All the better, if they do!" says Luisa, tears in her eyes for all the disappointment and the offence and the other awful feelings that keep welling up inside her.

Enrico puts on his jacket, yanking the sleeves in an attempt to smooth out the creases. He says, "And yet until yesterday afternoon you seemed all enthusiastic at the idea that we could buy the country homes of our dreams without having to ruin ourselves."

"Well, I'm not anymore!" cries Luisa. "Now that I know that I would have to take it from someone else!"

Arturo leans out of the window again; he says, "It's true that we didn't have a precise picture of the situation, Luisa."

"So you, too, knew that there were people living here?" says Luisa. "Margherita as well, of course?"

Enrico says, "Honey, let's try and be rational for a moment."

"Don't call me honey!" cries Luisa. "I don't want to be rational! I'm horrified by all this!"

"Let's not go too far now," says Enrico, trying to defuse her rage as he's preparing for a counterattack. "Don't start acting that 'Mrs. Right' part."

"Better than being 'Mr. Wrong'!" screams Luisa.

Alessio contemplates, with a pained expression, his loafers, which with yesterday's rain have gotten wide and stiff like small boats. He takes his spare ones out of his suitcase, wet as they are. He says, "Mrs. Guardi, even if you decide not to buy, those people would have to leave anyway. The only difference would be that you'd lose a once-in-a-lifetime bargain, and somebody else would snap it up instead."

"I'm not interested in this kind of bargain!" says Luisa. "Thank you very much!"

"But Mrs. Guardi," says Alessio, "didn't you see how those people live? No electricity, no telephones, no running water, with that awful outhouse in the backyard. They're nuts. You'll almost do them a favor, sending them away. Especially for the child." He puts on his spare shoes, carefully tying up the laces.

"Oh, sure," says Luisa. "It would be a philanthropic act on our part! Something to really be proud of!"

Enrico stamps his feet to flatten out the deformed soles of his shoes, making the floor tremble. He says, "Well, at least it would help them understand they're living in the twenty-first century."

"Don't they have the right to live in whatever century they choose?" says Luisa. "What entitles us to decide it for them? How can you be so arrogant?"

"I'm not arrogant," says Enrico. "You know I'm right."

"You are *not* right!" screams Luisa. "Not in the least!"

Enrico looks at her as if he's about to offer her a reason to change her mind; instead he says, "If you really want to know, I had no wish whatsoever to buy these damned houses!"

Luisa is taken aback. All she can say is "No?"

"Not at all!" says Enrico. "I was only going along with you, because I knew how badly you and Arturo and Margherita loved the idea. I just didn't want to be the one who betrays the wonderful collective dream and disappoints everyone. As for me, I've always hated the country!"

"Mr. Guardi, what do you mean?" says Alessio, with a dismayed expression.

"It's true!" says Enrico. "The country to me is isolation, dirtiness, cold, effort, ignorance, lack of choice, time that stands still! We've all had a chance to experience it, last night!"

"Come on, Enrico, that was just a piece of bad luck," says Arturo. "It could have happened anywhere."

"Not so!" says Enrico. "It could have happened only in the damned country! Throughout the last two centuries *millions* of people ran away from the country as fast as they could, the first chance they had, because to them the country was just a terrible nightmare. Even though they were peasants, they desperately wanted to live in the cities! Then fast forward to us today, and on the basis of childish dreams and ideological abstractions we start talking about the country as if it were some kind of *ideal*."

Arturo says, "If you compare it to the increasing inhumanity of the cities, it is."

"Of all people, you're the one who could never do without a city!" says Enrico. "And neither could I! I need the lights, the cinemas, the motion, the crowds along the sidewalks, the noise, the traffic, the variety, the choices, the surprises, the extended communication! I even need the *smog*! You all need it as much as I do, no matter what you say!"

"I'm not so sure anymore," says Arturo. "Perhaps I *could* do without cities, at this point in my life."

"Me, too," says Luisa.

"Sure, Luisa," says Enrico. "I'd like to see you if you had to live in a place like this, without any of the comforts you're used to. Without your job, your books, your authors, your editors. I'd like to see you, after one week. Being forced to spend your time with Lauro and Gaia and Mirta and Aria and all the other assorted creatures of the earth."

"Those are not even their real names, by the way," says Alessio. "That Lauro for example, his real name is Sandro Parente or something like that, it's written in the order of eviction."

"Right," says Enrico. "They even make up their own names, like in a school play."

"They picked nice ones, though," says Arturo.

Enrico doesn't even listen to him; he focuses on Luisa, saying, "You'd be *desperate* to get out of here, after a couple of days."

"What do *you* know?" says Luisa.

"Well, I think I know you a little bit," says Enrico. "I know that *I'd* be ready to do anything to get out of here."

"Let's go, then," says Luisa, coldly. Walking back to the straw mattress on which she slept, she folds up the blanket with sharp tugs.

Enrico must feel like he's on a roll. "I don't find it the least amusing, spending a night like last one. Maybe when I was seventeen I could have seen it as a fascinating experience, but today I really don't find any charm in it. None at all. And please don't tell me you do."

Luisa doesn't answer, she puts the blanket down.

"Okay," says Arturo, saddened by the way the situation is apparently beyond repair. "Come on, let's go to Turigi."

Alessio seems only now to realize fully that he's going to lose his clients and his commission, after entire months spent listening and reasoning and suggesting and making telephone calls and enquiring in at least three regions. "Excuse me, ladies and gentlemen," he says, "but let me make one last attempt with that Robin Hood guy. I'll explain to him where he stands legally, and make him an offer he can't refuse. Why give up the game now, when we still have all our cards to play?"

"I'm not interested in games," says Luisa, burning with indignation. "Especially not this kind!"

"We're past that, Alessio," says Enrico, coldly. "Let's leave those poor fools to their sorry life and get the hell out of here."

Arturo puts his tweed coat on; he says, "We better put everything on hold for the time being, Alessio."

Alessio smiles bitterly, shrugs his shoulders. "As you wish. I won't insist, the customer's always right. But it's a pity, let me tell you. A real pity."

As some sort of compensation, he walks over to Margherita who, incredibly, is still fast asleep, wrapped up in her blanket. He gives her a shake. "Wake up, Novelli. Unless you want to be left here with the natives."

Margherita tries to cover her head. She mutters, "Get him off me. I've been awake the whole damned night."

Enrico goes to tear the blanket off her, and says "Come on! Get up! We're leaving!"

Margherita rolls on her straw mattress, looking shapeless because of the three sweaters she's put on; she covers her eyes with her hands.

Luisa feels a little stab of compassion for her, cutting through the disappointment and the anger, the bitterness and the feeling of betrayal.

G aia is crouching in the vegetable garden, digging out some bulbs, Icaro helping her clean them and put them into a wicker basket. Luisa and the others walk toward them without exchanging any looks or words. Margherita limps behind them, trying to avoid the puddles, dragging her suitcase that with its mud-encrusted wheels seems even heavier than yesterday night. She has on her wraparound sunglasses and a foulard covering her hair, a pair of black patent-leather ankle boots that hurt her terribly at the heels and toes. She feels crushed, dirty, disheveled; her only wishes are a telephone line and a hot bath, she doesn't even know in what order.

The group stops near the vegetable garden; Luisa says "hi" and makes an awkward little gesture.

Gaia barely looks up, she doesn't answer. Her hands are dirty with mud, there's mud on her nose and forehead. Using a bent, rusty old spoon, she digs out another bulb that looks like an onion but probably is not, and hands it to Icaro.

Luisa says, "We're leaving then"—all composed and respectful as a visitor on an Indian reservation.

The others shuffle uneasily. In the light of day they all look pitiful, a thousand little pains and tensions and uncertainties running through them.

Gaia says, "Good," as if the matter didn't concern her at all;

she fills the hole in the earth with her old spoon. Margherita thinks that she's endowed with a kind of earthy femininity, with her high cheekbones, her round forehead creased by years of exposure to the elements without any protective creams, her strong calves poking through her worn out socks.

Enrico says, "Can you tell us which is the most direct route to town?"

Gaia makes a gesture; she says, "That way."

Enrico looks at her with a physical and ideological aversion too intense to hide. He probably sees her as the incarnation of everything he detests about the country.

Arturo says, "How many kilometers, more or less?"

"I don't know," says Gaia; she gestures to Icaro to bring the wicker basket closer.

"You don't even have an idea, after all these years?" says Enrico, harshly.

Gaia looks up at him blankly, to make him understand that his distaste is fully reciprocal. Icaro imitates her, with an insolent, fierce look.

"It must be about twenty kilometers, Mr. Guardi," says Alessio.

"Wonderful," says Enrico. "Are you sure?" Arms akimbo, he looks in the direction Gaia has pointed to, he's at least partially unaware of the way his formal dignity is undermined by his unkempt hair, by the creases in his overcoat and trousers and by the state of his shoes.

"More or less, Mr. Guardi," says Alessio. "That's what the navigator was indicating."

"Ah, that prodigy of accuracy," says Enrico.

Arturo says, "Hey, it's not such a terrible distance. It's about four hours' walk, at a good clip."

"It might not be so terrible for *you*," says Margherita, her head and body wracked with stress. "I can't even walk twenty *meters*."

"Would you rather stay here?" says Enrico, in an unbearably sharp tone. "With that wonderful suitcase of yours?"

Right now Margherita is much more susceptible to fear than to offense. She says, "Listen, there's no way I can walk for four hours on that road! My feet are destroyed, they hurt like hell even when I stand still!"

"You should have thought about that yesterday," says Enrico, "instead of going to the country with those disco boots on."

"They're not disco boots!" says Margherita, almost with tears in her eyes. "And besides, when we left Milan I didn't imagine I should suit up for a forced march!"

Alessio points to Arup, who's sitting on the side of a small hill digging out a tree trunk with chisel and mallet, pausing every now and then to look in their direction. He says, "Mr. Guardi, I'll go ask the Indian if they can give us a hand to pull our minivan out of the ditch."

"No," says Enrico. "We're not asking them for anything."

"But why?" says Arturo. "If Margherita here doesn't want to walk . . ."

"It's not that I don't want to!" says Margherita. "I just *can't*!"

"I refuse to ask these people for anything!" says Enrico. "We begged enough yesterday night!"

"You don't have to do it," says Arturo. "I'll ask."

"Bravo," says Margherita. "I'm sure they're eager to get rid of us, anyway." She turns to Luisa for some support, but her features are inscrutable.

Alessio pushes on the sides of his pigskin suitcase, trying to give it back its shape. He says, "I'll come with you, Mr. Vannucci."

"Please don't," says Arturo. "It's much better if you stay here." He walks determinedly toward the little hill where the Indian keeps hammering with his mallet.

The others watch him from the vegetable garden: Enrico stiff in his obstinacy, Alessio like a diplomat who has unreasonably been excluded from important negotiations, Luisa in an attitude of disassociation from the group.

Arturo walks up to Arup, he smiles to him, talks, gesticulates. Arup looks at him only intermittently, crouching in front of his partly hollowed-out tree trunk; finally he shakes his head. Arturo insists, using facial and body expressions that should be understandable in any cultural context. Arup shakes his head in a more determined way, then resumes hammering with his mallet.

Arturo walks back to the waiting group; he shrugs his shoulders, opens his arms.

Enrico says, "What wonderful satisfaction we've just given them."

"Well, at least we tried," says Arturo.

Alessio says, "If only you had let me do the talking, Mr. Vannucci."

"They would be shooting arrows at us now," says Arturo.

Enrico says, "Let's get a move on, we've already lost enough time."

"I told you I can't walk!" cries Margherita, in a desperate tone. "Do you understand this? I *can't walk*."

Enrico says, "If it's because of that damned suitcase, we're not going to carry it for you. Leave it here, we'll send somebody to pick it up later."

"It has nothing to do with the *suitcase*!" cries Margherita. "It's my *feet*! There's no way I can walk for twenty kilometers on that road! Do you want me to show you?" She crouches down to untie the shoelaces of one of her ankle boots, then she takes it off with much effort, and pulls the sock off to expose her right foot, all sores and blisters as it is. She cries "See? You think I'm exaggerating."

The others stare silently at her foot, then exchange dismayed looks.

Finally Arturo says, "Okay. There's no need for all of us to walk to Turigi. I'll go with Alessio, then we'll come back in a taxi and pick up the rest of you."

"Yes, Mr. Vannucci," says Alessio. "We'll be a lot quicker, too, without any dead weight holding us back."

Margherita looks at him as if she could kill him.

Enrico shakes his head. He says, "*I'll* go with Alessio. You stay here with the women, Arturo."

"The women?" says Luisa in a tone of cold fury, stepping out of her noble isolation.

Arturo stands face-to-face with Enrico: now it's become one of their recurring male confrontations. He says, "Listen, who's the better walker, Enrico, you or me?"

"That remains to be seen," says Enrico. "In any case I have some extremely urgent phone calls to make, I can't wait till you're back."

"Why don't the three of you go?" says Luisa. "The women can take care of themselves in the meantime."

The men don't answer for a while; they seem to hesitate between conflicting impulses. Then Enrico and Arturo exchange a nod. Enrico says, "You sure? Okay, if it's alright with you. We'll be back in a matter of hours, in any case."

Margherita stops lacing up her ankle boot, a shiver of fear running through her. She says, "You're kidding, aren't you? You can't leave us here all alone?"

"Margherita, come on," says Luisa. "We're grown-ups, and we're not among *cannibals*."

"That's what you say," says Margherita, with a frightened look at Arup banging his mallet on his wood chisel.

Enrico says, "As long as you don't talk to them or anything, you should be safe. Just act like you don't even see them."

"Don't you worry," says Luisa, coldly. "We're perfectly able to fend for ourselves."

Enrico draws closer to her as if to give her a kiss, but she backs away. He gives her what in his opinion is a deeply reasonable look, then he turns to the other two men and says, "Come on, let's go."

"Hey, don't abandon us here!" says Margherita, all her fears redoubled now that she sees them moving.

"We won't," says Arturo. "We'll be back in four or five hours at the most."

"It's too *long*," says Margherita. "I've got some terribly important phone calls to make, too!"

"We'll be back as soon as we can," says Enrico, with a last attempt to catch Luisa's eye.

Alessio says, "See you later, Novelli. I entrust this to you." He pulls his swollen and bruised pigskin trolley suitcase next to Margherita's, then hastens to follow Enrico and Arturo along the path that leads from the clearing to the dirt road. In a few minutes they're quite far in the distance, disappearing into the woods.

Margherita looks at Luisa apprehensively, only to meet her cold stare. She whimpers, "Are you angry with me, too?"

"I'm not," says Luisa, without relaxing her facial muscles in the least. Then she wanders off, her hands in her coat pockets.

Margherita finishes lacing up her boot, and moves as if to follow her but gives up. She kicks Alessio's suitcase, makes it fall into a puddle, and lets out a yell because of the stabbing pain in her right foot. Then she limps back toward the main house, dragging her suitcase behind her. She leans it against the wall and sits on it, her back to the old stones and bricks. She pulls the cell phone out of her handbag and stares at the blank little screen in dismay. She takes out a pack of cigarettes: there are only four left. She lights one up, breathes in the hot smoke, holding it down into the bottom of her lungs. It doesn't counteract the chill in her bones as she looks around: The inhabited house and the empty ones and the tower and the vegetable garden and the chicken coop and the horse paddock and the clearing and the woods encircling it all look like elements of a terribly foreign and dangerous landscape.

Enrico walks briskly at the head of the small group, along the dirt road that descends in curves among the tree-covered hills. Arturo and Alessio follow him closely, but it's Enrico who sets the pace. He doesn't feel bad, apart from his empty stomach and his unshaved beard itching a bit and some aches in his joints after the night spent tossing and turning on a straw mattress. He makes better progress than he would have thought, helped by the slope and by the satisfaction it gives him to react energetically to the circumstances, instead of succumbing to them. It seems to him that his intelligence gives him an advantage over someone like Arturo who would otherwise be more familiar with this kind of situation. In his opinion, this is a typical case of mental qualities prevailing over practical ones; after all, it's precisely here that the evolution of man differs from that of other species. A few pages of Nietzsche come to mind, which had left him rather perplexed when he read them in the sheltered comfort of his Milan apartment. In the present situation they take on an entirely different meaning, stimulating new chains of thought.

They go on walking for a good ten minutes, without saying a single word. There's only the sound of their steps on the damp ground, and of their rhythmic breathing in and out. Last night's desperation as they were dragging themselves in the dark and the rain seems nothing more than an unpleasant memory, now that all the right time-space relationships have been re-established. Twenty kilometers is indeed a minuscule distance by contemporary standards: nothing could prevent three healthy twenty-first-century males from covering it in a matter of hours.

At one bend Alessio stops and puts a hand over his forehead, looking at the undulating, thickly wooded waves of the landscape. He says, "Hey, there's not one single house in sight."

"Nice, isn't it?" says Arturo, without breaking his stride.

"I wouldn't say so, Mr. Vannucci," says Alessio, breathing rather heavily as he hurries to catch up.

"What do you mean?" says Arturo in mock surprise. "When you were trying to sell us those houses, didn't you say that this was one of the most enchanting parts of Italy?"

"I did, Mr. Vannucci," says Alessio, quickly. Mostly likely his brain is engaged in a series of rather complex evaluations concerning whatever chance he has of not losing his clients and his sale for good. Being forced to walk at this pace certainly doesn't help.

Enrico says, "So?"

Alessio must know he can't afford any more mistakes, if he wants to make one more attempt to salvage at least something. "Well, if it's the wilderness you want, there certainly is plenty of it here."

"But it scares you," says Arturo.

Alessio says, "Mr. Vannucci, please don't get me wrong."

"For heaven's sake," says Enrico, in a pressing tone that amuses him as much as the thought of forcing the pace, "tell us, would you buy Windshift, or wouldn't you?"

"Me, Mr. Guardi?" says Alessio, again experiencing some difficulty with the accent he must have worked on for years.

"Yes, you, Alessio," says Enrico. "You."

"Mr. Guardi, it would be way too large a property for me," he replies, torn between conflicting considerations.

"Let's suppose you had a lot of friends," says Enrico. "And children, dogs, whatever."

Alessio laughs nervously. "Mr. Guardi, as we know, in today's real-estate market, it's a rare opportunity."

"Forget about the opportunity," says Enrico. "What I want to know is, would you *personally* buy the house we spent last night in, and the others next to it?"

Alessio wonders whether this is only a cruel little game, or a way of giving him one last professional chance. Finally he makes up his mind. "To be honest, Mr. Guardi, between me and you, I see it a bit like you do, the countryside."

"Meaning?" says Enrico, without turning to look at him, concentrating on his stride.

Alessio says, "Meaning, nowadays we all agree one needs an outlet for the weekends. Especially the ladies, we know that. But personally, I'd look for a place within a forty-five-minute distance from Milan, no more."

"But forty-five minutes from Milan there's only the suburbs!" says Arturo.

"That's not true, Mr. Vannucci," says Alessio. "To the north there's the Brianza, there are some wonderful lakes. If you prefer to go south there's the Oltrepo, it's great hillside country. Good air, good wine and everything, but without having to cross half of Italy to get there."

"What do you call this?" says Enrico.

"Call what?" says Alessio, in a worried tone.

"Is this what you call redirecting the client?" says Enrico. "When the initial proposal doesn't work for some reason and you have to push toward a totally different solution before they lose any wish to buy anything at all?"

"Radical rerouting, it's called," says Arturo.

"Oh, come on, gentlemen," says Alessio, simultaneously

struggling to keep up with their pace and with the conversation. "You asked me what I would personally do. I would build myself a comfortable new home, amid greenery and with good air. But without this kind of isolation, where you can't see a car or a light pole or a bar or a gas station for kilometers. Without all these ugly thorny trees, without the owls and the giant weasels making scary noises as soon as it gets dark."

Enrico encourages him, chiding, "Without those rag-dressed, goat-cheese-eating savages prowling around with bows and arrows."

"Precisely, Mr. Guardi," says Alessio. "Let's face it, from an investment point of view it would be an entirely different matter, because a property here is stuff for connoisseurs, but one closer to Milan would have a *huge* market. Should you for any reason decide to sell it, there'd be a line of buyers waiting, at any time."

"That's true," says Enrico, enjoying this teasing as he drags him on at a fast pace back to civilization.

"Green Brianza," says Arturo in a mock dreamy tone, as if he was already sold on the idea.

Alessio is probably thinking of how to more precisely shape up his rerouting strategy, and this makes him lag behind even more; as soon as he realizes it he picks up his pace, his long blue overcoat hindering his stride.

Arup goes on hammering steadily at the tree trunk, producing a steady rhythm. Luisa observes him as she approaches him along an elliptical course aimed to be as unobtrusive as possible. When she's four or five meters from him, she makes a small gesture with her hand, smiling shyly.

Arup looks up at her for a moment, mallet in hand, then resumes hammering on his chisel, producing light-colored wood chips and curls. On the hillside behind him are other already excavated tree trunks, connected one to the other and to a rusty iron tank.

Luisa says, "We'll be going, too, in a few hours. As soon as the others come and pick us up. It's just that my friend didn't feel like walking all the way to town. Her feet are in a terrible shape."

Arup barely raises his head again, but he looks more embarrassed than hostile.

Luisa feels guilty and hates it; she's furious at the thought of having entrusted herself so passively to Enrico and to the others. She wonders whether this is due to a form of practical cowardice or to mental laziness, or both—Enrico might be right when he accuses her of letting him take the initiative only to find himself later in the position of being criticized if the results are unsatisfactory. She wonders if dealing with books is an excuse not to tackle more substantial matters; if her indifference regarding the practical side of life makes her, in the end, more vulnerable to it. She points to the partly dug-out tree trunk and asks, "It's for the water, isn't it?"

"Yes," says Arup, without looking at her. In the morning light, his hair has a bluish shade.

"Nice," says Luisa. She is reminded of some canoe makers she photographed years ago during a trip to New Guinea, who according to Enrico were working only for the tourists' benefit. She's also reminded of a remark Enrico once made about the division of roles in their married life: he as the initiative taker and she as the giver of judgments, probably referring implicitly to their sex life, too.

Arup hammers on the chisel with his mallet as if he was playing some percussion instrument, his eyes half closed.

Luisa is about to say something to him, but instead she puts her hands back in her coat pockets and resumes her walk. She feels cold and hungry and badly in need of a change of clothes; four or five hours is a long time and not even thirty minutes have passed since Enrico and the others left. She recalls her editor in chief's face; she asks herself how he must have interpreted her not calling him back after their tense phone conversation of yesterday afternoon. She thinks of the faces of the commercial directors and the managing director during their last meeting, their way of leaning back in their chairs and looking at her and exchanging glances between them as she talked.

There's a stockade enclosing a trampled-down, muddy portion of the clearing; five or six brownish horses crowd up near Lauro as he scatters hay with a pitchfork. Luisa gets closer, then stops with an expression that is both uneasy and uncertain.

The horses are rather short and shaggy; they tear away hungry mouthfuls of fodder as if they hadn't eaten for weeks, puffing and neighing, threatening to kick one another. Lauro thrusts his pitchfork into a compact bale of hay and scatters it around in a semicircle, with a vigor that seems purely functional but must at least be partly influenced by the fact that Luisa is watching. Finally he acknowledges her presence and stops, wiping the sweat off his brow with the back of his hand. He says, "How come you're still here?"

"They'll come back to pick us up in a few hours," says Luisa. "I had to stay with my friend because she can't walk." She gestures behind her, but when she turns Margherita is no longer near the house where she left her.

"I hope they hurry up," says Lauro; he resumes scattering the hay. In a few energetic movements he finishes the job, then pushes away a horse blocking his path and disappears with his pitchfork behind a shelter made of worn-out planks.

Luisa takes a few slow steps along the stockade; out of sheer nervousness she sings softly to herself a wordless little tune.

When Lauro emerges from of the shelter with a bundle of reins on his arm, he seems vexed to find her still there.

Luisa says, "Listen, I'm sorry."

"About what?" says Lauro. There's a scar on one side of his neck, and scars on his hands; his gray woolen loose jacket is torn and sewn up here and there.

"About our invasion," says Luisa. "About our wanting to buy these houses." She realizes that again she's talking with some kind of declamatory emphasis, as she does every time she has to deal with someone who for historical or political or social reasons seems to be in a more disadvantaged position.

"Why should you worry about it?" says Lauro. "It's not your fault if someone's living here, right?"

"I didn't *know*," says Luisa. "Really. You have to believe me."

"What about the others?" says Lauro. "They didn't know either?"

Luisa hesitates between several possible answers; she says, "We're different." Almost simultaneously she asks herself whether these words stem from moral honesty or resentment, from her wish to facilitate communication between two opposed cultures, from the fact that she has to spend several more hours here without anything to do.

"Different in what way?" says Lauro.

Luisa realizes she's put herself in a vulnerable position, but this has the effect of making her come out in the open even more, into a mentally black-and-white territory. She says, "In almost everything."

"And you realize this only now?" says Lauro.

"Yes," says Luisa. "No."

"It must be awful," says Lauro. There's a tension at the corners of his mouth which is not a proper smile; he turns, goes to take one of the horses.

Luisa thinks of other things she could declare with emphasis, but there's no longer any eye contact between them and she feels her words would fall flat. She makes a barely visible gesture, saying, "Anyway, we'll all leave as soon as they're back."

Lauro doesn't answer, nor does he look at her anymore; he sticks two fingers into a corner of the horse's mouth and slips the bite in, then sets the trapping, buckles it with confident, easy gestures.

Luisa waits for him to take the initiative and continue their conversation, but it doesn't happen, so she makes a half turn and slowly walks back toward the houses. She imagines that Lauro is looking at her from behind; the thought causes a strange tingle along her spine, influencing her way of walking. Then she thinks she hears him call out, "Hey!" She isn't totally sure about it, so she turns as if to look around: it doesn't come out very naturally.

Lauro is standing by the horse with a saddle in his hands, across the gulf of empty space that's widened between them.

Luisa hesitates, because she's still not certain that he has called out to her; measuring with the tip of her right foot the possibility of reducing the distance without exposing herself too much.

Lauro puts the saddle on the horse's back, then rests his hands on the stockade; he says, "What were you looking for, in a place like this?"

"Sorry?" says Luisa, even though she has heard him perfectly well.

"What did you think you would find here?" says Lauro.

"I don't know," says Luisa, getting two steps closer so she doesn't have to raise her voice too much. "It was an idea, more than anything else."

"What kind of idea?" says Lauro. Perhaps he doesn't want her to think he's too interested in this conversation, because he walks back to the horse and buckles up the belt.

Luisa touches her hair; she says, "Of a different life, perhaps. At least *bits* of a different life."

"And how would that different life be?" says Lauro.

"I don't know," says Luisa. Her temperament would normally make her stop here, but she forces herself to go on. "Perhaps a freer, more natural, more shared kind of life."

"Perhaps?" says Lauro.

"Yes," she says. "But it was all rather absurd, come to think of it."

"Why?" says Lauro, half hidden behind the horse's neck.

Luisa narrows her eyes. "Because we kept talking about it, while everything we do was in the exact opposite—toward a *less* free, less natural, less shared kind of life. We kept this idea of our place in the country like an animal in a zoo, to look at in moments of boredom."

Lauro is smiling now, even though it's not clear about what exactly; he says, "Sometimes you can free them, the animals in the zoos."

Luisa says, "Evidently we can't."

"Why do you talk in the plural?" says Lauro. "Didn't you say you were different?"

"Perhaps," says Luisa.

Lauro laughs. "You don't seem to have very definite ideas, today."

"You're right, I don't," says Luisa. She laughs, too, but with the feeling of having lost something she might need right now, even though she can't tell what it is.

Lauro goes on looking at her for a while, than he grabs a lock of the horse's mane and jumps in the saddle.

Luisa, standing on the other side of the stockade, says, "Are you going?" She's acutely conscious of how stupid her question sounds.

"Yeah, for a little ride," says Lauro; he prods the horse toward a gate in the stockade.

Luisa thinks of waving her hand nonchalantly, but instead she says, "If you're still out riding when we leave, bye."

Lauro says, "I don't think they'll be back so soon, your friends. It's a long walk, from here to town."

"I know," says Luisa, filled with embarrassment at the idea of having unnecessarily exposed herself. She lowers her eyes, bites her lips, puts her hands back into her coat pockets. She thinks of a nonchalant remark to get out of the situation with some dignity, but Lauro has already reached the gate and unlatched it without looking at her, he's already past it and back with a half turn to close it again, already galloping across the clearing.

A rturo follows Enrico who's walking too fast for the distance they have to cover. He knows that in a few kilometers he'll be breathless, but he also knows there's some kind of statement in the way he has been leading the march ever since they left. Alessio lags a few meters behind, his clothes totally in disarray. He's already showing signs of fatigue, stumbling every now and then. The landscape here is strange, the tree-covered hills showing portions of gray rock that look like North American canyons. Enrico checks his cell phone for the millionth time, he angrily puts it back in his pocket.

Arturo is right behind him. "Your extremely urgent phone calls," he says, "they're for work, right?"

"Right," says Enrico, without turning.

"Even on a Saturday?" says Arturo.

"I should have made them yesterday evening," says Enrico.

"Sure," says Arturo; he lets him lead by no more than half a meter.

Enrico tries to ignore his mocking tone, but eventually he turns and says, "What's so strange about it?"

"Come on, Enrico," says Arturo. "You can tell me."

"Tell you what?" says Enrico.

"If it's not for work," says Arturo. He wouldn't know how to explain this insistence, if not for the strange mood he's been in since yesterday evening when all their plans suddenly went to pieces. It's like a current pushing on gestures and thoughts unpredictably, almost against his will.

"It *is* for work," says Enrico.

"Yeah," says Arturo, "of course it is."

Enrico hastens his pace even more, as if to evade this subject. Instead, unexpectedly he says, "Okay, it's a girl. Are you happy, now?"

Arturo laughs, taken aback. He asks himself if this sudden breach in Enrico's defenses is due to the lack of sleep and food, or to the empty, endless landscape, to the distance that still separates them from the world of human activities. He continues through the breach: he says, "A girl?"

"Yes, a girl," says Enrico through tight lips, walking even faster.

Arturo easily keeps up with him. "How long has it been going on?"

"Since *what* has been going on?" says Enrico.

"Oh, come on!" says Arturo. Actually it's the first time since they've known each other that he's the one to poke into personal matters, instead of being prodded. He can recall countless conversations in which he was pushed to describe the inner workings of his private life, and when he saw the slightly ironic gleam in Enrico's eyes as he listened to him.

"What a nuisance you are," says Enrico. "Four or five months."

"And how is she?" says Arturo.

It looks as if Enrico has no intention whatsoever of telling him, but instead he says, "She's twenty-three, just got her degree. I didn't even want to hire her, it was my collaborators who insisted. Thin, light blonde hair. She talks in a slightly shrill tone, she can't pronounce the 'r's. She has a piercing through her navel, you know one of those little gold rings?"

Arturo laughs. "Wow."

Enrico says, "What can I do about it? You know how it is, when you spend years trying to live up to somebody's expectations, and all you seem to produce is disappointments and recriminations? Then you meet somebody else and, *wham*, you discover that with one tenth of the effort you can make her *happy*."

"Oh yes," says Arturo, "I know what you're talking about."

Enrico says, "And all this without first having to change into a different person. It's *you* she likes, exactly as you are. A *lot*, not just a little. With no reservation. You discover you have qualities you had totally forgotten about."

"That's what happened to me with Giulia," says Arturo. "After five terrible years with Jeannette, filled with continuous scenes, insomnia, headaches, stomachaches, I don't know how many hours of analysis."

"Yeah," says Enrico. "It's like some kind of miracle. All of a sudden you realize you're charming, reassuring, cultured, you've got a great sense of humor, you know life, you've seen the world, you've read a lot of books. You have an incredible advantage over other men, including those you thought were much better than you. And the best part is, it's a *simple* miracle, a natural one. There's nothing weird or frightening about it."

"Yes," says Arturo, images and feelings rushing back to him. "The only problem is, it's a *temporary* miracle. A year goes by, maybe a year and a half, then you wake up and you see you're capable only of producing disappointments and recriminations, just like before. Or to *be* disappointed and blame someone else, which is more or less the same thing."

"It's not inevitable," says Enrico. "It's not always like that."

"I'm afraid it is," says Arturo. "Look at how it ended between me and Giulia."

Enrico says, "But with you and Giulia it was clear from the beginning it couldn't work. You were the only one not to see it."

"Why didn't you tell me, then?" says Arturo. "If it was so clear?"

"You seemed too convinced," says Enrico. "What could I tell you, that you've married an arrogant, domineering, interfering, paranoid hyena who's not even particularly good-looking or intelligent? You would have been mortally offended, you would have never wanted to see me again."

"That's the point," says Arturo. "That's *exactly* it. There's some kind of automatic reflex that for some time blinds your critical ability completely, making you believe that there's an incredible difference between the new person you've met and the one you were with before."

"Sometimes it's true," says Enrico.

"Its seems to *you* that it's true," says Arturo.

"Sometimes it *is* true," says Enrico. "There are so many different elements that come into play. Mental and physical characteristics, habits, attitudes, aspirations, dreams, obsessions, vices, complexes, qualities, weaknesses, skills, things you know, things you don't know, fears, certainties."

"Yes," says Arturo. "Still, little by little the situation from which you ran away recreates itself, with subtle variations. It's not your fault, or hers. It's just *life*, there's nothing you can do about it. You can't really fight against this kind of thing. Even though when you were in the miracle phase you thought it could go on forever."

Enrico kicks a little stone; he says, "So, since I'm still in the 'miracle phase' let me think it could go on forever, okay? Do you mind terribly?"

"Not at all," says Arturo. "I'm happy for you. I didn't want to be a wet blanket."

"But you were," says Enrico. "Talking like a wise, bitter old aunt."

"I'm sorry, damn it," says Arturo. "Let's not talk about it anymore."

"Thanks a lot," says Enrico.

They walk in silence, far too fast. Arturo tries to find the right breathing rhythm, but he can't at first. He's embarrassed for having expressed his feelings in words so banal, so disheartening. He'd like to grab Enrico by the shoulder and shake him. He says, "And Luisa?"

"What about her?" says Enrico, sharply.

"Does she know?" says Arturo. "Have you talked to her about it?"

"Are you kidding?" says Enrico, as if he couldn't believe the question.

Arturo says, "You don't intend to leave her and to go live with the blonde?"

"Of course I don't!" says Enrico. "How can such an idiotic thought enter your mind?"

"I don't know," mumbles Arturo, a little intimidated by this reaction. "I thought that since everything with the girl was so dream-like . . ."

"But Luisa is absolutely essential to my balance!" says Enrico. "We've been together too long, we've been through too many important junctions, we're too complementary. I could never do without her."

"I was only asking," says Arturo.

Enrico breathes harder than he would like to. He says, "And it wouldn't be the same with the girl, if we saw each other day and night. We already work together, that's more than enough. It's great as it is, we have all the sparkle and passion we need. We can spend a weekend in some beautiful place every now and then, then she goes home to her parents and I go home to Luisa. To sleep in my bed, with my books and CDs on the shelves, my paintings on the walls, my clothes in the wardrobe, my food in the refrigerator."

"It's not a very romantic vision," says Arturo.

"On the contrary, it is," says Enrico. "Otherwise after a few months you inevitably find yourself back in the situation you wanted to escape from. That's where you make your mistake. If you break up a marriage only to throw yourself into another marriage, it's obvious how things will end."

Arturo looks at the trees, unconvinced. "As long as you have a foot in both camps."

"Why shouldn't I be able to?" says Enrico, quickly.

"You know perfectly well what I mean." Since they were in high school together, Enrico has had this way of prevailing on him in any discussion: he must see it as part of the basis of their friendship.

Enrico laughs. "It's a little more complicated, but after all you just have to put a little more energy into it."

"A little energy is not enough," says Arturo.

"Speak for yourself," says Enrico.

From five or six meters behind them, Alessio says, "Mr. Guardi, Mr. Vannucci, could you please slow down a little bit? I can't feel my legs anymore!"

Enrico and Arturo slow down, but Enrico wears an impatient expression. Even though he's probably glad to comply, as the pace was beginning to wear him out.

Margherita limps across the clearing around the houses with her suitcase in tow, all too conscious of how miserable she looks. Should some paparazzi appear with their cameras, she would have to hide rather than ask them to save her and give her a ride back to the civilized world. But the thought of paparazzi is so out of place, it almost makes her cry. She takes off her foulard and sunglasses, puts them into her coat pockets. She has a ferocious desire for a coffee and a desperate need of sugar; she tries not to think about it but she can't. She asks herself whether her beautician will be able to do something about her feet in a reasonably short time or whether she'll have to resort to a specialized doctor; how long she'll have to wait before she can put on a pair of elegant shoes again. Apart from such worries, she keeps wondering about possible developments in the sponsor situation and about other crucial matters concerning her program. Perhaps she should make up her mind and find herself a new agent; she's been too sentimental about it for too long, without considering her growing professional status. It maddens her to think that she can't make a telephone call or exercise any kind of long-distance control: she's filled with adrenalin that can't find any outlet.

She walks around the tower that she had wanted for herself when this place still existed only in her imagination, and she almost bumps into Mirta and Aria who are shepherding a small flock of goats with two long sticks. This scares her, but she tries to recover and says, "Hi there!"

Mirta doesn't answer; Aria stares at her with her wild eyes.

Margherita gestures to her and says, "We're not staying here for long. Only until the others come and pick us up."

Mirta barely nods her head; she looks at a small goat frantically suckling milk from her mother.

"It's beautiful, this place," says Margherita in a tone that sounds fake even to her.

Mirta still doesn't answer; Aria stares with too much attention at Margherita's unwashed yellowish-white hair, the sequins along the legs of her jeans, the patent leather ankle boots that are torturing her feet.

Margherita asks herself whether her ability to utter a sentence or even a single word in a natural way has been compromised permanently by her job. To test herself she says, "It's only a little cold, at night." The remark is supposed to sound like an admission of weakness rather than a complaint, but she's not at all sure of the result.

Mirta says, "You should come here in January, then."

Margherita doesn't know whether to interpret this as a hostile answer or as a simple observation; her difficulty of interpretation might be due to the physical discomfort of the place or to the mysteriousness of the local culture. To recoup the awkward situation she says in an almost childlike tone, "Are you angry with us because we wanted to buy your houses?"

Mirta looks straight into her eyes and says, without any kind of social niceties, "Yes."

"I can understand you," says Margherita, almost relieved. "I would be, too, if I were in your place. But we didn't know anything about you. I swear it."

"You didn't know that people were living here?" says Mirta, hard to fool.

Margherita tries to stick closely to the truth, to see what effect it has on her voice and on her facial expressions. She says, "We were told there was just a small bunch of poor peasants with a standing order of eviction."

"We *are* a small bunch of poor peasants," says Mirta.

"Oh, come on," says Margherita. "You're a lot more sophisticated and complicated than that. You're nothing like the people we were expecting to find."

Mirta scratches her right leg, she says "Why, would you have felt less guilty to kick out the people you were expecting to find?"

"No, not at all," says Margherita. "We've really been stupid. We hadn't thought of what it really meant, in real life." She tries to convey all the mortification and guilt she is capable of feeling through her voice and eyes. She's almost certain that she looks convincing now.

The tension at the corners of Mirta's mouth relaxes, and she looks away.

Margherita goes on in an even more grief-stricken tone, partly to consolidate the effect and partly because she's carried by her own words. "We felt so bad, when we realized our position. We felt *awful*. We felt like monsters. After you had taken us in so generously, without asking any questions. Wet and hungry and disheveled as we were." She dries a few tears with the back of a hand; right now she has enough reasons for being unhappy, she could cry rivers if she let herself.

Mirta looks at the goats, turns back to face Margherita; she extends a hand to touch her right shoulder and says, "Don't cry."

Margherita steps back, but almost immediately she recovers; she laughs, sighs, dries some more tears. "I'm okay, I'm okay."

The girl Aria seems even more moved than her friend, wide-eyed in front of this show of damaged feelings.

Margherita thinks that she could go on in a crescendo and make them cry, too, but she feels she's in too bad a shape to manage it.

Mirta says, "At least you realized you were about to do something awful." She smiles.

Margherita nods her head, swallowing her tears, sniffling. Then she changes mood and subject: she smiles, too, points at the little hamlet, and says, "Have you been living here for a long time?"

"I've been here for seven years, more or less," says Mirta.

It occurs to Margherita that, after all, asking questions is what she does best—and likes best, too—so she says "And how did you end up here?"

"Through a friend of my ex-boyfriend," says Mirta. "They left two years ago, together."

"Was that hard for you?" asks Margherita, in a concerned tone of voice that comes automatically to her. Everybody brings their tricks of the trade wherever they go, and these ones are hers.

Mirta shakes her head, she says, "No, he was an idiot."

Margherita turns to Aria and says, "What about you? You're so young, how did you get here?"

Aria doesn't answer. She looks away, prodding a goat with her long stick.

Mirta says, "Aria came here when she was six. She's Lauro's daughter."

Margherita says, "Really? She does look a bit like him. Same eyes, almost. What wonderful names you have, all of you."

Mirta says, "We chose them when we arrived here."

"Ah," says Margherita. "I see, now. I mean, it seemed so strange that you *all* had such suggestive names. And so in tune with the place."

"Except for Arup," says Mirta. "That's his real name."

Margherita would like to ask what their real names are, but instead she asks Aria, "And your mother? Where is she?"

Aria pretends not to hear her, bending down to check one of the goat's legs.

Mirta says, "She went away, too."

Margherita still has a good list of questions, but Aria puts two fingers into her mouth and emits a shrill whistle. The goats all spring off and she runs after them. Mirta makes a gesture and she, too, runs away.

Margherita stands there with her suitcase at her feet, looking around through half-closed eyelids. She thinks that if anybody offered her a hot coffee and a croissant with cream in a well-heated room with soft carpets and nice couches, where she could take off her patent-leather boots and make ten or fifteen phone calls in quick succession, she could cry out of sheer gratitude.

E nrico catches his breath as if he didn't really need to: arms at
his hips, he waits for his heart to slow down, pretending to
be very interested in the wooded landscape. Alessio, on the other
hand, pants shamelessly, his artificial tan contrasting strikingly
with his way of bending over at the side of the road. Arturo
inhales and exhales slowly, most likely for dramatic effect. He
says, "One should never run, in the mountains. What matters is
keeping a constant, regular rhythm."

"We're not in the mountains," says Enrico, filled with irritation
at the idea of having to listen to lectures on the outdoor life.

"Mountains, hills, it's all the same," says Arturo. "When you
have to cover a distance, the only thing is to set a pace and keep it
steady. It makes no sense to sprint for a few hundred meters and
then have to regret it for the rest of the way."

Enrico thinks that he must have kept these pearls of wisdom
ready ever since he took the lead; yet he doesn't want to get into
an argument, he keeps his eyes on the sloping woods. About a
hundred meters downhill he can see the road coming this way
after a long curve.

Alessio comes panting by his side, he looks down, too. He says,
"If we went straight down the slope from here we could cut out a
nice bit, Mr. Guardi."

"It's too steep," says Enrico. He has no wish whatsoever to

throw himself down a precipice right now, having up to this point exhausted all his competitive ambitions in leading the march at a furious pace.

Arturo leans out to evaluate the slope; he says, "It's true that we would save ourselves a lot of walking, Enrico."

Alessio dries his forehead with the sleeve of his overcoat. "We could cut out at least half a kilometer. Otherwise we'll never get to Turigi, Mr. Guardi."

"Come on," says Arturo. "What are you afraid of?" It's not hard to read a streak of defiance in his tone, and connect it with the observations he made a minute ago concerning what one should and shouldn't do in the mountains.

Enrico shrugs his shoulders. "Very well."

Arturo starts going down first, his steady feet supporting his strong legs, his energetic hands holding onto branches and boulders and brushes. Enrico thinks with growing irritation of how his movements reflect the countless weekends Arturo spent hiking and climbing and skiing and swimming, instead of reading books or asking himself some deep questions. On these very same weekends Enrico had been working in his studio, or at home absorbing Luisa's quiet dissatisfaction. This makes him even more anxious to return to civilization, where communications and travel from one place to another are quick and effortless and the only exertions are purely mental. He watches Alessio as he awkwardly puts down one foot after another, perhaps for fear of ruining his second pair of shoes, or because he's hampered by his long blue overcoat.

Enrico goes down the slope last, realizing after the first few steps that it's even steeper than it looked from the edge of the road. The leaves and the mold soaked with the night's rain slip under his feet, the tree branches he tries to cling to are dead and rotten and they immediately give way. Arturo has already descended quite far, but now Alessio seems to be having problems. He slips and slides and collides violently with a tree, and screaming "Shiiiiit!" he tumbles down like a blue avalanche with a noise of snapped wood and thuds and less distinguishable cries.

"Hey!" Arturo shouts, perhaps attempting to stop his fall but unable to, hurtling down after Alessio: the sounds of the falling men redouble in the undergrowth, with a frightful effect. Enrico feels his feet lose their hold, then he slips, lands on his bottom, tries to grab onto something but feels his hand burn and lets go, tumbles down, gropes about, hits his head and his left knee and his right shoulder, bruises his face, rolls over, gets mud in his eyes and nostrils and ears, scratches against rough barks and sharp branches, hits his back, hits his side, hits his head again but in a different spot. More than frightened, he's surprised, by how a descent that seemed only slightly risky has in a matter of seconds turned into a potentially fatal chain of events. He thinks that this must be the same kind of surprise that a swimmer must feel when he's sucked under by a whirlpool in the middle of a river, while his friends and maybe his girlfriend chat and laugh on the bank utterly unaware that they're witnesses to an absurd and banal tragedy. Apart from this, his brain is taken over by percussive and concussive and abrasive cracking and snapping and scraping and slithering feelings, mineral and vegetable smells reaching his nostrils with the same inexplicable aggressiveness of the images that flash before him, too close and too fast to make out in real time.

Then he finds himself lying still on the damp, muddy slope, his feet against a tree trunk and his back burning, a taste of mushrooms on his tongue, the last impact reverberating through his bones and in his ears. Very slowly, he raises his head, then turns it even more cautiously: a few meters downhill he sees the road they wanted to reach. A few meters uphill Arturo is sitting still with his knees bent, until he slowly stretches his legs and grunts and coughs and gets up by degrees, walks down holding onto the trees. His clothes are torn here and there and his face and hands are scratched and dirty with black soil; his hair is full of leaves and bits of wood. Spitting and laughing, he says, "Everything okay?"

Enrico doesn't laugh at all. He says, "Thank goodness it wasn't too steep, huh?"

From a point further down in the undergrowth comes an animal cry that is in fact human, that turns out to be Alessio, even though it's wordless.

Arturo turns serious with disconcerting quickness. "Coming!" he shouts, stumbling down through the tree trunks and brush, careful not to slip again.

Enrico touches himself where he hurts the most: the nape of his neck, his left knee, his lumbar vertebrae, his right hip, his right wrist. Apparently there are no serious damages, apart from the graze on his hands and the multiple bruises and the muddy black soil in his shirt and hair and under his nails and in his shoes and mouth and eyes and nostrils. He cautiously gets up, testing his balance, trying to wipe or shake off at least part of the debris. Then he walks down the slope toward the other two.

Arturo is crouched down in the attitude of an Alpine rescue-team member next to Alessio who's lying very still on his back, his head pointing downhill, his legs bent in an awkward way.

Not to be diminished, Enrico stoops down at once and grabs Alessio under the armpits and tries to pull him up, saying "Come on."

"Wait!" shouts Arturo.

Alessio lets out an even more piercing scream; he jerks back, his blue overcoat slipping through Enrico's hands.

"What's the matter?" says Enrico, his breath cut short from fright.

"His leg," says Arturo with a grave expression, although the dirt and leaves he's covered with make him look like a faun of the woods.

"Ahiahiaia!" says Alessio. "Ahaahiaahia!"

Enrico crouches down to have a better view. "Which leg?"

"The right one," says Arturo, in a low voice.

Enrico makes an effort to recall the instructions of a first-aid manual he leafed through once when he was a boy, but nothing useful comes to mind. He says, "Does it hurt a lot? Can you move it?"

"Yes! No!" cries Alessio. "I can't, Mr. Guardi!"

Arturo points to a bulge under Alessio's trouser leg that looks like a piece of stick that got in there during the ruinous fall. He mutters, "A really bad fracture, too."

"What fracture?" cries Alessio. "Where?" He raises his head, and as soon as he makes out the shape of his broken bone he starts shrieking and thrashing about like a stuck pig, scratching the earth with his fingers.

Enrico runs his hands through his hair. For some reason he thinks of a film set on a German U-boat during the Second World War, specifically the scene in which the captain and the second-in-command and the whole crew are stuck at the bottom of the sea and can't do anything about it, sweat dripping from their foreheads, water seeping in through all the seams.

Arturo puts his hand on Alessio's right shoulder. "Calm down, we're here with you."

But at this point Alessio is totally overcome by fear and pain, and he screams again, louder than anyone would have imagined he could.

Enrico feels a totally irrational kind of resentment toward Alessio; he looks at the dirt road only three meters downhill, with an irresistible urge to leave the wounded man behind and run back to the civilized world at all the speed his still sound legs are capable of.

Alessio's face is covered with sweat mixed with mud; he grinds his teeth and twitches his arms; he cries, "Help!"

"Help from *whom*?" says Enrico, in a sharp tone he can't suppress.

Arturo gives him a sharp look. "Let's straighten him up, at least. Let's carry him down. Careful. Don't hold him like that."

"How the hell am I supposed to hold him?" says Enrico, unable to get a firm a grip of his overcoat's blue wool.

Alessio struggles to resist their attempts to move him, crying, "Ouch! Let me go! It hurts too bad!"

All the same, Arturo and Enrico manage to carry him down, half-sitting him with his back to the slope, his feet touching the dirt road.

"What now?" Enrico says. His nose is running from the effort and the agitation.

"We'll walk to town and get help," says Arturo. "There's nothing else to do."

"Don't leave me here alone!" cries Alessio, in a barely intelligible voice. "The wild animals are going to eat me alive! Oh, God, I'm going to be sick!" He has a sudden retch; before Enrico realizes it, Alessio vomits on his coat's sleeve.

Enrico jumps back; he tries to shake off the strands of yellowish slobber, rubbing the sleeve against a tree trunk in disgust.

Arturo doesn't seem in the least shaken by the event. "One of us stays here with him, the other walks to town."

Enrico now hates Arturo's calm, practical attitude, and all that his words imply: the moral obligation toward someone he doesn't give a damn about, just because they were together when he broke a leg thanks to his very own stupid idea. He takes off his coat, taking care not to dirty his hands with vomit, and says, "I'll walk."

"I'll walk," says Arturo.

"Why you?" says Enrico in a defiant tone. He's so filled with anger, he could run a marathon with him on the road stretching before them.

Arturo preempts him: "Because you're already exhausted." He takes his tweed coat off and rolls it up, putting it under Alessio's head like a pillow.

"I'm not in the least exhausted," Enrico shoots back. He lays his vomit-soiled coat over Alessio, as if this, too, was an altruistic gesture.

"I'm going," says Arturo, definitively.

"Please be quick, Mr. Vannucci," whimpers Alessio, as if to declare him the official, victim-approved rescuer.

"Wait a moment," says Enrico, with renewed fury at the thought of being left in the middle of nowhere for who knows how many hours, taking care of an invalid real-estate agent.

Alessio moans again, as if he were dying. "I can't endure this much longer."

Arturo says, "I'll be back with an ambulance as soon as I can." He walks off briskly, in a demonstration of the perfect long-distance pace.

Enrico stares at him as he gets farther and farther away along the road, then he goes to pee against a tree trunk. The frustration caused by this delay in his return to civilization grows inside him in a devastating way, made worse by the acid smell of Alessio's vomit and by the sound of his laments, by the implacable neutrality of the unspoiled, observing nature all around them.

Arturo moves his arms and legs with a steady rhythm, estimating the distance he covers with each step, and what he'll cover in an hour. He picks a few leaves and sticks out of his hair and sweater, but he isn't overly concerned about it, nor about the scratches on his face and hands or the tears in his trousers or the soreness where he fell during his tumble down the slope. What worries him is Alessio's broken leg, and the thought of being at least partly responsible for it. He keeps reviewing the wrong moves with which he tried to stop Alessio's ruinous fall; he shudders at the thought of the consequences which the very same mistakes could have had in a truly demanding descent from a real mountain.

Aside from such worries, he is rather satisfied with the pace he's keeping. If it wasn't for the harrowing laments that still resound in his ears, he'd be happy to walk like this for hours. He has always favored extended physical activity, which doesn't demand burning dashes but a continuous, systematic application of energy. In sports like cross-country skiing, mountaineering, high-altitude hiking, once he gets into the appropriate rhythm he could go on indefinitely without getting tired or bored, transported far from the pressures and the besieging thoughts of organized life. He thinks of his very recent exchanges with Enrico regarding miracles and how situations tend to recreate themselves; he thinks of his ex-wife's voice, charged with claims and blackmailing intents. He thinks of the annoying faces of a Japanese buyer and an interior decorator from Dubai and a Monte Carlo–based couple with whom he has appointments for Monday, Tuesday, and Wednesday. He almost regrets having to emerge from the blind spot for cell phones; he wouldn't mind keeping out of contact for a little bit longer.

After twenty minutes of a vigorous downhill march, the road makes a bend at a reduced slant toward a more open landscape, where the woods are interrupted here and there by pastures. Arturo feels the lighter impact on his joints, and he adjusts his muscular engagement to the gradient. He scans the area in hopes of discovering an inhabited house, but he doesn't see any. What he suddenly sees is a metallic-gray pickup truck coming at full speed along another dirt road that connects to the one he's on. He recovers almost immediately from his surprise, and starts running. He is perhaps two hundred meters from the crossroads, and his boots are certainly not running shoes, but his advance is so speedy that he gets there a couple of seconds before the pickup. He stands in the middle of the road and waves his arms, shouting "Hey! Stop! Stop!"

But instead of stopping or at least slowing down, the pickup accelerates straight at him with a ferocious roar, its headlights and grille looking like the eyes and mouth of some motorized predator. Arturo watches it getting closer, a sense of disbelief immobilizing his legs; only when it's almost upon him does he jump sideways, rolling on the ground, hurting his hands and elbows and knees.

He immediately gets up again, and with a wave of fear and rage and incredulity, he picks up a stone and throws it in the pickup's wake, shouting "You criminal! You bastard! You pig!"

The pickup brakes with a screech of its big tires, then reverses at full speed, right toward him. Again Arturo can't really believe it; he shouts, "Heeeeeeey!" and again jumps to the side at the very last moment, feeling the air blast and the roar of the diesel engine. Then he stands on the side of the road, his arms and legs shaking, a thousand insults surfacing to his lips through layers of incomprehension.

The steel-colored pickup stops a little farther down the road with another violent screech, then the passenger's window rolls down. Arturo springs forward, propelled by an inarticulate fury that carries with it words and gestures of totally legitimate outrage and perhaps even a grabbing of shirt collars and an opening of car doors and a dragging out of who's inside to settle things face-to-face without the cowardly shelter of a mechanical means used to compensate for someone's personal vileness.

But when he gets there he doesn't see the face he expects to see. What appears in the open window are two small black circles that could be the eyes of an iron snake but are the holes at the end of a double-barreled shotgun. Arturo stands staring at them as they move toward him with determined slowness, his lungs emptying, a cold chill running up his spine all the way to the back of his neck and under his scalp. He feels unable to shake off the disbelief that again stops him in his tracks, and then, with a desperate jerk, he tears himself out of it and runs like crazy away from the road for the trees that seem far off even though they're only meters away.

His eardrums pound in anticipation of a blast, but when a shot really comes from behind him it cracks the air much more violently than he was expecting, making him close his eyes and fly forward and crash facedown among the branches and leaves. But, in spite of the chill in his stomach and in his bones, he isn't dead or wounded. He gets up again, his relief already overrun by other even uglier anticipations and by a terrible feeling of urgency that makes him zigzag like a rabbit and stumble and fall, get up again, and move his legs with all the speed he is capable of.

He doesn't have any mental space to reflect, or even to make some simple evaluations: his head is filled with images and feelings and impulses in frantic succession. He raises his knees up high and presses his heels down on the irregular ground to gain maximum traction, pumping with his arms to grab the air and the branches and whatever happens to be in front of him to pull himself forward. His only thought is to put as much distance as he can between himself and the road and the gray pickup and the two little black holes at the end of the shotgun's barrels, devouring space, stealing time.

He stops for a moment in front of a fallen tree that's blocking his way, and there's a second blast somewhere behind him. He jumps over the tree trunk as if he was flying and falls and gets up again and starts running again, his survival instincts wildly pushing him deep into the heart of the woods. He slips on the wet leaves and trips on the dead branches, scratching his face and hands with thorns and brushes but still he runs, sweeping away any obstacles.

He frantically climbs up a slope, fighting against the sprays of old-man's-beard that cling to his legs like odious deep-sea animals, against the rotten bits of wood that snap and give way under his feet and would make him stumble if it wasn't for his absolute determination to push forward, faster than any image or feeling that's trying to catch up with him. It's not a rational flight strategy, if there could even be one. He simply grabs and jumps and pushes and pulls and kicks almost blindly through the undergrowth.

At one point he dives headfirst into a thicket, cutting his way uphill until he unexpectedly comes out into a clearing. The open space and the light make him feel suddenly exposed, lost; he looks around like a hounded animal on its last legs, feeling he no longer has enough strength to throw himself back into the woods.

From somewhere along the edge of the clearing he hears a noise of broken branches. Arturo swerves, feeling his right ankle give way; he falls down. He lies on his back, eyes closed and heart beating fast, all his muscles contracted, his head full of terminal images piling one on top of the other. It's a strangely familiar feeling; rather like the critical moments of some of his sporting accidents, it can be traced back to the recurring nightmares he had as a child, in which he was chased by a fox or a wolf that caught up with him and sank its fangs into his throat. The mixture of surprise and rebellion and panic and resignation is the same as he experienced then, when he would wake up screaming and thrashing about in his bed, filled with the suddenness and the inevitability and the absurdity and the irrelevance of impending doom. His thoughts are jerky, severed from their habitual connections; he has a sharp perception of how futile it would be to put up any resistance or try to get up and run away again. He thinks that it will be only a matter of a sharp and briefly painful transition, over as soon as he's out of this body contained by physical laws and chemical reactions, dissolved and waking up elsewhere, turned into something else.

Then he feels something touching his forehead, but it's not the cold, hard pressure of a shotgun barrel, it's something wet and warm and breathing. He tries to keep his eyes closed but when he opens them, he sees the muzzle of a black dog, a bit distorted in a close-up perspective, and behind it Lauro on a horse approaching in slow motion and saying, "What are you doing here?" as if through a broken loudspeaker.

Arturo makes an effort to sit up, but it's not easy to go from a state of imminent death to a conversation, sparse as it may be. He points randomly to the woods, not even remembering where he's come from. He utters, "They shot. Me. With a. Shotgun. From a. Pickup. Truck." He isn't sure he's able to articulate the words he has in mind; he tries to guess whether he's succeeding from Lauro's expressions as he looks down at him from his horse.

Lauro seems to understand him, because he detaches his bow from the saddle and takes an arrow out of the quiver. He says, "Where are your friends?"

"On the. Road," says Arturo. "Eight. Nine. Kilometers. From your. Houses. The real-estate. Guy. Broke. A leg. I was going. To town. I tried. To stop. A pickup. Truck."

"A gray one?" says Lauro.

"What?" says Arturo.

"The pickup," says Lauro.

"Yes," says Arturo. "Metallic." He's surprised that he can extract this color from the confused, frantic overlay of objective and subjective details crowding his recent memory.

Lauro notches up an arrow and spurs his horse, galloping along the edges of the clearing, lowering his head to look through the trees. The black dog runs at his side, in great leaps.

Arturo observes the scene from his sitting position, feeling alarmed and reassured in almost equal parts. He doesn't even know if he and Lauro belong to the same team; if this gallop is an effective intervention or a symbolic gesture or an act of bravado; if he should feel safer or more in danger than before. He asks himself what the system of allegiances and rivalries is in this area; in what position the last events have put him; what chances does a man armed with a bow have against a double-barreled shotgun.

He gets up; the clearing seems to be whirling around him. Little by little he feels his face and hands burning from all the scratches and lacerations, his lungs and legs hurting from the prolonged effort. Sensations occur haphazardly—for example, it takes him a few seconds to be able to see straight, even more to perceive sounds without distortion. But a gust of wind is enough to recalibrate his senses, making his heart beat faster and his eyes dash along the edges of the woods with the selective focus of a prey, his hearing sharpened to the extreme in anticipation of a terrifying new blast that may happen at any time.

Lauro gallops back, reins in the horse before it almost runs over Arturo. His clothes are too coarse and his bow too handmade, his horse too rustic to make him look like an effective rescuer. Rather, he looks like some poor bandit of the woods, all alone with only a few more means of defense than Arturo. He says, "Hop on."

"Where?" says Arturo, without moving.

"Get on the horse," says Lauro. "Otherwise I'll leave you here."

Arturo reaches toward the horse's rump and makes an attempt to mount, but it's wide off the mark. He doesn't feel even remotely able to find the necessary muscular coordination, or the conviction; he smiles weakly at Lauro who's looking down at him impatiently. Then his sense of dignity and his sense of the ridiculous and his sense of balance all come back to him at the same time; he puts his hands on the horse's rump and leaps up, throwing his right leg over with force. Lauro grabs him by the sweater with a strong hand, locks him in place behind him. Then without even giving him a second to settle himself, he spurs the horse on; he gallops across the clearing and into the woods, along a narrow path that wasn't visible from afar. Arturo tightens his legs and holds on to the saddle, ducking his head like Lauro does to avoid hitting the branches that come at them.

M argherita eats bread and cheese with the utmost voracity, hating the texture of bran and the goat smell. But at this point she'd scarf down anything, just to give her desperate stomach some replenishment. She can't understand how Luisa can keep her good manners, sitting up straight on her stool, her polite hands taking a bite at a time and bringing it to her mouth without any trace of frenzy. Margherita has no intention of letting embarrassment restrain her; right now she's much more in line with the ways of Mirta and Aria and Gaia and Icaro, as they grab and chew and gulp down their food like a small group of primitives, unconcerned by any formal preoccupation.

There's barking outside; Mirta stuffs a piece of cheese into her mouth, goes to the door, and walks out. After a few seconds she appears again, saying "Lauro's here, with one of your friends."

They all go outside, into the strong light and the wind. Lauro is trotting on a horse across the level ground, with Arturo clinging at his back and the black dog running alongside. It's a curious and worrying vision, the worrying aspect prevailing as the human and animal figures get closer.

Lauro reins in his horse, which is sweating and puffing; the black dog comes over to sniff everybody. Arturo gets off the horse, heavily. He's moving awkwardly, looking like he doesn't know which way to turn. Only now does Margherita notice that he hasn't got his coat on and that his face and hands are covered with dirt and scratches, his sweater and trousers torn, small leaves and twigs in his hair. She feels a stab of fear and anger that makes her last bite go down the wrong way. She turns sharply toward Lauro, saying, "What did you do to him?"

"It wasn't him," says Arturo, in a slightly ragged voice. "Someone tried to kill me."

"Who did?" says Luisa, finally out of her perfect composure. "Where's Enrico?"

"Down the road," says Arturo. "With Alessio, who's broken his leg."

"What?" says Luisa. "How is Enrico?"

"He's fine," says Arturo. "At least, he was when I left him. A bit dirty and scratched from the fall down the ravine, but he was fine."

"But what happened?" says Luisa. "Why did you leave him?"

"Who was it?" says Margherita, in a panic. "Who tried to kill you?"

Lauro says something to Mirta, who at once runs toward the horses' paddock. He says to the others, "You'd better go inside."

"What about you?" says Gaia, pulling Icaro closer, under her protective arm.

"I'll go look for them," says Lauro. He prods the horse with his heels, makes it turn.

Arturo asks him, "You're sure you know where they are?" His lower lip is cut, there's blood dripping from his left cheekbone.

"Yes," says Lauro. "Go inside."

Luisa moves as if to ask him something, but he's already gone. Gaia is pushing everybody toward the house.

Margherita lets Gaia shove her inside and then goes back to the door to look out. She sees Arup come running in from somewhere and talking with Lauro; Mirta returning from the paddock with another horse which she ties to the first horse's saddle. Then they all scatter rapidly, Lauro galloping toward the woods with the second horse in tow, Arup in the opposite direction with the black dog, Mirta toward the house. She pushes Margherita inside, says "Sorry," and bolts the door.

Gaia fills a cup of water from the jug, she hands it to Arturo. He empties it in one long gulp, then hands it back to have it filled up again. He guzzles down the second cup just as fast, spilling water over his chin and throat; he asks for yet one more.

"Are you certain Enrico was all right?" asks Luisa, her pupils dilated by worry.

Arturo nods his head, but he looks like he's lost his bearings.

Luisa says, "What if they went and shot at him, too?"

Arturo stares at her, not knowing what to say. The child Icaro runs around, excited by the adults' tension.

Margherita has a series of terrifying images in her mind's eye, mostly of movie or television origin. She asks herself, what are my chances of being rescued from the outside in case the situation totally degenerates; she can't imagine any. She puts her hand into her bag to touch her useless cell phone. Again she feels like crying.

Mirta takes Arturo by the arm. "Here," she says, making him sit down on a stool.

"Why did they shoot at you?" asks Luisa. "What did you do?"

"Nothing," says Arturo. "I just wanted to hitch a ride."

Gaia pours another cup of water for him; he empties it as if it were the first.

"What about Alessio?" asks Luisa. "How did he break his leg?"

Arturo says, "He fell. But before. It was his idea." He shakes his head, sipping the remaining drops in his cup.

There are two sharp knocks at the door. They all start, but when Aria goes to check, it's Arup. He quickly walks across the kitchen, disappearing inside the house.

Mirta takes a cloth and dips it into the pitcher, and without saying a word, she starts to clean the dirt and the blood from Arturo's face. He lets her do it, with a kind of post-traumatic passivity.

Margherita says, "And you're absolutely sure they shot at you?"

"Well," says Arturo. He tries to laugh, but it turns into a kind of cough. "I saw the shotgun's barrel right in front of me. If I hadn't made it to the woods, I'd be dead now."

Mirta says, "Take this off." She makes him take off his dirty and torn sweater, then cleans his neck, forearms, and hands with the wet cloth.

Margherita can smell the pungent sweat soaking through Arturo's T-shirt; it adds to the other distressing signals she senses. The dog's barking outside frightens her even more, as does the irregular whistling of the wind against the window panes, and the alarm she can read in Mirta's and Gaia's very practical actions.

Mirta fetches a bottle from a cupboard and pours some dark liquid on another piece of cloth. She says to Arturo, "This is going to burn a little."

"What is it?" asks Arturo.

"A tincture," says Mirta, touching the cut on his cheek with the moistened cloth.

Arturo jolts. "Ouch!"

"Keep still!" says Mirta.

"It hurts!" says Arturo.

"Yes, but it also cures you," says Mirta; she continues, with firm gestures.

"It has a strange smell," says Arturo, already in a more manly tone. "What is it made of?"

Mirta says, "Propolis, dog rose, garlic, dandelion, and a lot of other herbs."

"Rosemary, verbena," says Gaia.

Margherita can hardly believe they're talking of herbs and folk remedies in a moment like this; she looks at the two women and says, "Do you have any idea who could have shot at him?"

Mirta says, "Those Cardoni bastards, for sure."

"Because you entered their territory," says Gaia. "They must have thought you belonged to our tribe."

Arturo says, "Their territory, your tribe . . . It sounds like the American Wild West at the time of the Indian wars."

"It *is* a kind of war," says Gaia. "It's been going on for years."

"You're crazy," says Margherita. "You're all out of your minds." She looks around; it seems to her that in the whole room there isn't a single person who could reassure her, even partially.

Arup crosses the kitchen again, with a crossbow and a quiver full of darts in his hands, walking to the door and out without saying a word.

"What if they shoot at Enrico, too?" asks Luisa.

"They're not going to shoot at him," says Mirta, it's not clear on what basis.

"Lauro will bring them back alive, you'll see," says Gaia.

Arturo says, "How the hell did you manage to get into a war, in this out-of-the-world place?"

Gaia brings to the table a bowl filled with little yellow discs that are perhaps legumes, she puts one into her mouth, breaking the skin with her front teeth, chewing on the pulp. She says, "The fact is, we never had a great relationship with the neighborhood."

"We never really did much to have one," says Mirta, as she keeps treating Arturo's scratches with her tincture.

"That's not true," says Gaia. "You weren't here yet, but when we first arrived we tried in every possible way. We invited them to our parties, gave them food, music, everything. But they only used to come to see if they could cheat us or use us in some way, and when they discovered they couldn't they turned into enemies."

Margherita points to the legumes in the bowl and asks, "What are those?"

Mirta says, "The parish priest encouraged them, too. Going around telling everyone we were a bunch of sinners."

"Lupins," says Gaia; popping more of them into her mouth, spitting out the skins into her hand.

"Why sinners?" asks Margherita. She takes a lupin from the bowl, nibbles at it cautiously—it has a salty, slippery taste which doesn't appeal to her at all. She spits it up whole into her hand, doesn't know where to throw it.

"Because we didn't have regular families, and so on," says Gaia.

"Because of all the nakedness, the tribal dancing, the home-made clothes, the music, everything," says Mirta.

"And what did you do, then?" asks Luisa.

"We tried to mind our own business," says Gaia. "But they just couldn't stand the idea that we were living here."

"They poisoned three of our dogs," says Mirta. "They shot at the goats, the chickens, the rabbits. They never stop spying and interfering, ruining everything they can. The cut down trees, drain the springs, try to widen the roads and have them paved by the municipality."

Margherita tries to catch a glimpse from out of the window, but she can't see anything. She says, "Okay, but what happens now?"

"We wait," says Gaia.

"Wait for what?" says Margherita. "For those guys to come and shoot us, too? I'm sorry, but I don't have anything to do with your wars! I don't want to be dragged into this mess and get myself killed!"

"Calm down," says Arturo, in a tone that doesn't match the reddish-brown welts covering his face and arms and hands.

"I won't calm down!" says Margherita. "And if you could only see yourself in a mirror you wouldn't be too calm, either!" She thinks of shouting some even more assertive words, but her nerves are too tense and her head is too filled with ugly images. She starts crying, a lot worse than she did in the morning—tears spurting out, sighing uncontrollably, her nose dripping.

The child Icaro runs for the shelter of his mother's arms; the girl Aria has a dismayed expression. Luisa, instead of at least attempting to reassure her friend, goes straight to the door and walks out.

Arup is sitting on a big flat stone near the houses, his cross-bow on his knees, scanning the semiflat space surrounded by the woods. Luisa moves toward him in cautious steps. When she's a couple of meters from him she says, "Am I disturbing you?"

He shakes his head and says, "You'd better stay inside."

Luisa ignores him by half closing her eyes and sitting obliquely on the flat stone. There's nothing moving, except for the geese and the chickens and the goats in their pens; the wind blows in erratic gusts. Luisa says, "Do you think Lauro will find them and bring them back?"

"Yes," says Arup, without looking at her.

Luisa turns toward the wood-covered hills behind them, and feels a sharp sensation of being literally off the charts and far removed from the logic she's familiar with. She says, "Those guys who shot at Arturo, could they come here?"

"I don't know," says Arup. His features are smooth, his skin soft; even close up it would be difficult to tell his age.

Luisa asks, "Has it ever happened before?" She asks herself if she shouldn't try talking to him in another language, using different words or a more expressive register, raising her voice, making gestures and faces, perhaps drawing on the ground with a stick.

"Only once," says Arup. He doesn't seem upset, yet it's clear that he isn't relaxed either, alert to even the tiniest signal with the utmost attention.

"What if they come this time, too?" asks Luisa.

"We'll see," says Arup.

Luisa thinks that she's never been without a net of institutional and social protection. She tries to trace back in her memory any situation that could even remotely compare with this one, but she can't find any. The closest she can recall is a motorcycle trip through Croatia with a boyfriend when she was eighteen, or a safari with Enrico, Arturo, and Giulia in the Serengeti national park. This makes her feel even more lost and vulnerable, surrounded by innumerable, nameless dangers that could appear in front of her or at her back without any warning. She is reminded of when she visited Nero's Domus Aurea in Rome with an American author, and when they got out he had asked her if she could picture life as it must have been so long before the advent of electricity and phones and TV and radio and newspapers. A totally unexpected anguish had swept over her at the idea of a world immersed in darkness, suspended in the feeble oscillation of unverifiable news. To shift her thoughts into any other direction she asks, "Are you Icaro's father?"

"Aha," says Arup.

"He's so nice," says Luisa. "He's so alert. He really has your eyes."

Arup nods, then says, "I didn't make him."

"No?" says Luisa, with a renewed feeling of disorientation.

"Gaia made him with another man," says Arup. "He went back home a couple of years ago, to the Faro Islands."

"Ah," says Luisa. She's disconcerted by his way of speech and conduct, by the apparent absence of any vocal or body language through which to represent himself.

They are silent. Every now and then Arup gets up and walks a few meters to have a better look, then goes back to sit on the stone. Luisa looks at the crossbow he's holding in his hands, with its smoothed wood and rather rough metal parts, the stubby dart on its guide. She's both fascinated and scared by the mixture of naivety and violence it reflects, the inadequacy and the determination. She too scans the horizon, but each time she thinks she sees something moving, she realizes it's an illusion created by the light and the wind among the trees. She thinks of a book she published on warfare in ancient times, which among other things described the silence and stillness that preceded the sudden terrifying explosion of sounds and movements of an attack.

She says, "Have you known Lauro a long time?"

"Yes," says Arup. "We were already brothers in some previous life."

Luisa smiles, and although this doesn't reassure her either, at least it belongs to a more familiar context, less difficult to define.

The winds blow through the trees and around the houses, throwing her hair into her eyes. She says, "This is why it's called Windshift, this place."

"Yes," says Arup.

Luisa thinks that a feeling of security consists in the answers you can give to your questions: in how quickly you can do it, leaving no margin for uncertainty.

M irta finishes medicating Arturo with her herbal tincture, then closes the bottle and puts away the cloth. "There you are," she says.

Arturo says, "Thanks. How kind of you." His face, neck, and forearms hurt more than they did before, but with a cool feeling that seems to tighten his skin and makes him want to sneeze.

Mirta looks at him with a funny expression; she says, "Now you need clothes. Yours are all ruined. Aria, go fetch some of Lauro's."

Arturo says, "Thank you, but I have mine in my suitcase. In the car, out there on the road." He makes a gesture, but when he tries to visualize the minivan it seems incredibly far away, lost in another dimension.

Aria in any case is already slipping out of the kitchen in her quick, silent way. Mirta moves the bowl of lupins closer on the table. Arturo tastes one, and hunger sweeps over him with long-delayed intensity. He puts a whole handful of lupins into his mouth, chewing and gulping them down skin and all, then takes another handful. Mirta smiles; she puts on the table a loaf of dark bread and some fresh goat cheese, pushing them toward him. Arturo grabs and tears the food with his hands, taking big bites, exalted by the essentiality of the taste and by the unaffectedness of the offer, as well as by the smells and textures of the feminine presence in the big room. He is unspeakably thrilled and delighted to be here tasting and feeling and seeing and breathing, instead of being dead somewhere along a dirt road.

Icaro observes him as if he was some strange animal, keeping close to his mother; Gaia and Mirta laugh. Margherita sits in a corner, looking like a war victim.

Aria comes back with a bundle of clothes; she hands them to Mirta who hands them to Arturo, saying "Here."

Arturo has a piece of cheese in his hand and doesn't want to leave it; he bolts it down almost without chewing on it. He looks at the home-sewn trousers and shirt, and the loose jacket also home-sewn, and says, "Shouldn't we ask Lauro, first?"

Gaia shakes her head; Mirta says, "Just put them on."

Arturo takes off his sweat-soaked T-shirt, he puts on the collarless shirt, then he takes his shoes and his dirty and torn trousers off. He thinks that he should feel embarrassed undressing in front of two strange women who instead of averting their eyes keep staring at him, but he's not: it's like a little tribal ceremony, both innocent and erotic. He takes the trousers Mirta hands him, and puts them on with a shiver running up his legs, tying them at the waist with a thin sash that functions as a belt. Finally he puts on the squarely cut loose jacket and turns around.

Mirta smiles. "You look good."

"Yes," says Gaia. "Much better than in your own clothes."

"Really?" says Arturo, not sure whether they are teasing him or not.

Mirta says, "Yes. You look like a totally different person, in your own clothes."

"What kind of person?" he asks, wavering between insecurity and attraction.

"The bored bourgeois who pretends to be free and easy," says Gaia.

"The city schmuck who goes to the country," says Mirta.

"Well," says Arturo, "that's what I call plain speaking!" He laughs, wondering whether it's really just a matter of clothes.

Mirta goes to put the tincture bottle back into the cupboard and says, "I'll give you a second treatment this evening."

"Well, thanks, but . . ." says Arturo. "We have to leave, before this evening."

"Isn't your car in a ditch?" says Gaia.

"And doesn't your friend have a broken leg?" says Mirta.

"He's not our friend," says Margherita, as if coming out of a trance. "He's a fucking real-estate agent."

"Anyway," says Gaia. "You certainly can't make him walk all the way to town. With those bastards on the road, too."

Margherita springs up with abstract determination. "But we can't be stuck here forever! Tomorrow is Sunday, I absolutely must be back in Milan! I must be back *tonight*! I have some totally vital phone calls to make!"

Gaia scratches her head. "Maybe we can help you pull your car out of that ditch."

"How?" says Margherita, a tiny flicker of hope in her eyes.

"With the horses," says Gaia.

"Really?" says Arturo. He looks at Mirta rummaging through the cupboard: for some reason he's sorry that she stopped taking care of him, even though she sees him as a city schmuck going to the country.

"Yes," says Gaia.

Arturo says, "But very likely something broke when we crashed into the ditch. So even if me manage to pull it out . . ."

"Arup can fix it," says Gaia. "He fixes everything."

"Well, that'd be great," says Arturo.

"You'd be saving our lives!" says Margherita, unable to stop herself from trembling.

From the other end of the kitchen Mirta says, "You really can't wait to get out of this place, eh?"

"It's not because we don't like it here," says Margherita, in a hasty attempt at being diplomatic. "It's because of work. I left a thousand terribly urgent things waiting."

"Me, too," says Arturo. "I've some important clients to see on Monday morning."

"What kind of clients?" asks Mirta.

"Furniture," says Arturo. He asks himself why it embarrasses him to talk about it now: is it because of the simple, functional beauty of the furniture all around them, or because of something much more difficult to define?

"You work in a shop?" asks Mirta.

"Well, it's a chain of shops," says Arturo. "I own them."

"Holy cow!" says Gaia. "You must be rich then."

Arturo laughs, looking at the wooden table, thinking that he'd rather talk about any other subject.

"Of course he's rich, Mr. Vannucci," says Margherita, in one of the automatic reflexes that go off in her whenever it comes to exposing somebody in front of an audience. "Richer than all of us."

"Ah, stop it," says Arturo. "Think of your golden contracts, paid for by millions of powerless television watchers."

"You son of a bitch," says Margherita, who's heard this kind of remark a thousand times and still hasn't found an effective answer.

Mirta says, "We don't have any money."

"What do you mean?" says Arturo.

"We don't have any," says Mirta. "At all."

"Oh, come on," says Margherita. "How do you buy things, then?"

"We don't," says Gaia.

"You barter then?" says Arturo. "Goat cheese and eggs and vegetables against the goods you need?"

"We did until three years ago," says Gaia. "Then we stopped, because after all, it was a kind of commerce, too."

Mirta says, "Now we make all that we need. So we don't have any use for money."

Arturo says, "In theory, it's flawless. In real life, I'm not so sure." He feels full of contradictions, unworthy of the clothes they have lent him with such generosity.

"Anyway, you can't make *everything* yourselves," says Margherita.

"Yes, we can," says Mirta. "Those dishes, for example. We use the clay we find down by the river."

"The jugs and the cups, too," says Gaia.

Margherita now gets into her unmasking attitude. Perhaps to keep the fear out of her mind, she says, "Come on, girls. How can you make, let's say, sanitary napkins?"

"We use cloth," says Mirta.

"And where do you get the cloth?" asks Margherita.

"We have tons of it," says Gaia. "Whole heaps."

"What about the gadgets?" says Margherita, even though she probably realizes she could think of better examples. "All the little things that make life more pleasant?"

"The *gadgets*?" says Mirta, as if she didn't understand what the word means.

Arturo keeps looking at her, and the more he does, the more he's struck by how affectless her way of moving and talking is. He doesn't think he's ever met a woman like her, except perhaps a little girl at the seaside when he was five years old, or an islander with whom he only exchanged a couple of broken sentences during a holiday in the South Pacific. But in this case Mirta is a grown woman who speaks his own language, with a combination of sincerity and sense of humor and natural grace that cause him a strange pressure between his stomach and heart and make his skin burn for reasons that have nothing to do with the abrasions and the herbal tincture treatment.

"What about *cosmetics*?" says Margherita, in a tone of feminine complicity that suddenly sounds terribly artificial. "To protect your skin from the constant wind and the icy cold water you have here?"

Gaia shrugs her shoulders. "We have all the herbs and the clay and the beeswax we need for that."

Arturo thinks that she isn't a bad-looking woman either, even though she bears the signs of her life choices, far from the influences of every magazine page and TV ad that come at you a thousand times a day, back in the civilized world. Mirta on the other hand could stand comparison with any film beauty or anorexic model with her scraggy shoulders and bony arms and affected poses and fake smiles, should she be interested in comparisons.

Margherita doesn't give up yet. "There must be something you can't make yourselves and can't find around here. *Toothbrushes*, for example."

"Elder sticks," says Mirta, with a luminous smile. "You just have to crush them on one end. Then we have walnut husks, and sage leaves for the gums."

Margherita gets up and reverts to her victim look. She says, "Which way to the bathroom? I can't remember."

"I'll show you," says Mirta.

"But, isn't it dangerous to go outside?" asks Margherita.

L uisa and Arup scan the horizon, each in their own way, sitting on the flat stone without saying a word. Suddenly Arup springs up, all his reflexes in action. Luisa stands up, too: She sees Lauro on his horse with Enrico behind him, and on the horse that follows is a sack which is in fact Alessio hanging widthwise. Her apprehension turns into a feeling of relief that goes to the very pit of her stomach, making her momentarily faint. Arup puts two fingers into his mouth and emits a sharp whistle in the direction of the houses, then runs to meet the small caravan. The black dog dashes out from behind a wall, running madly toward Lauro. Luisa makes only a few steps, surprised by how three-dimensional are the figures that she's been visualizing in the empty space.

Lauro rides up to the houses, nods for Enrico to dismount. Enrico slides down the horse's rump, almost falling. He's pale and ruffled, nearly as dirty as Arturo although with far fewer scratches: he would move her, if he didn't act so stiffly. Luisa tries to embrace him, but he sidesteps her. He looks first at Lauro and Arup, then at the house out of which the others are coming.

Luisa feels her relief turn into disappointment and the disappointment turn into anger, distance, boredom. These are not new feelings, even though they surprise her—they are as familiar as Enrico's features. She asks him, "How are you?"

"Great," says Enrico coldly, as if he held her in some way

responsible for what has happened. Or perhaps he's still annoyed with her from their quarrel.

Luisa doesn't want to think about it. She goes to see Alessio, who's tied with a rope across the second horse's saddle and has Arturo's tweed coat over him and two branches tied to the sides of his right leg to hold it straight. He keeps his eyes half closed and barely moves his lips, producing a raspy kind of groan as Arup busies himself untying the knots.

Lauro dismounts and helps him, wet with perspiration and tired as he is. Mirta and Gaia and Icaro and Arturo all crowd up around the horses, trying to help or at least give advice. Arup finishes untying Alessio, then he lowers him with caution, helped by the others. Alessio comes off the horse like a dead weight, with a weak cry of pain. Lauro picks him up and carries him on his back to the main house, followed by Gaia and Icaro. Mirta takes the two horses by the reins and brings them back to their paddock; Arup runs off in another direction. Luisa and Enrico stand looking at each other, without words. Enrico points to Arturo's face, to the scratches and grazes made even more conspicuous by Mirta's reddish tincture. He slowly shakes his head, saying, "You're in great shape, too."

"It could have been worse," says Arturo with a smile.

"How?" says Enrico.

"They could have killed us," says Arturo. "Like that."

"Okay, and what do we do now?" says Enrico. "Remain here as hostages to these lunatics, under siege by who knows who?"

Luisa once again is filled with physical and moral aversion; she says, "These lunatics have just *saved* you, Enrico."

"Yes, of course," says Enrico, coldly. "I'm deeply grateful. Anyway, we have to find a way to get out of here, and to take that poor devil to a hospital."

Arturo makes a gesture toward the main house. "They said that perhaps they can pull our minivan out of that ditch."

"By what means?" says Enrico. The right sleeve of his overcoat is soaked with a yellowish foam, giving off an acidic smell.

Luisa thinks she detests him right now, for his obstinate way of keeping his feelings wound so tight. For a moment she wishes to see him plunge deep into an even more serious danger, with his perennial skepticism.

"With the horses," says Arturo.

"The horses?" says Enrico. "But, even if they did manage to pull it out of the ditch, what if something is broken?"

"Arup can fix it," says Arturo.

"The Indian?" says Enrico. "How can he fix a broken axle, here? By replacing it with a wooden one, like in a Viking oxcart?"

"I don't know," says Arturo. "They say he can fix all sorts of things." He has a slightly unusual way of moving, perhaps because of the strange clothes he's wearing.

"I doubt it very much," says Enrico. "They haven't even reached the Iron Age yet, here."

"We might as well let them try, don't you think?" says Arturo.

"Sure," says Enrico. "As long as they get on with it. You've seen for yourself that it's not very healthy to stay in this place."

Arturo nods, he walks back to the main house. Luisa and Enrico stand there for a few more seconds, without exchanging a word and without even looking at each other directly.

M argherita comes out of the outhouse and finds Aria waiting with her back to the wall, a knee up. She says, "Ah, you're still here," with the kind of smile she uses with children and with very old or very provincial people.

"Yes," says Aria, slightly contracting the muscles around her eyes out of shyness.

Margherita looks at the water pump from which Arturo filled a jug for her in the morning; she doesn't touch it because it seems too hard to operate.

"Do you need help with that?" asks Aria.

"Thank you," says Margherita, even though she'd really prefer to retreat immediately into the relative security of the house.

Aria starts pushing the pump's lever up and down, her energy contrasting with her skinny frame.

Margherita washes her hands in the gush of ice-cold water, thinking that later her skin will probably flake in a horrible way. She says, "Thanks a lot," drying herself on her jeans, looking toward the door.

Aria says, "I wanted to ask you . . . you're Margherita Novelli, right?"

Margherita nods, flabbergasted, as if it was the first time in her entire life she had heard this question.

"I've seen you," says Aria. "*Crazy Stuff*, right?"

"But, where?" says Margherita, looking around. "Do you have TV, here?"

"No," says Aria. "In town."

Margherita tries to reorganize her thoughts; she says, "I thought you never went to town."

"I do," says Aria, in a slightly defiant tone.

"Ah," says Margherita. "For school, right?"

"No," says Aria. "On my own account. But don't tell anyone. If Dad finds out he'll get mad at me."

"Cross my heart," says Margherita, making the corresponding gesture with her two index fingers. She looks at the door again. "Shouldn't we go back inside?"

Aria is too caught up in her revelations; she says, "I rode there twice, without anybody knowing. I saw you on the TV in a bar. The second time I went on purpose, just to watch your program."

Margherita, in spite of all her fear and her eagerness to go back inside, now feels a little surge of gratification at the idea of someone willing to run some real risks to see her show. She says, "And did you like it?"

"Yes," says Aria. "I didn't see all of it, but it was interesting."

Margherita thinks that the network people and the major sponsors and at least a couple of chronically sarcastic critics should have a close look at this girl, names and photos and road maps included, to realize that what Margherita does is not mere, foolish entertainment. This thought gives her back some energy. She looks at the girl more attentively, asking, "What kind of school do you go to, Aria?"

"I don't," says Aria. "Dad and Gaia and the others teach me, here."

"And you don't have any problems?" says Margherita. "I mean, with the bureaucracy, the law and all that?"

Aria shakes her head, she says, "I took my exams as an at-home student. Legally, they can't do anything."

"Really?" says Margherita, in a good simulation of enthusiasm, even though her immediate priority is now just to survive. "Well, it sounds great, not having to sit in class every day. When I went to school, I didn't have a clue about some subjects. Mathematics, for example. Or philosophy. Not a clue. I had some kind of mental block, nothing came through."

"I'd like to go to school," says Aria. "It's Dad who doesn't want to have anything to do with the rest of the world anymore."

Margherita says, "It sure is rather absurd." She feels her way into the conversation, since she doesn't know what the girl really thinks and there's no audience from which to gauge the prevailing opinion. "I mean, it's a really strange situation. Fascinating, too."

"I don't know," says Aria, looking at the irregular paving of the backyard.

"What do you mean?" says Margherita. "Don't you like living here?"

"Yes," says Aria. "But I also get fed up."

"Really?" says Margherita. "You have such a dreamy place, all to yourselves." She thinks she hears voices and noises carried by a gust of wind, and stiffens.

"That's what bores me," says Aria, unperturbed. "There's never anybody new. Except for now that you're here. Nothing ever happens."

Margherita is now trembling with fear. "Frankly, it seems like too much happens here." She's certain that she hears the dog barking at the other side of the house. Temporarily she gives up her role and mission as interlocutor and walks to the back door as fast as she can, without letting Aria's eagerness for communication hinder her.

Alessio feels so ill he can hardly breathe, stretched out as he is on a bench in the squatters' kitchen, where he had sworn never to set foot again unless accompanied by a bailiff. But right now he's light-years away from any kind of legal or professional concern: He's totally overrun with physical pain and fear, thanks to his broken right shinbone. It seems to him that life has lost the shape he thought he knew so well, and has turned into a mish-mash of unexplainable events nagging him nonstop from the out-side in and from the inside out. He lays on his back on the hard wood, surrounded by the stench of goat-cheese and burnt wood and steamed cabbage, the muscles in his stomach and back and thighs still aching from the torture of a thousand shakes he endured while he was tied face-down to the bony back of a horse pawing and bouncing over unbearable hills and valleys. Each time he shifts, even by a millimeter, he feels a stab of pain running through him with the blinding violence of a white halogen light. He makes an intense effort to lie as still as he can, his forehead covered with ice-cold sweat.

The squatters and Vannucci and the Guardis get closer and move back and discuss and gesticulate, apparently with the intention of assisting him, but instead of reassuring him they only worsen his agony. The smells and the lights and the furniture and the voices and the faces are all wrong for this kind of situation. He thinks of the pictures in the brochure of the insurance policy he's been carrying for years mainly because it gives him a decent tax advantage: the photos of the mobile accident unit, the helicopters and the ambulances and the spring-loaded stretchers and the smart-looking ultra-specialized doctors in their white gowns inside operating theaters packed with constantly updated equipment. He would just like to have a remote control to press and change channels at once, to teleport himself somewhere else, to disappear from here.

But no matter how hard he imagines it, he remains stuck on the wooden bench in this primitive kitchen filled with voices and tramping noises, where every sound and motion makes him feel a little worse. The curly-haired girl who goes by the name of Mirta, for example, presses a clay cup against his lips, saying, "Drink." He takes a sip believing it's water and after a moment feels his mouth full of poisonous herbs and snake drool and dog vomit and rotten strawberries. He spits it out and screams, revulsion filling his every fiber.

Mirta doesn't give up: she presses the cup to his mouth again, saying, "You must drink," insisting. She has the pungent smell of a wild animal and scary eyes; all sorts of things could be hiding in her curls. Alessio shuts his lips, shakes his head while moving his body as little as he can for fear of another excruciating stab from his broken leg. The vision of the bone splinter through the cloth of his trousers keeps coming back to haunt him; he feels sick again, trembles all over, grinds his teeth.

Now the woman that calls herself Gaia takes the cup from Mirta and comes over to press it against his lips even more insistently. She says, "Come on, it's good for you." Alessio tries to push it away, he tries to scream that he doesn't want it, but Mirta holds his nose shut and forces him to open his mouth and Gaia pours all the disgusting beverage right down his throat, saying "Good boy, good boy." Alessio tries to spit it out but this time it's too late; it has already reached his stomach, it's already got into his blood-stream, with who knows what consequences.

Mirta nods to Vannucci and says, "Help me." He sits on the bench and holds Alessio's good leg. Mirta presses down on his arms with her strong, savage hands. Gaia comes back with a long knife that looks like it's out of some seventies horror movie, puts it near his broken right leg. Alessio desperately tries to wriggle free. "Leave me alone!" he screams.

"Calm down, calm down," says Gaia, all sweet and appeasing like a big crazy country mama. "I just want to take a look."

"Don't you touch me!" screams Alessio, although not as loud as he'd like to because the revolting stuff they made him gobble down must be starting to take effect now.

Gaia pretends she doesn't hear him. She slides the long blade under his trouser leg and slices it upward with a butcher's confi-dence. Alessio feels the cold steel slide against his leg; he arches back, trying to bite Mirta's wrists, screaming.

He hears Gaia's voice say, "Dear me!" They're all there looking at his exposed broken leg.

"Dear me what?" mutters Alessio in an even feebler voice, his heart beating like that of a calf in a slaughterhouse.

"Don't worry," says Mirta, in a suave voice that contrasts chill-ingly with the expressions of all the people around.

Alessio tries to raise his head but he can't, because Mirta presses it down and because he's too weakened by pain and dulled by the beverage they forced him to drink, and frightened at the thought of what he might see.

Mr. Guardi in a totally disapproving tone says, "I tried to con-vince Lauro that we should have brought him straight to a hospi-tal instead of here, but he wouldn't listen."

"It would have taken you three times as long," says Gaia. "He would have died of pain along the way."

Hearing this, Alessio almost goes into convulsions. He would fall off the bench if Mirta and Vannucci weren't holding him down with the determination of two accomplices in murder.

Mrs. Guardi says, "But what can we do here? He's in a terrible state."

"Arup will fix him," says Gaia.

Alessio is now certain that he's having a nightmare, but it's much more realistic than any nightmare he's had before, and he can't get out of it. He screams, "I want a doctor!"—his voice seeming to come from some other point in the room.

Mr. Guardi says, "So Arup fixes people, too, besides water pipes and cars and everything else."

"He's done it already," says Gaia. "He's fixed broken legs."

"Arms, too," says Mirta.

Alessio hears a shrill voice saying, "Oh, my God." He turns his head to see Novelli arrive from somewhere and freeze, staring at his leg as if it was a blood-curdling roadside massacre.

"I don't want the Indian!" screams Alessio with the little strength he's left. "I want a real doctor!"

Novelli's face is really white, she's on the verge of being sick.

Then the Indian arrives: He elbows his way to have a close look at the broken leg. He studies it from different angles in a pseudo-technical way, and this is not reassuring at all.

"Don't touch me!" screams Alessio, preemptively.

"So?" says Gaia. "Do you think you can fix it?"

"Yes," says the Indian, nodding, smiling.

"You're not fixing anything!" screams Alessio. "You're not a real doctor!" He wriggles on the bench, but Mirta has another cup in her hands and she presses it against his clenched teeth, holding his nose shut again. Alessio is forced to open his mouth to breath again, and immediately tastes the horrendous liquid pouring down to his stomach; he tries to cough and spit but he can't.

"Excuse me!" says Mr. Guardi. "Fixing a broken leg is a serious business, not a joke! You need X-rays, you need facilities, equipment, knowledge, years and years of study and practice!"

"Arup has already done it," says Gaia, in a soft tone that gives Alessio the creeps.

"He's fixed Orso's leg," says Mirta. "And Lauro's arm. And Mora's wrist."

Mrs. Guardi says to her husband, "Enrico, he's already done it several times."

"Obviously those weren't real fractures!" shouts Mr. Guardi. "They must have been mere contusions, small cracks at the most! How reliable can people with names like Orso and Mora be? How can you believe this kind of nonsense? What's in your head, I wonder?"

The guy called Lauro, who until now must have been outside, comes closer, asking Mr. Guardi, "What would you like to do, then? Let him suffer like a dog until whenever you can drag him to a hospital? So maybe in the meantime he loses his leg?"

"That's true, Enrico," says Vannucci. "Where could we take him? And how soon?"

"I've no idea," says Mr. Guardi. "But I know that you can't repair a fracture like this on a kitchen bench!"

"That's right," says Lauro. "Let's put him on the table."

Alessio feels himself lifted up by an untold number of hands: It's a bit like when he scored a decisive goal in a soccer match between real estate agents, years ago. Or like once in Ibiza when he tried a mini-hovercraft that floated with equal ease over sand and water. Although he wouldn't admit it, he feels almost no pain now. But it doesn't seem like a good sign—on the contrary, it's like a really bad one, and it's gotten so that he can't keep his eyes open or make out with any certainty the origin of sounds.

A voice that must be Mr. Guardi's says, "Silent as goats, all of you? Arturo? Luisa? Margherita? You don't have anything to say?"

There is no reply, or at least Alessio can't hear any through the thickening fog that surrounds him. A door slams, but it could also be a stool falling over, or both things, he couldn't tell. Then he's only aware of a diffused bustle: as if he was a large object to be repaired on some workshop's bench. All around him, people open cupboards and jars and bottles and mix and boil and cut and pound and blend and knead and roll up and unroll and saw off and whisper and cough and shuffle and get closer and put to his lips another glass of beverage that this time doesn't taste so bad but slows down all his perceptions until he slips into a dreamlike state which isn't actually a dream but it almost is.

Enrico paces furiously up and down the expanse around the houses, wiping down his quickly washed hands on his jacket. He's hungry, too; the thought that the others have already eaten while he was being dragged back by Lauro to this nut-house adds to the resentment brewing inside him. When he sees Arturo come out of the main house, he turns his back to him and sticks his hands deep into his trouser pockets, hastening his pace.

Arturo comes up behind him, saying "Enrico?"

"I'm not talking with you anymore," says Enrico.

"Why?" says Arturo.

"Because I have nothing to say to you," says Enrico. He thinks of the times in the past when he was exasperated or disappointed by his friend's character; of how their friendship has continued through the years out of sheer habit rather than a reciprocal, constantly renewed stimulation.

"What did I do?" says Arturo, following him with doglike persistence. "Could you please tell me?"

Enrico walks a few more steps without looking at him, then he turns, saying, "What *didn't* you do! You disappear for a couple of hours, and when I see you again you're totally on these lunatics' side, without the slightest trace of common sense anymore. Letting them paint your face like a striped monkey, thanking them if they let you eat some of their rubbish, indulging their every little whim!"

Arturo looks dismayed, under the cross-hatching of scratches covering his face. "Just what do you have against them? If anything, *they* should be angry with us."

"You see?" says Enrico. "This is the Stockholm syndrome, really!"

Arturo shakes his head and says, "If it wasn't for Lauro, it's entirely possible that those guys would have killed me. And didn't he bring you back, too?"

Enrico snaps, "He brought me back *here*! And it's *they* who created this situation, don't you see?"

"What do you mean?" says Arturo, as if he really didn't understand.

Enrico says, "I mean that when you decide to wipe out centuries and centuries of progress, the least you can expect is a few small side effects! Like finding yourself in a tribal feud with the neighbors, like being shot at!"

"But why?" says Arturo, seemingly shaken by the anger in his tone.

"Because this is what *happens*!" says Enrico. "Because the alternative to the contemporary Western world is not some bucolic idyll! It's a state of barbarism!"

"Not necessarily," says Arturo.

"It *is*!" says Enrico. "Otherwise it would be too easy! No telephones, no electric light, no heating, no engines, but at the same time the most wonderful sensitiveness and gentleness and generosity and harmony among all living beings, everyone behaving in a wonderfully civilized way! I'm sorry, my friend, but it's not so! When you decide to crank our civilization back to zero, you do it with *all* of it!"

"I didn't crank anything to zero," says Arturo.

"But you went along with them!" says Enrico. "Look at yourself! Rigged out like some poor cannibal from New Guinea! You thought it was such a nice and picturesque thing to do, eh?"

"They've been extremely kind," says Arturo. "They didn't have to help me."

"Look at those clothes," says Enrico. "How do you feel, in that wonderfully picturesque outfit?"

Arturo looks at his loose jacket and at his trousers, and in an embarrassed tone he says, "My own clothes were torn to pieces."

Enrico is not even listening to him anymore; he's beside himself with rage at the thought of finding himself back in a place he was sure he would never see again in his entire life, his prospects of getting out of it even more uncertain than before. He thinks that if they had stuck to the road instead of taking shortcuts they would be in town by now, back to a network of fast communications. He can't believe that his life got tangled up with that of an idiotic real-estate agent: he's filled with fury when he recalls the moral blackmail in Arturo's eyes after the fall down the ravine. He says, "You must be happy to be back here! It's all thanks to you and to that other genius, with your great idea of a shortcut!"

"Maybe they would have shot at us all the same," says Arturo. "At the three of us."

"They wouldn't have shot at us," says Enrico. "Not if we looked like civilized people, instead of having the appearance of forest zombies!"

"Anyway, it's happened," says Arturo, in an unacceptably fatalistic tone. "There's no point in going over it again."

"There *is* a point!" says Enrico. "Especially now that your great pals have decided to play sorcery with that poor devil, and not one of you had the courage to say anything about it! Not a single word, you were too fascinated by the local folklore!"

Arturo says, "Look, I had doubts, too, when they wanted to paint that tincture all over my face, but it's really working. My skin was enflamed, and now the burning is almost stopped."

"But yours are only *scratches*!" cries Enrico, fighting an impulse to shake him by the shoulders like a dumb child. "There is some difference with a broken leg, you'll admit!"

Arturo struggles to find the right words to reply; he says, "Let's just wait and see."

"Of course, let's wait and see!" cries Enrico. "After all, it's such a charming little game! Too bad if that poor wretch will be lamed for life!"

"Are you sure you care so much about Alessio?" says Arturo. "Or is it the idea?"

"Of course it's the idea!" cries Enrico. "Of course! I can see Margherita falling for it, with her television subculture. Or Luisa, with her populist, multicultural, political correctness. But to see you behaving in such an idiotic way!"

"Hey, don't you think you're overdoing it a bit, now?" says Arturo, not exactly in a tone of rebellion, but neither will he accept the blame with head bowed.

In the meantime the girl Mirta has got out of the house and she's calling out, "Arturo? Could you lend me a hand? Arup needs some herbs."

"Sure," says Arturo. "I'm coming." He glances at Enrico, as if to justify himself.

"Go on, help her get the herbs," says Enrico. "Have fun."

Arturo seems totally unaffected; he hurries towards Mirta.

The wind blows hard, the sky is covered with gray clouds again, the light is growing dim. Enrico kicks a piece of wood, walking in the relatively protected area. His blood is boiling and he has a hole in his stomach, he's cold but would never stoop so far as to return to the house and retrieve his overcoat, soaked as it is in Alessio's vomit. A sentence comes to mind, to the effect that you only know what somebody is worth when he's required to make a decision; as much as he tries, however, he can't remember who said it.

Luisa watches Gaia as she cleans Alessio's broken leg, just as naturally as if she was cleaning a fish or a vegetable or a household appliance. Mirta in the meantime grinds some leaves and seeds in a mortar with a wooden pestle. Arturo observes her from a short distance, seemingly held spellbound by her gestures. Arup performs some concentration exercises, then explains to everyone how to hold Alessio. They all take their places around the table according to his instructions, except for Margherita who sits in a corner shaking her head and Icaro who hides behind a cupboard, from which he peeps with morbid curiosity. Luisa holds down one of Alessio's rather inert arms, trying not to look at the broken leg. Nobody talks, the light from the lamps and the candle flickers, the wind whistles through the gaps in the window frames: there's an ancient, obscure, warm atmosphere that intrigues her and scares her in almost equal measure.

She thinks that she's taking part in an event that has no precedent in her life; she asks herself whether such a brutal immersion into such matters could help her get rid of her tendency to sublimation. Immediately afterward she thinks that perhaps Enrico is right, and that the scene in front of her eyes is as absurd and irresponsible as a game of unruly children; she is about to say something, but Arup takes a breath and starts tugging on the lower part of Alessio's broken shinbone. Luisa's eyes slip against her will down the table, to the strong, small hands that without any hesitation pull and turn the lower tibia bone until it matches with the upper part. Alessio has a small convulsion; rather than a scream, he emits a kind of loud yawn.

Arup backs up a bit without letting go of his hold; the room is filled with intent looks and hands, synchronized breaths. Mirta hastens to smear the herb-and-seed poultice on the fracture, Gaia wraps it up with a strip of cloth that perhaps was originally part of a curtain or a bedspread. Arup puts three wooden sticks along the wrapped-up leg, securing them with a second wrapping as if it were a rapid exercise of magic. When he's finished he says, "Done," and smiles. There's a collective release of tension, smiles opening up, hands touching shoulders and arms.

Gaia leans over Alessio, kissing him on the forehead. Luisa looks at him up close; his eyes are open and he has a dreamy expression, he doesn't seem to be suffering. Outside the window it's almost dark already.

S tanding in the backyard where all the light is now gone, Enrico
can't stand the wind and the cold any longer. He feels drained
and cut out, distracted by absurd worries for his survival, misun-
derstood by his wife and by his supposed best friends. But these
feelings are not entirely new to him: He has only to dig under the
layers of his acquired self-assurance to recognize this self-inflicted
exclusion as an integral component of his emotional landscape.
For example, he has a very detailed memory of when as a child he
was invited to a schoolmate's birthday party and at the very last
moment he had prevented his mother from ringing the doorbell,
because the party's voices and sounds filtering through the door
had suddenly made him feel extraneous. Another good example is
when, several years later, he had met a very pretty girl at the univer-
sity and they had chatted and flirted and had an aperitif in a climate of growing mutual attraction, and then when she suggested
they have dinner together he told her he had to study for an exam.
He didn't even ask her for her telephone number, and in fact he
never saw her again. These are only two episodes among many in
which he's renounced something significant for reasons he couldn't
pinpoint at the moment, convincing himself later of having acted
in the only possible way. He has no wish to analyze his past life
right now; he's simply tracing back the familiar, bittersweet nausea
that is spreading between his stomach and his heart.

The door at the back of the main house opens, and somebody carrying an oil lamp comes out: it's Mirta. When she sees him, she says, "Hey! What are you doing out here all alone?"

"Nothing," says Enrico, his hands in his pockets.

Mirta goes into the outhouse, then comes back out, busies herself with the water pump to wash her hands, fills a bucket with water, goes back into the outhouse to put it back. Enrico follows her movements by the light of the oil lamp. He thinks of the amount of energy that each person burns several times a day in banal activities like this one, when in a normal, civilized life it would take a simple push of a button or the turning of a tap. He thinks that he is literally surrounded by proof of his opinions, and yet this doesn't make him feel any better. Nor does it make him forget the hunger or the cold or the feeling of exclusion.

Mirta heads for the door and says, "Aren't you coming inside?"

"I'll be out here for a while," says Enrico, in what should sound like a nonchalant tone.

"You're not hungry?" asks Mirta. "There are some good things to eat."

"No, thank you very much," says Enrico. The feeling of being a solitary defender of principles is not enough to compensate for the agony of refusing the tender, generous offers of the world.

"As you like," Mirta says, in what seems like a slightly sad tone; she reenters the house with her lamp.

Enrico remains motionless in the dark for half a minute and then resumes walking along the perimeter of the backyard, now unable to distinguish the dividing lines between earth and sky. The wind whistles among the stone walls, seemingly charged with impending danger. Enrico stamps his feet and waves his arms to warm up a bit. Then he realizes the absurdity of his position: He goes back to the door, tries to open it but it's closed. He thinks that this fact should help him to be firm; but then he looks behind his shoulders and feels overwhelmed by the darkness. He knocks on the door again, in a breathless way.

After a while, a strip of light appears under the door. Arup's voice says, "Who is it?"

"It's me," says Enrico. "Enrico Guardi." Having to pronounce his name is like an embarrassing confession of weakness, even though he keeps repeating to himself that he doesn't give a damn about these people and that he'll never ever see them again anyway.

Arup opens the door, then makes way inside the house with his oil lamp.

Except for Lauro, the others are all sitting around the kitchen table in front of the remains of a rustic dinner, already polished off even though in the civilized world this would hardly be the time for an aperitif. There's a thick atmosphere, warmed up by the fire in the hearth and by the lamps and candles and the human presences; the smell is that of a cowshed or perhaps a sheepfold or of a primeval human settlement. And yet the country dwellers seem to have taken more care of their appearance, compared to the night before: Gaia is wearing a fringed shawl on her shoulders, Mirta a coral necklace, Aria a gored beret, Arup an Indian waistcoat over his rough woolen sweater. Luisa is pale and tense, her thin, light-brown hair drawn back into a tight bun. Arturo really does seem dressed up as a New Guinea savage; Margherita looks like a poor shipwreck, her eyes made small by worry and by insufficient makeup. Alessio is sunk into an old armchair, his splinted leg propped up on a stool, a glass in hand. In the other hand he is holding two Y-shaped sticks; he seems unperturbed.

Enrico feels everybody's eyes converge on him as soon as he walks in, and then they move away, to focus on Gaia who's telling an irrelevant tale about some escaped goats. Only Luisa still looks at him as he sits beside her, but in a way that only accentuates his outcast feeling.

"You must have really been worried for me," Enrico says, "judging from how you came looking for me."

"I thought you wanted to be alone," says Luisa, "the way you walked out like that, in the middle of the operation."

"Yeah, the operation," says Enrico sarcastically. But he finds it difficult not to let his eyes linger on what's left on the table of the bread and the cheese and the vegetables that the others have merrily devoured while he was out alone in the dark and the cold.

Gaia goes on with her story, fuelled by the wine and by the attention of the extended group: "It's incredible how high they can jump, when they're scared. Like they had springs in their legs, the go *ping! ping! ping!*"

"*Ping!*" cries Icaro.

"And then what happened?" says Arturo, sipping his wine, arranged in a convivial pose that looks to Enrico like the worst betrayal.

"I managed to catch them all," says Gaia. "Except for one who fell down the ravine and broke her spine. Poor Margherita. She had been with us for five years, she was so sweet."

"*Margherita?*" says Margherita.

"That was her name," says Gaia.

Alessio turns in his armchair, gazing mischievously at Margherita.

"Who are you smirking at?" says Margherita. "Even with a broken leg, you have the nerve to provoke me!"

"Come on, Margherita," says Arturo. "Show some sense of humor."

Margherita lets the matter drop: She must feel that even her loathing for Alessio is of little account, compared to the possibility of not being able to survive. At intervals she puts her hand into her handbag, perhaps under the illusion that by some miracle her cell phone might ring with offers of comfort and assistance from the outside world.

Gaia looks at Enrico, saying, "You're sure you don't want to eat anything?"

"I'm sure, thank you," says Enrico: straining to control himself.

"Not even a cup of wine?" says Arup, raising the pitcher.

"I'm fine, really," says Enrico, with a painful contraction that originates from his stomach and spreads to the muscles in his neck and mouth. He tries to see signs of pain in Alessio's features or in his posture, but apparently there aren't any. He leans toward Arturo, saying, "Do you have any idea what they made him drink?"

"Plant extracts," says Gaia, who must have developed a very sharp sense of hearing in her savage life, because she didn't seem to be listening.

"Really?" says Enrico. "Well, *curare* is a plant extract, too."

Gaia looks at him as if she didn't understand; she says, "We only use plants that grow around here."

"Thank goodness," says Enrico. He thinks that it's the obtuse imperturbability of her expressions that he finds unbearable: her way of talking and moving and taking care of the food and the house and the child and the others without ever showing any doubts about the meaning of the life she's chosen.

Luisa turns to look at him as if he was a wet blanket (a "light dimmer," to use the expression of a Scandinavian writer she's currently enthusiastic about). She says, "Couldn't you try not to be so negative, Enrico?"

Enrico twitches on the bench as if he's just received a stab in the side. "Sorry to spoil this wonderful atmosphere of quiet premodern anguish."

Margherita feels a new shiver of fear just to hear the word "anguish." She grabs the cup in front of her, gulps down more wine. The others give her some distant glances.

There's a noise at the door; they all spin round. It's Lauro, with his usual bow and quiver full of arrows, panting lightly, looking around.

The others seem relieved to see him, Arturo and Margherita and Luisa included. The polarity in the air changes, and this has the effect of increasing Enrico's bitterness, making him feel resentful and competitive in a way he hasn't felt since when he was in secondary school.

Arup says, "So?"

"Nothing," says Lauro. "Nobody. Neither uphill, nor downhill." He puts down his bow and arrows and takes off his loose home-sewn jacket, then he grabs some bread and cheese and vegetables from the table and fills himself a cup of wine, sitting down to eat and drink with brutish avidity.

Arup gulps down the contents of his cup and, picking up his crossbow, he goes out to relieve Lauro.

Lauro pushes the food into his mouth with both hands, chewing noisily. Enrico tries not to look at him, but his stomach seems to be working against him like an enemy, seriously undermining his dignity from the inside.

Gaia makes a gesture to include the townspeople around the table, and says to Lauro, "We told them that tomorrow perhaps we can pull their car out of that ditch, with the horses."

Lauro nods; he empties his second cup of wine. He says, "If they haven't destroyed it already."

"What do you mean, destroyed?" says Margherita, in a trembling voice.

Lauro tears out a piece of bread with his teeth; he laughs with his mouth full. He says, "Just joking. They have the greatest respect for cars, unlike for people and animals." He tries to fill his cup for the third time, but the pitcher is empty, so he gets up and goes toward the little barrel at the other end of the room. In passing he brushes Luisa's shoulder with his hand, causing her to quiver in a barely perceptible way.

Enrico notices this, surprised as he is by how sensitive to smells and looks and body signals he has become in the last few hours. Far from giving him pleasure, this causes a kind of disgust in him. But it's there, like some primitive legacy that resurfaces and simplifies his feelings, channeling them beyond his conscious will.

Lauro fills the pitcher from the barrel and returns to sit at the table, pouring himself another glass of wine, downing it in long gulps, devouring more bread and cheese and vegetables. His manners are so savage that they can't simply be due to hunger and incivility, they must carry at least an element of provocation. The others are silent; there's only the noise of Lauro's jaws and the whistling of the wind on the window panes and in the fireplace, the thin voice of Icaro whispering something in his mother's ears.

Enrico makes a last stand to resist the urges of his stomach, and then suddenly he gives in: he reaches out to the center of the table and grabs what's left of the goat cheese. He barely manages to suppress his impulse to devour it in Lauro's barbaric fashion. With trembling hands he takes an old knife and cuts a slice and puts it on his plate, then cuts off a morsel, bringing it to his mouth with a fork. His tongue and all his internal organs are possessed by a frenzy of acquisition; it costs him a terrible effort to chew slowly. He picks up some ironic glances from Lauro and Arturo and Mirta and Luisa and the others, but at the moment he's absorbed in his attempt to restrain the primitive impulses coming from his taste buds and salivary glands and chewing muscles. The food in his mouth has the same basic nature of the forces that spur him to devour it: He must put all his mental resources into play to keep up a minimal barrier of style and not be publicly overcome by bestiality. He pours himself some wine, takes a small sip, than cuts another morsel of cheese with the knife, sitting up as straight and composed as he can on the hard wood of the bench.

Luisa looks back and forth at him and at Lauro, as they eat in their opposite ways at the opposite sides of the table, all too conscious of each other and still pretending to ignore each other. Very possibly she's reminded of a confrontation between dogs that's described in a book she published last year, in which two male Beaucherons divided by a wire-net fence ran up and down to show they were masters of their own territories, until they found the right spot to snarl and bare their fangs and bark furiously.

Lauro finishes devouring the last bit of bread and cheese and the last spinach leaf from his plate, then wipes his mouth with the back of his hand, looking straight at Enrico. He says, "I've been wondering, what kind of architecture do you design? Army barracks? Supermarkets? Gas stations?"

Enrico swallows, looking in vain for a napkin. He says, "You're totally off target. I design apartment buildings, mostly."

"You mean tenement houses?" says Lauro. He takes another sip of wine: his eyes are charged with animal hostility.

"Yes," says Enrico.

"Big ones, huh?" says Lauro.

"Fairly big," says Enrico, holding his ground. "Fifteen-, twenty-story buildings, it depends."

"I can imagine them," says Lauro.

"I don't think so," says Enrico.

"Why?" says Lauro. "Are they more beautiful than our houses?"

Enrico feels Luisa's and everybody's eyes on him; he knows that he can't get out of it with just a witty remark. He says, "Let's just say they're different."

"How different?" says Lauro. He, too, is playing a part, for his usual audience and for the new one.

Enrico sighs, as if he had to explain it to a child. "Let's say they answer to another order of requirements."

"But are they beautiful?" says Lauro.

"Of course," says Enrico. "They have been published in several architectural magazines."

"Which makes them beautiful," says Lauro.

"It's the other way round," says Enrico, still with mock patience. "They get published because they are beautiful."

"Beautiful according to whom?" says Lauro. "To your colleagues, or to the people who live in them?"

Enrico has the feeling that the dividing line between this verbal confrontation and a physical one is getting thinner and thinner, but he has no intention of backing off. His ears are burning, his blood is running fast, words are pressing impatiently on his tongue. He says, "According to whoever is able to judge them on the basis of some evolved esthetic criteria."

Lauro has an insolent, uncivilized kind of smile. He says, "That is to say, not by the people who live in them."

"It depends," says Enrico, with a smile of civilized sarcasm. "They might not be a nineteenth-century landscape painter's dream, like this place, but you know, when you are designing buildings which are going to house hundreds of families, you have other guidelines to follow."

"Such as?" says Lauro. "Sticking as many people as possible in as small a space as possible, without caring too much about the kind of life they're going to have?"

Enrico says, "Dead wrong again. I care a great deal. I care

enough to fight against the ministry, the regional boards, the municipalities, the bureaucracy, the rules, the various lobbies in order to achieve the best possible living standard."

"So it's a kind of mission, your job," says Lauro.

Enrico says, "Well, perhaps in my own small way I try to improve the world a little bit, instead of hiding somewhere and pretending that the world doesn't exist."

Lauro smiles again, but you can tell he's been cut to the quick; he says, "I can only wonder at how you'd transform this place, once you got rid of us poor fools."

"I don't know," says Enrico. "What I do know is that going back a thousand years is not a very creative alternative to the contemporary world. We've made a few achievements, over the course of history."

"Such as?" says Lauro.

"Oh, there are quite a few examples," says Enrico. "We've managed to emancipate ourselves from ignorance, for one. From superstition, from sickness."

"From *some* sicknesses," says Lauro. "In exchange for even worse sicknesses."

"Worse than the *black plague*, just to mention one?" says Enrico. "Which in the fourteenth century wiped out a third of Europe's population?"

"There are some equivalent plagues, today," says Lauro.

"Not really equivalent," says Enrico. "And in any case we emancipated ourselves from a lot of other things that were just as horrible."

"Like what?" says Lauro.

"Like physical toil," says Enrico. "The exhausting, endless exertion it took to cultivate a field or shift weights, or walk from A to B."

Lauro turns to his friends, and it could be seen as a sign of weakness, too. He says, "I'm afraid that a few hundred million people must have been left out of your amusement park equipped with escalators and moving walkways. Which part of the world are you talking about?"

"Ours," says Enrico. "The part that achieved what everybody else will inevitably have access to, sooner or later."

"Sooner or later," says Lauro. "Too bad if in the meantime everything that was beautiful will have been excavated or poisoned or cut down or ground into pulp or covered with horrible materials and filled with stink and noise."

Enrico says, "You have a pretty grim vision of progress."

"Progress toward *what?*" says Lauro. "Toward an immense dumping ground which will eventually self-destruct?"

"Perhaps toward a steady evolution of thoughts and behaviors," says Enrico. "Toward knowledge, communication, unlimited variety of choice."

"Sitting in front of a TV set?" says Lauro. "Inside a room within a concrete building, with only other concrete buildings and sidewalks and cars to see from the windows?"

"Why not sitting at a table in a beautiful square?" says Enrico. "Or in a street full of people walking and talking and looking at each other. Or in a theater. In a cinema. In a bookstore. In a train. In an airplane. In one of the spaces we've managed to create through centuries of successive achievements."

Lauro makes a gesture that includes the house they're in and the area around it, and says, "We have no impulse to achieve anything, here. No wish to superimpose anything on anyone, to leave permanent marks. We're happy with just being here, as part of the whole."

"How cosmic," says Enrico with a sneer. "Too bad that you're so totally enslaved by your sacrifices. By the constant toil. By the cold. The discomfort. The isolation. The absurd feuds you got yourselves into. Maybe one day you'll discover that it's not worth killing yourselves to play the part of those who can survive on seeds and herbs. Maybe you'll learn to accept the fact that you're part of the contemporary world."

"We're not interested in the contemporary world," says Lauro.

"But you're part of it *anyway*," says Enrico. "Even though you live on its outskirts. Even though you don't even know what government this country has."

"We know," says Lauro, "but it doesn't concern us anymore."

"Of course," says Enrico. "Keep burying your heads in the sand. It's never taken anybody very far, though." He could go on, but he stops, looking at Luisa and Arturo and Margherita, hoping to force them to come out into the open.

They keep silent, their expressions wavering between complicity and dissociation. At last Luisa moves her lips, but it's to say, "Why don't you two stop being so contentious? Can't you talk in a normal tone?"

Enrico can't believe her not taking sides. He says, "Excuse me, who started being contentious, here?"

Lauro empties his cup and slams it on the table. "I'm not very interested in this kind of discussion, anyway. We've already talked about these things a whole lifetime ago."

"Good," says Enrico. "Because it sounds like a flashback from the seventies to me, too."

"Great," says Lauro. "I hope that tomorrow Arup will be able to pull your car out of that ditch, so you can hurry back to your wonderful lives."

"I hope so, too," says Enrico. "If he can't, I'll walk across the whole war zone rather than be stuck in this place another day."

There are a couple of seconds of general stillness, excluding Alessio who gently rocks in his armchair, humming something with his mouth closed. Then Lauro gets up, puts his loose jacket back on, and picks up his bow and arrows.

Arturo must feel it his duty to break the silence, because he turns to Icaro and asks, "Do you know the story of the Cat of the Seven Boots? I always tell it to my children; they love it."

"Wasn't it 'Puss in Boots'?" says Gaia.

"Or 'The Seven-Leagued Boots'?" says Margherita.

"Hey, people, this is how I know it," says Arturo, in his good-natured, ever adaptable spirit. "So. Once upon a time there lived a king who had two sons, a good one and an evil one . . ."

Lauro goes to the door and walks out. Aria and Mirta and Gaia follow him with their eyes, then turn to listen to Arturo.

Luisa says to Enrico, "You've been detestable."

"*I* have, of course," says Enrico. "It's wonderful how impartial you manage to be in a situation like this, without letting any personal feelings unhinge you."

She barely shakes her head; there's no trace of warmth in her eyes, not even sympathy.

Enrico tries to safeguard a dignified attitude, but then he gives in just as he did to his hunger before. "How come you're so intimate with that Lauro, now?"

"What are you talking about?" says Luisa.

Enrico makes a quick gesture, his hand trembling with jealousy and possessiveness. "I saw how he touched your hand."

"Are you out of your mind?" says Luisa, as if she were speaking to some deranged person in a public place. "He barely brushed it, by pure chance."

Enrico says, "It wasn't by chance, I'm not blind."

Luisa snorts and turns her back to him, sliding on the bench to get closer to the others, pretending she's terribly interested in Arturo's fable.

Enrico gets up, making a strenuous effort at self-control to prevent himself from shouting what he really thinks to the whole group, or even throwing some objects to the ground. He picks up his overcoat, still soiled with Alessio's vomit. He goes to the door and walks out, without anybody asking him not to do it.

Margherita has gulped down half a liter of sour red wine to relieve her fear, listening absent-mindedly to Arturo who's near the end of his children's story. Being surrounded by a sort of extended family in front of the fireplace seems to bring out unexpected qualities from him. He plays with his voice and accentuates the tension between a pause and an action, slowing down or quickening the pace. From a strictly technical point of view, he breathes in at the wrong times and his Milanese accent is too open on the vowels, but in this context it works, it holds everybody's attention. He says, "And so the cat with a giant leap reached the roof of the house."

"Why didn't he climb up?" says Icaro. The others laugh.

"He had his magic boots on, didn't he?" says Arturo. "Like a superhero. *Wooosh!*" he makes a gesture.

"What's a superhero?" says Icaro, looking at his mother.

Arturo says, "Well, it's like, you know . . . one of those guys who fly around in their colored suits and masks? I mean, not in real life. It's a cartoon . . . It's really stupid, anyway."

Margherita wonders whether she's drunk: her thoughts are growing confused and sticky. She turns to Luisa, refers to "our Enrico" in what should be a conspiratorial tone.

"What about him?" says Luisa.

"Pretty jealous, eh?" says Margherita, her words sounding hoarse, imprecisely enunciated.

"When?" says Luisa, with one of her just-fallen-from-the-Moon expressions.

"A few minutes ago," says Margherita, "with Lauro."

"Ah," says Luisa. "It was one of those stupid men's things."

Margherita draws herself closer to Luisa, putting a hand on her knee. She says, "Still, the guy seems to be rather interested."

"Who?" says Luisa, stiffly. "In what?"

"Lauro," says Margherita. "In you." She's always been a little jealous of Luisa's skin, of the way it absorbs and reflects light. She's always thought it rather unjust that such a gift should be bestowed on someone who not only doesn't put it to a professional use, but doesn't even like to be photographed by her husband during holidays.

"You're drunk, Margherita," says Luisa.

"So what?" says Margherita. "I saw how he was looking at you. This morning, too, when you went to talk to him."

"I didn't go talk to him" says Luisa.

"I saw you," says Margherita, like a fly on the honey. "I *saw* you."

"Stop it," says Luisa, pretending to listen to Arturo.

"You mean to tell me you didn't notice anything?" says Margherita.

"Of course not," says Luisa.

"Swear it," says Margherita.

Luisa says, "Drink some water, it'll help you get over it." Ever since they were little girls, she's always refused to play this kind of feminine game, seeing it as too stupid or vulgar. It's part of her always keeping at a safe distance from reality.

Margherita makes a wry face. She says, "Okay, then I'm wrong. But in any case he's rather attractive, the guy. It must be the call of the wild."

Luisa places her arms across her chest, to let the matter drop, turning all the way toward Arturo, who is saying, "So the cat put on his seventh pair of boots and went to Holland, where he received a hero's welcome and lived happily ever after."

They all clap their hands. Someone shouts, "Bravo!"

Arturo takes a bow, probably astounded at generating so much enthusiasm in a mostly adult audience. Margherita tries to imagine where else in the world something like this could happen: she can't think of anywhere.

Gaia says to Icaro, "Off to bed we go."

"No, I want another story!" cries Icaro, stomping his feet.

Alessio in a slurred voice says, "I can tell you the one about the goose with its head cut off, that ran around spouting blood all over."

Icaro runs to take refuge into his mother's arms. Gaia says, "Are you out of your mind? Just when he has to go to sleep!" The others give Alessio equally reproachful looks.

"But it's by the Brothers Grimm," mumbles Alessio, trying to turn in his armchair without moving his splinted leg. "Or perhaps it was Edgar Allan Poe who wrote it, I don't remember. Anyway, I saw the movie, with that bald actor, what's his name . . ."

"Forget it," says Gaia. She lifts up the whimpering Icaro, taking him out of the room.

Mirta and Aria clear the table, in one of their coordinated actions that amazes Margherita for how sudden and effective they are. Mirta picks up the dirty dishes and glasses and cutlery, and gives them to Aria who puts them into a tub while Mirta wipes the table clean with a cloth. Arturo and Luisa try to help, in a marginal and essentially symbolic kind of way. Margherita feels compelled to ask if she can give a hand, too, but she knows she's in no condition to do much and, in any case, nobody answers her.

Alessio is again humming a tune with his lips shut, he seems about to fall asleep.

There's a knock at the door; Aria goes to open it. It's Enrico: He looks around the room as if expecting apologies or comments of some kind about his argument with Lauro, but nobody says anything or even looks at him. Except Mirta who, without turning, says, "How is it, outside?"

"Fine," says Enrico icily. "I didn't hear any shots or guttural screams or excruciating laments." He stands near the table, waiting for a return of attention which doesn't happen; finally he says, "I'm going to bed."

"Goodnight," says Luisa, like a stranger, from the other end of the room.

"'Night," says Arturo, looking elsewhere.

"Take a lamp," says Mirta, pointing to the table.

Enrico takes one of the oil lamps; he's moving stiffly, and all the muscles in his face are contracted.

"But it's still early, Enrico," says Margherita, half disappointed by the fact that there is no explosive confrontation between him and Luisa.

Enrico doesn't answer; he walks out of the room with his oil lamp.

Luisa goes back to sit in front of the fireplace, close to Alessio who has slid back in his armchair and closed his eyes.

Arup comes back indoors, he puts his crossbow down. Aria disappears for a while and returns with a couple of small drums, which she hands to him. Arup sits near the fireplace and tunes one drum and then the other with a little golden hammer, listening intently. Luisa watches the fire. Margherita rummages through her handbag, finally taking out a pack of cigarettes which seems empty but in fact still contains two. Luisa shakes a finger at her. Arup places the two drums next to the other and starts tapping on them with his fingertips, producing a rhythm like a heartbeat. Margherita hesitates with her next-to-last cigarette in hand, then, spurred by an irresistible craving for a smoke, she puts on her lambskin coat and walks outside.

As soon as she is out in the dark, she is overcome by panic, and turns back to the door, knocking frantically. Aria opens it, staring at her with her attentive eyes. Margherita has an impulse to elbow her way inside, but then she thinks that she can't show herself to be so vulnerable to a girl who is in desperate need of a role model. So she forces herself to smile and says, "I just wanted to make sure you'll open up again." Aria smiles back at her, nodding, closing the door a bit reluctantly.

Margherita takes a few rubbery steps along the wall, as if she was walking along the edge of an abyss. Being drunk doesn't neutralize her fear at all, but it has the effect of making her feel strangely light-headed. The only thing like it is the day she had managed to swim naked from a boat, in a secluded bay along the coast of Corsica where there were no tourists or any lurking paparazzi. Just as she did then, she feels like an oblivious and yet acutely sensuous fish, exposed to the endless possibilities and dangers of the sea. The cold wind blows through her hair and on her face and neck, giving her goose bumps.

When she feels with her left hand that she's reached the corner of the house, she stops and puts the cigarette into her mouth. She takes out her plastic lighter, trying to protect the flame with a hand but the wind keeps blowing it out. She turns one way and the other, scratching the tiny dented wheel. Finally she manages to light up, inhaling the hot smoke down to the bottom of her lungs. She feels reactive and attractive, facing the black sea of the wild night with her back to the wall.

There's a swishing sound somewhere in the dark. Terror rushes through her, from the tip of her toes to the top of her hair. A voice that is much too near to her says, "What the hell are you doing?"

Margherita smacks the back of her head against the stones of the wall, but at the same moment she recognizes the voice as Lauro's. She can even make him out in the dim reflection of the stars that her eyes are only now beginning to adjust to. So, trying to bring her heartbeat back to normal, she says, "I know that smoking kills, but this is a pretty dangerous place anyway." It sounds to her like a funny thing to say given the circumstances, even though she knows she's slurring her words a bit.

"You shouldn't be out here," says Lauro.

Margherita tries to discern if he's at least smiling, but she can't. She's certainly not at the top of her form: every perception seems to reach her brain after a second's delay, leaving a long trail. She says, "I knew there was a brave paladin standing guard out here."

Lauro finally laughs, even though it's not clear if he's laughing at her words or at her. He moves in the darkness, but without going away. The black dog is there, too, brushing almost invisibly against their legs.

Margherita takes another puff from her cigarette, watching the red embers glow. Right now she feels like a character out of a film, rather than television: larger than life, fascinating and coura-geous, full of surprises. The very fact of walking out into such a potentially dangerous night is a true adventurer's deed; as is smoking next to an outlaw without letting him intimidate her.

Lauro says, "Mirta told me about the work you do."

Margherita says, "Should I be ashamed of it?" Even such a sim-ple sequence of words sounds like a tongue twister to her now.

"You should know," says Lauro.

"I do," says Margherita. "And I'm not in the least ashamed of it."

"Good for you," says Lauro.

"Thank you very much," says Margherita. "I don't know what you imagined. It's quite a nice program."

"Quite nice?" says Lauro, as if he was repeating an ambiguous expression.

"Listen, don't try to play these little games with me," says Margherita, still unable to make out his countenance. "It's a nice program, okay? In its own genre."

"And what would that be, its own genre?" says Lauro.

"Light entertainment," says Margherita: her "t"s sticking to her tongue.

"So you're proud of it?" says Lauro.

"Of course," says Margherita. "I also write it, this year. I write part of the scripts." She wishes she'd at least have a little more control over her vowels, since there doesn't seem to be much to do about the consonants.

"Really?" says Lauro.

"Sure," says Margherita. "It's a job like any other, and I try to do it the best I can. I'm lucky enough to have a lot of people who love me and follow me."

"Where do they follow you?" says Lauro.

"I mean, they follow the program," says Margherita, still not sure whether he's teasing her in a kind of erotic way, or having a philosophical argument with her like the one he had with Enrico. She wavers between these two interpretations, unable to decide. She asks herself if this is due to the darkness of the night, or to the wine slowing down her reflexes.

Lauro says, "Still, you seem ill at ease when you talk about it."

"Perhaps because I can't see your face," says Margherita. "Or perhaps because to you television is a total abomination."

Lauro laughs. He says, "No, I just think it's one of the means by which you have filled your country with rubbish."

"I've never filled anybody or anything with rubbish in my life," says Margherita. "And look, it's *your* country as well."

"You can keep it," says Lauro.

"That's easy," says Margherita. She inhales smoke from her cigarette, blows it out.

"I wouldn't say easy," says Lauro.

Margherita says, "Okay, maybe from a practical point of view it's not so easy, but *mentally* it's a great luxury, let me tell you. A great luxury." She considers other things she might say, but again she wonders if she's on the wrong track with him. According to how the wind blows, the beat of Arup's drums reaches them from the house: a rather suggestive soundtrack, underlying the two protagonists' confusion of feelings, suggesting developments. She throws down her half-smoked cigarette, stamps it out with an aching foot.

"Miss Guilty Conscience," says Lauro, in a childishly taunting tone, his shoulder brushing hers.

"Mister Peacock," says Margherita, with the right timing and even the right tone, miraculously. She feels a shiver run along the left side of her body, slowing her breathing down, making her temperature rise.

"Why peacock?" says Lauro.

"Because you're constantly playing the hard-to-get country dude," says Margherita, in an irresistible dash of sincerity that excites her as much as the darkness and his teasing and the moments of contact between them.

"What are you talking about?" says Lauro. He laughs, brushing his shoulder against hers, breathing a few centimeters away from her. He has a wild, male smell—musky hormonal compounds and volatile underbrush essences and sweat and leather and earth, light-years away from the eau de toilette scent of the men she's acquainted with.

Margherita turns toward him, but the stars' reflection is still not enough to make him entirely visible, so she takes out her lighter and scratches its tiny dented wheel: a little flame flickers on Lauro's face for an instant, before the wind puts it out. She thinks she glimpses the beginning of a movement, or perhaps just a look suggesting it. She's not even sure of this, so she remains suspended in an anticipation of contacts and pressures and consistencies. She narrows her eyes, even though in this darkness it doesn't make any difference: she half opens her lips and holds her breath, waiting for a sequence of events that might overwhelm her with its sudden brutality.

He puts a hand on her temple, runs his hard fingers through her hair; he says, "How come you've bleached it like this? I can see it even now, in the dark."

"It was a mistake," says Margherita, without thinking. "My hairdresser's mistake." The thought seems to her incredibly remote; she's swaying, feeling the circulation of her internal fluids alter.

There's a sudden explosion of sound: it's the black dog, barking and invisibly charging off in the darkness. Lauro withdraws his hand, pushes Margherita away, saying "Go back inside, hurry!" He disappears after the dog, into the heart of the black night.

Margherita goes from swooning to intense fear to primordial flight instinct so quickly, she doesn't even have the time to realize it. She rushes along the wall as fast as she can. The door opens before she can knock. Arup comes out, crossbow in hand.

Arturo finds it harder to sleep than on the first night. He keeps waking up abruptly with visions of gun barrels aimed at him point-blank, deafening sounds in his ears. It takes him several minutes to convince himself he's alive and in good health, on his straw mattress next to his friends. He falls back asleep out of sheer exhaustion, but after a while he's awake again, the scratches on his face and forearms and hands itching unbearably. He sits up and speculates what ingredients Mirta's tincture was really made of; cocking his ears to discern any barking or voices or more alarming sounds from outside. He lies down again, rolling himself in his blanket until his arms and legs are trapped. He kicks wildly to free himself, turns facedown, tries to flatten out his overstuffed pillow. Visions of Mirta pass through his head: Mirta grinding herbs and seeds in the mortar; Mirta walking, eating, turning, looking at him. They are too vivid and three-dimensional for a guy who desperately needs sleep; he can see the shape of her body through her home-sewn clothes, he can smell her light, amberlike scent.

The others are not sleeping very well either, judging by their relentless tossing and turning and snorting and grunting and moaning. Arturo thinks of their attitudes and appearances on Friday when they left Milan: it almost makes him laugh. He tries to relax his body, but his sight and hearing and touch and smell receptors are so overstimulated, they keep registering new images and feelings. Somebody is snoring, it's hard to tell who; the wind makes the window blinds creak. Arturo tries to immerse himself in sleep like a diver going underwater. He moves his arms and legs until the water is over his head, and he's totally submerged.

Somebody somewhere screams "MAAAAMMMMMAAAA!" in a terrible, blood-curdling register.

Arturo kicks furiously to come up from the depths of sleep; he struggles toward the scream and its meaning, without any stop along his ascent to decompress. In a second he's already thrown his blanket away, he's standing on his straw mattress with his heart beating fast. He turns his head around but can't see anything, the darkness is so thick that he thinks he's gone blind.

The scream occurs again, even louder and more excruciatingly. Arturo trips over the mattress next to his, falling on top of somebody, perhaps Enrico, considering the build of his body and from the inarticulate sound he produces. He gets up again, turning to what should be the room's center, bumping into someone else— Luisa, he supposes, who in her frightened voice says, "What's happening?"

"What?" says Arturo, his voice mixing with other voices and sounds that are difficult to distinguish in the total absence of light: "Damn it!" and "Oh my God!" and "Where are you?" and "Who is it?" and again "What?" and "AAAAAAAAAAAH!"

Groping around, overrun by his own impatience, Arturo shouts, "Margherita, your lighter!" Margherita screams, "Oh God, what's going on?" Another voice yells out: "Here!" Arturo tries to calm down, but it's not easy. He shouts, "Give me your damned lighter, for the lamp!" and searches for it blindly with his hands.

"Wait!" says Margherita, her voice distorted by fear. Arturo tries to grope his way in the dark, in the confusion of voices and breathing and sounds and movements and steps that make the unstable old tiles of the floor shake. He has a sudden flashback of a night camping in the Andes five years earlier, when he and his climbing companions had woken up in the dark inside a tent that was being swept away by a storm toward an eight-hundred-meter overhang. This overlapping of events has the effect of rendering him even more agitated, as if every gesture he makes was potentially his last one.

A little flame flickers on, illuminating Margherita's terrified face. Arturo grabs the lighter from her hand, looks for the oil lamp on the floor, fumbles with the wick, lights it up, causes a burst of light in the room. He rotates the lamp at arm's length: Luisa in a sweater and panties and long socks, with very white thighs and unruffled hair and pupils dilated by fright; Enrico in a sweater and trousers by the window, with a hand on his forehead; Alessio lying sideways on his straw mattress, bent toward his splinted leg that sticks out of the blanket. There's nobody else; the yellow light makes a second complete circle from wall to wall, returning to Alessio who says, "I thought it was just a nightmare, damn . . ."

Arturo exhales, relaxing his muscles; Luisa asks Enrico, "What happened to you?"

"Nothing," Enrico says, but he doesn't take his hand off his forehead.

Margherita says, "I don't believe it, you dickhead."

Enrico says, "He was screaming like a slaughtered animal."

Luisa says, "Let me see your forehead."

Enrico says, "I just hit something."

Margherita repeats, "Dickhead."

Alessio says, "I'd like to see you, waking up like this."

There's a sound of approaching footsteps, and a horizontal line of light growing more intense at the base of the door. They all freeze, not moving or saying a word until the light and the steps slowly recede.

Arturo asks Alessio in a low voice, "Does it hurt a lot?"

"A little," says Alessio. "But it's a weird feeling. I dreamt that a dinosaur was grabbing it, I couldn't get it free."

"A dinosaur?" says Luisa.

"You fucking dickhead," says Margherita again. She rummages through her handbag, fishes out a little wooden box, opens it, and pours three or four pills into her hand. She puts one into her mouth, then hands the others to Alessio, saying, "Take these" in a highly resentful tone.

"What is it?" says Alessio.

"Sleeping pills," says Margherita. "Even though you'd deserve poison."

"Take them," says Enrico, in a peremptory tone.

Alessio hesitates, muttering something indistinct.

"Come on, gulp them down," says Margherita, pressing the pills against his mouth.

"Hurry up, Alessio," says Enrico. "So perhaps we can try and get a little sleep."

Alessio takes the pills from Margherita, puts them into his mouth. He tries to swallow them but he can't, so he chews them.

The others go back to lie down on their straw mattresses, each with varying expressions of discomfort. Arturo waits for everybody to settle down in some way, then he puts out the lamp: the room plunges back into total darkness. He pulls the blanket up to his nose, tries to fall asleep again by degrees but it's even more difficult now, with the adrenalin still circulating through his body and the breathing and tossing and turning of the others who are just as awake as he is. He reaches out with a hand to check that the oil lamp and the lighter are close by in case he needs them again. He makes an effort not to think of what happened after they woke up five years ago in the Andes; or of Mirta sitting on the wooden bench in the kitchen, or the shape of her under her clothes. He remains wide awake for a very long time, then he sinks into a half-sleep, accompanied by the hissing of the wind and the barking of the dog, far off in the night.

From somewhere comes the raucous, insistent crowing of a cock. Enrico jumps to his feet, feeling a weak kind of satisfaction to see the others still asleep. He puts on his shoes at once, then opens wide the old, battered window shutters; the room fills up with light and wind. He watches the effect on the others, while placing a hand on his still hurting forehead where he hit it in the middle of the night.

Luisa sits up, rubbing her eyes with her hands. Arturo looks at his watch and grunts something. Alessio and Margherita lie very still, indistinguishable under their blankets.

Enrico looks outside, with no interest whatsoever for the landscape. About ten meters from the house Arup is pushing a wheelbarrow full of logs while having a furious row with Gaia. It's hard to make out what they're saying because the wind tears off their sentences: "I know, I know!"; "When?"; "Said so!"; "You never remember!" At one point Arup in exasperation unbalances his wheelbarrow and all the wood scatters on the ground. He turns as if to walk off, but then comes back and starts picking up each log. Gaia takes Icaro away, turning back after a few steps to make an angry gesture.

Enrico turns toward Arturo who's now sitting up on his straw mattress, and says, "You're really convinced these people can pull our car out of that ditch?"

"I hope so," says Arturo in a rather confused tone, his face still covered with reddish stripes of tincture.

Enrico consciously assumes one of the skeptical expressions Luisa detests, but right now she doesn't seem to take notice; she's putting on her pants as if she doesn't even see him.

Arturo massages his scalp; he says, "I think they've got good reason to help, since at this point it's the only way they can get rid of us."

Enrico says, "Supposing they want to get rid of us."

"Why shouldn't they?" says Arturo. "Do you believe they want to keep us here forever?"

"Maybe not forever," says Enrico. "But it probably wouldn't displease them to have some hostages to use in their tribal war. And an audience, for the first time since who knows when. Someone to preach to about their pseudo-ideological rubbish. The beautiful, sophisticated city women listening to them, all enraptured . . ."

Luisa keeps pretending not to see him or hear him; she puts on her shoes.

Arturo looks at his hands, then rolls up his sleeves to look at his forearms, then cautiously touches his face.

"What is it?" says Enrico. "Did the young shepherdess' magic potion have a miraculous effect?"

"Well, *yes*," says Arturo. "It doesn't hurt or itch anymore."

"Don't worry, you're still full of scratches," says Enrico. "You look like a sick jaguar. Tell it to that poor wretch, about the miracles they make here." He nods to Alessio who keeps sleeping in a crooked position, his splinted leg protruding from his blanket, his head thrown back as if he was dead.

Luisa walks to the door without a word.

"Where are you going?" says Enrico.

"To the bathroom," says Luisa, without turning.

"If you can call it a bathroom," says Enrico, to the door she has already closed behind her. "Now we'll have to queue up again for that elegant hole in the floor, and that wonderful, invigorating ice-cold water."

"Come on, it's not so terrible," says Arturo.

"Really?" says Enrico. "I'm happy to see you appreciate the local wonders."

Arturo doesn't answer; he does his morning knee-bends, a little less energetically than usual since his muscles must be aching from yesterday's run. Margherita and Alessio keep very still, breathing deeply from beneath their covers. Enrico looks at the door, looks again out of the window; all he wants is to get away from this place, as soon as possible.

Arup ties an old rope to the back of the minivan, then fastens it to the packsaddles of two horses that Mirta is holding by the reins, looking intermittently at his crossbow lying by the side of the road. The two horses look stubborn, and ill matched for such a well-balanced pair; Mirta has to shout to make them step back. Arturo tries to help her but he lacks any real experience with horses; he barely avoids a kick that could have easily broken his leg. Enrico feels an acute irritation as he observes all these gestures, alarmed by every little rustling from the woods.

"If they come, they'll come by the road," says Mirta. "Not from there."

"Ah, great," says Enrico, dryly. "It's nice to know."

Mirta nods her head, irony apparently not being among the nuances she's able to recognize.

Arup knots the old rope with an almost preternatural meticulousness; when he's finished he turns to Enrico and Arturo, saying, "One of you should take the wheel."

Enrico nods to Arturo to do it, a ceding of control that is in fact a show of noninvolvement. It seems to him that the only way not to debase himself further is to cultivate an attitude of detachment from the proceedings; to this end, all his muscles and nerves and thoughts are so engaged, they almost hurt.

On the other hand, Arturo gives in to the situation without the slightest reservation. He sits at the wheel and says, "Shall I start the engine?"

"Not yet," says Arup. He moves like a character in the Western movies Enrico used to watch as a child: He picks up his crossbow, checks the road, pricks up his ears, sniffs the air. Finally he nods to Mirta.

Mirta shouts, "Ha!" to the horses, pulling them by the reins. She, too, must have some kind of childish film reference in her head, judging from her frontier-woman's gestures.

This is what Enrico finds most exasperating: the mixture of fantasy and posturing consolidated by practice and time. He would be willing to run some pretty high risks to see this little game break down, the players forced to confront the inescapable laws of the real world.

Mirta shouts, "Ha!" again. The two horses strain in their uneven way, the old rope stretching and pulling taut, but the minivan doesn't budge. As seen from the side of the road, it's an embarrassingly pointless attempt. Enrico vividly imagines the rope snapping off, Arturo getting out of the minivan with a look of dismay on his face, Arup undoing the knots with the same absurd care with which he tied them, the little group disconsolately walking back to the house.

But after a few more attempts, the minivan starts to move. Mirta and Arup keep prodding and pulling, the horses strain on their harness, Arturo looks out of the side window, totally absorbed in the effort; the minivan's front wheels roll out of the ditch, they run free on the dirt road. Mirta and Arup and Arturo shout and laugh as if they have won some kind of victory, clapping their hands like children. Enrico keeps still by the roadside, unable to decide whether he feels relieved or disappointed.

In any case the minivan has a definite lean to the left and makes a noise of scratched metal as it is pulled backward. Enrico notices it at once and doesn't say anything, but a moment later Arturo shouts, "Stop, stop!"

Mirta and Arup stop the horses. Arturo leans out of the open window, he says "It seems to be tilting to the left."

"It *is* tilting," says Enrico. "The axle is probably destroyed." The relish he feels is caused by their disappointment, and it's now stronger than his worry over not having a means of transportation to get back to town.

"What do you mean, destroyed?" says Arturo, getting out to have a look.

Arup has already slipped under the minivan's front; he slides out and springs back to his feet. He says, "I believe it's the shock absorber."

"Can we drive to town in this condition?" asks Enrico, even though the slant itself is enough of an answer.

"Not as it is," says Arup, looking around. "Not on that road."

"So we might as well have left it in the ditch," says Enrico.

"Perhaps I can fix it for you," says Arup, in the mechanic-physician-sorcerer attitude he must have been cultivating all these years, in the sheltered environment of his tiny community.

"Perhaps?" says Enrico, in a cold tone.

"I must see, at the workshop," says Arup. "I'll be able to tell you more after I've taken the shock absorber apart." He narrows his eyes, looking rather self-assured.

"Let's hope," says Arturo, already full of renewed optimism.

Arup nods encouragingly; Mirta behind him smiles.

"Excuse me, but with what tools would you take it apart?" says Enrico. "I believe it's rather complicated, a shock absorber."

"I've got quite a lot of tools," says Arup, without placing any emphasis on his words.

Arturo goes back behind the wheel, Mirta and Arup spur the horses on; the little creaking, squeaking caravan gets moving again. Enrico follows it, with nothing to do but note pathetic details and look behind him for fear of seeing potential killers arrive, whose motivations are probably similar to his in this particular moment.

M argherita utters a shriek like a roused wild animal: she rolls on her straw mattress, thrashes about under the blanket, opens her eyes but can't immediately get rid of the dream-fog that's clouding her head. When she does, she sees Luisa with her hand on her shoulder and a worried look in her eyes, Gaia and young Icaro standing behind her. She sits up, panting. "What's happening?"

"Alessio won't wake up," says Luisa.

"Who?" says Margherita, looking around, trying to reconstruct the situation.

"Him," says Gaia, pointing to a bundle of blankets and clothes from which a splinted leg and a thrown-back head are protruding.

"Why?" says Margherita. She looks at her watch: it's nine, her sleepiness doesn't seem to her so monstrously unjustified.

Luisa says, "He doesn't react, not even when you shake him hard."

Margherita tries to smooth her hair a bit with her hands, even though she knows there isn't much to be done. What little makeup she managed to put on yesterday evening must have totally dissolved during the night, she's sure she has the small, naked eyes that mortify her every morning when she looks at herself in the mirror. Two years ago some paparazzi got some shots of her just after she woke up in the back garden of someone she was having a fling with, and when they were published in some trash magazine she almost had a nervous breakdown from the anger and the humiliation.

Luisa says, "What were those pills you gave him, last night?"

"Restfast," says Margherita, in a guarded tone because she knows they're trying to hold her responsible.

"How many did you give him?" says Luisa.

"I don't know," says Margherita, without seeing the reason for all this concern over a good-for-nothing real estate agent. "I think three or four."

"*Three or four?*" says Luisa. "Were you out of your mind?"

"Didn't you see the state he was in?" says Margherita, flaring up in self-defense. "It was just to help him sleep." She's getting back some of her reflexes, albeit not all of them: enough to remember the sequence of events.

"Yes, but *three or four* pills," says Luisa, with one of her deeply reasonable expressions that Margherita finds increasingly hard to tolerate.

"What's Restfast?" asks Gaia, in an even more accusatory tone.

"Sleeping pills," says Margherita, angrily. "I took a couple, too, and I'm perfectly fine, given the circumstances. One before going to bed, then another one when he started shrieking like a wounded eagle."

"But you're used to it," says Luisa, still in her even-handed vein. "And we had trouble waking you up, too. Imagine what effect three or four had on him."

Gaia shakes her head. "On top of all the herbal sedative he had drank, and the wine. It must have been a terrible cocktail."

"I'm sorry," says Margherita, who's beginning to worry about possible legal liabilities. "I did it for his own good. Make him drink some coffee."

Gaia stares at her as if she was the incarnation of all the world's evils; she says, "We don't have any coffee."

"Look, it's your free choice, not to have it," says Margherita. "Stop looking at me as if I was some kind of criminal. It's certainly not going to do him any harm if he sleeps a little longer."

Gaia doesn't reply; she goes back to Alessio, shakes his shoulder. Young Icaro contributes to the shaking, then Luisa does, too.

Margherita sniffs at her armpits through the triple layer of sweaters; she takes out of her suitcase a roll-on deodorant stick, applies it under her clothes with a gesture that should be almost undetectable, even though she's not one hundred percent sure of it. All of her perceptions have a rather wide margin of inaccuracy: signals reach her on a delayed basis, triggering thoughts that are equally slowed down. She thinks that this must be due to the combination of wine and sleeping pills and stress and all the mental anguish she's experienced since the car's breakdown. She struggles to react: she takes a black jersey out of her suitcase with MAKE IT written on it in silver letters, removes one of her sweaters, and puts the new one over the other two.

In the meantime, Gaia and Luisa have pulled Alessio up into a sitting position, they are slapping his face. At last he opens his eyes. "What time is it?" he mumbles. His words are slurred and his head is dangling, but at least he's not dead of an overdose, as someone was apparently suggesting only a few minutes before.

Luisa props him up as if she were a professional nurse, something she probably learned from a description she read in one of her books. She says, "It's all right, it's all right," in a soothing tone.

Margherita finds this a fake and irritating attitude, but she can't think about it for long. Her ability to concentrate is absorbed almost entirely by the act of putting on her black patent-leather ankle boots and lacing them up.

Gaia says, "Let's make him stand up," putting Alessio's left arm over her shoulders with the utmost caution. Luisa does the same with his right arm, saying, "Careful with his leg."

Alessio mumbles, "I can stand up by myself," hardly realizing how his pronunciation contradicts his words.

Gaia says, "Now we'll brew a nice herb tea that will wake you up."

"I'd rather have some of that red wine," mutters Alessio, swaying his head.

Gaia and Luisa pull him up, then support him by steps across the room and out of the door. Icaro follows them, enthralled by the drama of the scene.

Margherita finishes lacing up her ankle boots, then gets up. Her heels and toes still hurt badly; she takes some short, limping steps to the window. Outside a pair of horses are towing the minivan backward, guided by Mirta along the small dirt road that leads to the houses. Arup holds his crossbow in his hands, looking around. Enrico follows behind, his hands in his pockets and a noncommittal look on his face. Mirta stops the horses in front of one of the empty houses, the one that was once a barn. Arup unties the towing rope, and Arturo gets out of the minivan. They talk and gesticulate, then with Enrico's reluctant help they push the minibus inside. Mirta comes out at once, leading the two horses toward their paddock. The others remain inside the old barn.

Margherita tries to give another useless quick fix to her hair, then crosses the room, a twinge in her feet at every step, feeling like she's walking on the deck of a boat in rather heavy seas.

Arturo looks at Enrico who looks at Arup who's stretched out under the minivan. Hanging or leaning against the stone walls are tools of every conceivable kind, in various stages of rustiness: large and small sickles, whipsaws, jigsaws, hacksaws, rakes, shovels, hoes, pitchforks, hammers, bunches of nails, monkey wrenches, Allen keys, funnels, planes, files, rasps, screwdrivers, can openers, springs, bicycle wheels, a hand drill, ropes, hooks, rolls of wire, barrels, jars, planks, sticks, broken chairs, table legs, jerry cans, buckets, tanks, straw-covered and naked demijohns, metal and wooden boxes, tubes, chains, crown gears and other, harder to identify disassembled parts. There's a smell of dry wood and damp earth and chickenshit and spilled wine and goat cheese and olive oil, it gives Arturo a feeling of basic familiarity which cheers him up and fills him with nostalgia. He recalls that there were no such smells in his perfectly renovated and furnished Chianti house; to trace them in his memory he has to go back to when he was a child, visiting his grandfather on the Langhe hills in Piedmont.

Enrico, on the other hand, doesn't seem to be in the least impressed by the atmosphere. He paces up and down, giving Arturo an irritated glance every now and then, looking skeptically at Arup's legs protruding from under the minivan's hood.

Arup at last slides out from under, and wipes his hands with an old rag.

"So?" says Enrico, tensely.

Arup nods his head. He says, "It can be done."

"Great!" says Arturo. He's pleased not just about the minivan: He's happy to be involved in the experience, able to converse with a member of a different culture. It's like when he visited the tents of the nomadic shepherds in the Mongolian desert, or when he chatted with an old peasant woman while waiting at a bus station on an endless empty road in Guatemala.

"Aha," says Arup. It's clear that he likes this role of dispenser of surprises, but he doesn't overdo it, and contents himself with a light touch.

Enrico keeps his hands in his overcoat pockets, still wet after having washed off Alessio's vomit from the coat. He says, "How long do you think it'll take you?"

"A few hours," says Arup.

"That is to say, it'll be ready by the afternoon?" says Enrico.

"Yes," says Arup.

"Before dark?" says Enrico.

"Yes," says Arup.

"And we'll able to reach the town with it?" says Enrico.

"Yes," says Arup.

"Let's hope so," says Enrico, his level of confidence barely above zero. He opens the minivan's hatch, takes out his and Luisa's suitcases, and walks off.

Arturo watches him exit the barn, disappointed and embarrassed by his attitude. To compensate for his friend's rudeness he moves closer to Arup. "You're amazing, really. You fix legs, you fix cars, you fix everything." He injects warmth into his voice and eyes, and his smile is an attempt to eliminate any false politesse, to let honest feelings flow free.

Arup smiles, too, "Well, not really everything."

"What is there you can't fix?" says Arturo, his tone even more intimate, his head tilted to express comradeship.

"Hearts, for instance," says Arup, again producing a little surprise. Then he turns, because Icaro is at the entrance of the barn, regarding the minivan as if it was an apparition.

"Do you like it?" says Arturo, feeling a sudden pang of longing for his own children.

Icaro keeps still, leaning silently against the stone wall.

Crouching, Arturo walks up to him and says, "Would you like to sit at the wheel?"

Icaro doesn't answer, he keeps staring at the minivan as intently as a small animal gauging his chances for survival.

Arturo lifts him up with a sudden sensation of muscular gratification in spite of the difference in Icaro's weight to that of his children. He says, "Do you want to drive like the grown-ups do? Come on!"

The child is completely stiff, then he begins thrashing and kicking like mad, screaming, "Let go of me! Let go of me!"

Arturo is so surprised by the high-pitched intensity of his voice and by the desperate strength in his arms and legs, that he holds him for a few more seconds. Then he puts him down, shocked and deafened, without understanding.

Arup makes a gesture to Icaro with his open hands. "Hey, calm down, calm down. Don't you see it's not moving? It can't do anything bad to you. It's broken."

Icaro doesn't listen to him: he writhes convulsively, screaming, "I don't want it! I don't want it! It's bad! It's bad!"

Gaia enters the barn, her eyes and her whole body filled with maternal alarm. She opens her arms as the child runs to her. "What's happening here?" she cries.

Icaro climbs all over her, still shrieking, "I don't want it! I don't want it!"

Gaia looks accusingly at Arup; he points to the minivan, without saying anything.

Arturo doesn't know how to react; he says, "It's my fault. I thought it would amuse him to sit behind the wheel."

"He's scared of cars," says Gaia, without the least sign of a sense of humor or simple courtesy or adult maturity. "We're scared of them, too. And disgusted. We *hate* cars."

"I can understand you," says Arturo, even though this is really a bit beyond understanding.

"No, you can't!" screams Gaia. "Since that one is yours!"

"It's not mine," says Arturo, feeling a little pathetic. "The real estate agent rented it for this trip."

"It doesn't matter!" screams Gaia. "It's not this car in particular! We hate *all* cars, and the people who use them!" She's literally vibrating with indignation, the child sobbing and shaking in her arms.

Arturo turns to Arup in search of support, but Arup averts his eyes. These people must be crazier than he thought; maybe Enrico wasn't so wrong, after all. He says, "I'm sorry. Very bad idea. Please excuse me."

"You're sorry for *what*?" cries Gaia. Her screams have the effect of stirring up Icaro even more, who cries and convulses against her like a child possessed.

"For what has happened," says Arturo, in the calmest tone he's able to muster.

"You're sorry, my foot!" screams Gaia. "I'm not going to be taken in by your words, you know!" She's so beside herself with rage that for a moment she seems about to put Icaro down and grab one of the big sickles from the wall. Instead, she spins round, carrying the screaming, kicking child away with her.

Arturo looks around, raising his hands. He says, "It was really stupid of me. Should have thought about it."

"Don't worry," says Arup, in a soft tone partly contradicted by the dark light in his eyes.

E nrico pops his head into the kitchen looking for Luisa, and sees her intent on boiling some water on the hearth. He says, "I took our suitcases from the minivan, in case you need anything."

"Where have you put them?" says Luisa, as she takes a small, old pot from the fire and places it on the table in front of Alessio, who sits with a dreamy expression on his face. Aria is there, too, silently looking on, as she always does.

"Upstairs," says Enrico. "In the room where we slept last night."

"Good," says Luisa. She takes two pinches of herbs from a clay jar, pours them into the hot water. Enrico is taken aback by her actions even more than by her absolute lack of warmth, by the way she seems at ease in a setting that should seem as hostile to her as it does to him.

Alessio turns to him, and says in a raspy voice, "Mr. Guardi, did you see?"

"What?" says Enrico.

"My leg, Mr. Guardi," says Alessio. "He's worked a miracle, that Arup."

"Thank goodness," says Enrico. "How lucky, eh?" He'd like to go upstairs and change, but he stands there watching Luisa put the herb jar back into the cupboard as if she was in her own home.

Alessio proudly displays the two Y-shaped sticks they gave him last night. "I can actually walk, with these."

"A miracle, indeed," says Enrico. He moves away from the door, saying to Luisa, "I'll go upstairs and put on something more decent."

"I'm coming, too," says Luisa, unexpectedly. She looks at Aria, as if to entrust Alessio to her care; Aria nods her head.

They walk up the staircase without a word; probably picking up the same smells, the same vibrations from the old stone steps.

When they are upstairs Enrico says, "You really looked like you belonged there, in that kitchen."

"Did I?" says Luisa, casually. "It hasn't been easy getting him to shake off the effect of those sleeping pills, poor Alessio."

"Poor thing," says Enrico.

As soon as they are in the room where they slept, Luisa goes to open her suitcase, takes out her vanity case, a sweater, a pair of trousers, panties, a bra, knee-socks. She throws everything on one of the straw mattresses and begins to take off the clothes she has on.

Enrico says, "Don't you want to know about the minivan?"

Luisa takes off her dirty sweater. "What about it?"

"We towed it all the way back," says Enrico, as astonished by her indifference as by her general behavior. "One of the shock-absorbers is broken."

Luisa takes off her shirt and undershirt; she says, "Is it serious?"

"Of course, it's serious," says Enrico. He opens his suitcase, takes off his overcoat and jacket.

"You mean, the minivan's not working?" says Luisa; she takes off her bra, picks up the clean one from the mattress.

Enrico takes off his shirt. "It's all tilted to one side. We wouldn't last a hundred meters on that damn road."

Luisa removes her trousers, uncovering her pale thighs, reddened here and there.

Enrico peels off his T-shirt, looking at her as she balances on one foot and then the other to quickly slip out of her panties. He's reminded of the first times they undressed in front of each other; the thought suddenly makes him dizzy. He says, "The Indian claims he can fix it in a few hours."

"Why claims?" says Luisa, slipping her clean panties on and taking her knee-socks off.

"Because it's not a simple thing to do," says Enrico, filled with dismay at the distance that's grown between them, without them even noticing. Their bodies and the way they move are more or less the same today as they were years ago, when they used to produce an irresistible attraction. What happened, and when? Where has the attraction gone, along with the attention and the interest and the fun and the trust and the curiosity and even the mutual respect that came with it.

Luisa bends down to pick up her clean trousers. Her legs and bottom and back and arms are crossed by lines of tension that have nothing to do with their life together.

Enrico says, "It's a terribly complicated thing, dismantling a shock absorber and putting it back together again."

Luisa puts on her pants and zips them up, looking at him as though she didn't understand the reasons behind his tone.

Enrico with a desperate dash crosses the three meters of rickety floor that divide them and grabs her by an arm. "Luisa," he says.

She turns slightly sideways to evade his grasp: flexible but tough, inwardly out of reach. She says, "What's the matter with you?"

"I'm worried," says Enrico. He's aware of the naked feelings that fill his voice, but he can't do anything about it.

"Don't you worry," says Luisa. She takes his hand off, with a chillingly unconcerned gesture.

"I *do* worry," says Enrico, feeling stiff, cold, awkward, hungry. He grabs Luisa by the waist, pulling her against him, trying to kiss her. But she moves her head back, his kisses barely reach her chin and the base of her neck. The contact of their naked skin makes him even more desperate and insistent—it makes him try to squeeze and grab.

Luisa props her hands against his chest, pushing him away with all her strength; then she retrieves a clean undershirt from the straw mattress.

"Can you tell me why you are so distant?" says Enrico, short of breath, his stomach muscles contracted, disappointment coursing through his blood.

"I'm not distant," says Luisa, putting on her undershirt.

"What do you have against me?" says Enrico, feeling like a beggar.

"Nothing," says Luisa, putting on her shirt. She doesn't smile, doesn't even look at him.

"You treat me like a stranger," says Enrico. "You have barely spoken to me since yesterday."

Luisa puts on the pale green sweater he has seen her wear so many times; she says, "You haven't been very sociable, either."

"I was just tense because of the situation," says Enrico, in a tone so unsteady it embarrasses him. "Anybody would be, damn it."

Luisa takes a second sweater out of her suitcase, and puts it on top of the other. She says, "Last night you didn't even want to eat with us, you went to bed with that vexed air of yours."

Enrico wavers for a moment; he feels that he's entered an emotional landscape that fills him with dread. He decides to take a step back, to widen his angle of observation. Almost at once his dismay turns into annoyance, his fear into rationalizations. He fetches a clean T-shirt from his suitcase, puts it on with an aggressive motion. "I simply had no wish to play the city mouse drinking and singing merrily with the country mice. All slaps on the back and smiles, as if we had anything in common with them."

Luisa says, "We're guests at their place, aren't we?"

Enrico puts a clean shirt on, buttoning it up quickly. He says, "Why don't you stop treating them like the citizens of a small sovereign state with its own dialect and customs and its history? They're only a bunch of poor fools, Luisa. A bunch of poor fools out of time and out of reality, who have dragged us into their lives' nightmare."

"It's we who invaded their lives," says Luisa, "not vice versa."

Enrico changes his boxers, socks, trousers in quick succession; he says, "Their life was just as wretched as it is now, with or without us."

Luisa takes her spare suede boots out of a cloth pouch. "Why are you so *resentful*, Enrico?"

"I'm not resentful," says Enrico. "It's just that I'm extremely annoyed at the idea of being stuck in this place, with a very real chance of things degenerating even further at any time."

Luisa puts down her suede boots. "Come on."

"Come on, what?" says Enrico. "Haven't you seen what happened to Arturo? And Alessio? Do you need to see somebody *killed* to realize how serious the situation is?"

"What makes you think I don't realize it?" says Luisa; she puts a shoe on.

"I can tell," says Enrico. "You think you're in some kind of alternative holiday village, playing adventure games with the local entertainers."

There's a cold light in Luisa's eyes. She shakes her head as if she didn't understand him in the least.

Enrico says, "If the Indian can't fix the minivan within a few hours, we're walking out of here, before it gets dark. At the cost of having to drag you all the way to town, against your will."

"Stop calling him 'the Indian,'" says Luisa, putting on her second shoe. "He has a name, it's Arup."

"So sorry," says Enrico, his voice as controlled in tone as he can make it. "I didn't want to hurt your 'multiculti' sensitivities."

Luisa doesn't even answer him. She takes out of her suitcase the Scottish tweed jacket they bought together three years ago in a little shop in Edinburgh and puts it on. Then she crosses the room, without turning back.

M argherita walks out into the backyard in a clouded state of mind and heads for the outhouse. She puts down her handbag with the beauty case in it, then squats over the hole in the ground. She looks at the opalescent discs of the satinpod in the vase on the small table, and it seems to her that this attempt to embellish the room only makes it more squalid. She thinks of the warm, comfortable bathrooms in her Rome and Milan apartments: the Jacuzzi tub, the sauna-effect shower stall, the huge, brightly lit mirrors, the shelves and drawers full of bottles and tubes of nutritive and regenerating creams, the small jars of foundation cream, the little boxes of rouge, the eyebrow and lip-contour pencils, the powder puffs, the mascara and the lipsticks, the brushes and combs and tweezers, the nail files, the nail clippers, the 3-D-effect electric toothbrush with a built-in gum stimulator, the prescription drugs grouped by variety and easily accessed in their drawers, the sanitary towels and the tampons and the panty liners in their boxes, the soft, two-ply, jasmine-scented toilet paper, the tropical breeze of the electric heater in the mornings when the regular radiators are not enough with their silent work one takes for granted.

She pours a bucketful of water into the hole, then takes the jug and washes her bottom in the low sink that she assumes is there for that purpose, using a small cake of soap she took from a five-star hotel. The water is so cold, it almost hurts. She dries herself with a couple of tissues that shred at once; she gets tears in her eyes at the thought of all the soft cotton towels arranged by size and color in her wardrobes. She thinks that after less than two days of this life she's already near her breaking point, that if she has to endure another day without showering or washing her hair, she'll be on the verge of a serious crisis.

She takes a hand mirror out of her bag, follows with a pencil the outline of her eyes, puts a little mascara on her eyelids, a little rouge on her cheeks. But she's uncomfortable and she doesn't have the right light, and on top of it someone is knocking at the door. She pretends not to hear it, putting on some salmon-pink lipstick, spraying perfume under her armpits and behind her ears and on her wrists and then some in the room.

The knocking continues; she yells, "Just a second!" She takes her traveling brush out of her bag and brushes her hair, too hastily. The knocks at the door go on, insistently. She yells, "Coming, coming, *coming!*" and goes to unbolt it with an exasperated yank.

Outside is Lauro, with a hand on his hip. He says, "I thought somebody was barricaded inside."

"Excuse me, will you?" says Margherita in a tone that should be sharp but comes out rather dull. She hates for him to see her looking so shabby in this pitiless light, stepping out of their primitive toilet.

Lauro says, "The bucket and the jug?"

"What about them?" says Margherita, touching a corner of her lips where she can feel she has applied too much lipstick.

"Did you fill them up again?" says Lauro.

"I didn't," says Margherita. "Can't you see?" She tries to act nonchalant, but she can't understand whether he's actually reprimanding her or just continuing last night's teasing game.

He says, "They have to be filled again, each time. There aren't any waiters here to do it for you. You didn't do it yesterday either."

"So sorry," says Margherita, stiffly. "I'm mortified, really."

"It's not so bad," says Lauro, looking at her from a short distance with a kind of clinical attention.

She feels some of last night's magnetic warmth flow back into her, even though in full daylight and without the effect of the wine everything is now infinitely more complicated and tiring, every pleasant feeling offset by a negative one. She goes back into the outhouse, picks up the bucket and jug and comes back out, trying to move with some sexy elegance in spite of her aching feet. She goes to the water pump and tries to maneuver it like she's seen Arturo and Aria do, but as hard as she tries she can't manage to produce anything more than a squeaking sound and a few puffs of air; a whole catalog of curses runs through her head.

Lauro looks at her in a mocking way; he pushes her aside and grabs the pump. In a few energetic moves he manages to get an abundant gush out of it. He says, "See?"

"How wonderful," says Margherita. "You're a real champ." A few quick mental images of the two of them kissing comes to mind; of him being dragged away by the police.

"It's not so difficult," he says, apparently without picking up on the irony in her tone. "You just have to put some strength into it."

"I guess so," says Margherita. "But you know how we are, us poor city slouches."

Lauro smiles; he resumes pumping out cold water, splashing it on his face and neck and hair and into his ears. He seems satisfied; he dries his hands on his trouser legs. "Try it again," he says.

"I don't want to," says Margherita. She thinks that the only right tactic with him would be to not give him any attention, to find any excuse and walk away.

Lauro insists like an importunate child. Pointing to the pump, he says, "Come on, try. At this point it's a matter of principle, isn't it?"

"Not for me," says Margherita. "I prefer other matters of principle, really." But eventually she grabs the lever and pushes it down with all her strength, and a gush of ice-cold water wets her pants and patent-leather ankle boots before she has time to jump away.

Lauro doubles up laughing, as if witnessing the funniest scene in the world. He says, "Good! See?"

"What the fuck are you laughing about?" says Margherita, humiliation fueling her anger. "Asshole!"

Lauro doesn't stop laughing. "Is this the language you use in your TV show?"

"It's the language I use with assholes like you!" screams Margherita. She takes a tissue out of her bag to dry her boots, trying to choose a few outraged words among the many that come to mind. But the humiliation and the offence and the physical discomfort keep building up inside her to the point where she bursts into tears. She sobs uncontrollably: tears squirting from her eyes, nose dripping, lips trembling.

Lauro moves closer, with what seems like an authentically worried expression on his face, although at this point it's hard to tell. He says, "Hey, what are you doing? Are you crazy?"

"Leave me alone!" screams Margherita in a distorted tone. "It's none of your fucking business!"

"Look, I was just kidding," says Lauro.

"Do it with your shitty peasant friends!" screams Margherita. "Not with *me*!" Crying in front of him makes her feel even more exposed and offended, and these feelings make her even angrier; she struggles to control herself but she can't. She turns away so he won't see the tears on her face.

Lauro follows her around. "Listen, nothing serious has happened."

"Of course, it hasn't!" screams Margherita through her tears. "It only happened that we got stuck in a God-forsaken place, unable to make a phone call or take a shower or eat anything edible for days, with some murderers out there shooting at everything that moves, held hostage by a bunch of nutcases who amuse themselves by poking fun at us! You're right, nothing serious has happened!"

"Please calm down, now," says Lauro, patting her on the shoulder like he would do to one of his horses.

"Don't you dare touch me!" screams Margherita at the top of her lungs. "If you do it again I'll sue you! I'll send you to jail!"

"For what?" says Lauro, his puzzled look even more infuriating.

"For unlawful restraint and coercion!" screams Margherita. "And for all the illegal things that you've certainly been doing every single day in this place, for years!"

Lauro shakes his head, smiling sadly. He says, "Thank goodness *we* are the nutcases, here." He seems to want to stay and talk more, but then he turns and walks off.

Margherita is left alone in the backyard. She goes on crying, throwing into her tantrum all the reasons for self-pity she can find in her present and past life: her hurting feet and her wet pants and the discomfort and the cold, her present work problems and also the ones she's already overcome; episodes in badly ended love stories, disappointing gestures, the exceedingly long waits, extraordinary missed encounters on trains, images from a sad New Year's Eve, last week's telephone quarrel with her mother, the agonizing feeling of emptiness on a Sunday morning, even a fall from her bicycle when she was eight years old. It's all so vivid and immediate that she can almost feel the burning of her grazed knees now, the clanking noise on the hard ground covered with sharp little stones that tear her skin and pierce her raw, bleeding flesh.

Then it's over, leaving her with the same sense of indulgence and waste she feels after gorging herself on sweets: She's beyond satisfaction, in a zone of blank saturation. She feels as dumb as the worst participants in her TV program, the kind who, at the last moment, get scared in front of the cameras and can't live up to the expectations of the audience at home. She tries to recover her composure; she dries her tears with her last remaining tissue, she sniffs, she runs a hand through her hair, she looks up.

Alessio takes a few tentative steps with his two makeshift crutches in the kitchen. It's not exactly easy, but it's still huge progress for him, compared to lying upside down in the woods, waiting to be eaten alive by the wild animals. What's more, he's discovering an element of sport in this thing, and it provides an unexpected amount of satisfaction. It's like an asymmetrical, slowed-down version of the cross-country skiing that an ultra-athletic ex-girlfriend of his named Muni Maggi had insisted he try a few years ago. The main difference here is that there's only Aria looking at him in silence, showing no intention of wearing him out with a continuous barrage of prodding and correcting exclamations. This makes him feel free to experiment: for example, swinging his splinted leg back and forth, trying a couple of rotations, looking for a rhythm as he crosses the kitchen lengthwise. Strangely he's in a rather good mood now, except when the picture of the situation suddenly becomes sharp, with the sale gone to hell and the cell phone unable to pick up anything and his right leg broken and the minivan out of use and somebody with a gun almost killing a client, the crazy squatters holding everybody prisoner even though they treated his leg pretty well, his mother by now believing him dead, his girlfriend Deborah thinking he's run off with somebody else. Luckily, such thoughts only come in flashes; the rest of the time he moves from one end of the kitchen to the other as if he was floating, *hop hop hop* in this funny state of well-being that is due in part to the strange herbal brew and in part to the wine and in part to last night's pills and in part to the morning tea which tasted of licorice and aniseed and other unidentified substances, in part to not being able to do anything else but learn to walk with the two Y-shaped sticks and wait and see what happens.

At one point the girl Aria moves from her point of observation by the cupboard and says, "I've got a few things to do."

"Sure," says Alessio, making a half spin.

"But you stay here, eh?" says Aria.

"Who's going anywhere?" says Alessio. He looks at her bottom as she walks off in her stealthy way; she wouldn't be a bad-looking sixteen-year-old, if only she put on maybe a miniskirt or a pair of low-hanging jeans that would show her bellybutton and a bit of her panties, and maybe some high heels and a tight shirt instead of the home-sewn rags she's wearing, maybe some makeup on her face and some lipstick, maybe a designer bra to set off her tits a bit.

He walks another couple of times from one end of the kitchen to the other; then he feels he has exhausted all the potential of this confined space. Up to a second ago he was almost having fun and now he's fed up with it, filled with the boredom of a single-channel situation. He has withdrawal symptoms for lack of a remote control; he desperately needs to fill his eyes and ears with several simultaneous images and sounds, to avoid getting stuck with a single thought until he's swallowed up by it. He inspects the cupboards and the shelves, peeks into the corners; he can't believe there's not one single magazine or sports paper or brochure or mail-order catalog or calendar or any illustrated piece of paper with which to occupy his brain without engaging it in heavy work.

The only printed objects he can find are some coverless books packed with words, all underlined with a pencil and with notes scribbled on the margins. He begins to feel as if he's trapped in a sense-deprivation unit, and anxiety starts welling up inside him, making it difficult to breathe. Panting, he goes to the door and opens it. Looking left and right, he ventures outside.

As soon as he's on the grassy ground, the asymmetrical cross-country skiing feeling comes back to him and he immediately feels better. His uninjured leg propels him energetically, the two sticks invigorating him up to his armpits, his splinted leg pulling him forward like a magical pendulum. He's able to gain some speed, once he's found the right balance; he's able to change course almost with ease.

He pays attention not to get too far from the houses, of course: following the walls, crossing quickly the space between one building and the other. He turns a corner of the barn-house-workshop, and he sees the minivan, propped up on one side with a very rusty old professional jack. He stops to look at it for a couple of seconds, then swings his splinted leg forward and pushes with his sound one, gliding along the silvery metal side that shines in contrast with the stones of the wall.

At the end of it are Arup's legs and right arm sticking out, as he tinkers with a big monkey wrench. The left front wheel leans against the wall, near a partially dismantled shock absorber: a cylinder, a spring, nuts, oozed oil.

Alessio leans forward on his two sticks; he says, "Good morning." Talking clearly comes easily to him now; he almost enjoys feeling the vowels melt in his mouth like chocolate chips.

Arup emerges from under the hood. He looks at Alessio's splinted leg and says, "How is it going?"

"Okay," says Alessio. "*Okay*. It's amazing."

"Why amazing?" says Arup, looking straight at him with his dark eyes.

"I mean it, really," says Alessio. "You're some kind of wizard, I don't know. And to think that I never believed in such things."

"What kind of things?" says Arup.

"I don't know," says Alessio. "Yoga, gurus, alternative gymnastics, all that stuff. I even had a lot of discussions with my girlfriend, who's always there with her astrology magazines and Siberian eleutherococcus capsules and ionophoresis and the Pitigrin diet or whatever it is called."

Arup laughs. "It's not my thing, either."

Alessio isn't clear-headed enough to venture into subjects he knows nothing about, so he points to the minivan, saying, "Any luck?"

"Well," says Arup, "I have to fix the shock absorber's spring, straighten up the cylinder, put some oil back into it, and seal it again."

Alessio bows slightly, but he overdoes it and nearly loses his balance. When he finds himself in unfamiliar situations he has a tendency to draw from a repertoire of mannerisms he sorts by category: here we're halfway between science fiction and ethnological documentary, he should think.

Gaia pops her head in at the entrance, Icaro behind her digging his heels and looking at the minivan as if it was a monster. She asks Arup, "Still at it?"

"Yes," says Arup. They seem rather tense, but it's difficult to tell what a normal exchange is in this nuthouse.

She makes a gesture, saying, "I'm going to the chicken coop."

"Be careful," says Arup. "Whistle if you notice anything strange."

"Don't worry," says Gaia. She touches the child to reassure him, then leads him away.

"Take your time, madam," says Alessio. "I'll be here, in case the master needs any help."

She stops, looks in again with a strange expression of her face, and says, "I beg your pardon?"

"About the master?" says Alessio, slightly embarrassed. "But it's true."

"No, that other thing," says Gaia.

"That I'll be here?" says Alessio.

"No," says Gaia. "What did you call me?"

"Madam?" says Alessio, pivoting on his sticks to make a half turn.

Gaia bursts out laughing—a couple of dimples appear on her cheeks, and there are some gaps between her teeth. She says, "You know, I didn't think anybody would ever call me madam, in my entire life."

"Really?" says Alessio. He doesn't look her in the eyes for too long, as she's a kind of woman that scares him a bit.

Arup laughs too, seems really amused.

"Fantastic," says Gaia. "This proves it's true that wonders will never cease." Still laughing, she walks off, taking Icaro with her.

Arup says, "How come you don't call the blonde madam?"

"Novelli?" says Alessio. "It's different with her. She works on television."

"And so?" says Arup.

Alessio thinks about it, balancing on his sticks. "It's like she's always around your home and you don't even really know her or like her but she's there anyway, in the kitchen and in the bathroom, lunch and dinner, pretending she belongs to the family but she doesn't, acting as if she was a great friend but you know she really couldn't care less."

Arup is staring at him, an uncomprehending look in his eyes.

Alessio asks himself what someone like him could know of these things. For a moment the picture of the situation becomes sharp again and scares him. But he just needs to do another quarter turn on his Y-shaped sticks to float again in his vague feeling of well-being, no sharp turns intimidating him.

Arturo runs into Mirta who is prodding the goats with a long stick in her hands and carrying a bow over her shoulder. After the scene with Icaro he doesn't have much trust in his ability to communicate, so he smiles at her hesitantly and says, "How are you doing?"

"Fine," says Mirta. "And you? What about your scratches?"

"They're great," says Arturo. "Look." He moves closer to show her his face and hands, at the same time reading her expression.

She nods and smiles, seemingly satisfied, but a moment later she lets the goats lead her away, like a current.

Arturo darts after her, saying, "Where are you going?" He asks himself whether he should change into his own clothes, now that his suitcase is again within reach. It might help him feel more like his old self.

"There," says Mirta, pointing toward the edges of the small plateau. "There's no more grass here for them to graze on."

Arturo tries to understand if there is a latent hostility in her, as in Gaia, ready to explode on the slightest pretext. He says "Isn't it dangerous?"

"Maybe," says Mirta. "But they have to eat."

Arturo says, "Can't you feed them the horses' hay?"

"That's for the horses," says Mirta. "And besides, if I did, the milk wouldn't taste right."

Arturo looks toward the barn-house-workshop, trying to make

a rough estimate of how long it would take him to run to the minivan and take out his suitcase and rummage through it and choose the right clothes and put them on and run back after her: way too long.

Mirta says, "Then, I have this," touching the bow slung across her shoulder.

"Do you know how to use it?" says Arturo.

Mirta stares at him as if she didn't understand the question. "Don't you?" she says.

"I've tried a couple of times," says Arturo. "While on vacation. But it was one of those compound bows, you know, with a double pulley, carbon fiber, et cetera."

Mirta shakes her head, then runs to chase away two goats who are nibbling at some vegetables in the orchard.

Arturo runs after her; he says, "Can I come with you?"

"If you want," says Mirta. "If you're not afraid."

"I'm not afraid," says Arturo. Being close to her stirs up a kind of vibration inside him, making him move in a lighter way than usual. It's true that he isn't afraid when he's near her. On the contrary, he'd be happy to have a chance to display his courage, his ability to withstand pain, his intelligence, his sense of humor, any other resource he may possess.

Mirta puts two fingers between her lips, producing a sharp whistle; the goats spring forward, gathering themselves in a group.

Mirta and Arturo hurry after them, both looking sideways at intervals to check the situation. Arturo anticipates a vision of armed men emerging from the woods, and tries to imagine a variety of defensive reactions, most of them spectacular.

Every now and then Mirta prods a goat with her long stick, clicking her tongue or whistling to direct the small herd. She is a strong walker, a country woman who for years has used her legs as her only means of transportation.

Arturo is close enough to her to perceive her light smell of smoke and ambergris and perhaps patchouli or other mysterious vegetable essences and certainly of goat. He keeps trying to think of something to say but he doesn't come up with anything—all his feelings are too mixed and confused.

They reach a sloping pasture where the grass is a little less frost-bitten than elsewhere. Mirta pushes the goats uphill, then leans on her long stick, watching them graze ravenously.

Arturo lets her get a few steps away, so she doesn't get the impression that he's clinging to her. He makes a slow, panoramic spin, then ends up looking at her again. From five or six meters away he says, "Do you know you look like a girl in a painting?"

"Which painting?" says Mirta, sounding more perplexed than flattered.

Arturo thinks about it; he says, "*La Bergère*. By Dumartin."

"What does she look like?" says Mirta. "A rough peasant with a hale and hearty face and thick arms and crooked legs?"

"She's one of the most *enchanting* women in the history of art. So delicate, energetic, balanced, noble, sunny, luminous, transparent, palpitating."

Mirta is perhaps embarrassed by these words, because she walks up the slope to a point from where she can overlook the little scattered herd. She takes the bow off her shoulder, sits on the grass.

Arturo waits a little while, then walks over to her and sits beside her on the damp, cold turf. It could be dry and warm, the way he feels right now; it could be burning hot.

They sit still and silent, a few inches apart, looking at the goats as if they were extremely interesting. The moment is so fraught, it seems about to suddenly evolve into something else, but it remains suspended.

Arturo has to make an effort to turn his head and look at Mirta in profile, with her short, straight nose and her full lips and her knotted hair. Without thinking he says, "I told you a lie."

She looks into his eyes, saying "When?"

"Five minutes ago," says Arturo. "The thing about the painting. It's not true. There's no such painting. There's no Dumartin either, at least not that I know."

Mirta looks at the goats again, her hands clasped around her knees; she has some thin lines around her eyes, perhaps indicating a slight sadness or disappointment.

Arturo panics. He says, "The fact is, you *were* like a woman in a painting. Only, in a painting that doesn't exist yet. In a painting that should be painted now."

"You mean earlier," says Mirta.

"It was only five minutes ago," says Arturo, with a feeling of apprehension he can't explain. "Not much can have changed in the last five minutes, can it?"

Mirta doesn't answer, nor does she look at him.

Arturo realizes that he hasn't at all been able to explain what he meant, and in the meantime he has perhaps spoiled everything irreparably. He expects an outburst of hostility any time now, and his eardrums are already hurting in anticipation. In a desperate attempt to limit the damages he says, "Did you know that men and women see things in completely different ways?"

"Yes?" says Mirta, apparently not too interested.

"I read it in a book," says Arturo. "Men have a tunnel-like vision, because originally they were hunters and had to focus on prey, ignoring everything else."

"And women?" says Mirta, without averting her eyes from the goats.

Arturo feels he has to keep the conversation moving at all costs.

"Women have a much more developed peripheral vision, because they originally had to check the territory around them and keep track of a thousand little details." He doesn't know why he's saying this, of all the things he could have said; perhaps to stress the fact that he's a man and she's a woman and there are some deep differences at play between them as they sit side by side without moving.

Mirta turns toward him, with a look that seems anything but peripheral. Without any warning she moves closer, grabs him by the shoulders and kisses him on the mouth.

Arturo is caught so off guard that he can't even manage to move his tongue or arms, nor can he isolate a single thought among the many overlapping in his head, mixed with the impulses that are picked up by the receptors scattered throughout his body. When she lets go of him, he falls back, breathless.

"Are you okay?" she says, knitting her eyebrows in a funny way.

"Yes, yes," says Arturo, struggling to pull himself together.

"You sure?" says Mirta, staring at him at close distance.

"Yes, of course," says Arturo. "It's just that that was so . . ." Groping about for the right word, he feels his vocabulary at a loss.

"So?" says Mirta.

"Unexpected," says Arturo, at last.

Mirta laughs, but it's not the most reassuring of reactions. She says, "Yesterday I noticed the way you were looking at me."

"Which way was that?" says Arturo. He tries to remember how he had looked at her, but he can't because he's too caught up in looking at her now.

"You know," says Mirta. "Why did you look at me like that?"

Arturo makes a gesture that doesn't explain anything and smiles in a way that makes the muscles around his mouth ache. He looks at the goats, looks at Mirta again; he says, "Because I liked you."

"What does that mean?" says Mirta.

"That I found you beautiful," says Arturo, his face burning.

"That's all?" says Mirta.

"Plus everything else I told you before," says Arturo. "Speaking of the girl in the painting."

Mirta smiles, but in a manner different from before, and only for a moment. Immediately afterward she punches him in the stomach with all the strength of her very strong right arm.

Arturo lets out a kind of yelp. Feeling all the air being sucked out of his lungs, he doubles up, then tries to get his breath back. "Are you crazy? That hurt!"

"Really?" says Mirta. "I didn't know you were so frail." She doesn't seem to be poking fun at him; she sounds genuinely surprised.

"I'm not frail at all," says Arturo, trying to get over the shock quickly, straightening up, returning to a normal expression. He musters all his sportsman's resources; in a few seconds he can even smile.

Mirta smiles, too. "Thank goodness." Then she springs to her feet, grabs him by a hand and pulls him up, dragging him toward a thicket further up the hill.

Arturo lets her drag him, feeling there a time lag between these events and his reactions.

A lessio circles around Arup who lines up the shock absorber pieces on the worktable and runs his hand over them, as if this were a way to put everything back in its place.

Alessio says, "You were good with those drums, last night." To be honest, his memories of last night are shrouded in a thick fog, but he can still hear the pulsating rhythm in his ears.

"They're called a tabla," says Arup.

"Ah, tabla, tabla," says Alessio, the name fascinating him, and at the same time making him feel a little less at ease.

"It was my job, before," says Arup.

"Really?" says Alessio, leaning forward on his Y-shaped sticks.

"Uh-huh," says Arup; studying the shock absorber's spring closely under the light of an oil lamp.

Alessio says, "How come, with all the things you can do, you are holed up in this place out here?"

"Because I like it," says Arup.

"Okay," says Alessio. "Okay, okay." He gets a reckless kick out of talking to this wild, ultraradical, non-European, lawless squatter who should hate him but for some mysterious reason has fixed his broken leg and now even wants to repair his minivan. It's the kind of feeling he experienced as a child at the circus, when he saw a lion tamer stick his head into a lion's mouth, with a big smile on his face.

Arup puts the spring back on the table, examining with equal attention the metal cylinder casing.

Alessio smiles like the lion tamer of his childhood. "Didn't it ever occur to you that if you lived in a city you could play in a band, cut some CDs, make a bit of money?"

Arup says, "I've done that already. I've played for years."

"Didn't you like it?" says Alessio. It's strange, because now he feels perfectly clearheaded, while just a second ago he might as well have been on Mars.

"I liked it while I was playing," says Arup. "But not always, even then. It depended on where I played, and with whom. In any case I was never in a situation that I liked all the time. There were individual moments I enjoyed, but until I found another one, I had to endure a lot of others I didn't like at all."

"Whereas here . . . ?" says Alessio. Saying "here" is enough to make his clearheadedness vanish again, like in a broken DVD where the image freezes and breaks down into a myriad of pixel fragments.

"Whereas here it's the *whole* I like," says Arup.

"The whole?" says Alessio, without the slightest idea of what he means.

Arup nods his head.

"Okay," says Alessio. This, on the contrary, is a word that reassures him. He enjoys repeating it—"okay, okay, okay"—feeling that the world gets recognizable again before his eyes. He would make the sign with his thumb and index finger, too, if he didn't have to hold on to his walking sticks.

Arup says, "What about you?"

"What about me?" says Alessio. He makes a quarter turn to the left, and then to the right.

"Do you like everything in your life?" says Arup. He has these

~ 241 ~

delicate, tensionless features; it's hard to tell whether he's thirty or forty, or more.

"Yes," says Alessio. Now his head is clear again, and he realizes he's not in the best of shape. The thought depresses him.

"Really, everything?" says Arup, his eyes shining as if it were a trick question.

Alessio nods. He feels a slightly aggressive instinct cropping up, but it's a defensive impulse against whatever might be behind Arup's question. He says, "Well, I've done quite a lot of nice things, in the ten years you've been living here."

"Like what?" says Arup, with an otherworldly calmness that confuses Alessio all over again.

Alessio moves his eyes as if to look into a mental rearview mirror where things appear to him clearly defined; he says, "Let me see . . . I sold fifty-one apartments, twenty-three office spaces, nineteen country houses." These numbers pop up with a surprising sort of autonomy, before he can actually think of them, dragging whole chunks of his life behind them through the fog that shrouds him intermittently.

"And besides the selling?" says Arup.

Alessio hesitates on the meaning of "besides"; he says, "I've made heaps of money, I invested it in the stock exchange and it went up substantially."

"Yes?" says Arup.

"Oh, yes," says Alessio. Whole ready-made sentences form in his mind, not requiring any effort or thought. "You missed it, out here. Okay, you also missed the bursting of the bubble and 9/11 and the recession and all that. But since then it's been steadily climbing for quite some time because the economy always goes in cycles—the stock exchange goes up and then comes down and then goes up again, so all you have to know is when to get in or out of it. Bear-bull, bull-bear, it's all like that."

"Bear-bull?" says Arup, gently shaking his head.

"Bear-bull," says Alessio. "Bull-bear-bull, bull-bear-bull-bear-bull-bear." He finds it no longer easy to connect a meaning to these sounds.

"And besides the bulls and bears?" says Arup. "What other nice things have you done?"

Alessio struggles to recall a sequence, in the same way in which he usually can recall a phone number. "I convinced my mother to sell her house in Usmate and I made her buy a hundred-and-twenty-square-meter apartment in Milan for the price of an eighty-meter one. Close to viale Piave, fourth floor with a lift, nineteen-fifties building in need, of course, of renovation. In the last four years its value has already gone up by thirty-five percent."

Arup puts the shock absorber cylinder down. "And you went to live there with your mother?"

"Absolutely," says Alessio, with a sudden longing for the absolute and for his mother. "Why should I throw money away living alone and eating frozen food and having to clean things up and anyway having to bring my laundry bag to my mother once a week?"

Arup slants his head. "And then?"

Alessio rattles on automatically, a name evoking a shape evoking a price evoking a shop evoking an acquisition. He says, "I made myself a king's bathroom and bedroom, with a wardrobe filled with so many Armani and Versace and Hugo Boss clothes they don't fit into it anymore, a NASA-tested mattress with the self-adapting micro-springs, a forty-two-inch Panasonic plasma TV set with 5.1 Dolby surround system, an authentic Jacuzzi bathtub, a Super Howitzer multifilter tanning station with all the EEC certifications."

"Those are things you *bought*," says Arup. "What are the nice things you *did*?"

Alessio suspects that the Indian is now taking advantage of his miraculous healer's position to X-ray his life and prove some kind of thesis, even though it's not yet clear which one. But if he thinks about what he says too much, the words and their meanings tend to dissolve in his head. To make them stay whole he says, "Holidays in Riccione, Ibiza, Formentera, Malindi, the Seichelles. Four soccer world championships, three America's Cups, three Olympic games. The best discos on the Adriatic and in the Balearics, I don't know how many restaurants in the Michelin guide. Five girlfriends, two generations of Playstation, two generations of Volkswagen Rabbits, three generations of 3-series BMWs, five generations of personal computers, six generations of cell phones."

"Wow," says Arup: it's not clear whether impressed or frightened or what.

Alessio would like this seemingly unstoppable current to carry him on, but he suddenly gets stuck on the echo of "six," just as the minivan got stuck in the ditch: the sound breaking the circuit and preventing other names and numbers from running on, dissolving all contours.

"You did quite a lot of nice things," say Arup.

Alessio looks at him, not understanding what language he speaks or where he comes from. He looks at the shock absorber parts on the table, and they look like unidentifiable objects from outer space. He feels uncontrollably tossed between contrasting concepts: precise-vague, pleasant-unpleasant, safe-dangerous, close-far, his-nobody's. He struggles to redirect his thoughts toward some indisputable mental image, but he doesn't seem to have any anymore. He sniffs the air in fear, he looks at the walls' stones and the roof's beams, at the shiny and opaque and rusty tools, at the hooks and shelves, at the variously shaped containers: they all have the same meaningless coating. He tries to say "okay" again, but for some reason it doesn't work anymore, and this fills him with even more dread.

Luisa walks up to the horses' paddock with a feigned, absent-minded gait, as if she was conveyed there by the undulations of the ground rather then by her own will. This doesn't prevent her from feeling stiff, with too many sweaters under her too tight Scottish tweed sports jacket. She thinks that her extreme care for detail is embarrassing in this context: from the cleanliness of her suede lace boots to the neat creases in her hazelnut velvet trousers, to her inability to move in any kind of situation without feeling the implacable judgment of the world upon her. She's only too aware of how formal her way of walking must actually appear. It must betray the paralyzing self-consciousness behind her every gesture.

In the paddock there's a saddled horse standing very still, eyes half closed. The black dog springs out of the small wooden shed and comes to sniff at Luisa's crotch. Embarrassed, she says "Stop it," pushing it away, looking around.

Lauro comes out of the shed, a saddle and reins in his hands. He puts them down on the ground, barely looking at Luisa. Then he takes another horse by its noseband and puts an old, faded green saddlecloth on its back.

Luisa nods to him: a wooden gesture; she hates it.

Lauro apparently doesn't notice it; he puts down the worn, flattened-out saddle on the saddlecloth, adjusting it with a few

well-tested gestures, tightening the girth. The horse seems trust-
ful, it doesn't move. Lauro says, "How is your husband?"

"Fine, I believe," says Luisa, dryly. She turns and checks the corners of her eyes with a fingertip, because she's not sure of having
washed her face properly with the pump's cold water and because
she hasn't looked at herself in a mirror since yesterday.

Lauro says, "We're really two kindred spirits, me and him."

Luisa thinks that she probably should either defend her husband or laugh, but instead she says, "I'm sorry for yesterday
evening. Sometimes he manages to be intolerable, I know."

Lauro doesn't comment. He finishes putting the bit on the second horse.

Luisa says, "Why did you saddle up two horses?"

"To go for a ride with you," says Lauro.

Luisa doesn't understand if this is a joke or a real proposal; in
doubt she takes a step back, smiling uncertainly.

"So?" says Lauro, patting the saddle.

Now Luisa is acutely aware of having a totally out-of-place
hairstyle, a stupidly straight nose, cheekbones that are too high;
she feels like an expensively dressed dried female cod. She says,
"What do you mean?"

"So?" says Lauro. His stares and smiles at her, with an insistence that could be shy or curious or brutal or perhaps just
unknown.

When Luisa was a little girl she never played with this kind of
boy, because they both frightened and attracted her. She says,
"How did you know that I would come here?"

"I saw you," says Lauro.

Luisa turns away in embarrassment. She gestures toward the
woods, saying, "Isn't it dangerous, with those armed people
around?"

Lauro shrugs his shoulders. "Everything is dangerous."

"That's not true," says Luisa, too quickly. "Not everything."

"*Almost* everything, then," says Lauro. "Everything that is worth doing, anyway."

Luisa wonders whether this is just a witticism in his slightly naïve, outlaw style, or whether it could simply be true. She considers a possible ironic answer, but at the same time it all seems like a childish skirmish to her, so she doesn't say anything.

Lauro says, "Are you mounting or not?"

Luisa says, "I can't ride." But immediately afterward she steps under the wooden fence, reducing the distance between them more than she actually intended to.

"Try," says Lauro. He makes her move closer to one of the horses, bends down to pick up her left foot at the ankle.

Luisa lets him do it only because she's too surprised to react in time. She puts her foot in the stirrup, feeling intolerably slow and awkward.

"Good," says Lauro, taking her left hand and putting it on the horse's mane.

Luisa feels a shiver from this unexpected touch. It mixes with her embarrassment and with her resistance, making her even more self-conscious. She says, "The only time I tried riding was when I was eleven, and according to the riding-master I didn't show any kind of aptitude."

"He must have been an idiot, for sure," says Lauro. Then, before she realizes what he's doing, he puts a hand under her bottom and pushes her up and onto the saddle.

"Hey!" says Luisa indignantly, struggling to find a balance, frightened by the sudden height and by the horse apparently shying away.

Lauro laughs, but whether out of innocent amusement or for

the sadistic pleasure of humiliating a Milanese editor in the wild countryside, it's not clear. He puts the reins into her hands, presses her fingers on the leather strap, then walks around the horse and adjusts her right foot in the stirrup, pushing her heel downward. These are competent gestures that take only the necessary time, but all the same they generate quick chains of feelings, rapid, conflicting thoughts.

Luisa acts as if the extremities of her body didn't overly concern her, trying hard to correspond to the pictures of horsewomen she's seen in books and museums. But she doesn't have enough data upon which to find a posture, and on top of that her horse keeps jolting sideways. She says, "What is he doing? Hey! Stop it!"

"Don't worry," says Lauro, without even looking at her. "Just relax."

"But he's too high-strung!" says Luisa. "He's trembling all over!"

"It's a she," says Lauro. "Her name's Frieda. All you need to do is show her you're in control."

"But I'm not!" says Luisa, looking at the ground from her all too vertical perspective, squeezing her legs as much as she can around the horse's restless sides.

"It's good if you know it," says Lauro. He jumps on his horse and comes up alongside her, leaning over to adjust the reins in her hands. Then he immediately moves off, past the unsaddled horses.

"Wait!" says Luisa. She tries to pull the reins but to no effect, as her horse starts to follow Lauro's.

Lauro rides up to a gate in the paddock, leans on one side to unlatch it without dismounting.

Luisa has a feeling of increasing precariousness. She says,

"Please let me get off!" But her horse follows Lauro's through the open gate, making her right leg brush against the wooden stake, and leaves the paddock.

Lauro turns his horse around, goes back to close the gate again. The black dog follows him; he says "No, you stay here." The dog lowers its head and puts its tail between its legs, trotting off toward the houses. Lauro glances at Luisa to check on her and spurs his horse, setting it to a trot.

Luisa's horse springs forward on the rolling ground, making her bounce on the saddle, without anything to grab onto safely or any way to check the horse's speed or direction. She feels certain she'll fall at any time now. She cries out, "Hey! Stop! Make it stop!"

Lauro doesn't listen to her, he doesn't turn. The two horses trot at a brisk pace, one after the other across the small plateau, the group of houses slipping by to the left.

Luisa hasn't been so scared since she was a child. She clings to the saddle with one hand and to the reins with the other but it doesn't help much. She bangs her bottom, gets unbalanced on one side and then on the other, the pounding reverberating through her bones as her horse frantically moves its legs and back to catch up with Lauro's.

Lauro finally turns. He laughs and shouts, "Don't be so stiff! Try and feel the rhythm!"

"What rhythm?" shouts Luisa, all the muscles in her body tensing spasmodically, her head flooded with alarm signals to the point of excluding any other thought.

"The *rhythm*!" shouts Lauro.

Luisa shouts, "I'm scared!" She sees the ground slipping too fast underneath her, anticipating the violence of the impact, the pain and the humiliation, the very likely permanent damages.

"Just relax, keep flexible!" shouts Lauro, in an unconceivably cheerful tone.

"Like hell I'll relax!" shouts Luisa. Now she has no more doubts about the fact that he has intentionally put her into this situation to mortify her and ridicule everything she represents to him. The thought fills her with so much fury, it takes all her effort to not let him get his way: she holds onto the reins and tightens her knees, trying to find a better posture and slow down her breathing, recovering at least a little bit of her ability to think logically and coherently.

Lauro digs his heels into his horse's sides, making it break into an even faster and more alarming motion.

Luisa's horse does the same, in its obsessive determination not to be outdistanced by more than a couple of meters. Luisa feels she's being jerked forward with an impulse that's impossible to resist, the clearing and the woods and the hills dissolving around her in colored waves and stripes, the wind blowing into her ears and making her eyes water.

Lauro turns and shouts, "Is it better?"

Luisa doesn't answer, even though she'd like to shout at him all the worst insults she can think of. She is right to think that to fall off now wouldn't mean just getting hurt, it would most probably get her killed, and this overlays her fear and anger with an unexpected kind of detachment. It seems to her like a clear-cut and rather noble way to get rid of everything that tires and depresses and bores her in life—all the commitments and duties and responsibilities and ambitions and expectations and pressures and demands and personal limitations and defects and professional roles, the delays and repetitions, the chains of disappointments. She feels like she can look at herself objectively with even a subtle thread of humor, as she bounces and jolts through the landscape rushing by.

It's the same sensation she had when as a small girl vacationing at the seaside she would speed on her bicycle down a steep asphalted road with other children, thinking that each time could be her last.

Then all of a sudden Lauro is turning his horse and waving his arms so as to block Luisa's horse, until after some shying off and jerking and snorting and quivering both horses are moving at a walking pace.

It takes Luisa a few seconds to register the transition, her detachment turning into fear and fear into anger, anger into relief and relief into anger again. Her cheeks and ears feel frozen, her eyes are full of tears, her wrists and knees are trembling, her lungs are burning, her heart beats frantically.

"Everything all right?" says Lauro. His face looks serious, but here, too, it's hard to tell whether he's really concerned or just looking for another way to mortify her.

"Perfectly all right," says Luisa. She breathes in with her nose, struggling to assume an indifferent air even though she realizes it's almost impossible in so little time.

Lauro says, "Please forgive me. I'm sorry."

"Don't mention it," says Luisa, all her muscles and nerves still overrun with survival impulses, her brain overloaded with disjointed thoughts and feelings.

Lauro dismounts with a jump, and comes over to take her reins. "Really," he says, "I've behaved like a fool. You could have hurt yourself."

Luisa would gladly kick him, now that she's in the right position to do it; but in the coldest tone she can muster she says, "After all, this was supposed to be a demonstration of how *everything* is dangerous, wasn't it?"

"*No*," says Lauro. "It wasn't supposed to be anything. I just let it get out of hand."

Margherita walks into the room where she has spent two dreadful nights, and looks around. On the floor and on the straw mattresses is a confusion of blankets and pillows, dirty clothes, open suitcases. She rummages into hers, takes off her clothes, puts on fresh ones. She takes her hand-mirror out of her beauty-case, looks at her face in sections: left eye, right eye, left eyebrow, right eyebrow, nose, lips, chin. She takes out a salmon-pink lipstick and applies it to her lips with all the care she's capable of; then she takes out the brush, tries to fix her hair a little. There isn't much she can do: she feels dirty, with heavy hair and mangled feet, even her fresh clothes smelling of must and boiled vegetables. There's someone opening the door; she spins round, saying "Who is it?" in a shrill voice.

Aria peeks in, an embarrassed expression on her face. She enters and walks over to Margherita, handing her Margherita's Mp3 player. She says, "I broke it. I'm sorry."

"So that's why I couldn't find it anymore," says Margherita. She tries to hide the annoyance that instantly wells up inside her, but without really succeeding, because a top network manager gave the thing to her as a gift only a couple of weeks ago and it was important to her. She turns it over in her hands, feeling the sense of irreparable loss that overcomes her whenever she finds one of her possessions damaged or even just worn out by use. In a blind attempt, she takes two spare batteries from her suitcase and substitutes the old ones: the little display lights up at once.

"I'm sorry," Aria says again. She seems crushed.

Margherita says, "Come on, it's not so bad," her feeling of loss slowly fading. "You just drained the batteries, that's all." She smiles, as if to suggest that it wouldn't have been so bad even if she had in fact broken it, which is light-years away from the truth.

Aria has the attitude of a guilty puppy: downcast eyes, bent head. She says, "I just wanted to listen to the music. I know I should have asked you."

Margherita's facial muscles relax, letting a magnanimous expression surface. She knows perfectly well that her possessive relationship with objects dates back to her early childhood, when her younger sister systematically stole every puppet and illustrated book from her, along with their parents' attention. She must have gone over this with her analyst a thousand times, but she knows by now that identifying a knot and untying it are two entirely different matters. Right now she can't forget that her role as a TV host requires her to adopt a form of generalized amiability—unless, that is, she's dealing with unbearable boors like Alessio or Lauro—so she smiles and says, "Did you like the music?"

"Yes," says Aria, a little unconvincingly. "It just hurt my ears a little bit."

Margherita says, "You must have set the volume to the max, you blessed creature. That's how you drained the batteries." She observes her closely: a kind of young girl very unlike the ones who audition for her show. In all probability, no more than two or three of her kind must exist in the whole of Italy, provided there are other middle-of-nowhere places like this one.

A sudden flicker appears in Aria's eyes. She says, "Would you like to see my room?"

"Sure," says Margherita, in a simulation of enthusiasm that clicks in like a conditioned reflex.

Aria walks quickly to the door, turning to wait for her before going down the stairs.

Mirta pushes Arturo to the ground and covers him with her hair: pressing lips to lips and tongue to tongue and forehead to forehead, hot and heavy and insistent, with her smoky herbal smell, clinging to him with her strong arms and legs.

Arturo tries to lift his head enough to get a better look at her, but she pushes him back against the grass, pressing him even more strongly. He thinks he would need some perspective to be able to find the right response to Mirta's aggression and her movements, and to the sense of alarm caused by the isolation of this spot and to the arousal he feels. He struggles to meet the kisses and the touch and the caresses that displace clothing and generate heat, but his thoughts lag behind his feelings, and his feelings behind facts. He makes a half-hearted attempt at turning Mirta over, and strangely he succeeds almost at once. She rolls onto her back, looking up at him with dilated pupils, half-closed lips, reddened cheeks. Arturo lies on top of her, wavering between attraction and anxiety, with a leg between her legs, doubts and hesitations and fears hammering at him, until she gets tired of waiting and upturns him again and presses against him with even more impetuousness than before. She kisses him on the mouth and neck and ears, fumbles with his loose jacket and shirt and with the strip of cloth that holds his trousers up, sliding a hand in, brushing his skin.

Arturo says, "Wait a second," and tries to stop her, but there's not enough space between their bodies and she doesn't listen to him at all, her mouth and fingers getting more insistent as he struggles like a predator astonished by the sudden possibility he's turned into prey.

Mirta stops, lifting her head with a perplexed expression. "What's wrong?"

"Nothing," says Arturo. He slides back a little, propping himself up on his elbows.

"Don't you like me?" says Mirta, her hand retracting through layers of cloth.

"I do like you," says Arturo. "Of course I do. It's just that I'd need a little time."

"For what?" says Mirta. She looks disappointed, confused.

"To talk a little," says Arturo, fastening his trousers.

"About what?" says Mirta, tilting her head to one side.

"About us," says Arturo. "About this. About why we are here."

Mirta shakes her head slowly; her pupils are contracting.

"Just to understand what's happening," says Arturo, suddenly afraid that, in fact, things have already stopped happening. He's filled with disappointment, at himself and at his reactions; he feels slow and overcomplicated, unable to face the spontaneous unpredictability of natural life.

Mirta looks away, running her fingers through her curls.

Like a very careful instrument, Arturo is able to sense her breath normalizing and her body heat decreasing, her energy being reabsorbed after her frustrated rush. The distance between them seems to increase by the second, now that he's managed to thwart the desire for contact and the instinct for exploration that brought them so close with such intensity only a few minutes before. He sees himself already standing, stretching his lips into a weak smile and nodding toward the houses, walking out of the thicket, pointlessly concentrating on the style of his gait.

Mirta says, "It's okay," and takes a blade of grass out of her hair.

"No, it's not," says Arturo. Probably she is seeing him like she did in the beginning: the city schmuck who goes to the country. He thinks that he's always gone wrong with women, even when they shared the same background; there's no reason why it should be any different with someone who lives with a group of back-to-nature nutcases. He feels relief mix with disappointment, along with a sad, somber wish for order and normality.

"You needn't worry, anyway," says Mirta. She gets up, brushing her clothes energetically with her hands.

Arturo does the same, in a kind of absurd, symmetrical pantomime. He's so ill at ease that he'd like to run away as fast as he can; but a moment later he turns and bumps into her and looks into her eyes at zero distance, and he feels an incredibly taut spring going off in some ancient hidden part of his being, making him grab her by the arms and pull her close and kiss her savagely and push her back to the ground and hold her wrists with one hand and wildly caress her hair and neck and hips with the other and then slide it up her skirt, looking at her and sniffing her and breathing against her so closely and frantically that his thoughts and feelings and motions overlap and melt into one another. Now she is putting up a resistance that's not a real attempt to defend herself, it's part of a furious muscular and mental play inviting him to squeeze her and press her with all his weight and strength and might, his hand climbing up between her strong smooth thighs, toward the humid warmth that's kept inside them. This is not the circumscribed, localized attraction he's experienced before with other women—it's a torrent that comes in a flood, that can't

~ 258 ~

be stopped or analyzed or even observed, hurling him about without leaving space or time for a single breath or reflection or consideration or name. He feels swept back to the origins of the world, pulled under by the current, kicking and grabbing on to Mirta's curls, stretching out between her arms and legs, penetrating the elastic tension of her feminine essence with a pressing, panting, pulsating urgency of possession and communion which he certainly has never before experienced and yet is utterly innate to him. She pushes against him and pulls back and pushes again with an intensity that increases and increases as if it could go on forever and instead suddenly breaks into a breath that wells up from deep within her and turns into a scream that turns into a shudder that shakes her through and through and makes her tighten her thighs and makes Arturo leap forward in a spasm that transports his feelings beyond the fusion of their bodies and extends to the firm damp ground to the thicket of trees to the open space of the small plateau to the surrounding woods to the white light charged with energy surging from down below.

Margherita limps after Aria across the backyard, toward the tower where she had dreamed of spending enchanting weekends of regenerating rest. Now she looks at the gray stone building with its narrow windows and she feels stupid, betrayed by reality.

"Your room's in here?" she says, a little dismayed by the rubble in the entrance and by the steepness of the stairs.

"Dad's, too," says Aria, starting to climb the unstable steps. She goes up two, three, four flights of stairs like a young goat, Margherita panting behind her. At last she stops in front of a door and opens it, letting Margherita in and closing it again with a strange latch.

Margherita breathes heavily; she thinks that she should definitely give up smoking, provided she's not forced to do it by an absence of cigarettes. She glances at the low bed in a corner, the Indian or African fabrics, the irregular, homemade furniture, the brightly colored drawings hanging on the walls. When she looks at these up close, she sees that they all depict city scenes: skyscrapers, cars, shops, crowded sidewalks, streetlights, billboards, signs, as if from a visiting extraterrestrial's point of view. She asks, "Who made these?"

"I did," says Aria, averting her eyes.

"You're good," says Margherita. This is not merely to get in the girl's good graces; she's truly impressed, both by the choice of subjects and by the expressive strength through which they are represented.

Aria now stares at her with a kind of intensity similar to her father's, albeit a less disquieting version.

Margherita says, "Seriously. I wouldn't have expected it, from someone who grew up out here."

Aria nods her head, thoughtfully.

It occurs to Margherita that, as in any power game, she shouldn't overdo it with flattery. She walks along the wall, pointing to some drawings which are more difficult to decipher. She says, "What are these about?"

"Traps," says Aria.

"Traps?" says Margherita. "You mean, to catch animals?"

Aria shakes her head. "To catch cars."

"You mean, traps for *cars*?" says Margherita. She realizes she's definitely slower than usual, even though this is entirely justified by the fatigue and the stress and the intolerable level of hardships she's had to endure.

Aria says, "We invent new ones all the time, of every kind."

"And then you actually set them up?" says Margherita.

"Yes," says Aria. "Along the road and the paths that lead here."

Margherita says, "You mean to say that the ditch we ended up in with our minivan was in fact one of your traps?"

Aria laughs. "Me and Mirta dug it up. Then we put branches and leaves and earth on top of it, so it was practically invisible."

"You sure fooled us," says Margherita, struggling to restrain an impulse to grab her and give her the good spanking she deserved.

Instead of showing contrition, Aria seems proud. "It's based on the same principle as the traps the bushman set in southern

Africa. Except, of course, they dig much bigger holes for elephants, and put a lot of sharpened poles on the bottom."

"Sure," says Margherita, with a thin-lipped smile. "In our case it's just as well you didn't include the sharpened poles."

"Yes," says Aria, gnawing on her thumb.

Margherita says, "So that poor idiot Alessio was right, when he kept repeating that the ditch wasn't there." She laughs, but only about Alessio and only for a moment; as for the rest, she's simply appalled by the apparently unwitting delinquent tendencies of the people that hold her hostage.

"Yes," says Aria. "It was very well made, he could never have seen it."

Margherita continues her exercise in self-control. In a simulated indulgent tone she says, "You sure are crazy, all of you. I bet it was your father who taught you how to build traps."

"Yes," says Aria. "But Arup is also very good at inventing them. Mirta, too. Once she made a trap with a fine iron net she had found in a field. She set it up down on the road, near the crossroads. It was January, so even from a few steps it looked like some bluish fog. A huge tractor drove right over it, and the net got all stuck in its giant wheels and gears, *straaaak*, like that. We watched it from the woods, then we ran as fast as we could."

Margherita thinks they should all be locked up in some kind of institution. She says, "Now I understand why you don't have a great relationship with your neighbors."

"It was them who started it," says Aria. "All we did was react."

Margherita looks out of the window. "Do you get along well with your father?"

"It depends," says Aria. "Sometimes I do, sometimes I don't."

Margherita says, "A while ago he was unbelievably rude to me." Only to talk about it renews her humiliation, making her voice tremble with feelings of revenge.

Aria apparently feels no need to come to the defense of her father. All she says is, "He can be difficult, every now and then."

"Difficult is a bit of a euphemism," says Margherita. "You've got a daughter's heart, really."

Aria stands on tiptoe to swing a little wooden bird that hangs from a ceiling beam. "When I was small he was more good-natured. He was always making up new games. Once he built me a tree house."

"And your mother?" says Margherita.

Aria stares at her, perplexed.

"What did she do?" says Margherita. "Besides living here and being with your father?"

"She paints," says Aria, striving to look nonchalant.

"Ah, that's who you got it from," says Margherita. She thinks that the only thing she's really mastered in her job in television is her ability to make people talk about things they would prefer to keep to themselves. "How was it, between her and your father?"

Aria says, "I don't know."

"But you must have *seen* something," says Margherita, "or heard something."

Aria says, "Dad once said that with her he felt cut out of all of life's surprises."

"Wow, that's pretty tough," says Margherita. "Always the gentleman, eh?"

Aria shrugs. "That's the way he is. He can't stand the idea of *having* to do something. He does a lot of things, but only if it's from his own free choice."

"That's very original, for a man," says Margherita, in a sarcastic tone that is certainly wasted here. "Believe me, I never heard it before."

Aria looks at her without understanding. "He's occupied with

~ 263 ~

a lot of things: us, the houses, the animals, the trees, the water, the roads they want to enlarge."

"They who?" says Margherita.

"The others," says Aria. "The rest of the world."

"Tell me the truth," says Margherita, lowering her voice a little. "Between me and you, now that nobody is listening. Don't you think it's a slightly paranoid vision? Windshift against the rest of the world?"

"Yeah, a little," says Aria.

Margherita points to the drawings on the walls. "Wouldn't you like to go and see it with your own eyes—the rest of the world beyond Turigi? To form your own idea of it?"

"Yes," says Aria.

Margherita sees this as a small victory, even though it doesn't compensate her for what she's gone through recently. She says, "Well, in a couple of years you'll be in a position to decide for yourself, won't you?"

"Yes," says Aria, in a doubtful, or perhaps dreamy tone.

Margherita says, "You could maybe enroll in an art school, spend time with kids your age, broaden your horizons."

Aria says, "What I'd really like to do is be an actress."

"Really?" says Margherita.

Aria nods her head, her expression wavering between absolute naivety and obstinate willfulness.

Margherita says, "It's a pretty tough job, huh."

"How's that?" says Aria.

Margherita makes a vague gesture. "It's like a big market crowded with truly ugly people, bustling about all the time with their monkey faces and dog faces and snake faces and kitty faces, talking and talking and talking ceaselessly about themselves."

"And you?" says Aria.

"I don't do too badly," says Margherita, irritated at the idea of being dragged into the picture.

"Yes?" says Aria, studying her face.

"Uh-huh," says Margherita. "You need to have a pretty high level of self-esteem if you want to give it a try. And it doesn't do you much good, either. The thing is, you have to convince yourself you're the center of the world. You have to spend hours in front of a mirror, always keep your telephone at hand. You have to have a lot of close friends who aren't really friends at all."

Aria lowers her head, but she doesn't seem to be put off at all. "I want to try it all the same."

"Of course," says Margherita. "Who doesn't?"

"I know," says Aria, without looking at her.

Margherita doesn't know whether to feel bitter or wiser or simply more realistic; come to think of it, it's been quite a while since she last gave someone advice without the motive of provoking a response to entertain her TV audience.

Lauro leads the two horses by their reins down to a little stream. Luisa follows him, so full of resentment that she'd rather walk all the way back to the houses, if she weren't afraid to run into the snipers. She takes off her glasses to dry the tears caused by the wind and by tension; she doesn't put them back on, sticks them into a pocket.

Lauro lets the two horses drink from the stream, then ties their reins to some low branches. He walks along the narrow bank, as though he was sure that she would follow him, at least with her gaze.

Luisa realizes this and stops, looking at the water that runs over a succession of shallow stone pools. There are some tall poplar trees and a couple of ancient oaks, smaller elms, a weeping willow, and thickets of reeds by the water. But it's only a thin feeder of some bigger stream, and winter is beginning to spoil the vegetation; she can't see anything charming in this scenery.

"It's not really a river," says Lauro, "but in summer you can swim in it. The water warms up over those flat stones, so you can stay in for hours."

"Really," says Luisa flatly, without even the courtesy of an interrogative inflection.

"Yes," says Lauro. "Downstream from here there are a couple of bigger pools where you can actually swim a few strokes. Every now and then some little fish come and nip at your legs."

"How wonderful," says Luisa, in a tone intended to reflect her detachment.

Lauro turns around and says, "Do you really like it?"

"Very much," says Luisa; she can't believe he's unaware of the distance between them.

He looks around, then turns toward her again, with a totally different expression from just a minute ago.

She expects him to make an attempt to get her to ask him a question, so she keeps silent, pressing her hands into the pockets of her tweed sports jacket. She wonders whether she should put her glasses back on to feel less exposed, but she leaves them where they are.

Lauro gestures toward the sloping meadow they have descended. "This isn't what we had originally imagined when we came here, ten years ago."

Luisa looks at the running water, biting her lower lip.

He says, "The idea wasn't only to hole up somewhere and survive."

"What was it, then?" says Luisa, just to hasten the end of their conversation.

"There were a thousand different things we wanted to do," says Lauro.

Luisa's lips spread into a cold, thin smile, but in fact she's caught a bit off guard by the sudden vulnerability of his words. Is this a calculated effect on his part, or is he sincere? "Such as what?" she asks.

Lauro says, "Like playing music, painting. Growing all kinds of plants, raising every species of animals. Sculpting wood and stone. Printing books. Or writing them by hand, in just one copy. Digging den-houses in the earth, covered with grass, with hidden skylights. Building houses on treetops. Building a *whole village* on treetops. Having people come here from all over the world. Talking in ten different languages. Making up a language *of our own*. Creating endless surprises, without ever letting ourselves be overwhelmed by the weight of things as they are."

"Like in an illustrated fairy tale," says Luisa. In her opinion, he hasn't the slightest idea of how sharp and hard and cutting she can be when she wants to be—enough to put in their place some international writers with egos even more raging than his.

Lauro shakes his head. "Like in a dream come true."

Luisa continues to wonder whether he's being pathetic on purpose, to win her sympathy. "You had a really nice plan, anyway," she says.

He keeps wearing a disarmed expression. "But it *can* be done, making a dream come true. You just have to believe in it, and go on believing in it."

Luisa smiles as she would to an overbearing and ingenuous child. Still, even though she wouldn't admit it, a part of her is touched by the feelings that seem to run through his voice. She thinks of all the things she has dreamed about in her life: of what she has imagined, what she has expected, and what has actually happened. She says, "So, how did it go?"

Lauro says, "Little by little we let ourselves be overwhelmed by the weight of things as they are. By the need, by the repetition. By the lack of surprises. We got into a closed circuit of gestures and feelings we already knew."

"Perhaps that's inevitable, don't you think?" says Luisa. It embarrasses her to put herself on his level, albeit with the protection of a detached look and accent. But she can't help asking herself whether there really is a way to get rid of the weight of necessity and repetition, to move instead into a territory where everything flows in a pure state and generates endless surprises.

She asks herself how long it would last, provided one could even get there.

Lauro says, "The inevitable was one of the first things we wanted to get rid of."

"Still, you've managed to do it, haven't you?" says Luisa. "At least in part."

"Which part?" says Lauro, as if he had no idea.

Luisa is unsure what kind of game they're playing, and who's playing which role. She says, "Well, you've rid yourselves of quite a few things that for most people are not exactly optional."

"Like what?" says Lauro.

"Like money, or timetables," says Luisa. "Transfers, job relationships, phone calls, dressing codes, accessories, social niceties, manners. Even *words*. If you could only see one of my average days, you'd know what I'm talking about."

"How is it, one of your average days?" Lauro looks at her with a disconcerting level of attention.

Luisa says, "I don't even want to think about it."

"Give me an idea," says Lauro pointedly. "Just an idea."

Luisa shrugs; she says, "A continuous zigzagging between a thousand things."

"A quick zigzagging?" says Lauro.

"At times," says Luisa. "At others, agonizingly slow."

"And these thousand things, are they interesting?" says Lauro.

Luisa doesn't know whether to answer or not. "Some of them are, some not at all."

"In what proportion?" says Lauro.

"I don't know," says Luisa. "I never thought about it."

"Think about it now," says Lauro.

"Fifty-fifty," says Luisa, careful not to let any communicative warmth reach the corners of her eyes or lips.

Lauro says, "But aside from that, do you actually *like* some of these things?"

"Of course I do," says Luisa.

"In what proportion to the ones you don't like?" asks Lauro.

Luisa thinks that she shouldn't have let him begin to ask questions. "What is it, this need of yours to renew your catalog of miseries of the civilized world?"

"No," says Lauro, looking perfectly serious. "I just want to know what's the proportion of the things you really like to the things you do only because you have to."

Luisa says, "I told you, I don't know."

"But you must know," says Lauro. "Don't you even have a vague idea?"

"I have a very vague idea," says Luisa, "but it's my own business, don't you think?"

"Of course," says Lauro, in a tone which at this point can only be either absurdly fake or absurdly authentic. "I was just asking."

Luisa looks at the water running by. What a minuscule stream, she thinks, as imperfect as the two horses they rode here on and as the small cultivated fields and as the vegetable garden and as the houses and as the community of survivors who live in them. This awareness produces inside her a strange mixture of detachment and compassion, freedom from Lauro's stare two steps away from her but also from the world's judging eye. It seems to her that she's already in an afterwards and in an elsewhere, far away from this moment—the discomfort and the embarrassment already filed away in her memory with the reflections on the water's surface and the rustling of the wind among the trees. She says, "It must be one to a hundred, the proportion. Perhaps one to a *thousand*. And even the things I like are probably substitutions of other things I don't have."

"For example?" says Lauro; he doesn't seem surprised by her words.

Luisa thinks about it; she says, "For example, I like working on a book that is written in a fascinating style and full of ideas. But I think I'd rather be in a *real* situation that gave me the same feelings, if I had a choice."

"Doesn't it ever happen?" says Lauro. "With your husband and your friends?"

"Hah!" says Luisa.

"*Never*?" says Lauro, with what now looks like a compassionate expression.

"Every once in a while," says Luisa, her embarrassment returning for a moment. "Provided you plan everything in advance and with great care, and you have the incredible luck of all the pieces fitting together."

"What do you mean, the pieces?" says Lauro.

Luisa says, "The spirit, the mood, the time, the intentions, the place, the people, the infinite essential coincidences, et cetera."

"And all this happens only once in a while?" says Lauro.

"Once in a while," says Luisa. She makes an effort to look at him only through the corner of her eyes, without facing him.

"How often is that?" says Lauro.

"I don't *know,*" says Luisa.

"More or less?" says Lauro.

"Not often," says Luisa. She'd like to end the conversation here and now, put a stop to it.

"I can tell that by the way you smile," says Lauro, pointing a small stick at her.

"Which way?" says Luisa, on the defensive.

"You have a controlled smile," says Lauro. "As if a part of you was keeping watch on the other part all the time, never letting it do what it would like to."

"It's not true," says Luisa, blushing a little. "How should I act, all exuberant and impulsive?"

~ 271 ~

Lauro laughs. "No, it would be enough if you got rid of your inner watchdog."

Luisa regrets having revealed herself to him on this point, but a part of her keeps trying to push herself to further revelations. Her facial muscles and nerves are almost hurting from her effort to contain herself.

"Well, as long as you're happy with things as they are," says Lauro.

Luisa says, "What gave you that idea?"

"It's your life, isn't it?" says Lauro.

"So what?" says Luisa, with some of the resentment she felt when she got off the horse.

Lauro says, "If you weren't happy with it you'd change it, wouldn't you?"

"With what?" says Luisa.

"With another life," says Lauro.

Out of sheer exasperation, Luisa laughs and says, "A life is like a face. Everybody would like to have a different one, at least every now and then. But you have the one you have, there's nothing you can do about it."

"You know that's not so," says Lauro. "You can have the face you want, if you have enough ideas and curiosity inside your head."

"What a stupid thing to say," says Luisa.

"But it's true," says Lauro.

"Oh, come on," says Luisa. "You can think like that when you're sixteen, perhaps. When you still don't have the slightest idea what life is like."

"Did you think like that?" says Lauro. "When you were sixteen?"

"Probably," says Luisa, quickly. "Like everybody."

"And what exactly did you think?" says Lauro.

Luisa looks at the tied horses grazing, with an impulse to walk right over to them and jump back on the saddle and gallop away before making any other stupid revelations. Instead she says, "I thought I could be a thousand different people."

Lauro smiles as if he'd just won a bet or proved a point, or as if he was glad for a more basic reason.

Luisa goes on all the same, saying, "I thought there was an unlimited variety of possible lives waiting for me to choose from. Each with its own ways, places, its own thousand possible details."

"Like what?" says Lauro.

"I don't know," says Luisa.

"Yes, you do," says Lauro. "Stop being reticent."

"I'm not being reticent," says Luisa, feeling her cheeks redden up even more.

"Be more specific, then," says Lauro.

Luisa looks at the trees on the other side of the stream. "I don't know, one day I thought I could be a dancer, the next day a scientist."

"Really?" says Lauro. He seems unaccountably moved by her words.

Luisa says, "Or an explorer, an actress, an adventuress, a nursery school teacher, a kept woman, a thief, a bank clerk, a housewife. I thought I could live in a thousand different houses, in a thousand different cities. With a thousand different men. I thought I could learn countless languages, adapt to any sort of climate. I thought I could have two or three or five children, or none at all, or be somebody's child instead."

"And then?" says Lauro.

"Then I grew up," says Luisa.

"And?" says Lauro.

"And I realized those were just immature ideas," says Luisa. "That real life is different."

"What is it?" says Lauro.

"It's what you have," says Luisa. "It's what you do. The people you know. The place you live in. The things you're familiar with."

"But it's not *true*," says Lauro, with sudden vehemence. "Life is what you imagine. It's what you want. What you *dream*. You only need to have the energy to discover it and to pursue it, without letting yourself be paralyzed by fear of being disappointed or judged or ridiculed by somebody else. Because we're not *this*, anyway."

"This what?" says Luisa, with a feeling of growing uncertainty.

"This," says Lauro: he beats a hand on his chest, on his legs. "Our bodies are just good temporary instruments, as long as they last. But it's ridiculous to think that we *are* our bodies, or faces, or names—to believe it to the point of being paralyzed by them."

"I'm not afraid," says Luisa, mostly because she doesn't know what else to say.

"Yes, you are," says Lauro.

"I'm not," says Luisa, furious over this exchange, and for how she doesn't know how to get out of it.

"You *are* afraid," says Lauro, "otherwise you'd change your life. You'd recognize that this one isn't what you dreamed about when you were sixteen and you'd change it. You'd try, at least."

"So how come *you* don't do it?" says Luisa, in an exasperated tone.

"I've already done it," says Lauro. "Years ago."

"But now you're again unhappy with your life," says Luisa.

"What do you know?" says Lauro.

"You said so," says Luisa.

"I didn't," says Lauro.

"Yes, you did," says Luisa. "You said this wasn't what you had imagined when you came to live here."

"It's not what I *originally* had in mind," says Lauro.

"So it isn't," says Luisa, unrelenting.

"Ah, stop it," says Lauro, turning his back to her. He picks up a small flat stone, makes it bounce off the surface of the little stream.

Luisa thinks that he's decidedly pathetic, but that she is, too—that neither of them is in a position to pass judgment on the other.

A ria toys with a small wooden object that looks like a spider. She asks Margherita, "I wanted to ask you, on *Crazy Stuff*, do the boy and the girl really kiss, when you send them into the love room?"

"It depends," says Margherita.

"On what?" says Aria, staring right into her eyes.

"On what types they are," says Margherita. "On what the plot is."

"The plot?" says Aria.

Margherita feels cold, she touches the three-layered New Zealand lamb's wool sweaters that a fashion designer gracefully tossed into a box for her last week. She says, "Me and the other authors decide what is going to happen. We write it down."

Aria says, "*Everything* that is going to happen?"

"More or less, yes," says Margherita, as if she was confessing to a crime by degrees to the jury of a naïve country that doesn't have the means to punish her anyway.

Aria says, "So it's not real, what you see? When for example the boy falls in love with the girl or the two of them have a fight or cry?"

"Well, it is real, but we plan it beforehand," says Margherita. "It's a bit like in a soap opera, okay? Except it's all done live, of course, and there are no professional actors."

Aria shakes her head in disbelief. "But you seem so surprised, when you get back in touch with them and find out what happened when they were in the love room all alone."

"That's part of the format," says Margherita. "It helps to emphasize the turning points and feed the attention of the audience at home."

Aria says, "It's a fraud, then."

"It's not a fraud, Aria," says Margherita. "It's television."

But the disappointment in Aria's eyes is so intense that Margherita feels welling up inside her the constant fear of betraying everybody's expectations. Of this, too, she's talked a thousand times with her analyst and her astrologer and her manicurist and her friends and boyfriends, but talking about it hasn't helped at all. She suddenly feels failed, shallow, fake, with a whole life of wrong choices behind her. She tries to find a way out, forward and backward. She says, "Did you know I was in avant-garde theater? The Electrical Penguin, have you heard of it?"

"No," says Aria, shaking her head.

"Don't worry, it's not because you live in such an out-of-the-way place," says Margherita. "We toured all over Italy for years, and at the most, a hundred people saw us."

"That's a lot, a hundred," says Aria.

Margherita laughs in an awful, raucous way. "Consider that now, even when I'm really doing badly, I have at least *four million* viewers. I gave my soul to the theater for eight years, and nobody ever recognized me in the streets. Then when the first episode of *Crazy Stuff* had barely gone on the air, *everybody* out there was stopping me and asking for my autograph. Even my concierge, who until then had simply hated me."

Aria looks at her uncertainly. "That's good, isn't it?"

"It depends," says Margherita.

"On what?" says Aria.

"On who you are," says Margherita. "At times I feel like I ended up in somebody else's life."

"And which life would yours be, instead?" says Aria.

"I don't know anymore," says Margherita. "Perhaps playing in half-empty theaters, doing some experimental and abstract and intense stuff that no one really understands and dining in terrible restaurants at one A.M. and returning alone to an ugly hotel room and smoking and touching myself under the covers thinking of some purely imaginary man."

Aria half closes her eyes and says, "I don't believe you. You don't really mean it."

Margherita nods her head. She feels like the whole game has gone totally sour: She can't find anything amusing in it anymore. Plus, she's shivering and she needs to pee. She says, "I want to go and see how Arup is doing with the minivan. I absolutely have to be back in Milan by tonight."

"Tonight?" says Aria, as if she had expected her to stay forever.

"Absolutely," says Margherita.

Aria puts her little wooden spider back on top of her home-made lopsided table, looking bereft.

Margherita walks to the door, then comes back. "Listen," she says, "don't tell Alessio about that trap on the road. Let's keep it between you and me, okay?"

"Okay," says Aria, nodding her head.

Margherita fumbles with the door latch, but it's too complicated and she can't make out how it works. Aria opens it for her, then looks at her quizzically as she limps down the steep stairs.

Arturo smoothes out the borrowed clothes he has on, leaning out of the thicket to look at the sloping meadow.

"What are you looking at?" says Mirta. Now she really looks like a forest woman, with her wild eyes and her flushed cheeks, her curly hair full of dry blades of grass and twigs.

Arturo says, "I just want to check how the goats are doing." He's overheated and hyperventilating, his temples are throbbing and his knees are burning. He feels shaken out of all the languages and feelings he's familiar with, and doesn't even know whether to feel euphoric or in the grip of some shapeless anxiety.

Mirta glances down the slope and says, "The goats are perfectly okay."

Arturo takes a leaf out of the collar of his loose jacket; he looks toward the woods behind them, then toward the houses. He says, "Are you sure it's okay to be so far away on our own? Without even having told the others?"

"They know where we are," says Mirta. "We keep an eye on each other all the time, here."

"You mean that even before . . ." says Arturo. He is about to lean out of the thicket again but he thinks better of it and he ducks back in.

"What is it?" says Mirta. "Are you ashamed of what's happened?"

"No," says Arturo, "but I thought it was a private thing. I didn't have any intention of sharing it with anybody else."

"Not even with me?" says Mirta.

Arturo laughs, but he's not entirely sure that she's joking. At this point, he isn't entirely sure of anything.

Mirta looks at him in her mysterious way, picking up non-verbal signals. She says, "If you feel uneasy, say so."

"Why should I feel uneasy?" says Arturo, uneasily.

"I don't know," says Mirta. "You have this perplexed attitude."

Arturo tries to laugh again, but he can't; he feels he's in a no-man's-land, lost in the ebb tide of the devouring, mad urge that swept over him only a few minutes before. He doesn't even know what she means by perplexed: weak, uncertain, unspontaneous, tied up, rigid? He says, "I'm surprised, not perplexed."

"Surprised by what?" says Mirta.

"By everything," says Arturo. "By you."

"Why so?" says Mirta.

"Because I'm not used to it," says Arturo.

"To what?" says Mirta.

Arturo picks a twig out of her hair, and just placing his hand near her gives him a shiver akin to fear. He says, "You're so instinctive."

"You mean rough," says Mirta.

"No, no," says Arturo. "You're the first truly natural woman I've met in my entire life."

"You mean I have a goatish smell?" says Mirta. She sniffs under her right armpit, her wrist; she leans forward to smell her right knee.

"You have a wonderful smell," says Arturo. "I could sniff you all day."

Mirta clenches her right fist and says, "Are you pulling my leg?"

"Not at all," says Arturo, backing down a little. "I swear."

She keeps staring at him, a series of different lights passing across her hazel eyes.

Arturo says, "Why are you looking at me like that?"

Mirta says, "The other women . . . you know, what are they like?"

"Not like you," says Arturo. "Not at all." He feels as if he's already had this conversation, but he is certain that it isn't so; he wonders where this feeling of familiarity comes from.

"You mean in sex?" says Mirta.

"In everything," says Arturo. "But in that too, yes."

"Why?" says Mirta. "How is it, with them?"

"Rather frustrating," says Arturo, looking away.

"In what sense?" says Mirta.

"I don't know," says Arturo, scratching his head. Actually he could put together a rather precise collection of ways of breathing and looking and moaning and gesturing and speaking.

"You said frustrating," says Mirta. "Explain."

"I don't know," repeats Arturo. "It's always seemed to me like an endless pursuit of an almost unreachable goal."

"What are you talking about, exactly?" says Mirta. "Their orgasm?"

"Everything," says Arturo, wavering between embarrassment and relief. "You know when something keeps moving back whenever you feel you're getting closer to it?"

"Always?" says Mirta.

"Almost," says Arturo. "And even the few times when with the greatest patience and effort you do get there, they let you know that wasn't exactly the point. It wasn't that essential, compared to a million other essential things."

"Really?" says Mirta; the changing light in her eyes makes the skin of his face itch again.

"Yes," says Arturo, scratching his forehead. "I always thought it was my fault. Inadequacy, you know? A lack of sensitivity, call it what you like. That's why you see me like this now. I've got to get used to the idea."

"What idea?" says Mirta.

"Of the way you are," says Arturo. "Of the way it has been."

Mirta smiles, but it's a light, not totally convinced smile.

Arturo brushes his clothes with his hands. Then, in an attempt to change the subject he makes a gesture that includes her and the surrounding landscape. "I can understand why you don't want to be kicked out of here by some bored city dwellers with money in their pockets. It's so beautiful, here."

Mirta takes another twig out of her hair. "Still," she says, "so many things have changed, since the beginning."

"Like what?" says Arturo. Now he would like to know everything about her, and at the same time know nothing more than he already knows; he's afraid of sinking into a sadness of details.

Mirta says, "Everything used to be so much more fun. Crazier. Lauro always said we should act like we were in a waking dream, where you can make happen anything that comes to your mind."

Arturo says, "It's a nice idea." But he wonders if this isn't a little sad, given the circumstances.

"There were a lot more of us," says Mirta. "We were about to become a real tribe."

"And how would a real tribe be?" says Arturo. He wonders whether the sadness of the situation resides in the slight absurdity of these ideas, or in the fact that they have been eroded by reality; or simply in the fact that he wasn't there.

Mirta says, "We thought we would know, at the right time."

"What were the others like?" says Arturo. He tries to remember where he was six or seven or nine years ago, and this makes him even sadder: he thinks of the endless engagements and attempts to concentrate, all the down time, the partial joys, the vicarious satisfactions, the attention given out of duty or courtesy—or lack of any alternative—to wives, relatives, acquaintances, clients, suppliers, designers, climbing mates, sailing-crew members, table companions, accountants, barbers, salespersons, estate managers, caretakers, garage owners.

"All kinds of people," says Mirta. "They all went through a transformation, after they got here. You know how, when you take a duck that grew up far from the water and you put it on the edge of a pond or a river, and it stands there a little perplexed for a while, but then it dips its bill into the water and goes in and starts swimming like crazy and dipping its head and splashing all over and going up and down with the most incredible joy, and you're looking at it and you wonder how it could have ever lived out in a world without water?"

"Yes," says Arturo; he laughs, but with a feeling of loss made much worse by these images. Then his head fills up with the thought of the other men with whom she must have spent these past years, while he was so far away from here: names faces hairstyles eyes mouths legs penises feet arms heads, ways of laughing and walking and running and gesturing and hoeing sowing dancing talking caressing her taking her looking at her.

"We were always laughing," says Mirta. "We marveled at all the little things, even the most ordinary ones. We really had a ball. It was like a never-ending party."

"And then?" says Arturo, his heart beginning to hurt in a serious way.

Mirta looks down. "Then it ended. We started fighting over everything. You know, all the stupid, ugly things we thought we had forever locked out of our lives came back with a vengeance."

"Like envy and jealousy?" says Arturo. "Suspicion and possessiveness and touchiness and discontent?"

"Yes," says Mirta, looking surprised.

"Did it happen all of a sudden?" says Arturo. "Without any
warning?"

"Yes," says Mirta. "One day it seemed like we were all living
in perfect harmony, and the next day we were full of reasons to
feel bad."

"And then?" says Arturo. In spite of his tone of concern, he's
unutterably relieved at the idea that the never-ending party in
which she took part without him finally ended. He's ashamed of
it, but there's nothing he can do about it. It is what it is.

Mirta shakes her head. "Somebody fell ill, somebody left somebody else, somebody got tired. It had happened before, but now
every little thing seemed terribly serious. You would get up in the
morning to find an empty bed, a good-bye note in the kitchen, or
not even that."

Arturo thinks that at this point he should make a gesture or say
something to confirm and explain what happened between the
two of them a while ago, but he doesn't know what. He says,
"Thank goodness you stayed."

Mirta nibbles at the skin around a scratch on her hand. "Perhaps it was just because I didn't know where else to go."

"You mean that otherwise you would have left, too?" says
Arturo, dismayed.

"Maybe," says Mirta, shrugging her shoulders.

"But how can that be?" says Arturo. "You shock me."

"Why?" she says.

"Because you're so much a part of this place," says Arturo. "I
can't imagine it without you. And I can't imagine you out in the
ordinary world, either."

"I can," says Mirta. "Even though I don't really know what it's like anymore, the ordinary world."

"It's rather ugly," says Arturo. "Rather squalid and meaningless."

"But you live in it," says Mirta.

"Perhaps because I didn't know where else to go," says Arturo.

Mirta looks at him in a cutting way. "Now you *are* pulling my leg."

"I swear I'm not," says Arturo. "I'm absolutely serious."

She says, "Anyway, you could never live here."

"Why?" says Arturo. "Maybe I could."

"You see, you're saying maybe," says Mirta. She gets up, tidies her dress, looks around as if she was sniffing the air.

"Okay," says Arturo. "Very likely I'd have a few problems adapting at first, but that's normal."

"A few," says Mirta.

"Yes," says Arturo.

"Like having to give up things?" say Mirta.

"That, too," says Arturo. "Sure."

"What would you have to give up?" says Mirta.

Arturo says, "A few things."

"Like what?" says Mirta. "Tell me which things."

"I don't know," says Arturo. "Going to work through the morning traffic in my green car, with the stereo on. Meeting people I know too well and people I don't know at all. Reading newspapers full of news that worries me and outrages me and puts me in a bad mood. Working in a constant struggle to improve the taste of people who have no intention of seeing it improved. Eating in restaurants that are supposedly sophisticated but are only fake, from the waiters' smiles to the Chantilly cream. Spending whole afternoons trying to stimulate and convince and motivate people who don't know what they want or who they are. Driving back home to listen to the suggestions and proposals my answering machine has gathered. Deciding whether to eat frozen food and listen to some record or watch a DVD on my own or go fetch my children and take them to the circus or to the movies—provided my ex-wife agrees—or else call someone to go to some art exhibition or to a dinner at friends' or in some Mexican or Vietnamese restaurant or to some rock or jazz or classical concert or to see some comedy or some serious movie or maybe to a party, or else if it's Friday or Saturday driving all night to get to a seaside or mountaintop hotel and waking up the next day in different scenery just to refresh my eyes and breath some clean air . . ."

He's so concentrated in this attempt to make an accurate list that he keeps staring straight ahead without focusing his eyes on anything. When he does turn toward Mirta she is no longer there listening to him—she's going quickly down the sloping meadow.

Gesturing pointlessly, getting up too slowly, Arturo shouts, "Hey! Wait!"

She has already picked up her long stick and her bow from the place where they had first sat down, and she's already going downhill in big leaps, pushing the goats ahead of her.

Arturo runs heavily after her down the slope, on the wet, thin grass that doesn't give enough grip to his cleated soles and almost makes him tumble down several times. It takes him a few minutes to catch up with her, and he manages to do it only because she is slowed down by the goats trying to escape and graze some more. He says breathlessly, "Hey, what happened? Did you get upset for something I said?"

Mirta doesn't answer, she doesn't turn. She walks on unstoppably, whistling and shaking her long stick to keep the goats together as if she was in the greatest hurry.

Arturo says, "I was just trying to give you a precise idea of what

I would be missing if I decided to live here. It was *you* who asked me to do it."

Instead of slackening her pace, Mirta hurries up even more, evading with a furious stubbornness his attempts to explain.

Arturo says, "It was just to tell you that I *could* adapt to a life here."

At last she says, "Why should you give up all those wonderful things that fill your life now?"

"They're not wonderful at all!" says Arturo in desperation. "I could very well do without them!"

"It's not true!" says Mirta. "But don't worry, nobody is asking you to do without them! Nobody wants to deprive you of your Mexican restaurant!"

With a desperate sprint, Arturo manages to overtake her, running backward and looking right into her eyes, his arms open wide. But she has no intention of letting anybody block her way; she hastens her pace even more, pushing him away with such force she almost makes him fall on his back. He realizes how little she actually put her defensive power into play when he had grabbed her behind the thicket; he desperately chases her, trying to establish some eye contact with her. He says, "I don't give a damn about the Mexican restaurant, or any other restaurant! I was serious when I said I could live here! Maybe even *work* here! Maybe put in a small handcrafted furniture workshop, find the right distributor! It's not such a totally absurd idea! I mean, I certainly couldn't do it all by myself, but with the right woman I could!"

"So go find the right woman!" shouts Mirta. "And take her to one of your seaside or mountaintop hotels! So you can refresh your eyes together!"

Arturo goes on running beside her for a while, then he gives up, looking at her stream past him like an unstoppable force of

nature. He tries to estimate the distance between where they are
and the houses, and the speed at which she is crossing it: a few
minutes of total loss that sucks the air out of his lungs and the
blood out of his heart and the strength out of his legs.

nrico turns a corner and almost bumps into Alessio; in an
instant of overlapping fear and anger he says, "Pay attention, damn it!" Then he looks at the splinted leg and at the two
rudimentary crutches and he remembers he's dealing with the victim of a serious accident. He contracts his lips into an awkward
smile.

Alessio balances on his sticks and says, "Mr. Guardi, is everything okay? You look a bit so-so."

"Everything's okay, everything's okay," says Enrico, with wasted
sarcasm. "We're walking pretty swiftly, eh?"

"Yes, Mr. Guardi," says Alessio. "He's incredible, that Arup."

"How is he doing with the minivan?" says Enrico.

"He's working on it, Mr. Guardi," says Alessio.

"Yes, but when does he think he'll finish?" says Enrico, even
though he knows it's useless to expect any accurate information
from a broken-legged idiot doped up to his eyeballs with narcotic
beverages.

"Oh, soon," says Alessio.

"Blind faith," says Enrico, with a new angry impulse at the
thought of how the moral and cultural capitulation has spread
throughout the group.

"Yes, Mr. Guardi," says Alessio. "He really knows what he's
doing." He swings his splinted leg in a demonstrative way.

Enrico says, "The power of suggestion is huge. But I'm afraid it doesn't work as effectively with cars."

Alessio looks at him as if he didn't understand, leaning on his homemade crutches.

Enrico walks away quickly, without giving him another look. He realizes that the endless delay is having a devastating effect on his nervous system: His head is full of frustrated impulses, unfinished sentences, suspended instructions, contradictory excuses, unexpressed requests, unused adjectives, nicknames held in reserve. He feels like he's been stuck in this minuscule enclave of nothingness for an inordinate amount of time, with the collusion and the adventure-holiday spirit of his wife and his friends. He's come to the very end of his patience; he could explode any time now, on the slightest pretext.

He walks into the barn-workshop as if he was walking into the garage near his home in Milan. Going directly to the side of the minivan, he says to Arup in a sharp tone, "How are things going here?"

Arup is standing in front of the workbench, all the disassembled shock-absorber parts aligned before him like some mysterious finds. He looks at Enrico in his enigmatic way and says, "Very well."

"Excuse me, what exactly do you mean by that?" says Enrico, without the slightest attempt at being gracious.

"It's disassembled now," says Arup. "All the parts." His tone is too soft not to be calculated, at least as calculated as his country-guru smile.

"This much I can see," says Enrico. "The point is, how do you plan to put everything back together again? Just by staring at it very intensely?"

"No," says Arup, as if he was answering a terribly naïve question.

"Too bad," says Enrico, in a crescendo of irritation. "It would have been wonderful."

"Very," says Arup, nodding his head.

Enrico would like to continue in this sarcastic vein, but exasperation runs through him like a high-voltage current burning fuses along its way. "So how are you going to do it?" says Enrico. "Above all, *when*?"

"Soon," says Arup, from beyond his ineffable screen.

"And what does 'soon' mean, in this place?" says Enrico. "Five hours, five days, five weeks, five months?"

"Soon," says Arup again. He smiles, probably with deliberately provocative intent.

Enrico can't control himself anymore. "You don't even have the vaguest idea? Do you intend to place your trust in Shiva or whichever your favorite divinity is?"

"You're getting upset," says Arup, in a tone he could use with a child.

"Of course I'm getting upset!" screams Enrico, in a blinding outburst that almost lifts him off the ground. "I can see that in your wonderful condition of detachment time is of no importance, but for me it's absolutely vital! I have a billion important things to do, I can't afford to throw away one more hour of my life with these kinds of tricks!"

"Which tricks?" says Arup, barely moving his head.

"The tricks you're playing now!" screams Enrico. "The little magic feats by which you fix anything even though you haven't got the faintest idea of where to start, and without any adequate tools either! When all that matters to you is keeping us here as long as possible, so as not to lose the audience you desperately need!"

Arup smiles again, as if these words aroused in him a mixture of disbelief and compassion. "Why do you think that?"

"Because it's the pure truth!" screams Enrico. "But you know what, Mister Guru? We're sick and tired of being your audience! We'll walk all the way to town, you can keep the minivan! Disassemble it all, while you're at it! You'll see how many nice parts it's made of!"

Arup seems about to say something, but Enrico has no intention of paying attention to him; he turns his back on him and stomps furiously out of the barn, heading toward the main house.

L uisa and Lauro sit on the bank of the very small stream. There is a smell of clay and rotten leaves, a cold light outlining the branches of the weeping willow; there are no sounds apart from the running water and the intermittent gusts of wind. Luisa says, "Perhaps it's better if we go back."

"Better in what sense?" says Lauro.

"In the sense that I'd like to go back," says Luisa. They don't look straight at each other, and this sharpens the acuteness with which they attend to each other's every motion.

"Yes?" says Lauro.

"Yes," says Luisa, but she remains seated on the hard ground.

"All right," says Lauro, getting up first.

Luisa jumps to her feet at once, then hesitates between moving in two or three possible directions. "Why, did you want to stay longer?"

"No, no," says Lauro. "It's perfectly okay to go now." He picks up another flat stone and throws it, bouncing it five times down the stream.

Luisa says, "Anyway it's beautiful, here." She doesn't know why she feels this, since the place seems sad and cold and damp to her, out of season and out of spirit, out of time.

"And yet you can't wait to get back to Milan," says Lauro. He throws another flat stone: it bounces six times on the surface, like a little silvery fish.

Luisa presses her hands deep into her jacket pockets. "I have a lot of things to do."

"And you miss them?" says Lauro, in a strange tone that could be absentminded or all too attentive.

"No, but still I have to do them," says Luisa.

"Of course," says Lauro. He walks along the bank, looking for more flat stones.

Luisa says, "Don't you ever miss anything, here?"

"No," says Lauro. He throws a stone. This time, it bounces only once.

"*Never?*" says Luisa.

Lauro shrugs his shoulders; then he says, "Yes. Of course I do."

"What do you miss?" says Luisa, scared by the way he's looking at her. Her heart is beating fast; she struggles to slow it down, keep her features relaxed.

Lauro says, "The feelings I don't have. The things I don't do. The people I don't meet. The lives I don't live."

"Why?" says Luisa. "How many more lives would you want? Didn't you say that you were satisfied with the life you have?" She hates her stiff, upper-class Milanese accent now; she also feels that her lips are too thin, her eyes too close to one another, her hands and feet too small.

"I *am* satisfied with it," says Lauro; he throws another stone, and it doesn't bounce at all, cutting right into the water. "And anyway, in your built-up, organized world out there, there's only one kind of life, with minimal variations, and it's a slave's life."

Luisa feels afraid again, although her fear is difficult to define. She says, "Don't you ever think that the world could get better?"

"Yes," says Lauro. "Maybe in fifty, or a hundred, or a thousand years. Through a slow evolution, or in the aftermath of some terrifying catastrophe. For the time being, the most useless, harmful enterprises born out of purely bad intentions are winning hands down."

"Perhaps you're right," says Luisa.

"Perhaps?" says Lauro. "This is a world in which if you don't *own* things, or at least dream of owning them, the whole meaning of life vanishes before your very eyes."

Luisa nods her head; it's not about these things that she would like to talk. Still, she thinks that as dangerous as the subject is, it's safer than others.

Lauro says, "Your husband, isn't he a perfect inhabitant of this world?"

"I don't know," says Luisa.

"How come you don't know?" says Lauro.

"Because to him the meaning of life is in what he *does*," says Luisa. "Much more than in what he owns."

"It doesn't make much difference," says Lauro.

"He thinks it does," says Luisa. Talking like this about Enrico with someone who detests him makes her feel guilty and at the same time subtly excites her. She thinks that she should stop; or that she should go on.

Lauro rips a twig off a branch and chews on it. "What do you see in him?"

Luisa thinks about it for a moment. "I know him."

"You mean, you know how he functions?" says Lauro.

"Yes," says Luisa.

"And that's a good thing," says Lauro.

Luisa undoes her bun, letting down her hair. "Compared to not having the slightest idea of what another person thinks or feels, yes."

"And does he know how *you* function?" says Lauro.

"I think so," says Luisa. "Well, perhaps not entirely. But he's rather patient. He usually is, at least."

"Does one need to be patient, with you?" says Lauro.

Luisa turns toward the water. "That's what they tell me."

"Why?" says Lauro.

Luisa feels her face burn on the side he's looking at, while the other half is cold; she has only to turn a little to alter this flow. "I'm too demanding, too critical, too restless. I pay too much attention to details, ask too many questions, talk too much, read too much, have too many opinions. I stay up too late."

"How late?" says Lauro.

"It depends," says Luisa. "Until there's something to say or read or think."

Lauro laughs. "I usually go to bed at nine-thirty, more or less."

Luisa laughs, too, but tensely. "But you also get up really early, don't you?"

Lauro picks up another small stone and throws it into the water without even trying to make it bounce. "Once I used to go to bed really late, too. At times I didn't go to bed at all."

"When was this?" says Luisa. She realizes that she's probably too near to him now, but she doesn't back up.

"When I used to live in the world," says Lauro.

"Were you very different from now?" says Luisa. She looks at the scar on his neck, at his right ear, at the hair which he probably never combs.

Lauro shakes his head; then all of a sudden he seizes her by a shoulder and says, "It's true, you do ask too many questions."

Luisa feels her knees go suddenly weak; she puts up a little resistance but still moves a few centimeters closer to him before being able to stop. They look into each other's eyes and at each other's lips, breathing at an extremely short distance. She feels all her senses working at peak capacity, her skin temperature rising, her sweat glands and her other glands secreting fluids, her inner rhythm altering, her sense of balance becoming precarious.

Lauro withdraws his hand. "We'd better go back to the houses."

Luisa runs her eyes from his lips to his chin to his clothes, down to his widely stitched, homemade boots. She says, "Yes," with what sounds to her like an imperceptibly questioning inflection. She thinks of all the requests and offers that are implied in his way of standing there and looking away, like the currents of a subterranean stream. She feels relief at the thought of going back, and an almost equal amount of loss, abandonment, waste, nostalgia, absence, uselessness, disappointment, regret.

They both turn, with the same thinly concealed reluctance, and walk toward the two horses tied to the tree.

E nrico barges into the kitchen as if he wanted to knock down the door. "Where's Luisa? I've been looking for her all over the place!"

Margherita and Alessio and Gaia and Icaro are sitting around the table, nibbling at some bread and cheese and vegetables as in the most idyllic of country settings. They turn to him with a collective look that takes him aback.

"What happened?" says Margherita, vaguely alarmed.

"It happened that the Indian took the minivan's shock absorber apart with great gusto and now he doesn't have the slightest idea of how to put it back together again!" says Enrico, without a single pause for breath.

"How do you know?" says Margherita.

"I *saw* it!" says Enrico. "I *asked* him! Go ask him yourself, if you don't believe me!" He can't stand still; he gesticulates in such a frantic way that his wrists are hurting.

"Why are you so upset?" says Margherita with a sideways glance at the others, in one of her unbearable expressions of common sense, made for the sake of her audience.

"Do you think I should instead be relaxed and unperturbed?" barks back Enrico. "Stuck for the third day in this vile place, without being able to get out of it?"

"*You* are vile!" says Gaia, red in the face.

Enrico points his finger at her. "What a bunch of poor nut-cases! It doesn't take much to understand that! It only takes a look! Nevertheless, you've been going along with them, appeasing them, telling them how nice and sweet and good they are for living this ghastly life!"

"Listen, you horrible man," says Gaia, in a fighting attitude, "we never invited you here! You begged us to let you in!"

"Only because I didn't know what was waiting for us!" screams Enrico. "Otherwise I would have walked the whole night in the pouring rain!"

"I wouldn't," says Margherita, exuding a fake neutrality.

"You automatically adjust yourself to the lowest common denominator!" screams Enrico. "Your number-one priority is to cultivate the audience, no matter who it consists of! It's more powerful than you, and you don't even realize it anymore!"

Aria slips into the kitchen in her usual silent way, hiding beside the cupboard.

"You seem a little bit off your head, Enrico," says Margherita.

"Can you hear the jargon you're using?" says Enrico. "Can you hear your own voice?"

The door opens—it's Arturo, in a state of extreme agitation. "Is Mirta here?"

The others look at him without answering; only Gaia shakes her head.

Margherita tells him, "Enrico claims that Arup is not able to fix our minivan."

"I don't claim it, that's the way it *is*!" says Enrico, feeling like the victim of a conspiracy. "And even if he is able, he has no intention of doing it!"

"Mr. Guardi, I think he does intend to fix it," says Alessio, slurring his words.

"What you think has no relevance at all!" says Enrico. "Your ability to assess things was close to zero before you broke your leg. You can imagine where it stands now!"

"But why should he take the shock absorber apart, then?" says Arturo.

"Why?" says Enrico. "To act the part of the great all-knowing guru! To keep us here as prisoners! For fear that we might take their houses away from them! Maybe to slice our throats tonight, and bury us somewhere in the woods!"

"Hey, Mr. Shithead!" says Gaia. "How dare you throw this load of crap at us?"

"Yes, don't you think you're exaggerating a bit?" says Margherita, her show of impartiality beginning to cost her an increasingly bigger effort.

Enrico says, "I was expecting you to say that! I'm exaggerating, of course!"

Arturo looks out the window. He tells Gaia, "She put the goats back into their pen, but then I didn't see where she went."

"Let's all worry for little Mirta, now!" says Enrico, beside himself with rage. "And for her little goats, maybe!"

"I thought she had come back here," says Arturo, without even raising his voice.

Margherita says, "Guys, let's be reasonable for a moment, please." But fear has started to flood back into her. Obviously she doesn't really believe she can play the role of the moderator.

Enrico says, "There's little to be reasonable about, Margherita! The only thing to do is get out of here while we still can!"

"And how are we going to do that?" says Margherita, in a desperate tone.

"We walk!" says Enrico. "If you don't feel like doing it I'm willing to push and drag you all the way to town!"

"But there are those guys out there with the guns," says Margherita, now about to burst into tears.

"I'd rather be shot than be stuck here forever!" says Enrico. "And, anyway, they're not going to shoot at us!"

"The did shoot at *me,*" says Arturo.

"That's because they thought you were one of these nutcases!" screams Enrico. "You still don't get it? This is a dispute between them, what the hell have we got to do with it? If we meet those people we'll just tell them the truth, that we were held here as hostages! Most likely they'll be better than this bunch, too! At least they live in the same century as we do! They have cars!"

Gaia is overcome by a primitive kind of anger. "You really are a horrible man!"

"You don't know how affected I am by your judgment, countess," says Enrico, with the best sarcasm he can muster. "Keeping in mind that your male role models are a school-play witch-doctor and a third-rate holiday-farm hero, with their little arrows and crossbows and their pitiful little clip-clop horses."

Gaia and Margherita and Arturo seem about to react to his words, but before they can say anything Aria takes a jar from a shelf and flings it at Enrico.

Enrico recoils from the impact and the surprise and the thudding sound, fragments of glass and spatters of a reddish liquid and wild cherries soiling his jacket and beige corduroy trousers.

Aria looks at him with wild eyes, then crosses the room quickly and walks out, slamming the door.

Gaia says, "You deserved it," and she follows her, Icaro on her trail.

Enrico turns toward the others, as if to gather declarations of solidarity.

Margherita has a face fit for a television screen in a day of catastrophes.

Arturo walks to the door, says "I'll be right back," and runs out.

Alessio takes another sip from his glass, with the utmost slowness.

Enrico feels a bitter mixture of disbelief and disgust. He takes a rag from a shelf, cleans himself up as best he can. "I'll go look for Luisa, then you'd better make up your minds whether you want to come with me. Otherwise, so much the worse for you, I'm nobody's guardian."

Margherita points a shaking finger at Alessio, saying, "What are we going to do with him? There's no way he can walk, with that leg."

"We leave him here," says Enrico. "He seems quite happy, anyway. We'll send for him and our luggage later. You really have no idea where Luisa might be?"

Margherita slowly nods her head.

"Where?" says Enrico.

"I saw her with Lauro," says Margherita, making a vague gesture. "They were going that way."

"And you're only telling me now?" says Enrico, in a tone that sounds appallingly savage to himself.

"When should I have told you?" says Margherita. "You were doing all the talking."

"Didn't you try to stop her?" says Enrico. "You let her go like that, without doing anything?" He looks at the door, his possessive instincts making his arteries contract, making his heart beat furiously.

"What was I supposed to do?" says Margherita. "They were far off, on their horses."

"On horses?" says Enrico, overwhelmed by more violent feelings, whose existence he wouldn't even want to acknowledge.

Margherita nods again. "They were galloping that way," she says. As she adds details, her expression becomes more stolid.

"Do you realize what she's done?" says Enrico walking up and down. "I've seen it before! I was sure of it! Someone who publishes novels filled with poor neurotic women who swoon over the first man they meet from some third-world country, either real or imagined."

Margherita stiffens her face muscles in a desperate attempt at an acceptable expression. "Enrico, please, let's try not to lose our heads."

"I'm not losing my head at all!" screams Enrico. "Only I have a little problem with my wife who's let herself be ensnared like an idiot by a dangerous lunatic who thinks he's living in the year one thousand! Who knows where he's taken her, now!"

"Let's ask the others," says Margherita.

Enrico shoves her aside as he walks to the door. Margherita hesitates, then she follows him, turning toward Alessio with yet another accusing look.

Arturo runs between the houses in search of Mirta but he can't find her; he starts to fear she might have dissolved like a figment of his imagination. The wind blows strong, increasing the air's resistance to his frantic movements. The goats are in their pen; the horses in their paddock; the chicken and ducks and geese are pecking around; the clothes hanging out to dry flap on a clothesline; the black dog barks, it is not clear at whom or what. Arturo feels there's too much empty space around the stone buildings; he zigzags across it as fast as he can, as if this was a way of connecting one point to the other, keeping everything together, at least until he finds Mirta.

He runs back toward the main house, and amazingly she's there, in a small but noisy, gesticulating cluster that includes Gaia and Icaro and Aria and Margherita and Enrico. He stops, and then approaches them by almost controlled steps. Mirta barely gives him a glance, immediately averting her eyes.

Gaia is saying to Enrico, "We don't tell everybody what we do here."

"Of course not!" says Enrico. "Here rules the deaf and blind law of the primitive clan! The code of silence in its purest form!"

Gaia seems about to grab him by his overcoat collar, then refrains from doing so perhaps because of the attention with which Icaro is watching her.

Margherita says, "Calm down," trying to hide behind one of her ready-made attitudes but she can't even decide which one.

Mirta nervously plays with one of her curls. She seems difficult to reach, having returned to the solidarity of her tribe. Arturo puts out a hand to touch her, stopping halfway.

Enrico says to her, "You don't know anything either, of course?"

"No," says Mirta, shaking her head.

"Of course," says Enrico. "What could she know, the little shepherdess? She takes care of her little goats, and doesn't ask herself too many complicated questions!"

"Hey, dickhead," says Mirta.

"Enrico, cut it out!" says Arturo, giving in to a defensive impulse that would make him draw his sword, if he had one.

Mirta turns to look at him, but her features show none of the palpitating feelings they had when they were together behind the thicket.

Enrico says, "Please forgive me if I was disrespectful to your pastoral muse. I saw you together, a while ago."

"When?" says Arturo, almost hoping to have him as witness of what has happened between them. He stares at Mirta's lips, with the incredibly recent and yet distant memory of her smile; he tries to meet her eyes again but she looks away.

"You were really moving," says Enrico. "The leopard man and the little shepherdess, with your nice primitive clothes."

"I said cut it out, now!" says Arturo, with a feeling of revulsion at the thought of not being able to go back to the scene of half an hour ago.

Margherita must be smelling a trend, because she finally chooses an attitude. Flashing a fake smile at Mirta and Gaia, she says, "Anyway I'm sure your Lauro has a favorite place to bring his prey of the day, doesn't he?"

The two women look at her in disgust, without answering.

"I bet you have a notion of where he might be," says Margherita, in a debased version of the winking style she uses in her program. "Something tells me that in all these years both of you must have gone for a little ride with him."

"You rotten pumpkin," says Gaia.

Mirta says, "You talk like that because last night you were terribly disappointed, when you discovered he wasn't interested in you!"

"What do you know about last night?" says Margherita.

"I saw you," says Mirta.

"You didn't see much, sweet curls!" says Margherita. "Because it was pitch dark, and I don't believe you have infrared eyes!"

Mirta says "You were acting like a cat in heat, with your mewing, your poses, your cigarettes."

"I'm sorry to disappoint you, my dear spy!" says Margherita in a shrill tone. "If you're so interested, it was him who was coming on to me as hard as he could!"

"Liar!" says Gaia. "We saw how you were looking at him, from the first night! As if you wanted to jump on him!"

"You're two miserable gossips, both of you!" cries Margherita, growing strident. "Rather than jumping on a guy like that I'd throw myself out of the window! What a disgusting expression, too! Fit for a barnyard, really!"

"But it gives a pretty good idea!" says Gaia.

"To *you*, perhaps!" screams Margherita. "To me, it's just revolting!"

"Listen," says Enrico; he's gone pale, with trembling hands.

Margherita screams, "That lout dares to play king of the chicken coop only because he has two hens like you at his disposal! Otherwise you'd see how he would come off his high horse!"

"You're the hen!" screams Gaia. "With that fake dyed hair of yours!"

"Fake!" shouts Icaro.

"You shut up, you parrot!" screams Margherita. She turns as if to look for support from her audience. She seems mystified at not hearing any applause, or seeing any cameraman ready to amplify her expressions with a close-up shot.

Enrico stands on tiptoe to gain a little height, and says to her and Arturo, "Could we stop dwelling on your sordid sexual dealings for a moment and try to understand where Luisa might be?"

Margherita says, "How the fuck do you dare? I haven't had any sexual dealings with anybody!"

Gaia says, "You really are an idiot."

"Idiot," says Icaro.

Enrico makes a tremendous effort not to stoop to their level. He takes a deep breath, says to his friends, "I still can't believe that such a pocket of material and moral backwardness can exist in twenty-first-century Italy, and that you were sucked into it to such an extent! But it's your own business, I don't care! All I care about is retrieving my wife and getting out of here!"

The black dog cocks its ears, springing forward. Aria turns in the same direction; she says, "Daddy."

The others turn, too. They see two human figures on two trotting horses, the dog catching up with them, circling around them in big leaps.

Enrico seems about to start running toward them, but he remains motionless in the small group, watching them approach.

Lauro and Luisa ride up to the main house, Luisa holding on to the saddle with one hand; their horses are wet with perspiration. Lauro dismounts, with a jump that is obviously calculated to produce an effect on who's watching; he holds the reins of Luisa's horse.

Enrico addresses her with barely controlled fury, saying, "Can you tell me where the hell have you been?"

She says, "We just went for a ride," She doesn't have her glasses on, her cheeks are flushed; she pants slightly.

"How romantic," says Margherita in a low voice, from behind.

"A ride?" says Enrico. "A *ride*?"

"Yes," says Luisa. "Is there anything wrong with that?" But she's too flushed by the ride to look as innocent as she would like to appear, and her position up in the saddle makes any pretence of a balanced dialogue seem ludicrous.

Enrico must realize that, by contrast, he's in the position of a medieval petitioner. He becomes even more furious, saying, "Would you mind getting off that beast, at least?"

Lauro holds out a hand to Luisa; she dismounts, if a little awkwardly. She looks at Margherita and Arturo and at the three country women and at the child, as if to distribute the tension among several witnesses.

Enrico struggles for self-control, with very poor results. "How did you get such a wonderful idea?"

Luisa puts her glasses back on. "We just did it," she says, as she tries to mingle with the group.

Lauro points to the horses and tells Aria, "Take them back to the paddock."

Aria takes the horses by the reins and leads them away, looking back with the long sideways glance of someone who would rather stay and watch what happens.

Enrico keeps on at Luisa like a ravenous dog, his composure totally undone by visceral impulses. "So? Are you going to give me some explanation?"

"There's nothing to explain," says Luisa, smiling uncomfortably.

"There's *everything* to explain," says Enrico.

She says, "We'll talk about it later, okay?"

"Let's talk about it *now*!" says Enrico. "It's no use sneaking off like a cowardly, deceitful little girl!"

Lauro grabs him by the shoulder and says, "Don't you dare be so arrogant with her."

"She's my *wife*!" says Enrico, his whole body vibrating with tension.

Luisa looks at Lauro as if to ask him to keep out of this; he releases his hold, unwillingly.

"I asked you a question!" says Enrico. "At least have the decency to answer!"

"Leave me alone!" says Luisa. "I'm an adult, and I go where I want, with whom I want!"

"Not *here*!" screams Enrico. "Not *now*! Not with *these people*!"

"Is it a kind of limited freedom, that she's entitled to?" says Lauro, with a defiant flicker in his eyes.

"I'm not talking to you!" says Enrico, even though it's clear from the way his body is shaking that he would like to punch him, if only he could.

"No?" says Lauro.

"No!" screams Enrico, so loud that the veins in his neck swell up and his face goes purple, tiny drops of his saliva forming in the cold, sharp light.

Luisa says, "Don't assume that the louder you scream, the more you are right."

"I'm not screaming!" screams Enrico. "And you know perfectly well that I'm right!"

"Okay, come on, we get the point," says Margherita, her features again dominated by fear that the situation could totally degenerate.

"You haven't got a damned thing!" yells Enrico. "None of you has the slightest idea what loyalty is, or even what our common goal is! All you know how to do is flirt with the enemy!"

"Hey, slow down, love!" says Margherita, in the pseudo-Roman inflection you wouldn't expect from her unless you had seen her program.

Enrico screams at her, "You, too—I can't understand how you can have drooled over someone like that! Who knows what third-hand fantasies you must have had in your head! It's the subculture of your programs, really!"

"How the fuck do you dare?" screams Margherita. "I've never drooled over anybody in my entire life! Unlike you!"

"What are you talking about?" says Enrico, screwing up his eyes as if he couldn't even see her clearly.

"You know perfectly well," says Margherita.

"No, I don't," says Enrico.

"Yes, you do," says Margherita.

"I *don't*," screams Enrico. "And I'm not in the mood to get into one of your idiotic quiz games!"

Margherita says, "Have you forgotten about four years ago in Sardinia, perhaps?"

Aria comes back, swift and silent, standing at the edge of the group.

"What does Sardinia have to do with all this?" says Enrico, wavering between disbelief and indignation.

Margherita says, "When I was sunbathing in the nude on the terrace and you brought those drinks on the tray?"

"So what?" says Enrico. His eyes are almost closed now, as if preparing for an onslaught.

Margherita says, "Towel around your waist, with that suggestive look on your face, hinting to me that Luisa was staying in the sea and nobody would disturb us?"

"It was just a joke!" says Enrico, but he backs away half a step. "You've been dealing with your small television circus for so long, you can't even tell the difference between irony and vulgarity anymore!"

"You know perfectly well there wasn't any irony there!" says Margherita. "You were drooling over me, with your tongue out!"

"I feel pity for you!" says Enrico, trying uselessly to smile. "Pity and disgust!"

"I feel pity for you, too!" says Margherita. "And as for disgust, I just have to think of your face on that terrace when I laughed instead of taking you seriously! You never forgave me that one!"

Arturo looks at Mirta and Aria and Gaia, who are observing the scene with a kind of anthropological curiosity.

Enrico turns toward Luisa, saying, "I hope you're not listening to her! These are just the self-gratifying ravings of a poor, complex-ridden neurotic!"

"What complexes are you talking about, shithead?" says Margherita.

"About your legs being too short!" says Enrico. "And your chin being too long and your ears sticking out and your cellulite and all your other parts you can't accept because they are not up to your stellar parameters!"

"I don't have any cellulite, you asshole!" screams Margherita. "Not one ounce!"

"Certainly not in the pictures you send to the magazines!" says Enrico. "In those you're as smooth as a supermarket apple, the digital-retouch professionals know how to do their job! But on that terrace you didn't make for an exciting view, I can assure you!"

"On that terrace you were so excited you had a pathetic hard-on!" screams Margherita, as if she was going to burst into pieces.

"I could see your stiff little prick under your towel! You would have sold your soul to the devil to fuck me!"

"This is really worthy of you!" screams Enrico. "The failed avant-garde actress recycled as television clown and swindler!"

"You should talk, you would *die* to be on television!" screams Margherita. "The only time they invited you, you telephoned everybody you knew and rushed to Rome as if you had won the Nobel Prize for architecture, even though it was only a shitty morning show and they let you talk for two minutes between a faded politician and an old singer, for an audience of housewives and retired persons and invalids!"

"I certainly couldn't hope to have the audience you have!" screams Enrico. "Since I'm not the perfect mirror for a mass of illiterate Peeping Toms with tattoos on their buttocks and not one single evolved thought in their brains!"

"You're the Peeping Tom!" screams Margherita. "You deserve to be a cuckold!"

"You pathetic cow!" screams Enrico. "You short-legged, ignorant, vulgar, cheap bitch!"

Arturo interposes himself between them, raising his hands. "Now, knock it off, both of you."

Enrico screams at him, "You'd better shut up! Our transcultural excursionist, infatuated with the little troglodyte shepherdess! I wonder what lofty communication goes on between the two of you!"

Arturo morphs from peacemaker to injured party in an instant. "I wonder what lofty communication goes on between you and your twenty-three-year-old colleague!"

"Which colleague?" says Luisa.

"Arturo, you'll pay for this!" screams Enrico.

"Which colleague, Enrico?" says Luisa.

Enrico gestures emptily, screaming, "You're not listening to him I hope, Luisa? It's only a miserable diversionary tactic!"

Arturo screams, "At least I separated from my wife, when I fell in love with somebody else! I didn't go on keeping my foot in two shoes like a hypocrite!"

Enrico lashes out, "You separated from Giulia only because she caught you red-handed with that Swedish salesgirl of yours and she kicked you right out of the house! Otherwise you'd still be there, playing the phony perfect husband and father!"

"It's not true!" screams Arturo, overcome with fear at the thought that Mirta might replace this image of him with the one she has, whatever it may be. "I had already decided to tell her! I would have left her anyway!"

"But as chance would have it, you didn't!" screams Enrico. "As chance would have it, you waited for her to find out!"

Luisa screams to Enrico, "You have the courage to make a jealous scene, and all the while you've been having an affair with a twenty-three-year-old co-worker for who knows how long!"

"Luisa!" screams Enrico. "Don't believe this idiot! Margherita, tell her it isn't true!"

"Don't expect any cover-ups from me, asshole!" barks Margherita. "I don't know anything about your squalid secret life, but the twenty-something colleague fits perfectly into the picture!"

"I would have divorced my wife anyway!" screams Arturo, more at Mirta more than at anybody else. "There wasn't anything between us anymore!"

"Luisa, listen to me!" screams Enrico.

"You make me sick!" screams Luisa.

"Mirta," says Arturo, in a desperate attempt to establish a line of communication with her in the midst of this furious brawl. She gives him only a glance, then turns her back on him.

"You too, Luisa," says Margherita. "If you hadn't been so fond of your role as the perfect woman, maybe you would have woken up earlier!"

"The fact is, I *work*, Margherita!" Luisa points out. "I don't spend my days surrounded by manicurists and hairdressers and makeup people and assistants, looking at myself in monitors!"

"Look here, I work just as much as you do, darling!" screams Margherita. "Or more! Except that every now and then I also get some gratification out of it, instead of having to cater to a bunch of pain-in-the-ass editorial rats and narcissistic authors nagging me with requests!"

Luisa screams, "Still, when you were dying to publish that foolish booklet of anecdotes of yours, you didn't seem to hold them in such contempt, the editorial rats! You tried to win them over one by one with your simpering, in the most embarrassing way!"

"Please excuse me if I have embarrassed you!" screams Margherita. "The poor, wise, intellectual little Libra, who thinks that books are so much nobler than real life and, in the meantime, doesn't even realize that her husband is fucking his twenty-three-year-old assistant at work!"

"Luckily, not all women are like you!" screams Enrico. "Filled with hasty vulgarity down to the roots of your bleached hair!"

"Wash your mouth out before you talk to me, okay?" screams Margherita. "You're dogshit!"

"And you're a poor slovenly bitch filled with failed ambitions!" screams Enrico.

"I want nothing to do with you anymore!" screams Luisa to Enrico.

"But Luisa!" screams Enrico. "Please try to be reasonable!"

"I've had enough of being reasonable!" screams Luisa. "I've been reasonable for ten years!"

"Thanks a lot, eh?" screams Enrico to Arturo. "You disloyal, gossipy imbecile!"

"Who started with the insults?" screams Arturo. "And acting like a hypocrite?"

"You've always been a poor blockhead!" screams Enrico. "Ever since we were in high school! If your father hadn't left you his shops, you would have never gotten anywhere in life!"

"He left me *two* shops, my father!" screams Arturo. "I opened the other five! Entirely by myself!"

"How admirable!" screams Enrico. "What a benefit to the whole nation! Did you tell your little shepherdess how much one of your armchairs costs? A clerk's monthly wage, more or less? But it's made using entirely natural materials and processes, mind you! With the utmost respect for the environment!"

Arturo is staggered for a moment at this thought, then he cries out, "What about you? How did you win that contract for the new housing project where you'll cram a thousand people in like chickens? How come you became such good friends with the local politicians? Did you discover that they really are wonderful people, in spite of their dishonest faces? Or was there something else that it wouldn't be so nice to discuss?"

"What?" screams Enrico, stepping even closer to him. "How dare you make these ignoble insinuations?"

"Stooooooooop it!" screams Margherita, on a frequency that cuts through all the other voices. "I can't stand you anymore! All of you! I just want to go home!"

Enrico steps back, catching his breath. Pointing to the country squatters he says, "Do you realize the satisfaction we're giving them, with this scene?"

"It was you who started it, you know," says Lauro.

"I already told you I'm not talking to you!" screams Enrico.

"What are you trying to distance yourself from?" says Lauro, in an eerily calm tone.

"I'm trying to distance myself from your *barbarism*!" screams Enrico. "From the utter uselessness and meaninglessness of your life!"

"I'm sorry for you," says Lauro. "But it's the life we've chosen. We wouldn't exchange it for any other."

"Are you talking on their behalf, too?" screams Enrico, gesturing angrily toward Mirta and Aria and Gaia and Icaro. "On behalf of that poor wretched child, too? You really think they wouldn't run away from here as fast as they could, if it weren't for your constant moral blackmail?"

"*You* are the poor wretch!" screams Gaia. "You snail-eaten cabbage-head!"

"You're the one involved in blackmail," says Lauro, "trying to make everybody stick to your rules, so you'll feel less alone."

"We live here because we've *chosen* this place!" shouts Gaia. "And because we've chosen *each other*! And because we don't *ever* want to have anything to do with people like *you*!"

"Wonderful!" screams Enrico. "So stay in this earthly paradise! I wish you good luck! As long as you don't want *us* to be part of your pitiful playacting!"

The situation degenerates completely: mouths and eyes and hands moving frantically, thoughts and feelings and mental pictures hurled at each other in an almost indistinguishable, furious overlapping of words and gestures and facial expressions.

Then Arup arrives, stopping at the edge of the quarrel. With stupefying composure he waves his arms and says, "Your car is ready."

Everybody stands still—all sounds and images suddenly frozen.

After some time Enrico says, "What do you mean?" His words seem to surface with a slight delay over the motion of his lips.

"I mean, I fixed it," says Arup. "More or less. Enough for you to drive to town."

Enrico is at a loss for words; Luisa looks down; Margherita has a relieved expression, tinged with disbelief.

Arturo can't even think about it. The only thing he'd like to do is grab Mirta by the arm and drag her somewhere where the others can't see them, be intimate with her as they were a while ago, trying to translate into very simple words and very simple acts what he feels inside. But he's not at all sure how she would react, so he watches her without moving, concentrating on every hint of an expression on her face, all too conscious of the implacable acceleration with which time and space and a thousand other forces are working to separate them.

Alessio Cingaro looks at the woods through the minivan window, trying like the others to discern any potential movements of armed and hostile people. At the same time he feels strangely detached from everything: from danger, from the splinted leg that prevents him from driving, from the minivan's pronounced tilt to the left where Arup put back the patched-up shock absorber. It's the mental and emotional equivalent to the soundproofing of the Lexus that Alessio tried out at a dealer's a week ago, so thorough it made him lose touch with the pulse of the traffic. Right now, it doesn't bother him; on the contrary, it relieves him of his anxiety to keep up with the events and to anticipate even the less predictable variables and overcome all adversities to finally bring the result home. He feels lucky enough to bring himself home, in this situation; he wouldn't ask for more.

He looks at Mr. Guardi as he holds the wheel stiffly; at his wife Luisa sitting as far as she can from him in the last row; at Novelli gazing intently at her cell phone's display; at Arturo Vannucci looking like an overgrown child forcibly dragged away from a playground. In a normal return trip with clients Alessio would try to imagine what they're thinking about, and he would be able to do it rather accurately, but at this point he doesn't care. He doesn't care about the lost sale either, or about the complaints he'll certainly get from the director in Milan for all the wasted time and the damaged minivan. Except for a few flashes of apprehension, his conscience is clear—he feels he has done everything he could, until destiny, or whatever you want to call it, swept over him and the whole situation.

They're out of the woods now, the road descending with a gentler slope toward the cultivated fields. The left front shock absorber is working very badly, but it can probably hold for a few more kilometers, provided they steer clear of potholes and ditches. They all keep looking out their windows, their nervousness decreasing as they slowly approach the mellow expanse of the plain.

Arturo Vannucci says, "So it's true that they respect cars more then people," sounding almost disappointed.

"Perhaps they respect the fact that we don't have anything to do with those lunatics," says Mr. Guardi.

The two women don't talk, pretending in their own different ways as if they weren't there.

At long last the minivan reaches level ground, running on the dirt road through the fields toward the asphalt road. When they finally get to it, Mr. Guardi slows down and flicks on the indicator, turning with the utmost caution toward Turigi. His muscles relax visibly; he even risks stepping on the gas pedal a bit, although on the smooth surface the tilt to the left seems even more pronounced than before.

Suddenly an overexcited little tune spurts out of Novelli's cell phone. She springs forward, says, "Hello?" like someone breathing again after having spent an unbearable amount of time underwater. The connection fails at once, but now the others also start going through their bags and pockets almost automatically; in a matter of seconds, four slightly different sounds confirm that they're again connected to their networks. A few more seconds later, a whole weekend of text messages reaches them in a cacophony of trills and beeps and buzzes, as if the minivan had been invaded by a swarm of hunger-frenzied insects. It goes on for a while, with an intensity that has the effect of paralyzing every gesture or expression.

When the sounds eventually subside, Alessio contemplates the idea of calling his mother and Deborah, but the thought of doing it publicly almost makes him sick; he decides to wait till they are in town.

Already there's Novelli talking frantically into her phone, her voice rising in pitch as if to compensate for all the calls she hasn't been able to make in the last two days. She cups a hand to better convey her words, saying *"Im-me-di-a-te-ly"* in a machine-gun way. She must also be trying to get back as much self-esteem as she can, after all the ugly things that have been shouted at her recently. She says *"I . . . I . . . I . . . I . . ."*; she says "Who's the *host* here?"; she says "Who's putting *her face* on the screen?"; she says "What's *my percentage* on the advertising?"; she says "From the channel or *straight from the sponsors?*"; she says "For how many *weeks?*"; she says *"On the contract* or off the book?"; she says "Gianni, perhaps you should remind them that *I'm* the fucking *star?!*"

Mr. Guardi, on the other hand, pretends to be too concentrated on driving to notice the *trrrrp trrrrp trrrrp* that's coming from his phone. Perhaps for the time being he just needs to know that contact has been reestablished; and most likely he'd rather read his messages when his wife is not sitting two rows behind him.

His wife right now seems to have quite different things on her mind, judging from the way she is sitting with her face turned toward the first houses that slide by along the road. She looks either very tired or very absorbed in her thoughts, it's hard to tell which. Strangely sexy, too, with her ruffled hair and her cheeks still flushed from the quarrel and the horse ride and whatever she did with the guy Lauro before that. Alessio thinks that he hadn't noticed this sexiness before, when she came to the agency with her husband and the others to talk about the houses they wanted to buy. He had always seen her as a stiff, cold, intellectual Milanese woman. Now all the irregular feelings running through her don't do her any harm, even though she probably isn't too aware of the effect.

The minivan proceeds at a snail-like pace, compared to the cars zooming in the opposite direction or coming up from behind without the least consideration for its obvious handicap. An ultra-high-strung Alfa Romeo is madly flashing its headlights while tailing the minivan almost bumper to bumper, finally dashing forward in a dangerous overtaking, the man at the wheel hurling insults and raising his middle finger before roaring down the road at four times the legal limit. Luisa mutters, "bastard," in a low voice.

Arturo Vannucci keeps his knees pressed high against the backrest in front of him, his head leaning against the window, not looking at anything inside or out. When they reach the concrete walls and the billboards and the supermarket at the outskirts of Turigi, his phone rings. Slowly, he takes it out of his pocket, as if doing so cost him a great effort. He says, "Giulia. I didn't call you because I couldn't. I didn't *turn it off*, I wasn't getting any signal. I didn't. . . ." He moves the cell phone away from his mouth, saying, "What? I can't hear you! What? Hello? Hello?" Then he presses the off button, and cuts the communication.

Mr. Guardi pulls up in front of a bar and turns off the engine, with a look of intense relief on his face. Arturo Vannucci's phone rings again, with the lighthearted tune he must have chosen when he was in a very different mood. He lets it go on for a while, then as soon as Margherita slides the side door open, he throws the cell phone out of it. The others all turn to look at it, with disturbed expressions. The damaged phone keeps producing its cheerful little tune, albeit in a slightly distorted way. Vannucci gets out of the minivan and tramples on it savagely, smashing it into pieces of silver and black and transparent plastic, exposing the tiny printed circuits.

The others get out of the minivan, too, careful not to step on the remains of Arturo's cell phone, as if they are afraid of some radioactive or psychological fallout.

Mr. Guardi looks back at the minivan, he seems happy to be rid of it. He takes his cell phone out of his pocket and says, "I'll call a cab," to no one in particular.

Without looking at him, Novelli says, "Call two. There's five of us."

"One's enough," says Arturo Vannucci. "There's only four of you." He opens the trunk, takes out his red-and-blue waterproof sailing bag, and puts it down. He certainly looks strange right now, his face covered with dark reddish stripes, his Irish tweed coat over the home-sewn clothes that for some reason he didn't give back to the Windshift people.

The others look at him, without saying a word.

He closes the trunk, shoulders his bag, then looks in the direction where they came from.

"What's the meaning of this, now?" says Mr. Guardi, in a strained voice.

"I'm going back up there," says Vannucci, without turning. "If I'm still in time." He sets off, with the steady gait of someone who could cover dozens of kilometers without exerting himself or altering his pace.

Mr. Guardi shakes his head in disbelief, turning to look at the others. His wife, Luisa, looks down, her hands deep in her coat pockets. Novelli says, "I need a coffee and a cigarette *this minute*."

She walks toward the door to the bar, already frantically punching another number into her cell phone.

Mr. Guardi makes a gesture to his wife, saying, "I'll go in, too, to ask for the cab number."

His wife, Luisa, finally looks up at him. They seem about to say or shout something to each other that they haven't already said or shouted back at the houses; or perhaps whisper something to each other, or even start crying. But they remain silent, as if they are stuck in a giant, very finely detailed digital photograph.

At last Mrs. Guardi takes off her glasses, puts them in a pocket. She says, "Call *two* cabs. I'm not going back with you."

Her husband stumbles for a moment, as if about to fall.

Alessio leans on his two Y-shaped, homemade crutches. They already seem highly inappropriate for this semi-urban scenery, with the contemporary Western world quickly closing in.